Vikings

Taken

The Great Heathen Army series – Book 1

By Ceri Bladen

Acknowledgments

Without the love and understanding of my family, my books would never happen.

Thank you, I love you.

Also, I'd like to thank Shirley Miller and Val Tobin for their help. It is very much appreciated.

To my readers

I would like to say a big 'thank you' for choosing this book to read. I hope you enjoy it.

If you would like to give any feedback on the story, please contact me at ceribladen@gmail.com

Or, if you have the time, a review of the book on Amazon.com, or any of their sites, would be very much appreciated.

https://www.amazon.co.uk/-/e/B00AS0256Y

Thank you,

Ceri Bladen

Contents

Chapter 1

Year of 865 – Dunwich Fortress, East Angles.

High upon a tower of her Dunwich fortress, Rosfrith squinted against the sun, while she looked into the distance. Stretched up on tiptoes, she took a deep breath to steady herself and attempted to control her breathing, fast from her run from the seashore. Suddenly, she sobered and bit her bottom lip. *Should I have mentioned my haste to the guards, instead of rushing past to get a better view?* After a little thought, she shook her head. Unfortunately for the people living in and around her home in East Angles, Rosfrith's two and ten winters hadn't made her wise to life.

Eager to watch the goings-on down at the shore, she leaned as far as she could over the ledge, excitement making her forget the danger of falling. A smile spread on her lips. She was right, there *were* ships landing. Ones she'd never seen before. They were huge wooden vessels with oars sticking out of both sides, and large sails. Brightly coloured flags flapped in the offshore breeze, but she was too far away to distinguish the black raven that decorated them.

A shout from below her vantage point, and the ringing of a bell, drew her gaze from the sea. Rosfrith looked down and saw people hastily gathering items. They were pulling children and livestock from the villages to the fortress. Those who had already arrived were heading for the main hall. She wasn't naïve. She knew the bell signalled a problem, but for reasons unknown to her, she stayed where she was. Ignoring what she knew she should do, Rosfrith glanced back towards the boats, too interested in them. If she squinted enough, she could observe figures getting off the vessels, the sunshine reflecting off what she assumed were helmets. Abruptly, she backed away from the wall. Helmets meant armor. A worried frown touched her forehead.

"Mistress Rosfrith?"

Rosfrith turned towards the angry voice. "I'm here." She watched her maid, Edith, come through the opening. Rosfrith's brow puckered. It was unusual for Edith to be angry with her—frustrated at her antics, yes—but angry?

"Come." Edith waved her hand indicating for Rosfrith to take it. While she waited, Edith took a second to search for her breath. "We must go quickly." She stepped forward to grab the girl's hand.

"Why? What's wrong?" Rosfrith asked quietly before she spun her head back to observe the advancing party of men from the boats. "Oh," she whispered. In all the excitement of seeing something unusual, she hadn't stopped to assess any danger they might be in. It wasn't because she was silly, it was because she hadn't needed to before. Her home had never been under threat.

"Quick, Mistress. We must hide you."

"Is Papa and my brother back?" Rosfrith tried to quell her fear when she saw worry replace the anger on Edith's face.

"No, they are still somewhere in Northumbria. Safe," she added under her breath

Rosfrith could feel Edith's anger towards the men in the inflection of her voice, but something told her she didn't have time to ask why. She stepped forward and grabbed Edith's hand tightly. "Mother and my sister?"

"Waiting for you in the hall. Come, we have wasted enough time."

After a couple of steps, Rosfrith stopped, pulling Edith to a halt. "Please be honest with me, for I am old enough. Who is coming?" Noticing Edith pale, Rosfrith suddenly didn't feel mature anymore, but she said nothing.

"Oh, Mistress, you shouldn't be asking me such things."

"But I need to know so I might be of use," she said sullenly.

"You'll be of better use if you hide, my girl."

Rosfrith noticed Edith glance over her shoulder. She could now hear distant screams, but Rosfrith stood firm, determined to know why she was so concerned.

Edith huffed and then tugged firmly on Rosfrith's hand. "The Vikings."

Chapter 2

Dunwich Fortress, East Angles – The Great Heathen Army

After muttered prayers to *Óðinn* and *Thór*, and the ritual banging of weapons on their circular shields, the warriors, far from home, jumped off their warships, called *langskips*, into the water. They moved swiftly into pre-arranged groups, splitting off into various directions, covering the small coastline.

Large men, carrying all manner of weapons, crept like a thick fog along the coastline, each one's mind filled with the battle that would face them. Some welcomed it, some had no choice, some hoped they wouldn't be the next in line to visit Valhalla. But, regardless of their thoughts, each followed their leader, ready to take any risk they faced.

Without turning around to look at his men because, without question, he trusted they followed him, Ubba Ragnarsson waved his group to a halt. He crouched behind the scrub to get a better view of their target—Dunwich fortress. The bell ringing in the distance told him their arrival had been noted. A smile played on his lips because he wasn't bothered. Fear of imminent attack confused people, making them less organised and easier to conquer.

Concentrating, Ubba scanned the area in front of him. It appeared unguarded. They'd been informed Lord Guader lacked protection, having never been attacked before, but Ubba was too wise. It could be a trap. Just because it was quiet, didn't mean the fortress's soldiers had gone inside the protective walls. Surprise was a crucial element in warfare.

Happy that, so far, there were no soldiers to concern them, Ubba glanced to his left, seeking out his right-hand man, Gunnar. They nodded at each other. Years of fighting together, side by side, had eliminated needless conversation. Gunnar indicated his wish to advance, but Ubba held up his hand to stop him for a moment. "Lord Guader is not to be harmed, nor anyone that is *not* attacking us." He flicked a glance at the warriors crouched behind him. "Do what you need to the ones holding weapons." He looked away as they acknowledge his command.

"That's not the order your brother gave, Ubba," said Gunnar, keeping his voice low, so others didn't hear. He wouldn't want to disrespect his *chieftain* in front of the men.

Ubba turned his steely, blue gaze on his fellow warrior, noticing his friend twist his axe in his large hands, eager for the fight to begin. He sighed. "Ivar thinks differently from me. The thirst to avenge our father's death runs deep within his blood, but it makes him reckless. We need to use Lord Guader. He understands both our tongues." His gaze returned to the front to finish assessing the situation they were walking into. He wanted to change the conversation, he didn't want revenge to make him unable to think rationally. "Besides, why kill more people than we need to?" He gave a quick snort and chuckled. "They only start smelling when they rot."

Ubba ignored his friend's grunt because he was used to the bloodthirsty views of his kin. Not many agreed with his reasoning of keeping alive the local people, who knew how their crops, land, and weather worked. It was Ubba's wish that some of his people would settle peacefully in this new, more hospitable, land. But, saying that, he also understood the majority of Norsemen just wished to conquer and plunder.

Gunnar shrugged. "Ivar has come to avenge Ragnar's death and to take the spoils of war back to our homeland."

Ubba grunted. "He is too much like my sire, and look what that got him—thrown into a pit full of snakes by King Ælla of Northumbria. Besides, we have no fight here in East Angles. King Edmund pays us handsomely for his peace."

"Granted," said Gunnar. "But, *Thór's teeth*, that son of a whore, Lord Guader, has double-crossed us."

Ubba rolled his large shoulders with irritation. It was probable Lord Guader knew Ragnar was walking into a trap. Gunnar's voice interrupted his thoughts.

"Will King Edmund mind us attacking Lord Guader's land? After all, his land is under King Edmund's protection."

Ubba shrugged. "Not our concern. The King can take it up with Guader. Besides, if Edmund does protest we can sort him out later." Turning away from any more conversation, his eyes narrowed, scanning the darkness of the forest to the left of them. He nudged Gunnar and nodded. There were definitely soldiers hiding in there. He could tell by the wildlife—they were being disturbed.

Gunnar nodded and indicated the threat to the men behind them.

Ubba unconsciously turned his axe in his left hand waiting to hear the battle cries of his brothers before he gave the order for his men to commence. He was so accustomed to his weapon, he didn't feel its weight. It was part of his being—whether chopping wood or protecting himself. When he heard the whistle, he momentarily tensed, psyching himself up for battle. "Come on, let's go. The soldiers' attention is spread enough. My brothers will be making their way to the fortress."

"Which way are your brothers attacking?"

"Every side," replied Ubba, ready to give the signal to move forward. "We need to go before my brothers do too much damage, and there are no lives left to save."

Chapter 3

Dunwich Fortress

"You must hurry," said Edith, fear tainting her words. She dragged Rosfrith as fast as she could.

"Where's my mother and sister?" Rosfrith asked again.

"You cannot worry about them at the moment, mistress Rosfrith. They will already be hiding. You must hurry, we are running out of time."

Rosfrith tried to stop, but the greater strength of her maid wouldn't allow her. "But what about you?"

"You must not worry about me, mistress Rosfrith. I will be safe with the other servants."

Rosfrith couldn't see Edith's face, but she'd known her maid since she could remember, and she had a strong feeling she was lying.

They reached the kitchen building first and Edith hesitated, unsure whether to keep to her original idea of taking Rosfrith to the main hall. She shook her head. *No. If the barbarians get in, Rosfrith will be a sitting duck in the hall,* she thought. *Better to hide her amongst the servants.* "Come, in here, mistress." She swung the door of the kitchen open and stopped in the doorway.

They both watched as frantic women scurried around, hiding anything of worth behind the wooden slats of the walls.

Edith snorted. She knew the servants had orders to hide valuables if they were under attack. It was just a shame that valuables were more important than servants' lives. They needed to hide themselves, not the material goods.

Turning away from the scene, Edith looked at Rosfrith and squeezed her hand. To her, this little girl, whom she had nursed from a baby, was more important than gold. "Quick," she said as she pulled her across the room. "In here." Edith indicated towards a small, dark cupboard, full of wooden utensils. "Promise me, you will not make a sound, or come out, whatever you hear going on." She squeezed Rosfrith's small hand, trying to relay her message without spelling the danger out.

Rosfrith felt tears welling in her eyes. She glanced around and saw the fear on the faces of all those she knew. "I promise, Edith."

Edith gave an encouraging smile, as though nothing was wrong. "Good. Now get as far back as possible. And remember, whatever you overhear, *do not* come out."

"All right," Rosfrith whispered. When she stepped into the darkness, she prayed to God everything would be all right and that Edith's false smile wasn't the last thing she would see. As the room darkened, Rosfrith turned around and wiped her sweaty hands on her shift. "I'm all right, Edith," she said, hoping that Edith didn't catch the hitch in her voice.

"You will be safe, mistress," Edith said as she closed the door. She turned back towards the chaos. "No one is to enter that room, other than me." If the servants heeded her request, they nodded, knowing the mistress needed to be protected; the others were too busy to care for someone else's safety when their own was at risk.

Once she placed a chair in front of the door, Edith went to stand with the others. If the Norsemen defeated their men and entered the kitchen, they would all be found. Attempting to hide behind tables and chairs wasn't going to stop the barbarians, but she knew the act of trying to protect themselves made everyone feel a little safer.

Rosfrith huddled towards the back of the dark cupboard, behind large wooden serving platters. She strained to hear what was going on. Initially, she heard loud whispers of urgency and the muffled footsteps of soft leather on earthen floors. But soon, an eerie silence took over. She closed her eyes and tried to recall her favourite tune, humming it in her mind, in an attempt to ward off the fear that kept threatening to engulf her. She hadn't sung to the end of the first tune before the screams and clashing of metal became louder.

Rosfrith knew the warriors had breached the outside walls. Feeling scared, she put her fingers in her ears. She wanted to block out the sounds of clashing metal, and the screams of people gasping for their last breath on earth.

Although her hearing was muffled, and her eyes screwed tight, the smell of burning wood and reeds nearly had her bolting from her hiding place. It made her feel sick, but she had promised Edith to stay put, and one thing she would never do was go back on a promise. So, she curled up further and prayed to God her exit from this life wouldn't be by burning.

#

The air was crisp, but sweat poured off Ubba's brow as he continued to fight with his men in the village just outside the main walls. He knew most of Guader's soldiers were inside the fortress, but there were still enough of them to make him work for every step he took.

When he yanked his well-used axe out of his next conquest, Ubba wiped his brow with his free arm, his other too busy swiping at more men who blocked his way. Not that they stood there for long—his aim was too good, his fighting technique too perfected, and his axe too lethal for a long battle against their swords. The spilling of blood and innards would sicken him if he had time to think during battle, but he didn't. It was theirs or his insides that would colour the earth at his feet, and he preferred it theirs.

Once he finished off the last soldier in front of him, he took the opportunity to scan the destruction around him, ignoring the metallic smell of blood in the air. He grunted with disgust. Plenty of men, both Lord Guader's and his, lay on the ground, their lifeless eyes, missing limbs, and open wounds indicating nothing could be done for them. But, regardless of the bodies strewn on the ground; the clashing of metal, grunts, and cries continued, all indicating others still fought fierce battles of their own.

Ubba's attention narrowed in on movement. Through the smoke from the burning village, which billowed around him, Ubba noticed two more of Guader's men coming for him. He squatted a fraction, his large thigh muscles pumping as his strong arm swung the axe menacingly. Roaring loudly, he barely hid his smile when the two advancing soldiers thought better of it—they turned and ran towards where they thought they would be safe. But they weren't. His hand gripped his axe while a couple of his men finish them off.

A while later, and more men dead around his feet, Ubba stood tall. He watched the last of the Anglo-Saxon soldiers retreat. They'd obviously had enough.

He whistled for his men to regroup. He was aware their battle was not yet finished—they still had to make it through the burning village and up to the main stronghold, to the hall— but he needed to find out who had made it so far. He studied each man as they regrouped, mentally noting who he'd lost. "We advance quickly, but beware of anyone left in the village. Leave them if they are unarmed, but Guader's soldiers will be lurking in the shadows."

Ubba looked at his men. They nodded their agreements, each covered with sweat and blood—their own and others. Ubba sighed, through weariness and regret. Once they returned home to Ranaricii, he would have to visit the families of the fallen, to offer condolences and help. It was a job he disliked. Crying women weren't his thing, but as their leader, it was his responsibility. He pushed his melancholy thoughts away. It wouldn't do him any good to think soft thoughts while in battle. He waved his hand, indicating it was time to go.

Carefully making their way through what was left of the village, Ubba ignored the destruction of property and lands—thatched cottages, barns, crops burning around him, sending their putrid smoke into the already heavy atmosphere—even some of the hounds had their throats cut. The village had been completely ransacked by his brothers and their men.

Ubba's jaw tensed as his eyes scanned around. Everything that was ransacked was of no use to man nor beast. *What is the point of razing buildings and valuable food to the ground?* He thought. The food and shelter would be useful if they stayed around the area, but Ubba knew his brothers didn't think while in battle—they acted like *berserkers*. They had a thirst for blood.

Ubba grunted and turned. For now, he ignored the death and destruction all around him. He had a job to complete, so he stepped over yet another mutilated corpse and continued onwards, fighting along the way.

#

Rosfrith slowly removed her fingers from her ears and ceased repeating the song within her head. Compared to the noises from outside the walls, it was deathly quiet in the kitchen. Wondering what was happening, she leaned forward, as quietly as she could. The floor squeaked underneath her hand. She pulled her hand off the offending plank, which covered the stores below. Safely back in her corner, her brow furrowed when she heard muffled voices. They were quiet, but she knew they were not speaking her language. Fear made it difficult to breathe, but she listened carefully to heavy footsteps nearing.

Time seemed to blur and slow down. She heard a sharp whistle, before a loud shattering of wood. The servants screamed. Whoever was outside, had broken the door down. The servants were no longer keeping quiet to avoid detection—they had been found.

Over the din of screams and shouts, Rosfrith picked out Edith's familiar voice. She was chanting, over and over, "Protect us, O Lord, from the wrath of the Norsemen." A loud roar stopped Edith in her flow. Rosfrith jumped with fear for her maid. Tears sprang to her eyes, so she put her fingers back in her ears, trying to block out what was happening outside her hiding hole. She knew she could do nothing to help.

Asmund Jensson breathed heavily, axe in the air. He scanned the room he had burst into. A smirk grew on his lips when he noticed the room full of servants, huddled together, trying to hide their eyes from his large form. He let out a snort and lowered his weapon. There were no fighting men. He turned to search for his friend and fellow warrior, Bard Klaussen, but turned his gaze back quickly towards the servants. You could never be entirely sure an Anglo-Saxon soldier wasn't hiding amongst them. "Bard, let's get these thralls out of here and take them to Ivar."

Bard nodded until another spoke up. "Not all of them, Asmund. There're some comely ones here to entertain us for a while," said Eirik.

Asmund glanced at him and narrowed his eyes. "What did you say?"

Eirik shrugged away Asmund's cold tone. "I'm saying, I could do with some loving. A couple of these women look very agreeable." His brown eyes narrowed as he rubbed his beard, nodding at the men who seemed in agreement with him. "And, it's been a long journey..." His words trailed off when his glance focused on one of the women that interested him.

Asmund hesitated, but only because he'd been on strict orders from Ivar to bring all the women into the hall. They needed to find Lord and Lady Guader, their son, and both daughters. He glanced at the group again. *Surely, they would not hide in the kitchen with the servants?*

Bard, not one to care about orders from anyone, even Ivar the Boneless, stepped forward. "Take your pick, Eirik," he said, before laughing at Asmund's hesitation. He shrugged. "What? Don't you think that the brothers will get theirs? Besides, they are no ladies in here, only thralls."

Bard moved into the room, shoving Asmund to the side. He motioned to three men, who already stood in the room, to move forward. "Ivar wants all the hostages in the hall as soon as we can round them up," said Bard, before he smirked and slapped one of the men on his back. "Although, Ivar can wait a while longer for *all* of them." Bard watched as more men moved forward, but they were still waiting for Asmund to give the order.

"Take your pick," Bard said, encouraging them. He turned and winked at Asmund, knowing that he was his friend before his leader. When he moved forward, some of the women screamed. Puffing his chest out, he thanked the gods for their good fortune. It was fate that they checked the kitchens. There was plenty of time to have their fun, and get the ones they didn't want to Ivar and his brothers, Sigurd, Ubba, Bjorn, and Halfdan.

Asmund finally nodded. "Take your pick, men."

The men laughed and turned their gazes onto the women.

Edith didn't understand their tongue, but the intent in the men's eyes was enough. She had been married, she understood that look—unlike some of the maidens standing with her.

Not feeling brave, but knowing as one of the oldest, she had to do something, Edith took a breath, and stepped forward. She wanted to conceal some of the younger women and hopefully, give the heathens time to change their minds. Not that she held much hope.

Asmund eyed the group of crying women until he noticed an older one, with greying hair, step forward. His eyes narrowed at her, to scare her back. To his annoyance, she didn't flinch. She could be trouble. He flexed his hands. If she turned out to be, he'd soon stop her—with his axe, if needs be.

One of the men who'd also noticed Edith pointed. "Is she offering herself?"

The others sniggered.

Bard glanced towards the woman. "Not her, she's too old."

"Unless she *is* offering," one of the men behind them laughed.

"Still too old," countered Bard.

"But, with more experience," another replied.

"Calm down. You will have your pick," said Asmund. Truthfully, he wanted to be rid of the wenches, let Ivar deal with them. But, it had been a long and lonely journey. He glanced at the men and nodded at the youngest one. "You, Magnus, take some of these thralls to the hall. Ivar awaits. If he asks where we are, tell him we are locked in battle with the enemy." He chuckled at his poor humor. When he finished laughing, he ignored the scowl on Magnus's face. The lad barely had hair on his chin—what would he do with a woman? He was the leader, and the lad best remember that. He stepped forward and grabbed Edith, pulling her forward, easily with his greater strength.

Almost falling onto the floor, Edith found herself being thrown towards the doorway, towards another lumbering beast. Once she found her footing, she turned and noticed other women being torn from the group. It was the older ones being singled out. Her heart sunk at the innocent faces of the ones left. A sharp shove whipped her head back around. She growled at the man, but he merely laughed at her.

They were being taken out of the kitchen to goodness knows what fate. Her heart ached for the women left and for poor small, innocent Rosfrith. She feared she might not see her again. Unconcerned the enemy would understand her, Edith shouted. "Be still, mistress Rosfrith. Remember, stay where you are. Whatever you hear, don't come out. Remember your promise." A hard slap across her face quietened her.

Bard continued to pull the older and less desirable women from the group and pushed them towards Magnus. "Take them. Kill any which misbehave."

Magnus growled and stepped towards the women to frighten them. He sniggered when they recoiled. *I might be young, but I still scare these wenches into doing what I wish.* He waved his axe to get them moving. He followed them as they screamed and ran across the open courtyard towards the main hall.

"Now for some fun," Bard said, watching Magnus disappear around a corner. He shut what was left of the wooden door. He didn't need any more men in on their party. His narrowed gaze returned to the women. A sneer appeared on his lips. "Choose yours, men," he said, stepping forward and grabbing a servant with an ample bust. The other men grabbed their own.

Rosfrith tried to hold down the bile she felt rising in her throat. Even from her darkened corner, she knew what was happening to those women. Although it didn't sound entirely like the coupling she'd heard, she was old enough to understand the situation. Besides, she understood the women's pleading and prayers even if those beasts couldn't.

Rosfrith desperately wanted to help them, but, like them, she was outnumbered. Being a child wouldn't stop them defiling her. So, much to her horror, she stayed where she was. Tears slipped from her eyes.

After what felt like an eternity, the women's screams, scraping of wood on the floor, crashing objects falling to the ground, sounds of flesh hitting flesh, and laughter of the men became quieter. The sound of sobbing took its place.

"Come on, let's get these up to the hall. We've wasted enough time on these wenches," said Bard. He pulled up his trousers and tightened his drawstring. "I bet Ivar is wondering where we are." He joked, not the least bit concerned. To his way of thinking, Ivar the Boneless had pretty much given them leave to do whatever they wanted to the people. Everyone, except the family. Ivar wanted them himself. He pulled his tunic down and grabbed the woman off the table, unconcerned that she hadn't had time to cover herself.

Asmund glanced around the room. He ignored the woman, now he'd satisfied himself. The carved pots, which were strewn over the floor, piqued his interest. His bedmate would love some of those. "You go, I'll see what's here to take, first."

Bard's eyes narrowed. He didn't want Asmund to find more valuables than him. "I'll look, too."

Asmund shrugged, unconcerned, for there was plenty for all of them.

"Move," said Bard as he pushed the woman he had hold of, over to the corner of the room. When the others didn't immediately move, he made a jerking movement. He smirked when they all followed—like the sheep on his holding back at Ranaricii.

Asmund stooped down and picked up a couple of wooden pots to inspect them. They were of good quality, but well used. He moved around the room, growling towards the women where their sobbing escalated. They quietened. With his attention divided between the women and a pot, he failed to notice the chair's leg sticking out in front of him. His leather boots caught it and he stumbled. He righted himself and scowled at the laughter from his fellow warriors. When one still sniggered, he turned and threw the pot at him. The laughter stopped. He glanced at the offending chair. His eyes narrowed. He noticed a door behind it.

He signalled to his men, as he grabbed his axe. Each of them swiftly, but quietly, grabbed their weapons, unsure what was going to be behind the door. He pulled the chair away.

"Nay," said one of the women. She was terrified the beasts would find their mistress and inflict the same vile acts on her.

Asmund's head quickly turned to silence her. His eyes narrowed. He didn't understand what she had said, but it could have been a warning to whoever was in there. He lifted his chin to one of the warriors, indicating that the women needed watching. He turned back around and reached to open the door. On a deep breath, and poised ready for the possible battle, he opened it.

From the darkness of her hiding place, Rosfrith controlled her panic when she heard the chair scrape along the floor and the door squealing open. All was quiet before she heard a low voice.

"Now, what do we have here?"

Rosfrith looked in horror at the beast of the man, whose words she did not understand. He filled the whole space, blocking out the light from behind. She closed her eyes tight, hoping against hope he was referring to the pots and pans that hung in front of her. Her heart stopped when she heard the floorboard creak. That meant he was near. She made herself as small and inconspicuous as possible. When her arm was roughly grabbed, the breath she was holding escaped as a loud squeak.

"Another one to join in on the fun," said Asmund, as he hauled the kicking girl out from the darkness. He held her in the air. When he looked at the angry, red face, he realised she was a child. A feisty one at that.

"Now, that one *is* too young," said Bard stepping back in case her flailing kicks landed on him.

"Já," replied Asmund, not at least bit interested in a girl of this age, although it didn't deter some of the men. He'd just witnessed that. "Come on, let's go. We don't want to annoy Ivar too much."

Through fear and anger at being found, with all her might, Rosfrith tried to kick the beast who held her in the air. Unable to aim any of her kicks, she screamed and cursed at him. Be damned with being lady-like.

Eventually, the beast threw her, like vermin, towards the rest of the women who were huddled in the corner. When Rosfrith joined them, a couple of them nodded at her. Although she felt a little of her fear dissipate, she was also very aware they weren't out of danger yet.

"Gather what you can, and let's go," said Asmund as he glanced around. He noticed his orders were unheard—the men were pillaging what they could find.

While he scanned the scene, Asmund's eyes narrowed. He'd noticed the women gather in front of the young girl he had just found. They pushed her behind them, sheltering her. He rubbed his beard while he considered their actions. It couldn't be because she was young, there was another female who looked about the same age, already in the room, sobbing into the breast of another. His head tilted to the side. Amongst the drab clothes of the others, the young girl's attire was brighter, more quality to the cloth. He turned his head. "Hey, Bard. How old is the Lord's daughter?"

Bard heard nothing over the din of the room being plundered.

"Bard," Asmund shouted, now more confident in the way he was thinking. This would be a great find. "Bard, what's the age of the Lord's daughter?"

Bard stopped and rubbed his beard with his free hand, the other balancing utensils. "Young, I think. He has two. One a young adult, one too young to breed, yet."

A smile spread across Asmund's lips. "I think we've found all the treasure we need."

Chapter 4

Main Hall, Dunwich Fortress

Ivar was not happy. He stalked back and forth across the reeded floor of the hall, a scowl firmly on his handsome features. The axe, strapped over his muscly shoulder, dripped with fresh blood. "Have none of you found the Lord or his family?"

"No," said Sigurd Snake-in-the-eye, a matching scowl to his brother's. To demonstrate his annoyance, he swung his axe and chopped a chair in half.

The captives, who huddled together in a corner, jumped. They tried to stifle their screams because they did not want to draw *that* temper in their direction. Their situation was dire enough.

Ubba stepped forward. "We have started to ask, but none of them understand us, yet," replied Ubba, trying to calm his brother down. When Ivar and Sigurd were in foul moods, there was no telling what they would do with the captives within the hall. "A little more time and we will find both the Lord, his wife and their children."

Ivar's lip curled with disgust. "How can we not have found anyone of importance yet?" He waved his arm towards the group of people. "Just their thralls."

"We…" Ubba stopped in mid-sentence when the hall door burst open and a group of women, most looking worse for wear, were herded in. He flinched but hid his disgust at the state of the women—it was plain to see what had happened to them, but there was no point in voicing his disapproval. It was the way of the men to take what they wanted—whether materialistically or from the people.

"Ari. Ask this lot," Ivar waved over to the women, "where the Lord and his family are."

Ubba watched Ari, one of Ivar's kinsmen, walk towards the group. He veered towards one of the elder ones and gestured for her to come forward. After some hesitation, she did.

"Where are your Lord, Lady, and their children?" Ari asked bluntly.

Ubba sighed, the woman obviously didn't understand what he was saying.

"Guader?" Ari tried again, knowing the servant would understand the name.

Hesitantly, she pointed towards the door. "Gone, before you came," she said in a fearful voice. She quickly lowered her eyes.

Ari forced the woman's chin up, making her meet his eyes. "Lady Guader?"

She flinched under his cold stare.

"Where?"

The old lady shrugged.

Sigurd growled while watching the non-verbal exchange. "She's lying, Ari. If not the Lord, the rest are here. None have left the area since we breached the walls. They are hiding," he said and glanced at the group. "I'll try and get answers out of her."

But, before anyone could cross-examine the woman, the door opened again, and more captives were herded in.

Ubba's blue gaze watched as the terrified men and women ran over to the rest of the captured thralls. When he turned away from them, he noticed Asmund smiling. He was gripping a young girl, not allowing her to run with the others.

Ubba didn't need to be a genius to know she was the youngest mistress. He hoped Ivar wouldn't take all his frustrations out on the youngster.

Ivar turned towards the commotion by the door, but not before he noticed the look of horror on some of the captive's faces. He followed their gazes, which landed on Asmund. It told him everything he needed to know. *Well, at last, someone has found someone of importance.* "Well, well. What do we have here, Asmund?"

Asmund strode into the room, barely giving Rosfrith time to put a foot on the floor. "I found her hiding in a cupboard, Lord." He placed Rosfrith down but held her tightly by the arm. She was still trying to attack him, and after the ribbing he'd had off Bard when she'd managed to bite him, he wasn't taking any chances. "She's a feisty one, and I think she is the Lord's youngest."

Edith cried out when she saw Rosfrith unceremonially hauled in. A stern look and an indiscreet flexing of an axe arm from one of the brutes guarding them, stopped her running forward. She'd be no good to her mistress if she were dead herself, so she glanced over at Rosfrith, who apart from fighting like a caught rabbit, seemed unharmed. Unlike some of the women, they had brought in.

"Mistress Rosfrith, I do believe," said Ivar, nodding as the smile widened on his lips.

Rosfrith stilled when she heard her name. She didn't understand what was said, but her name was clear enough. Her spirits deflated. *Mayhap I shouldn't have fought so much, then I wouldn't have been singled out?* Quickly, she pushed her thoughts away. Regardless of what she thought now, when the blond beast barged through the women to grab her, her instincts had kicked in. *For that, I will pay the price.*

"Mayhap, with some persuasion, she will tell us where her parents are?" suggested Sigurd, stepping forward, a smirk growing on his face.

Ubba felt a prickling on his scalp. His brother possessed powers he did not fully understand. He knew, when Sigurd extracted information from someone, they experienced pain, but at least there was no physical bloodshed, for somehow, he was able to read a person's mind. Ubba stepped nearer Ivar, so less men would hear his request. "Is there any way you can find out that information from the child, Sigurd?" He gave Rosfrith a quick glance. "Without hurting her too much?" He ignored the grunts of disagreement from the other warriors who'd heard—they were more in tune in the ways of his brothers; more comfortable with inflicting torture. He shrugged his large shoulders and turned around to face the men, laughing, pretending he was unconcerned, when he heard the muttered heckling. He didn't know why he cared whether the child was hurt or not, but he knew he would have to justify his reasons to the men who had just stepped off a battleground. "She might be of use in the future." He turned back and looked directly at Ivar. "We could ransom her?"

Ivar let out a snort and then carefully regarded his brother. *Mayhap my soft-hearted brother has a point?* He swivelled his head to engage Sigurd. "Sigurd, do what you can..."

"Já, don't hurt her, brother," Ubba reiterated, not realising he had interrupted Ivar in mid-sentence.

Ivar's gaze narrowed on Ubba and his jaw clenched. It would not do his reputation any good to have someone seem to make his mind up for him. It had been agreed he was in charge while in *Bryttania*. *Mayhap my brother needs reminding of that fact?* "Halfdan Ragnarsson, step forward." He waited for his other brother to stand in front of him. Ivar crossed his arms across his chest, and flicked a quick glance at Ubba, daring him to defy him. He noticed the tension in Ubba's stance, but he was pleased that Ubba was wise enough to keep quiet. "If Sigurd Snake-in-the-eye can't extract any information from her, you can use your method."

Ubba's gut clenched but he nodded tightly, holding back his thoughts. He noticed a smile appear on Halfdan's lips while he fingered his weapon, and something inside him stirred. He didn't analyse it, but he knew, in his gut, he didn't wish the child to experience pain. He scanned around the room, trying to work out how to handle the unfolding situation, but before he could react, he made eye contact with Ivar. He was raising his eyebrows in warning. Ubba knew his place, so fighting his instincts, he stayed still. Although Ivar was not the oldest sibling, *he* was the leader of this raid and it had been agreed that he was to be obeyed—even by his brothers. Ubba's hands fisted at his side in frustration—there was nothing he could do to protect the girl. If she didn't give any information to Sigurd Snake-in-the-eye, she would have to deal with Halfdan—and he'd witnessed the mess his brother made with his knife. His nostrils flared and he cracked his knuckles. Like it or not, he had to stay where he was.

"Sigurd?" said Ivar. He clicked his fingers for Rosfrith to be brought forward.

Ubba widened his stance when she was pushed forward and landed harshly on her knees in front of Sigurd and Halfdan. It would have hurt, but she scowled at them instead of crying. He was impressed. The only indication of her nerves, that he could tell, was the biting of her bottom lip when the men talked, their attention no longer on her. He hooked his thumbs into his weapons' belt. She had a strong character, for one so young. Not to show fear was commendable, but unfortunately, it could also mean her youth didn't allow her to comprehend what was about to happen to her.

His icy gaze narrowed on his brothers while they conversed. He was too far away to know what they said so he glanced back at the girl. Her face now, pale as snow. His teeth ground together. He would not allow the child to be physically harmed. Warning from Ivar or not, Ubba planted his feet apart and fingered his weapon, bracing himself for a fight, if needed.

When the men turned back towards her, Rosfrith felt her body shake. She used all her strength to stay still. She was terrified and wanted to cry, but she would not show these brutes that. She hadn't understood what they had talked about, she didn't understand their

Norse language, but when one of them walked towards her with a smirk on his face, she knew it was not going to be pleasant. Although she heard the sound of her heartbeat thrashing in her ears, and could barely take in a raspy breath, she narrowed her eyes and stared at him—determined not to let him see her tremble and cry.

To take her mind off what was going to happen, she concentrated on him. He was dressed entirely in black. He was of smaller build than the other beasts, with none of the bulging muscles they possessed, but, even in her youth, she didn't underestimate him. When he neared, he bent down towards her. Her breath hitched. One of his eyes was milky white. She panicked, never seen anything like it before, but despite her surprise, she pushed her chin higher and stared directly into his eyes.

"Stay still, pretty one," said Sigurd. He placed his hands on either side of her face. He wasn't worried about her moving away because a warrior held her fast, her arms rammed against her back. "Let's see where your sire, mother, and siblings are, shall we?" He knew she didn't understand his words, but the images that would appear when he closed his eyes would tell him what Ivar needed to know.

Within seconds of feeling his hands on her, Rosfrith screamed. The pain in her skull was excruciating. Before she could catch a breath to scream again, Sigurd jerked away. The pain instantly stopped.

A puzzled look flittered over Sigurd's face and he stilled, his hand still wavering in the air. His dark gaze narrowing on the young girl. *What have I just seen?* He pulled his arms down and turned to look at Ubba, who had a frown on his face. *Interesting, I will have to talk to him, later.*

"What do you see, brother?" asked Ivar, impatience lacing his words.

Sigurd hesitated before turning towards him. "I see nothing, my brother." He flicked another glance at Ubba, then looked back towards Ivar. If anyone thought it was unusual, no one said anything. "Let Halfdan have his turn. I see nothing," he mumbled, moving out of Halfdan's way. "Your turn." He walked over to Ubba and placed his hand on his arm to keep him where he was. "Say and do nothing. I will explain later."

Although Ubba was puzzled, he nodded at Sigurd. He was too interested in Halfdan, at the moment, to worry about Sigurd and his visions.

"See if you can triumph where your brother has failed." Ivar the Boneless's voice echoed around the hall.

Once her dizziness subsided, Rosfrith opened her eyes. The sick feeling of pain still remained. She focused and noticed a different, larger man standing before her. The look on his face indicated he might cause her even more pain than the last one. Her eyes widened when she saw him remove a sharp knife from his belt. She struggled against the human restraints and shouted, "Nay." Before a large hand clamped over her mouth, cutting off her protests.

"Pray, cease."

A hush filled the room.

"Cease, I say." Lady Brigitta Guader stepped out from the group of captives she was hiding amongst. She side-stepped the large beast who guarded them.

From beneath the hand covering her mouth, Rosfrith tried to shout for her mother to stop, but no audible sound came out. Distressed that her mother had made herself known, Rosfrith fought against the hands on her shoulders and arms. She wiggled wildly, but more hands appeared to restrain her. She saw the worry in her mother's gaze as she looked at her quickly, before looking at Ivar.

"Pray, be still, Rosfrith. They have me now, hopefully, they will leave you and your sister be. She is safe with the others."

Her mother was addressing her, not Ivar. He wouldn't know as he would have no idea what she was saying. She settled under the hands. At least she knew her sister, Edeva, was safe.

Ivar's gaze zeroed in and inspected the woman, who was dressed in ordinary servant's ware. He nodded to his man to let her through, he wasn't scared of a lone woman. His gaze narrowed, she was apparently talking to him, but he wasn't fooled. He'd witnessed the quick glance she'd given the young girl—there was love between them. He rubbed his beard in thought, resisting the urge to smile at his fortune. He was impressed that the lady of the house had donned servant's clothing in an attempt to fool him. Now she neared, and he had the time to inspect her, her beauty shone through despite her attire. *Very clever.*

Brigitta stopped in front of Ivar.

He could see her hands shaking. She was brave—but afraid. "Speak," Ivar commanded, waving his hand. When she stood, quietly rubbing her hands together, he could feel his patience slip. He crossed his arms and tapped his foot. "Lord Guader?" He prompted, knowing she would understand those two words. When she shook her head, his jaw clenched. This might not be as easy as he first thought. "Lord Guader?" he repeated. "Here?" He pointed to the floor and raised his brows in question.

Again, Brigitta shook her head.

He was glad to see her flinch when she heard the growl deep in his chest.

Brigitta fought her tears and anger. She didn't know where he was. Her husband, Lord Arter Guader, had received a missive only a couple of days ago. He had packed immediately and disappeared, mumbling something about going to meet someone. At the time, she hadn't thought much of it. Arter often disappeared to have council with King Ælla or King Osberht of Northumbria. They respected her husband. *But if Arter knew these heathens were coming?* She clenched her hands tightly, trying to compose herself. She had to be strong, now her husband was gone. She had to protect her children, so she glared at the dark-haired brute in front of her. *But by God, if Arter knew these barbarians were coming and left me and his daughters to deal with them, I'll never forgive him.*

In the silence, with every gaze on him, seeing how he handled the situation, Ivar could feel his temper boil. He didn't appreciate being duped by the weasel lord. When they had landed on the shoreline, it was obvious that Lord Arter Guader was not there with a welcoming committee—like he'd promised in a missive. Luckily, Ivar had predicted his betrayal. It was the reason he'd amassed an army before coming. He didn't want to end up like his departed sire, unprepared for betrayal—and dead.

For years, East Angles had honored a peace agreement with his father, Ragnar Lothbrok. In exchange for information and gold, Ragnar had vowed not to attack King Edmund's land, which included Dunwich fortress. However, his sire had his sights on the lands of Northumbria and Lord Guader, while communicating for King Edmund, had promised him he would talk to the Northumbrian kings, King Ælla and Osberht, to arrange a similar agreement to King Edmund's. But when Ragnar Lothbrok had arrived expecting the deal to be finalised, he was betrayed and killed by King Ælla—thrown into a pit of snakes.

Ivar's gaze narrowed on the woman in front of him while he scratched his bearded chin. His plans would have to change. They had come for compensation for their sire's murder and a peace treaty—not to attack Northumbria—but now he was stuck in a room with a load of prisoners, no one had any idea how to communicate with, and a run-away traitor. He stepped forward to stand directly in front of the Lady, using his bulk in an attempt to intimidate her. She was Arter's wife, and he was no doubt she knew where he was. He would have to break her—one way or another.

From the sidelines, Ubba watched the dark-haired woman, her back straight with dignity. It wouldn't take his brother long to break that pride. For her sake, and that of her young daughter, he hoped she would tell Ivar where her husband was.

Everyone within the room watched silently when Ivar stepped forward and reached out to stroke Brigitta's cheek. He laughed when she flinched away. He glanced around at his men, a smile flickered on his lips. "So," he said, turning in a circle before his gaze returned to Brigitta. "This lady doesn't like to be touched." He, and the men around him, laughed. "Mayhap, she doesn't like her husband touching her, either?"

Brigitta tried not to flinch when the heathens in the room roared with laughter. Whatever the brute in front of her had said, it was obviously something at her expense. Suddenly, she was glad not to be able to speak their filthy language. She didn't want to know what they were saying, or know what was to become of them all. She stood as still as a statue, waiting for her fate at the hands of the brutes. But while she did, Brigitta silently cursed her husband to burning hell.

Chapter 5

On the road to Northumbria

Lord Arter Guader ran his sweaty palm over his face. He gazed, unseeing, at the passing countryside. When the carriage hit yet another bump, he grabbed onto the seat, save him falling at the feet of his son.

Once he'd righted himself, he glanced at Bryan, who still wore the same scowl on his face—the one he'd had since leaving Dunwich. "We should be there soon," Arter said in an attempt to pacify his son of five and ten winters. He ignored the grunt his son returned him.

Annoyed, he looked out of the window again. He understood Bryan hadn't wanted to join him on this journey, but what his son failed to understand was this journey might save his life. "For goodness sake, son, cheer up. This day is stressful enough without you making it worse."

Bryan slid his father a glance before he turned away.

Incensed by his son's insolence, and the never-ending journey, he said. "I'm warning you, Bryan. Cheer up." When he didn't get a response, he glanced back out of the window. *Mayhap I should have left him with his mother and sisters?* If Bryan weren't the sole heir to Dunwich, he would have.

Another large bump in the road caused both their heads to bash onto the roof.

"Sorry, this track is very holey. But not in a religious way," shouted the driver, laughing at his joke.

While Bryan rubbed his head, he glared at his father. "Pray, why did you bring me on this journey? You've never wanted me to assist you before." He held on as the carriage rocked. Once it settled he carried on whining. "I had my falconry tuition lined up," His lips parted in his first genuine smile since leaving Dunwich. "You should see Conyan."

"Conyan?"

The smile fled from Bryan's lips. "My bird." Under his breath, he added, "You'd know if you took the time to watch."

Once again, Arter chose to ignore his son's jibe. *Does Bryan think I have time for leisure pursuits? I have to mollycoddle two temperamental Northumbrian Kings, and keep back an invading Heathen Army!* If his son didn't buck his ideas up, he'd have to impart that bit of information to him.

"Why couldn't we bring our horses, instead of being thrown around this thing?" said Bryan, after bumping his head once again.

"Because we have too much luggage to carry," Arter said, only supplying part of his reason. His cases were heavy because they were filled with valuables, jewels, coin, and gold. Anything he could take without his wife becoming too suspicious.

"Oh."

Arter's thoughts wandered to his wife. He hadn't wanted to leave her, or his daughters come to that, but he hadn't a choice. He was only hoping that on his return, the Norsemen and his wife, would understand his reasons for leaving. He was confident that the Norsemen wouldn't attack his home because King Edmund paid them to keep East Angles safe. He hoped. "Keep the horses straight," he shouted when the carriage swerved again. *By the time we get there, half of my luggage will be left on the tracks!*

"Aye, m'Lord. I'm trying," said the driver, tutting at his passenger.

Arter took in a frustrated breath. Eager to get there, he tried to gauge the scenery. He had made this journey often enough to realise they were over halfway, so he attempted to gather his scattered thoughts.

The mission in front of him wouldn't be easy. He was off to meet King Ælla and his brother King Osberht of Northumbria to tell them about his recent missive from the Danes. They were on the way! Arter hoped King Ælla would either give them the coin he owed for killing their father or if not, an army to defeat them. Realistically, the only way to get an army to defeat the heathens was for the two Kings to join forces.

Arter felt his heart racing with panic. He'd acted as a peacekeeper long enough to witness the jealousy and sibling rivalry between the brothers. So, he knew it was nigh on impossible to persuade them to act together. He exhaled. In fact, at present, there was a mini civil war going on between the two, which, unfortunately, the Danes were taking advantage of.

He sighed heavily, running a hand over his mouth and chin. If only he could get the brothers to join forces, they might be able to defeat the Great Heathen Army, which, if his timing were right, would be landing on their shores very soon. He'd already had a resounding no from King Edmund about joining forces with the North. He wanted nothing to do with the Vikings because he paid handsomely to keep them away. A sweat broke on his brow. *What will King Edmund think now they are coming through his lands?* Starting to feel sick by the turn of events, Arter tried to close his eyes in an attempt to block out what was happening.

After a couple more hours of bouncing around on the hard wooden seat, they arrived at King Osberht's stone fortification. Unusually for the times, King Osberht had not used timber for his fortress, but the stones left by the Romans. Arter wished he'd had the same foresight. His timber fortress in Dunwich wouldn't take long to overthrow if the Heathens were angry with him. He shuddered, and then pushed his thoughts away because it made him think of his wife. "We are here, Bryan."

"At last," he mumbled under his breath, trying to hide his true feelings of excitement, now he'd seen the impressive building. It wouldn't do for his father to think him content.

Stretching his travel-weary body, Arter nodded at the servants who arrived to deal with his luggage. As custom, they would be taken to a chamber he normally vacated when in residence. It was only small, and he would have to share it with his son this time, but Arter feared he wouldn't see much of it on this trip. He would be too busy trying to sort out this mess. He rubbed his chin and realised he needed to wash his dusty face and get changed before he met with King Osberht, the divine counsel, and nobles in an attempt to unite their forces and form an army with King Ælla. "Come, Bryan. Follow me."

Lord Guader was not happy when he finally returned to his bedchamber. His body, tired due to the late hour, and his mind, tired due to the meeting. Throwing his surcoat on the bed, he sat heavily on the chair next to it.

"Is all good, Papa?" asked Bryan. He didn't really care what his father's answer was. All he'd been interested in was a tour of the building, and now, it was too dark. He glared at his father's back.

Arter's head swivelled, and he let his gaze flick over his son, catching the tail end of his son's scowl. He sighed deeply. "No, no, it isn't."

Forgetting his adolescent mood for a moment, for his father's disposition was peculiar, Bryan suddenly felt a chill. He'd thought he'd been dragged up to Northumbria to keep his father company, but now, he wasn't quite sure. His eyes narrowed. *Thinking about it, we did leave in a rush.* "W-w- what's wrong, Papa?"

"What isn't?" Arter mumbled, running his hand over his face in an attempt to clear his mind. *Mayhap I shouldn't have drunk so much alcohol during the meeting?* It certainly hadn't made anything better. He bent to take off his boot and then indicated for Bryan to help him when he noticed him standing watching his struggles. *For Lord's sake*, he was so frustrated—with both the Kings and his son!

During the meeting, it hadn't mattered what his arguments were about joining forces to defeat the Danes because King Ælla hadn't even bothered to turn up. The war King Ælla had with his brother, Osberht, was making him immune to reason and blind to the dangers of the Heathens! And Ælla was the one who'd started this mess by killing Ragnar.

He lifted his other leg for Bryan to take his boot off.

Without the help of King Ælla, or King Edmund come to that, there was no way he was able to persuade King Osberht to intercept the Great Heathen Army. None of this affected Osberht yet—the Danes were in East Angles, nowhere near Northumbria, and their anger was towards Ælla, not him. He couldn't understand that the Vikings would eventually want his land. The fool! He closed his eyes and pinched the top of his nose. *If only the Kings understood that lethargy will be their downfall!* As his chest tightened with anxiety, he finally remembered his family he'd left and tears welled in his eyes.

"Papa?"

His son's voice interrupted his thoughts. He glanced at Bryan and realised his usually sullen son looked frightened. He let out a quick breath, his lips pursing. *Do I tell him the truth or lie? Would Bryan be glad they ran to potentially save their lives, or mad at him for leaving the women?* Maybe, for now, he'd tell him a bit of both.

Chapter 6

Dunwich Fortress

A couple of hours later, Ivar was satisfied Lord Arter Guader, his son, and elder daughter had disappeared. He was disappointed Guader had fled. He'd hoped to receive their compensation and leave, and if not, his fight would only be with that back-stabbing King Ælla. But he shouldn't have been surprised. The Lord had always reminded him of a wily fox.

While he sat down at a large rectangular table, Ivar studied those who sat with him. He was pleased that apart from some cuts and bruises, all his brothers were with him—Bjorn Ironside, Halfdan Ragnarsson, Sigurd Snake-in-the-eye, and Ubba Ragnarsson. He leaned forward to grab their attention. "So, we have some planning to do, brothers."

Bjorn's hand slapped the wooden table, making the girl who had been released to serve them ale, jump. He laughed at her scuttling away, before glancing back at Ivar. "Já, we do. We need to avenge our sire's murder now it is obvious King Ælla is not going to pay compensation."

Ubba watched his brothers, and the other warriors around the table, nod their agreement. When they quietened, he asked, "So, what do you propose, Ivar?"

"We must go North, into Northumbria. There we will find that coward, King Ælla," said Ivar, taking a sip of his ale—it helped take away the bitter taste in his mouth.

"And his brother, King Osberht?" Bjorn asked.

Ivar shrugged his shoulders, then banged his mug down with force. "We don't need to bother him—yet. Besides, we've reason to believe Kings Osberht and Ælla are fighting amongst themselves." He looked around the table, seeking out his future-seeing sibling. "They might kill each other before we get there and their lands will be for the taking," he said, laughing, before sobering quickly. "Sigurd?"

Sigurd gave a small nod before he closed his eyes. He grabbed the arms of his chair, while he let images float in his mind. A small smile crossed his lips when the images finally faded.

"So?" Ivar's eyebrow rose with question.

Sigurd waited for a moment, gathering his thoughts. "Siblings may fight, but once an outsider lays a finger..." He didn't need to finish his sentence.

"They unite and fight together," added Ivar. He was quiet for a while, thinking about his brother's words. Catching Ubba's eye, he nodded and stood up. He glanced at all of those around the table and then threw his fist into the air to motivate the battle-weary men around him. "So, we take the two whoresons instead!"

The room erupted with cheers.

Ubba smiled, but inwardly sighed. He wasn't as jubilant as his brothers and kinsmen about another war. *Two Kings to fight, and potentially King Edmund, too, because we've broken our agreement and are on his land?* Too many good men would be lost, never to return home to their loved ones.

"Will all of you stay to fight by my side?" Ivar's gaze glanced around at his brothers, landing on Ubba. He knew out of all of them, he had the least stomach for fighting—even though he was the most gifted fighter.

Ubba nodded. He didn't have a choice. He wanted to return to Ranaricii, but his loyalty was to his murdered sire and brothers. Besides, he valued Ivar's wisdom, and mastery of strategy and tactics in battle. Therefore, he'd go with him, willingly. "And when we defeat King Ælla, and mayhap Osberht, we will return home or stay here?"

"You can return." Ivar paused. "Or stay, if you prefer this land that will be ours to rule."

Ubba smiled at the wink Ivar gave him.

"Let's celebrate!" Ivar commanded, picking up his ale. Everyone cheered.

Once the room had settled, Ubba noticed Sigurd move nearer to him. He gave his brother a side glance when he pulled his chair near. "Já?" Ubba's eyebrow rose in question while he took a slurp of his ale.

"About before," said Sigurd.

Ubba stopped drinking and looked at his brother. "Before?" He wasn't sure what Sigurd was getting at until he noticed him glance in the direction of Lord Guader's daughter.

"That one," Sigurd said, before returning his gaze on Ubba. "She is in your future."

Ubba stayed quiet.

"She'll cause you trouble..." he said, looking in Rosfrith's direction once more and becoming silent.

Ubba shrugged but said nothing. He had no reason to doubt what Sigurd saw, for he didn't fully understand his brother's visions, but they didn't always tell the whole story. Sometimes his visions would change due to events. "Whatever you say, Sigurd."

Ubba couldn't stop his gaze flick over to Rosfrith. Her mother and an older servant were protecting her. He snorted and tore his gaze away. If she were going to cause him trouble in the future, perhaps *he'd* need to keep a closer eye on her? His father's words popped into his head—*My son, keep your friends close, your enemies closer.* Suddenly, he laughed. *How ridiculous Sigurd's words are. What on earth can a little girl do to a warrior such as me?*

While he gave his beard a scratch, he decided to put Sigurd's words out of his mind. He wasn't one to worry about what you couldn't control, and besides, as soon as they left Dunwich, he wouldn't see the black-haired child again.

For tonight, he would enjoy their partial victory and Lord Guader's ale.

Much later on, while nursing his warming ale, Ubba's gaze encountered Rosfrith's. He couldn't help a smile play on his lips when she scowled at him. *That little girl has guts.* His gaze narrowed on her to see if she became frightened, but she continued to glare back at him. Ubba took a mouthful of beer to hide his smile, somewhat pleased by her character. When she finally stuck her nose up and looked away, Sigurd's words came back to him. Only a couple of hours ago, he'd convinced himself to ignore his brother's warning about

Rosfrith—now he was having trouble forgetting them. There was something about her that bothered him and something he admired. He put his ale down and leaned forward to grab Ivar's attention. "Ivar," he said, shuffling nearer to Ivar so he could be heard over the noise within the hall. "What will we do with the servants of Dunwich when we leave?" Ubba hoped they'd leave them. Then Rosfrith wouldn't be a problem, but perhaps his brother had other plans?

Ivar looked around the room. "I don't know, yet," he said, shrugging. "Maybe we'll leave them here in Dunwich, especially if they are lazy."

"Or we can take some for slaves?" interjected Asmund, overhearing the brother's conversation.

Ubba flicked a glance at Asmund and then ignored him. "What about the Lady and her daughter?" he directed at Ivar.

Ivar waved his hand. "It depends if Lord Guader appears with our coin and we go straight back home. If he does, we'll leave them all. If he doesn't return," he paused, "we'll leave them anyway. I don't want to feed and look after any Britons if we have to travel to find the Kings."

Ubba relaxed. The girl would be out of his life.

"Mayhap we can take a couple—to keep us entertained?" Bard sniggered, elbowing Asmund in the ribs.

Ivar glanced at Bard and shrugged. "Mayhap."

For reasons he didn't understand, a coldness crept into Ubba's veins. If they took women from Dunwich, the chances are the girl would be taken, too. Perhaps he had no choice and *Loki,* God of mischief, was meddling in his fate? He sighed heavily, annoyed at his mixed feelings.

After some thought, Ubba decided if his fate were already marked, all he could do was keep an eye on her. He interrupted his brother's conversation. "When I return to Ranaricii, I'll take some of the women as thralls. Of course, I'll pay for their upkeep in between."

Ivar revolved his hand in the air. "We have plenty of them. Take whomever you like."

Ubba stood and pointed in the direction of the captives. "I'd take her, and her, and her..."—he pointed at Rosfrith—"and a couple more of the women as my thralls."

Ivar's eyes narrowed on him. "You're keen, brother."

Ubba laughed, hoping it covered the tension in his voice. "Just picking out the strongest, Ivar, before any of my brothers do."

Ivar gave a snort.

"Why do you want them as thralls, why not sell them as slaves? You'll get something out of them then," Bard butted in.

Ubba bristled under Bard's questioning. At home, in Ranaricii, Bard would never question Ubba's authority because he was his Chieftain. Whether it was the euphoria of battle or the ale, Bard was pushing his luck. Ubba made a mental note to keep an eye on him and although he was agitated, he let nothing show on his face. He shrugged at Bard's question. He couldn't appear too keen about the fates of captured ones, otherwise, he had a feeling

Ivar would be liable to sell them just for the hell of it. He ignored Bard and looked back at his brother. "I'm in need of the extra hands for work when we return north."

Asmund snorted a laugh. "In the *bed-closet*, no doubt."

Ubba shrugged his large shoulders again. "Mayhap." He watched the smiles spread on the faces of the men around him. Slaves were often passed around for bed sport, but, this was completely the opposite motive to why he was doing this—he wanted to protect her from that. For some reason, the Gods wanted their fates to be entwined. He didn't know why, but he'd keep her near enough to watch—especially if she was to bring him misfortune.

Ivar flicked a glance at the women before his gaze rested back on his brother. "We'll discuss it later. For now, they can all work and get us some food."

Ubba realised as soon as Rosfrith was out of his sight, she was at risk from any of the warriors—for whatever they wished. He pointed at the child and her mother. He needed to keep his reasons for keeping them near something Ivar could relate to. "Those two there, the Lady and her daughter, are too valuable to go missing. Keep them near."

Ivar said nothing for a while before he grunted and nodded to his men. "Tie them to those chairs. You," he looked at Asmund. "Guard them. Do not let them go anywhere."

Ubba put his ale down when he noticed Ivar looking at him. "Já, brother?"

Ivar grunted and sat back in his chair. "So, are you thinking of returning to Ranaricii so soon?"

Ubba became aware of the interest of the men around him. He waited a moment before answering. "Not until our sire, Ragnar, has been honored."

A smile spread slowly over Ivar's lips. "Good, I thought my warrior brother had grown too weak bellied to continue the fight."

Ubba ignored the guffaws of the men around him. He tilted his chin up and forced a smile on his face—he didn't want his brother, or anyone else come to that, to know what he was thinking. "Who wouldn't be eager to get back to their bedmate as soon as possible?" He ignored Gunnar, for it was his sister, Astrid, that he was talking about. He waited for the laughs to settle down before he continued. "However, I will stay here as long as it takes to revenge Ragnar Lothbrok." He lifted his ale into the air and watched the other men around him show their respect.

"There are many bedmates available here," Bard interrupted while scanning the room.

Ubba didn't want to explain he wasn't interested, so he just said, "Já, many. But the battle has taken it out of me." His gaze pinned Bard. "Mayhap you didn't fight as hard as the rest of us, Bard?"

The men laughed when Bard scowled at Ubba.

"Brothers, we will talk about the plans later, in more detail. Now, we eat and enjoy our success," said Ivar.

From her hard, high-backed seat, which she'd been forced to sit on, Rosfrith could overhear the banter from the main table. She scowled, frustrated she didn't understand what the big beasts were saying to each other. Rosfrith wished she'd taken more notice of her father, who'd insisted she'd learn the Heathen language—she hadn't been bothered.

Rosfrith looked around the hall—the hall that only yesterday, belonged to her father. Apart from the furtive glances between the servants, the hall looked like any other day. All except, it wasn't her and her family sitting at the main table—it was a bunch of barbarians.

For a while, she quietly watched the activity going on around her—servants feeding and watering the beasts, who, by the looks of it, were enjoying her father's ale stock. She shut her eyes. She'd seen enough. Rosfrith tried to control the tears that threatened. It was so unfair. *Where are Papa and Bryan? Did he know these beasts were coming?* She hoped he didn't—that would be the ultimate betrayal.

Feeling stiff, Rosfrith wriggled her shoulders in an attempt to get feeling back into her arms and wrists, which were tightly bound. She gave a long, frustrated sigh. There was no way she was going to get out of the knots. She and her mother were helpless. Rosfrith tried not to think of their fates because she had a feeling it wouldn't be kind. Swallowing the ball of fear, which had started to choke her, and tried to focus on the one positive—her sister, Edeva, hadn't been noticed. Rosfrith blessed God for giving her sister their father's mousy colour and average looks. Hopefully, it would protect her from unwanted attention.

Her mother, muttering prayers over and over, interrupted her thoughts. "Mama, are you faring well?" she whispered.

"Aye," was all her mother managed to reply before Asmund growled at them to be quiet.

Once again, they sat in silence, and Rosfrith watched the one she assumed was the leader, leave the hall. With him gone, and Asmund's attention off them, Rosfrith thought it safe to look for her sister, who earlier she'd seen pick up plates of food to serve. She hoped her Edeva's inexperience of serving wouldn't show. As long as those beasts thought she was the same as the other servants, she would be as safe as any of them.

When Rosfrith found her, she resisted the urge to smile. Edith was near her, covering any mistakes she made. Edith was such a blessing to the family.

When Rosfrith noticed the barbarian coming back into the room, even though he didn't glance her way, she looked away from her sister.

Ubba glanced at the men seated at the wooden table. The mood within the hall was jubilant, as was expected after a battle won, even though their main objective of finding the Lord had failed for now. He watched his brothers and the higher commanding warriors talking and drinking ale. They quietened when Ivar strode back in and sat at the head of the table.

Ivar looked irritated. Wherever he'd just been, the news had not been good. Ubba watched him stand and gain the attention of those around the table. They'd all soon find out what was wrong.

Ivar glanced at his men. Before he started, he grabbed the ale in front of him. He took a swig. Using the back of his hand, he wiped the liquid away from his beard. "We have been unable to find Lord Guader, his son, or his oldest daughter. We can take it that's he's fled.

He's taken all his coin and valuables, too." Ivar grunted his disdain for the weak Lord. "Too frightened to face what he started."

Or to protect his family, thought Ubba.

To his right, Halfdan spoke up. "King Ælla started this when he killed our sire."

Ubba noticed his brothers nod and grunt in agreement. He felt the same, revenge was in his blood—but he was just interested in King Ælla. To be honest, the weasel, Lord Guader, and his family were inconsequential to him.

"Já, he did," replied Ivar.

While he watched his brother, Ubba noticed a smile form on Ivar's lips. *My brother is up to something.*

"Which is why King Ælla will pay." Ivar's gaze flicked towards the back of the room. "Lord Guader, too."

Ubba followed his brother's gaze. It landed on Lady Guader and her daughter. His heart sank. This wasn't the right time to ask what Ivar intended to do with them—emotions were flying high, and his brother had consumed too much ale. All Ubba could do was try to divert his brother's attention. "Do you think Lord Guader fled to warn King Ælla and Osberht of our appearance?"

Ivar nodded.

"No doubt," sneered Sigurd. "I advised you not to send a missive to him. It forewarned him of our arrival."

Ubba could see Ivar bristle under Sigurd's reprimand, but surprisingly a smile appeared on his lips.

"Well, dear brother, not all of us can see the future like you." Ivar's gaze narrowed on Sigurd, as his false smile disappeared. "I will make sure to use more of your powers in future. Hopefully, you will get your predictions correct. *All* of the time," he stressed before turning away, ignoring the surprise on Sigurd's face. He addressed the rest of the men. "Back to business. You all know Lord Guader paid our sire coin, from King Edmund, not to attack East Angles." He waited for their replies. "Well, he was supposed to be arranging the same deal with the Kings of Northumbria for Ragnar." Ivar became serious. "But, when our sire came over, in peace, I might add, King Ælla disposed of him—killing him with snakes."

Ubba watched his brother pace back and forth. The clenching and unclenching of Ivar's fists indicated that his brother was getting more wound up.

"Mayhap they have forgotten the destruction we caused at the abbey in Lindisfarne or the death we caused at Portland Bay? Mayhap we need to remind them of what we Norsemen do to our enemies?" Ivar continued, his mood lighting up when he heard the roars of encouragement from his men. After a while, he held up his hands for quiet. He continued, "I have decided, for now, if Lord Guader doesn't come back with coin, we will enjoy the winter in East Angles." He picked up his ale and held it high. "On Lord Guader's expense." He stopped briefly, waiting for the cheers to settle. "Then, we'll march to Northumbria and the capital, Jórvík, to fix our business there." He waved his hand in a circle. "Who knows? Mayhap we might be able to kill two kings with one stone?"

Halfdan banged the table with his large fist and stood, gaining everyone's attention. "I like that idea. Get rid of both Ælla and Osberht in one go." A large smile parted his lips. "March on Jórvík and conquer it. Mayhap I will become King instead?"

All those around the table laughed and nodded in agreement.

Halfdan looked towards his brother. "Sigurd Snake-in-the-eye, do you foresee this in my future? I fancy being a king in England."

Sigurd glared at his sibling. He hated it when people, especially his family, jested about his powers. But, regardless of their mirth, he did have strong powers to envisage the future. "As it so happens, I foresee you a King of Jórvík." Sigurd waited for the roars to subside. "But, even though I picture two areas of rule for you as King, you must be wary of battles."

"Why?" asked Halfdan Ragnarsson.

"Because you will die in battle on an island far from here."

After a moment of hesitation, Halfdan shrugged and raised his tankard. "In battle is the best way for a warrior to die!" He turned in a circle, saluting all the rowdy warriors with his ale. "Valhalla awaits," he roared before plonking himself back down on his seat.

While the rest of the men started to grow rowdy, through the free-flowing ale, Ubba nursed only one. They were in an unknown land and didn't know what surprises it had in store, so he preferred to keep his wits about him.

Eventually getting fed up with the boasts of some of the jarls, warriors, and freemen around the table, and sensing Ivar was starting to brood again, Ubba got up and went to sit at a table on the other side of the room. If he was truthful, it was nearer Lady Guader and her daughter. There was no telling how the mood would continue this eve, and the women were too valuable to be caught in the crossfire. If he could help them, he would, but he'd have no choice if Ivar thought differently.

With drink fuelling his system, Ivar became more annoyed that things hadn't gone to plan so far. He scanned the room looking for something he could take his frustrations out on. He didn't fancy getting into a fight himself, his reactions too slow with the ale he had consumed, but he wanted something to happen to fire his blood.

It wasn't long before he found his target.

He clicked his fingers to gain Bard's attention. "Take Lady Guader to her bedchamber for the night," Ivar said.

A puzzled look ran over Bard's face, his thoughts slowed down by alcohol.

Ivar rubbed his beard in consideration as his attention returned to Lady Brigitta Guader. *Já, I'll enjoy taking my frustrations out on her.* "Bard. Take her to her chamber, guard her until I come to keep her company."

A smile slowly spread on Bard's lips, and Ivar laughed.

"In fact, why don't we share her hospitality?" Ivar stood suddenly, gaining the attention of the men near him. "When I leave—you," Ivar pointed to one man before making a sweeping gesture. "And the rest of you can enjoy Lady Guader's hospitality, too."

From the other side of the room, Ubba watched the exchange between his brother and Bard. His ale stopped halfway to his lips when he noticed Ivar, and then Bard, stand up quickly. Within seconds, those around Bard were laughing and talking, and even slapping each other on the backs, raising their ales to Ivar. His eyes narrowed. *What's going on?*

Slowly, Ubba lifted his ale to drink, all the while watching and assessing. He tensed when Bard strode across the hall towards him—but more importantly, towards the women. His nostrils flared when he glanced at the main table and saw one of the men stand and grab his groin. Ubba gripped his tankard harder. He had a good idea what was about to happen, but there was nothing he could do for Rosfrith or her mother without being disloyal to his brother. With his jaw clenched tight, he forced himself to stay seated. He hoped it was Lady Guader, not her child, which had caught the interest of the men.

Rosfrith glanced towards the source of merriment. From below her long lashes, she glared at the beast who stood up, swaying in his drunken state. She knew they took no notice of her glares, but it made her feel better. When some of the beasts stood, she looked away and stared at the floor. *How dare those foul beasts laugh. How dare they eat all our hard-earned provisions. How dare they keep my mother tethered to a chair with no care for her needs!*

Rosfrith felt her tears threaten but pushed them away. They had no place here. She didn't want anyone to know how frightened she was so she tried to concentrate on her loathing instead. Caught in her thoughts, Rosfrith failed to notice one of the Danes walk towards them, but her mother's scream of distress had her tear her gaze from the floor. "Mother," she shouted, while she watched the huge beast pull a knife out in front of her mother's face. *Lord, he was going to kill her!*

In a matter of seconds, the beast bent and cut the tethers, which tied her mother to the chair. "Come," Bard said as he hauled Brigitta up to her feet.

Rosfrith noticed her mother stumble into the beast, no doubt her legs were numb from hours of being in one position. When her mother pushed away from the large chest she'd fallen into, Rosfrith noticed her usually rosy complexion was pale. The roar of laughter from within the room, and the unsure feeling for her mother's fate made Rosfrith's head spin. Feeling sick, she tried to push the feeling aside and struggled to get out of tethers. Unfortunately, all her efforts were only rewarded with her chair toppling over—much to the delight of those watching.

"Be good, my daughter. Remember, whatever happens to us, the Lord will protect," Brigitta managed to say before being forcibly pushed out of the hall.

A muscle flexed in Ubba's jaw when he watched Bard take Brigitta away. When he saw Ivar step down and exit the room, he had a fair idea where his brother was off. Sick to his stomach at what was happening, he strode over to Rosfrith and righted her chair. She weighed so little. He looked down at her and ignored the tears falling down her face. He let out a breath when he caught the look of loathing in her violet eyes because he couldn't blame her. The dark-haired lass was young, but not silly—she would know her mother was in danger. But, he couldn't do anything to help the Lady. He cursed himself for it but decided not to get involved. Lady Guader was an adult. Instead, he would stay to keep an eye on the terrified little girl. He returned to his ale, keeping her in his peripheral vision. He only glanced at her again when the noise in the hall quietened. Her head was bowed, and her long black hair hid her weeping. A muscle flexed in his jaw before he tore his eyes away. There was nothing he could do.

When Ivar eventually returned, Ubba watched, hour after hour, as various men made their way out of the hall. When they returned, he caught snippets of their sickening tales of their time with Lady Guader. He was glad her daughter didn't understand what was being said.

Suddenly, he decided he'd had enough. Ubba stood, ready to put an end to Lady Guader's suffering. It wasn't her fault her husband was a fool. He marched over to the main table.

"Brother?"

Ivar turned from his conversation with Halfdan. "What is it, brother?"

"It's about Lady…" Ubba never finished his conversation. A commotion had them all turning towards the door, each grabbing their weapons.

Ivar stood, and relaxed marginally when he saw Asmund enter the hall. His eyes narrowed on the blood covering his face and tunic. He grabbed the hilt of his axe. "What's happened? Are there more of Lord Guader's soldiers?"

"No," said Asmund. He walked towards the table, wiping the blood off his face with the back of his hand. "It's the Lady."

Ivar's eyes narrowed. "Brigitta Guader?"

Sensing his sire's disapproval in his voice, Asmund changed what he was going to say. "Um, já. Lady Guader. She's dead."

With the grace of a large cat, Ivar leaped forward and grabbed Asmund around the neck. "What have you done, you fool?"

Asmund pulled at the hands around his throat. He could feel his eyes bulging with the lack of air in his lungs. "Nothing, she killed herself."

Ivar released his hold and threw Asmund backward, away from his reach. Agitated, he pushed his hand through his hair as he watched Asmund gasp for air. "She killed herself?"

"Já," said Asmund, still gasping for breath. "When I arrived…" he glanced up at Ivar who was towering above him. "She had a dagger."

Ivar let out a noisy breath while he watched Asmund try to stand up.

"I don't know what she said, but she looked at me and then stuck the dagger into her chest," said Asmund, still a little hoarse from his choking.

"She's dead?"

Asmund looked down at his tunic and hands. "Já, there was too much blood for her to survive."

While he listened to the conversation, Ubba's gaze whipped around to where Rosfrith sat. She didn't know what was going on—that was for the best. He stood and walked over, towards Ivar and Asmund. "I'll get Gunnar to sort out the mess," Ubba said to his brother.

"And my men," he looked around, "the sober ones, will guard the rest of the hostages tonight."

Ubba leaned forward, towards the table, and picked up a spare ale. Winking at Ivar, hoping his actions seemed normal and his brother wouldn't realise how desperately he wanted Rosfrith out of harm's way, he took a sip before slamming it back down. "Don't worry about Lord Guader and King Ælla. We will avenge our sire. You can count on it." He felt his muscles relax slightly when his brother beamed at him.

"You are right, Ubba. Tonight, we'll carry on celebrating capturing Dunwich."

Chapter 7

Winter of 865 – Dunwich Fortress

Rosfrith glanced down when sharp pains shot up her arms. Her cold hands were red and stiff, so she rubbed them together in an attempt to warm them, but they remained cold in the brisk air. She eventually gave up and bent to pick up the pale of water she'd been carrying.

When she entered the kitchen, Rosfrith took in a deep breath. The warm kitchen air hit her rosy cheeks, making them and her hands tingle, painfully.

"Please, mistress Rosfrith, put that down," said Edith, stepping forward to take the load from Rosfrith's hands.

She gave Edith a tired smile as she shut the cold out. "I keep telling you, I'm not a mistress anymore." She noticed Edith bristle.

"By the Lord, this isn't right. Those," Edith looked around just in case they were overheard. "Those barbarians are devils. They are not fit to walk this earth."

"But there is nothing we can do, Edith. We must wait until they decide to leave."

"Or hope your Pa and brother will come back and retake Dunwich?"

Rosfrith's heart missed a beat before she let out a small breath. She had long finished hoping for that to happen. It was months since the Norsemen had invaded and changed her life forever. Her father, if he'd cared, would have surely come back by now? *No, my Papa isn't returning.* He would have heard what had happened to her mother, and if that didn't make him want revenge...

Rosfrith shook her head, knowing the past was long gone. Her future was not in her hands, and it was a luxury to think it was. "We can only pray that he does," she said in an attempt to move the conversation on. "How many more trips do I need to take?"

Edith peered into the large water container—it was just over half full. "About five more, I'm afraid."

Rosfrith felt her shoulders sag but pushed them back quickly. There was no point complaining about the work needing to be done. The water had always needed to be hauled, she'd just never had to think about how before because she had servants to do it. "I'll go back out now before I defrost too much," she said in a joking tone, although she felt far from it.

"Mistress Rosfrith?"

She stopped and turned back towards Edith.

"Remember, God gave you this life because you are strong enough to live it," said Edith, before giving Rosfrith a quick nod.

Rosfrith gave a sorrowful smile—she certainly didn't think herself strong enough at the moment. "Thanks, Edith," she said before turning to go back out for the next haul.

Rosfrith faltered as she stepped out of the doorway, ready to go back to the well for more water. The winds were cold. It wouldn't be long before mid-winter would be knocking at their doors. A shudder went down her back, and she used her free hand to rub her arm. She used to love the snow, playing in it with her brother and sister. But, this year would be different. She closed her eyes, trying to halt the tide of sadness washing over her. Once she felt more composed, Rosfrith opened her eyes and a movement made her swing her gaze towards the barn.

The man she knew was called Ubba was watching her. She swiftly nodded in his direction, and he nodded back. From her quick glance, she could see he was leaning against the wattle fence, cutting what looked like a stick, while his breath made clouds in the brisk morning air. Not wanting to tarry, Rosfrith started to walk, picking up her pace as she neared the well. She wanted to get away from him. It wasn't because Ubba frightened her, not like some of the other Norsemen whose looks sent chills down her spine, but he unnerved her because he was always watching her.

Watching me with those icy blue eyes.

On a couple of occasions, she'd been close enough to him, she saw his eyes were the lightest blue she had ever seen. Her parents had always told her she had the rarest coloured eyes, but after seeing Ubba's, she disagreed.

At first, Ubba never spoke to her, not that she knew what he was saying. But lately, if she served him, he tried to teach her his language, pointing at objects and saying words unfamiliar to her ear. She was still wary, but grateful. Her knowledge of their language might help her overhear their plans, or might even aid in her escape. Even seeing what happened to those who were caught, didn't deter her. Running away, if the opportunity arose, had to be an option. She was now three and ten winters, and to her disgust, had observed some of the barbarians didn't mind such a tender age.

While she made her way down the slope, Rosfrith gave a backward glance. Satisfied Ubba was still standing in the same spot, unconcerned, she made her way to the well.

When she reached it, Rosfrith chucked the pale down at an angle that would not disturb the silt at the bottom. She waited for the splash, leaning over the well to grab the rope. Out of the blue, two large hands heaved it towards her.

"Let me haul that for you," Ubba said, knowing she wouldn't understand his words.

"Nay, sir. I'm fine," she replied hastily, once she understood what he was doing. She didn't want his help because she'd seen what happened to those who didn't do their jobs. The Norseman called Bard, left in charge of the servants, was not a kind person.

"But you are a child, and this is heavy," muttered Ubba, more to himself. He was irritated she was expected to do the job of an adult. He never required the children of Ranaricii, even of slaves, to do such back-breaking work.

When Rosfrith realised he was going to get it, whether she wanted him to or not, she took a step back. She watched as he lifted the container and water as if it weighed nothing.

"I'll carry it back." Ubba turned to face her and motioned his intent, nodding towards the building.

Rosfrith shook her head, fear rising in her throat. "Nay, you must not." She reached forward to grab the container, but he lifted it out of her reach. Frustration flittered over her face. "Nay," she said again, and wanting for him to understand, she said, "Bard." She saw a muscle twitch underneath his beard. She hoped he wasn't mad at her.

Ubba took in a deep breath to control his anger. He'd witnessed the treatment Bard had given out to some of the thralls. It wasn't to his liking, but even though he'd mention it to Ivar, nothing had been done. It annoyed Ubba even though he was Chieftain of Ranaricii and his orders were to be obeyed there, in Dunwich they meant nothing. Ivar was the leader. Sometimes he cursed the fact he'd given his word to avenge his father's death.

Catching sight of the fear in the young girl's large eyes, he sighed and handed her the container back. He watched her glance around before taking it, presumably to check who was watching, with a guilty look on her face. He hoped he hadn't made trouble for her—it was the last thing he wanted to do.

His gaze narrowed on Rosfrith as she hurried away, as fast as she could with the weight. It was a shame one so young had been abandoned by her parents. Even though he hadn't always see eye-to-eye with his sire, Ubba always knew they'd had each other's backs.

Still watching Rosfrith, he nodded when she reached the door and turned to give him a brief smile before disappearing through the entrance. She'd be back out. He'd watched her often enough to know she'd make at least ten trips. He walked over to a broken log, and sat to wait, unconcerned about the cold air swirling around him. It was what he felt he needed to do.

A month later, when they still hadn't heard anything from Lord Guader, Ivar started to talk about invading Northumbria to find King Ælla. Ubba and all the men had agreed. They were like sitting ducks, waiting in Dunwich, giving King Ælla enough time to establish an army.

Even though Ubba knew how impatient his brother was, he suggested they waited in Dunwich until the winter had finished, where the stores were still plentiful. It was different in their homeland, for they knew what prey was available to them when they were away from home. But, walking during the winter in an unknown area, without the prospect of regular food, would be foolish. Ubba was glad his brother had listened to reason, although, to be fair, his brother's decision might have had more to do with the ale and plentiful bedmates rather than logic.

End of winter...

Bored and brooding, Ivar's eyes scanned the room, quietly taking in the scene. His gaze narrowed. Lethargic men surrounded him; chatting, drinking, and playing the board game, Hnefatafl. The servants of Lord Guader were busy with their chores, but they too looked settled, no longer afraid of him and his men. He grabbed his ale and took a large swig. He slammed it down. Very few reacted. *If we stay much longer, they will all become as peaceful and docile as the dogs lying by the fire.*

Ivar stood, scraping his chair along the floor. Some men glanced in his direction. When they noticed the scowl on his face, they nudged the others. Satisfied that, at last, he had some attention, Ivar banged his hand down on the wooden table, calling his brothers and a couple of senior men to join him.

Once everyone was settled, and ale placed in front of them, Ivar started their rendezvous. "We have stayed in Dunwich long enough." He waited for the grunts of agreement to settle. "The winter is nearing its end, Lord Guader has not returned, so we need to seek out King Ælla ourselves."

"Where will we find him?"

"North," Ivar replied to Halfdan Ragnarsson.

Ubba pushed back in his chair, leaning back for Rosfrith to fill up his mug. When she finished, he watched her fill up Sigurd's. "When will we leave?"

"Soon, we have secured enough horses for our travels." A large smile crossed his lips. "King Edmund and the people of East Angles have been very giving with their help. I think they are trying to pay us off."

Ubba gave a small snort and nodded. That was normally the way—people would pay handsomely for them to leave. "Have we enough provisions?"

Ivar nodded.

"Good," said Ubba as he scanned the hall. It was about time they made a move. Apart from the feeling of restlessness amongst the men, which only led to trouble, Ubba wanted to avenge Ragnar, and then get back to his life in Ranaricii. "Any plans?"

"Not yet, but we can talk, now." Ivar nodded at Sigurd, who produced a badly drawn map.

Everyone was quiet while Sigurd unrolled it on the table. "We found this in Lord Guader's chambers," he said before looking down onto it. "If this is correct, we are here." He pointed to East Angles. "And King Ælla's kingdom is around here," he circled Northumbria with his finger. "Jórvík will be the biggest town around, one King Ælla will, no doubt, want to protect."

"How will we know King Ælla will be there or come to protect it?" asked Halfdan.

Ivar laughed before he slapped Sigurd on his back. "Because, dear brother, our brother here has had a vision."

"What?" asked Halfdan.

Sigurd straightened. "A vision that shows we will find and defeat the Kings of Northumbria."

"Both Kings?" Ubba interrupted.

"Já," replied Sigurd.

"But I thought them to be battling each other?"

Sigurd shrugged.

"But that isn't the whole of it, is it dear brother?" Ivar laughed and placed a hand on Sigurd's shoulder.

Sigurd scowled at his brother.

"No, our dear brother sees *his* future, too. Marriage and children," Ivar said before making a show of pretending to stifle a laugh. "With King Ælla's daughter, no less."

Most of those who overheard the conversation laughed at the absurdity—all except those who knew how powerful Sigurd's visions were.

"Well, that's good then," said Ubba, realising if they didn't get off the subject, Sigurd could end up battling with Ivar himself. "What happens if Ælla is not there when we arrive?"

Ivar shrugged. "Then we'll wait."

When he recapped over their meet, Ivar said, "It's decided. We will plan to cross the mouth of the Humber River, and move onto Jórvík. Unless Lord Guader has managed to get the Kings to form an army before we arrive, it should be easy going."

"We'll kill them all," said Bard, laughing, and taking a large swig of his ale. He motioned to Rosfrith to fill his mug up. He was finding he was partial to the English ale.

Ivar glanced at Bard and nodded. "Our priority is King Ælla, then anyone else who gets in our way. Let's see if we can't get that whoreson to come out of his hiding place. If he does, we've got a nice death planned for him," said Ivar, lifting his ale in salute.

Once the cheering had quietened, Bard's gaze flicked to Rosfrith. Throughout the meet, he'd been only half listening to Ivar, because his interest centered on one blonde-haired, comely looking thrall serving them beer. But, when Ivar slammed his mug back down, the other serving wench, Rosfrith, caught his attention. His eyes narrowed on her. She looked an innocent enough child, pouring the ale, but something wasn't quite right. She was the Lord's daughter, not that she looked any different from any other wench now. But, she was a little too interested in their discussions for someone that couldn't understand what they were saying.

Bard picked up his ale and took a big slurp, finally ignoring the thrall he was previously interested in. He'd seek her out later, if needs be. *Does the young wench understand what we are saying?* He would find out. "*Mugge, taka.*"

Without thinking, Rosfrith turned to reach for Bard's ale mug to take it away. She stopped abruptly, realising what she'd done. With her hand wavering in the air, she glanced at him. His slow smile, spreading across his lips, told her he knew her secret. She moved away from the main table quickly and went across the room to serve the men playing the board games instead, not daring to look at Bard again.

After she had filled the last mug, Rosfrith spotted Edith stoking up the fire in the hall. She wandered over to her, taking her time, so it wasn't obvious where she was going. Still holding onto the half-filled jug of ale, she nudged Edith with her elbow. "They're leaving."

Edith put down the poker and gave the men at the table a sideward glance. "When?"

"I don't know, but I think it's soon." Rosfrith shrugged. "I tried to find out, but that one,"— she nodded towards Bard—"seems to know I can understand some of their language."

Edith's lips thinned. "That won't do. It could be dangerous for you if he finds out."

"I know, but I think he realises. It was the look he gave me."

Edith stretched out her hand to take the ale off Rosfrith. "I'll serve them, you go into the kitchen, away from his eyes."

"Why?"

"Because you need to protect your knowledge—your soul holds no secret that your behavior does not reveal," Edith explained, taking the jug from Rosfrith. "Go now, before they notice you've gone."

Rosfrith smiled at Edith's wise words. "All right, you be careful, too."

Edith let out a short breath. "Aw, don't go worrying about me, mistress Rosfrith. They aren't interested in an old servant who doesn't understand a word they are saying. Quick, now, go."

Though it wasn't obvious to anyone else, Ubba watched Rosfrith talk to Edith, and then leave the Hall. He hadn't failed to notice the incident with Bard and Rosfrith, either. He'd overheard and witnessed her picking up Bard's mug without hesitation. Ubba rubbed his beard. *Mayhap I shouldn't have taught the girl so well?* He'd done it to help her, but had he? He yanked his look towards his ale. There was nothing he could do about her being a quick learner. To him, it was beneficial for her to be able to speak their tongue, especially if he was thinking of taking her back to Denmark, but it did mean the others could use her for unsavory situations. He looked towards the closed door, glad she was clever enough to make herself scarce. *Mayhap Bard will drop it?* He huffed, he knew Bard too well.

Rosfrith stepped into the kitchen, away from the brisk morning air. She was glad the winter snow was finally gone, but the nippy atmosphere still indicated summer was a long way off. She smiled when she noticed Edith. "I've finished my morning task," she said as she passed a heavy wooden bucket containing milk to Edith.

Edith turned from the pot of porridge she was serving and took the pail. "Good, come over here and have a little of this to warm you up. Blythe come here and take this." She held out the container. "Use half of it to make some cheese."

Blythe nodded and took the milk.

Rosfrith shook her head. "No, Edith, we can't. It's for them to break their fast." She lifted her chin.

Ignoring her, Edith grabbed a wooden bowl. "They won't notice a spoonful gone. Besides, mistress, you are looking thin."

"What about the others?" Rosfrith looked around the room at the servants busy with their jobs.

Edith smiled. "Ssshh, I've given them a little, too." She winked at Rosfrith when she added a good dollop of honey.

Feeling her stomach gurgle, Rosfrith finally reached out for the bowl. She would be no good to anyone if she became ill with starvation. She sat down on a stool, near the fire, with her porridge. In the quiet, Rosfrith stared at the flames. For the first time in ages, she felt content. It wasn't that she would choose the life she was living, but the comradeship she had found with the other servants had been heart-warming. Even her relationship with her sister had improved. They had become closer in their grief about their mother and bonded over their new situation during the long dark evenings. She continued to eat in silence before a shout from outside the kitchen brought Rosfrith out of her thoughts.

Edith started instructing some of the younger servants to grab serving plates. "The Danes want to break their fast early today." She regarded Rosfrith. "Perchance the rumors are true?"

Rosfrith nodded. She hoped the conversations she'd eavesdropped were correct about the beasts leaving Dunwich. *If they left, maybe everything will return to normal?* She could only hope.

After the food had been consumed in the hall and tidied away, Rosfrith, Edith, and some other servants huddled together in the kitchen. Now, they definitely knew the Norsemen were on their way. The tense but excitable atmosphere in the main hall last night and this morning indicated the change.

"Let's hope they leave something in our stores," one of the servants stated.

"Who cares, as long as they just go. We can get back to normal."

"Aye, especially when Lord Guader comes back and claims back what is his. If he's not happy somewhere else, forgettin' about us folk, you know what Lords are like."

One of the girls nudged the other, suddenly remembering Mistress Rosfrith was standing with them. "We didn't mean no harm, mistress."

Rosfrith smiled at them. She wasn't offended. The truth was, over the winter both Rosfrith and her sister had become so much part of the workforce, carrying out the same amount of chores, they'd forgotten they were born a different class, so spoke freely in front of her. "I've taken no offence."

Edith eyed the two young girls and shook her head. They were naïve to think things would ever go back to normal. Even if the beasts did leave without harming or taking any of them, from the looks of things, there would be very little left at Dunwich for the Lord's return. "Come on, let's get our chores completed."

A couple of hours later, all the people of Dunwich were summoned to the main hall. Rosfrith, Edith, and her sister all followed the other servants and crowded in. They all silenced when Ivar shouted for their attention. Even though most of the servant still did not understand what the Heathen wanted, his tone told them to quieten. Before long, Norsemen mingled between the servants of Dunwich and started splitting them into groups.

While Ivar barked orders to his men from his elevated position on the dais, Ubba watched Bard push his way through the crowd. Some servants tried to step out of his way, but most were too packed to move. He could see Bard make his way towards the darkest haired one. Ubba tensed. He knew he was after Rosfrith, but he had to stay where he was. He watched Bard smile and stretch out his hand, grabbing Rosfrith roughly by the arm.

"We'll take this one with us," Bard shouted. The room became quiet when they realised who he had.

Ivar stopped instructing his men, interested to see what Bard was shouting about. His eyes narrowed on the girl he was pulling. It was Lord Guader's daughter. The only way he could tell was because, under the layer of dirt, he could still see her midnight coloured hair.

Ivar fingered his beard. *What's Bard up to?* They'd already picked out most of the thralls and slaves they were going to take—ones that were strong and worth the price of the food they would consume. This one was a child. Besides, apart from his initial excitement of finding her, she'd been no use after. "Why would we take her? She is of no use. She's young and weak. Besides, Lord Guader doesn't think her worthy of rescuing, he hasn't even responded to our missives asking to exchange her for money." Ivar squared his shoulders. "No, we leave her."

Ubba kept quiet at their exchange, a muscle twitching along his jaw. He was unsure whether it was safer for Rosfrith to come with them, so he could keep an eye on her, or for her to be left behind at Dunwich to take care of herself and anyone that was left behind.

Not giving up, Bard roughly hauled her forward. "Because, she,"—he scrutinised her before smiling at Ivar—"can speak some of our tongue, and of course, theirs. She can communicate for us."

Ivar's gaze sliced onto her, his interest in her reignited. "Is this true?" Rosfrith's paling face told him all he needed to know. "All right, take her." *Perhaps she is worth the trouble?*

Ubba sighed deeply. It seemed as though he had his work cut out keeping her safe, especially as Bard had her in his sights.

Chapter 8

Autumn of 866 – Outskirts of Jórvík, Northumbria

The brisk autumnal winds cut through Rosfrith's clothes as she gathered firewood for the evening's warmth. She was bone tired after walking North on the Roman roads, along the Humber. But, as a Viking's thrall, she didn't have time to rest, so she scanned the floor, searching for kindling. Her feet ached, as did her muscles while she moved through the fallen leaves of various colours. In fact, she could swear her bones ached, too, from the pounding of her feet on the ground. All of the thralls had walked, while most of the heathens had ridden on horses or in carts. The irony was that the majority of the horses had been her father's, or given to the Danes, willingly, by the Anglo-Saxons, regardless that they were the same people that they kept as slaves.

She sighed wearily and eyed the ground, it appeared soft. *Mayhap if I lie down and sleep, no one would notice?* She gave a light laugh, of course, they would. They wouldn't notice her gone but they would notice an absent fire. She moved forward through paths the trees allowed her access to—unfortunately, not having much luck finding what she wanted because most of the wood was damp.

Finally, after hours of scouring, Rosfrith straightened and stretched her back. It was getting dark and she'd have to go back, before she got into trouble. She picked up the sparse bundle she had amassed and hoped the others had collected enough. Not that she cared about the fire—the only time she got near to its warmth was to tend it, but the consequences of not feeding and warming the Danes was dire. She yawned. She didn't need luxury tonight, she was so exhauseted, even a thin fur on the leaves would feel extravagant.

Rosfrith made her way back to camp in the dimming light, only stopping briefly to right the twigs, which frequently slipped out of her arms. She scowled, becoming frustrated when one fell, again. At the moment, she was frustrated with everything—her life, the Heathens, and even her own people. *Don't the villages we pass on our travels, who willingly gave the barbarians food, horses, and coin to leave them alone, realise they help make the Norsemen stronger—fuelling them with more energy for raiding and battle?* It was a strange situation, to be sure.

Once she was back in camp, she disposed of her meagre wood offerings on the pile, well away from the make-shift constructions, in case of fires. When she finished her other chores, Rosfrith lifted the flap on the main tent and walked in, ale in hand. Although the moon was fully in the sky and the stars were twinkling between the clouds, she hadn't yet finished for the night. She stepped in, most of the men inside barely glanced at her. She knew she was truly a thrall to them, for they didn't even stop their conversation. She moved swiftly, wanting to finish in order to go to bed. She waited for Ivar to raise his jug for her to fill. After his was full, as efficiently as she could, she filled each man's jug. The only one who gave her any acknowledgment for her service was Ubba. He nodded, and she gave him a brief smile in response. After over a year, Rosfrith was still unsure how to act with him. Sometimes he took time to teach her new Norse words, other times he didn't notice she was there.

When she refilled the last jug, she caught her father's name being uttered. It dragged her out of her thoughts of sleep and she hesitated. She glanced at Ivar, who had mentioned him, but she tried not to react. Obviously, they'd forgotten who she was—or didn't care. Her spirits lifted. *I'll possibly get to see my father again?* She moved closer to listen to the conversation, only to move quickly away when she noticed Bard's gaze narrow on her.

"Fill, wench," said Bard holding his jug high.

Rosfrith felt herself redden. He'd obviously remembered her talent with their language. She watched the ale turn into a trickle. She had nothing left in her jug to warrant her hanging around. "I'll get some more, *vikingar*." She bowed slightly and exited the tent as quick as she could.

A couple of days later, a long whistle made Rosfrith look up from her mending task. Someone was coming into their camp. Uninterested, she resumed her work. It wasn't unusual—Norsemen left and returned numerous times a day. This time, however, as the noise of horses neared, her interest aroused. She could make out the distinctive tinkle of chain mail armor and noticed more warriors move towards the crude, temporary gate. When the advancing group neared the heavily guarded entrance, she noticed a man on a horse carrying a white flag, and next to it, the flags of both Kings of Northumbria.

She threw her work down, mindless of the cloth getting dirty and stood, the same moment her name was called.

"Your sire requests you," the warrior in front of her said, indicating to the largest tent.

Hiding the smile on her face, she ran towards the main tent, where Ivar, his brothers, and the other leaders were. Hesitating only a fraction to wipe the smile off her face, she lifted the flap and entered.

Ivar glanced at Rosfrith when she entered. He knew who it was Lord Guarder arriving into their camp and hoped that the addition of Rosfrith would startle him into not thinking properly. "Ah, good. Let's see if all that food you have consumed has been of good use. We need you to translate for us," he said. "We have a party arriving..."—he scanned the faces in the tent—"hopefully with coin for our coffers." He shrugged before an enormous smile erupted on his face. "If not, at least we can get ready to fight." His gaze whipped back around to Rosfrith, and his eyes narrowed on her before he said, "Let's go."

Rosfrith stayed in the same spot and kept her gaze towards the earth floor, unsure of how to act. If they were soldiers of either King Ælla or King Osberht, they might have news of her father. Only when the men exited, and she raised her gaze ready to follow, Rosfrith noticed Ubba hadn't left. He stood with a quizzical look on his face, his blue eyes narrowed on her. "Sire," she mumbled quickly, before leaving the tent and catching up with the party.

Rosfrith's heart beat faster, not only from her rush to follow the long-legged men but with excitement and nerves. She stopped behind them, noticing they all had their hands casually on their weapons. She scanned the Northumbrian men as they neared. *He's here! My father is here!* Standing on tip-toes, Rosfrith tried to get a better view of him from behind the large Danes. Luckily, he sat astride one of the horses so she could see him, aloft. It took all her self-control not to run up to him.

As Ivar welcomed them with customary pleasantries, Rosfrith scanned the rest of the party, noticing her brother, Bryan, before she glanced back at her father, inspecting him. He appeared aged, much older than just over a year would account for. *Maybe he knows what has happened to mother?* She pushed her sadness, which always churned her stomach when she remembered her mother, away, and continued to watch and listen, waiting to be called upon by Ivar.

From his high position on his horse, Lord Arter Guader noticed his daughter straight away, hanging behind the welcoming group. He was surprised, but he didn't outwardly react. He averted his eyes from her. Ignoring Ivar's greeting, he didn't know how he felt at seeing her. To be honest, he'd hadn't expected to set eyes on her again—no one left at Dunwich fortress knew where either of his daughters had gone.

When Arter had eventually returned to Dunwich and found it ruined, with barely a soul to tend to it, he heard the fate of his wife. When he was informed, he'd thrown up, but then he quickly composed himself. Although it was against his religious belief that Brigitta took her life—only God should choose the moment you die—he was also, in some way, glad she had. It pained him, but he didn't think he'd have it in his heart to love her, or even touch her again after she'd been debased by the barbarians.

His gaze rested briefly on Rosfrith before he noticed a smile flicker on her lips. She recognised him. He jerked his gaze away, not returning her smile. *Nay, she is better off left here with the Norsemen.* No doubt they had defiled her too, and if she came back with him, he'd have no chance of marrying her off to anyone of worth. He just hoped Rosfrith wouldn't make a scene when he left without her. *If* he got out alive. He glanced at the white flag to check if it was still flying. His tension increased as he dismounted his horse. He stepped forward and hoped the Heathens would let them go peacefully after he informed them neither King Ælla or King Osberht were willing to give them any silver or gold—for compensation or to not attack Northumbria.

"So, Lord Guader, I presume you got our missive," said Ivar once the men had dismounted. Keeping one eye on them, he waved Rosfrith forward, ready for when he needed her. He noticed Arter didn't make eye contact with her, but he could tell that he was rattled. Good. "Have you come to give us good news? Has King Ælla agreed to my terms in regard to my sire's death?" He didn't fail to see the Lord tense, but he hadn't expected anything else. It had been too long to wait for payment, so now he was going to have some fun with the kings before he engaged in the fight his mind and body was craving.

"Hmm, we'll talk about the compensation, after," Arter said, hoping it wouldn't be brought up again. "In your missive, you stated that for exchange for peace with the King to be near his lands, you only ask for as much land you can cover with an ox's hide?" Arter asked, a frown on his head, the request was so peculiar—but then, not much of what the heathens did made sense.

Rosfrith listened to her father's rough attempt at speaking. He knew the basics of the Dane's language, but not enough to make sure their business went smoothly. She translated her father's words properly, and jumped when Ivar roared with laughter.

Ubba, standing to Ivar's side, studied his brother with a side glance, wondering what he was up to. They had amassed an army and acome to this land to get coin or to kill King Ælla, why on earth was he asking for the peace deal his father failed to get?

"Já, that is all we ask," replied Ivar.

Arter clicked his fingers and a soldier brought an ox hide forward, placing it on the floor between them. "We are confused, is this what you mean?"

Ivar raised his eyebrows his men to the sides of him, and chuckled. "Já."

Arter stuttered, "If that is the case, King Ælla agrees to your terms. He will give you the land you have asked for, if you promise never to wage war against him." Arter indicated for the soldier to pick up the hide when listening to Rosfrith translate, a little annoyed she spoke the language better than himself. She's never been interested when he'd tried to teach her and now, just over a year, she was truly a Heathen. There was no hope for her.

"Wait," Ivar said firmly. All eyes looked at him as he removed a sharp dagger from its sheath. "Ask the soldier to give me the hide," he said to Rosfrith. Once he had it in his hand, his smile returned. "Help me, brothers," he said, indicating for them to stretch it out. He then proceeded to cut the hide into fine strands.

Once Arter understood what he was doing, he paled. "That's not what we agreed, there is enough hide there to envelop Jórvík," he stammered, backing away. "I'll have to explain to the King."

Ivar, looking all innocent, shrugged. "Best be quick. You have given me his promise already."

Rosfrith looked quickly between them both, knowing Ivar had duped her father and King Ælla. There would be trouble.

With the meeting turning bad, Arter made sure the rest of the meeting was swift. He wanted to leave.

Rosfrith sensed the tension in the Anglo-Saxon men, it was so unlike the jovial mood of the Vikings. When she saw them preparing to go, she was relieved her translating was coming to an end, but it saddened her that her father hadn't acknowledged or thanked her. *Mayhap he didn't recognise me? Have I changed that much?*

Just before Ivar turned to leave the meeting, he grabbed Rosfrith's arm. She jumped, not expecting the contact. He glanced between Rosfrith and Lord Guader, then snarled. "Lord Guader?" She pushed her forward, still holding her arm tightly. "There is some more negotiating you might like to conduct?" He turned his attention onto Ubba. "Let them talk. The Lord might be willing to pay some of *his* coin to get his daughter back."

Rosfrith's heart swelled at the thought. *I could go home to Dunwich. Surely father will pay?* When she heard the small amount, Ivar whispered into Ubba's ear, her heart took another leap.

Ubba nodded at Ivar. "Come," he said to Arter. When one of the soldiers took a step forward to stand shoulder-to-shoulder with Lord Guader, Ubba's hand instinctively went for his axe.

"It's all right, he's my brother," said Rosfrith, stepping between them.

Ubba raised his brow briefly before huffing and walking towards one of the tents. "Come."

Ubba lifted the tent flap and indicated for them to enter. Although their weapons had been removed when they'd entered the camp, he still didn't trust either of the men who were Rosfrith's family. They would hurt her—there was something in their eyes that didn't sit right with him.

Once they went in, he followed and closed the flap. Ubba rested his hands on his axe and watched while the two men settled, before Rosfrith took her seat. He grunted to himself. He wouldn't understand what was going to be said, but he had the feeling Rosfrith would be upset by the end of it. *There is no way her father will pay us any coin.*

Rosfrith's gaze flickered back and forth between her father and brother willing them to speak. She waited, but they were silent. "It's—it's been a long time, but I'm overjoyed to see you, Papa." She considered her brother. "You, too, Bryan."

Arter gave a weak smile, his skin crinkling around his eyes. "Aye, Rosfrith, it's been a long time, much has happened."

Rosfrith felt her heart speed up. *He does know me! Does he know about dear mother?* She, herself, hadn't known all the facts of her death—until recently when she could understand the Norsemen tongue and two warriors were discussing it. Their words had torn her heart in two, but at least she finally knew her mother had killed herself, that she hadn't been murdered. "Mama?" she quietly questioned.

Arter nodded. "I know. I've been back to Dunwich fortress."

The mention of her home made her smile. "Is it standing?"

Arter nodded again.

She sat forward. "Is Edeva and Edith there?"

Arter shook his head.

Rosfrith saddened. She would love to know what had become of them both after they'd been separated. She hoped Edith was with Edeva. Once she composed herself, her gaze returned to her father's lowered one. She licked her dry lips. "I would love to return to Dunwich." When neither replied, she moved forward to the edge of her seat. "Can I come home, Papa?"

Arter gave a little cough and Bryan examined the floor.

"Well, there's a problem there," Arter nervously coughed again. "We haven't the coin at the moment to spare."

Rosfrith's brow furrowed. *Surely I am more important to him than his coffers?* "Haven't you been paid handsomely by the Kings of Northumbria for all your efforts?"

Arter didn't respond.

Desperation started to claw at her. "But, Papa, I will find a way to repay you. The Danes are fair in their ransom for me, because of what happened to..." Rosfrith felt her voice falter. "Mama."

Arter gave a small uncomfortable laugh. "There's more to it than that, child."

"What?" she questioned, looking at them both for an answer. She noticed the sly look her father gave Ubba. "Oh," she whispered when she understood their train of thought.

Getting up from her seat, Rosfrith threw herself on her knees in front of her father. She was not too proud to beg, after all, being a thrall was the lowest she thought she could go.

Ubba tensed when she neared the older man, but he didn't move from his position. It would only take him one large step to pull her out of harm's way.

"I have not, I swear, Papa. I am not dishonored. Please, take me with you," she pleaded, grabbing for his hand.

"You cannot believe her, Papa. You can't tell me that those," Bryan raised his chin towards Ubba, "haven't ruined her yet? She's lying."

Stunned at brother's only words, she pleaded, "I always tell the truth, Bryan. I wouldn't lie to either of you. I am your sister". Rosfrith felt tears well in her eyes. *When did Bryan become so heartless?*

Bryan's eyes glanced around the tent before returning to meet her gaze. "I have no mother," he paused, "or sisters."

Pain sliced through her heart when she watched him stand, turn, and walk out of the tent.

"I must go," Arter said quietly, also watching his son leave. His son was his concern now, the one to pass on the Guader name. Painful as it was, Rosfrith was the past, and he must forget her.

Rosfrith regarded her father, squeezing his hand. *Maybe he's shocked at seeing me, and needs time?* She needed reassurance everything would be all right. "Will you come again, Papa?"

Arter moved his hand from hers and stared at her for a moment before standing. "No, no, my dear girl. I...," He patted her head then paused, trying to find a way to say he wouldn't see her again. "I have work to attend with both King Ælla and Osberht. Then I have to travel to Jórvík to attend the *All Saints* celebrations, before heading to meet King Edmund. My priority is keeping peace in this land." He paused, the pursuit of peace was something that had personally cost him dear.

Hope sprang into her soul for the briefest of seconds. "So, if there's peace, you will return for me?" Even though he muttered, *perhaps*, Rosfrith knew by the look on his face, he wouldn't. She didn't rise from the floor when he stood to leave. She was defeated. Another of her family was leaving her to fend for herself.

Ubba swivelled his head and watched Lord Guader leave the tent. He didn't have to follow him, he'd already instructed his men to keep watch for them. Turning back, he viewed the broken girl in front of him. He didn't know what was said. When her eyes closed, in an attempt to stop crying, he stepped forward.

Rosfrith glanced up. For the briefest of moments, she hoped her father had returned. When she saw Ubba, her heart sank. To be truthful, she'd forgotten he was there—she was so used to him watching her.

"Are you troubled?"

She shook her head and slowly stood. "*Nay*." No, she wasn't troubled, it was deeper than that.

"Is your father returning?" Ubba spoke slowly, knowing her upset frame of mind might hinder her translating.

She shook her head. "He is busy." She glanced at him when he gave a large snort of disgust. She looked away, so he didn't see her tears.

Ubba was furious. Ivar had asked for hardly any coin from the man in exchange for his daughter. *But, Lord Guader couldn't even give them that for her!* He sighed. He hadn't understood what was said, but the Lord and his son's action indicated Rosfrith was going to be staying with them. It appeared he would be watching over her for some time yet. Her shaky voice drew his attention back to her.

"I have some information for you. It might be of use."

Later on, after a brief conversation with Ubba, Rosfrith was left alone in the tent where her father and brother had broken her heart. She knew the information she'd just told Ubba would be used, but her father's betrayal deeply hurt her. *If I am to be left with the barbarians, it's better I protect them, not my former people.* She owed them no loyalty.

Ivar eyed his brother when he walked into his tent. "You've been a while, brother. I was going to send Halfdan to find you. What tidings do you bring, brother? Did Lord Guader pay his money and take his daughter?"

Ubba shook his head.

Surprise flickered over Ivar's face. "Not even for the token gesture we asked for?"

"No." Ubba moved towards a seat and sat.

"We should have killed him, like we originally thought."

Ubba shrugged. "Listen, I have something to tell you; something that I have found out about the Anglo-Saxons." Ubba told his brother the events within the tent with the lord and his son, and then about the information Rosfrith had imparted to him. Once he'd finished, he watched as a wide smile spread across Ivar's lips as he nodded.

"All of them will be in their church, you say?"

"Já," Ubba replied. "They celebrate something the Christians call '*All Saint's Day*,' which means everyone will be in church for the celebrations. Easy pickings." As Ubba spoke to his brother, his stomach clenched. He felt awful betraying Rosfrith's trust by telling his brother of the ways of the locals, but it had to be done. He was loyal to his family, not to a thrall.

"So, we attack then?"

Ubba nodded at his brother. "We will prepare."

While they completed their daily tasks around the camp, Rosfrith and the other servants carefully watched and listened. There was a strange atmosphere around the camp, euphoric and excitement. The servants were nervous because it was obvious the barbarians were preparing for battle. Because of the day, 1st November 866, Rosfrith knew where they were going to attack—Jórvík.

While she watched them don their weapons and smear dyes on their faces, Rosfrith had a moment of regret for her loose tongue. Her chest squeezed with anxiety, making it hard to breathe. *What if Papa is at the church when the Norsemen arrive? What about the innocent women and children there? What have I done?* Panicking, she glanced around for Ubba. Although she didn't fully trust him, out of all the Norsemen, he was the least bloodthirsty. When she spotted him exiting a tent, she ran over. He hadn't noticed her, so she called, but he didn't respond.

Ubba, lost in his thoughts about the upcoming battle, felt something grab his arm. Instinctively, he grabbed his axe, turned and raised it in the air. Ready to kill. Luckily, before he brought it down, he paused. It was Rosfrith. She looked terrified, her violet eyes staring at him in shock. He was annoyed he hadn't heard her near him. *I'd better be more prepared for the upcoming fight.* Ubba growled with annoyance at his error and noticed her shrink back before straightening back up.

"Can I talk to you, Lord?" It took all her efforts not to cower from his icy glare. Ubba obviously was in no mood for a conversation, but she had to proceed, for her peace of mind. When he finally raised an eyebrow in question, she took in a breath. She needed to make sure. "If there are women and children at the Church, will you spare them?"

Ubba's gaze narrowed on Rosfrith again. She was standing in front of him—on the one hand, looking scared of him, and on the other, being bold enough to ask him to spare lives in a battle.

"Please?" she asked again. "I told you about the Church, and I fear God will be angry with me if innocents die."

Ubba huffed and tore his gaze away. He didn't care about her God, and he certainly didn't have time to question his actions in battle, especially when he was mentally preparing. He'd *never* intentionally killed any woman or child, but he wasn't going to explain that to her— she was, after all, only a thrall. "I'll do whatever I need to," he said before nodding and turning to stride away.

Rosfrith watched him go. She wasn't going to badger him again, he appeared too cross, but she hoped she'd planted enough of a seed for him to do the right thing.

A couple of days later, loud cheering indicated the returning of warriors back to the empty camp. Rosfrith stopped her chore and stood, scanning the group when they entered through the parted gateway. They appeared bloodied and tired after their battle. Her eyes narrowed on them and she noticed neither Ubba, nor his brothers, had returned. *Mayhap they are all dead?* A frown marred her forehead. The returning men didn't look defeated, and their cheers indicated victory, which would mean the Danes had won the battle. She bit her bottom lip, unsure of how she felt.

"You, there," one of the men shouted at Rosfrith as he neared the fire, bringing her out of her thoughts.

She turned her head to look at him.

"You, tell the rest of your kind to help pack up the camp. We are leaving for Jórvík in the morn."

Rosfrith gave a quick nod, before moving away. She sighed, knowing more warfare was coming because the Kings of Northumbria wouldn't take kindly to that.

Chapter 9

Jórvík (York) – Winter 868

Ubba scanned the large hall, located in the middle of Jórvík. *Thór's teeth,* he was bored. They'd captured the area over a year ago, and nothing exciting had happened since. There wasn't even any news about King Ælla or Osberht trying to take it back, even after Ivar's trick with the ox hide. In fact, the people of Jórvík and the area around were more than happy to provide food and all manner of luxuries to them. Bored to death, Ubba wanted to return home to Ranaricii. He watched another of his kin fall to sleep by the fire, and knew he'd had enough. He got up and walked up to Ivar who was sitting in a straight-backed chair near the fire.

"Ivar?"

Ivar glanced at his brother, before returning his attention to the fire. "Brother?"

"I have an itch."

"Go and wash, then," laughed his brother, Bjorn, who was sitting next to Ivar.

Ubba let out a snort. "Not that type of itch. I need to return to Ranaricii," said Ubba.

Ivar was quiet for a while before he finally glanced back at Ubba. "Not yet, brother. We received information that King Ælla and King Osberht are finally putting their differences aside, and amassing an army to try and retake Jórvík," Ivar shrugged. "They are nearly ready for battle."

Ubba's gaze narrowed on his brother. *How did I miss that piece of information?* Boredom was making him soft.

Ivar grinned. "Don't look so worried, Ubba, they won't succeed."

"I'm not worried," Ubba replied, sounding almost angry. He rubbed his hand over his face. "Sorry, brother. This battle has been a long time coming. I'm glad it's almost time."

Ivar nodded and then sobered up. He glanced at the group of men in front of him. "I need all of you to stay for a while. To be ready to fight."

Ubba nodded, along with the other men. Their duty was next to Ivar—even though Ubba knew they could be talking years.

Two years later...

Ubba put down his knife and pushed his plate aside. "Ivar. It is time. I'm going back to Denmark. I need to go to Ranaricii and check on things."

"Don't you like it here?" Ivar questioned, his mouth filled with food.

Ubba took the time to glance around the hall. "It's not that, Ivar, for we have plenty," he said, glancing at the plentiful food covering the tables. "But we've been away five winters."

We have done what we needed to do. Both Kings, Ælla and Osberht, are dead from our hands."

"Killed," interrupted Sigurd. "By a blood-eagle, don't forget."

Ubba grunted. He'd never forget the battle or seeing King Ælla's back cut open, his ribs torn out, and lungs folded to represent an eagle's wings. He hoped he wouldn't witness it again. "Já, Sigurd," he said, knowing his brother saw worse in his visions, so the battles didn't affect him. But, he was tired of fighting—or worse still, hanging around becoming lazy. He turned his attention back to Ivar. "But, Ragnar Lothbrok has been avenged. I have followed you to Mercia, fought against the joint forces of Mercia and Wessex, wintered in Nottingham, and now come back to Jórvík." He puffed. "But I need to head North before my people forget I am their Earl."

Ivar rubbed his beard. "I know how you feel, brother. I would like to return home, but..." he shrugged, "I think we might return to East Angles, see if we can't get King Edmund to give us more coin to leave him alone."

Sigurd sniggered. "And get him to renounce his precious Christ to become a pagan. Or kill him."

Ubba's gaze narrowed on Ivar, ignoring Sigurd. "But who would protect Jórvík if you leave?"

Ivar stood up. "There is no one left to fight for it now the Kings are dead. I'll leave a puppet king here..." He glanced around the room. "Mayhap Egbert? He can collect the tax for us. There's nothing left here. No challenge," Ivar said, displaying a line of teeth.

"You love fighting, brother," Ubba flatly stated the fact.

"What else is there to life?" Ivar sobered as his eyes narrowed on Ubba. His brother was unhappy. "All right, you can go back to Ranaricii and take your men." He looked around at the others. "The rest will come with me. I have a fancy for ruling all of *Bryttania*."

The room erupted with cheers.

Chapter 10

Spring 870 – On the way back to Ranaricii

Ubba was in a jovial mood. He was finally going home. None of his brothers were coming, they were too busy killing and conquering *Bryttania* to return. He'd had enough.

Ubba stepped upon the higher ground and surveyed the goods he was returning with— livestock, weapons, coins, and captives. While he observed the going-ons, his gaze fell on Rosfrith's long black hair, which, for some reason, was loose. It was hard to miss, shining in the sun. His brow puckered as he paused and rubbed his beard. *Why does she always draw my attention? Is she always going to be a curse on me?*

He had considered long and hard about taking her back to Ranaricii. But, whether he could admit it or not, Sigurd's words, nearly five winters ago, about their entwined fate had spooked him. Those mutterings had inflicted within him a need to watch over Rosfrith. Whether to protect himself or her, he wasn't sure.

During those years, he could admit she had not been a worry for him. Although he guarded her carefully at first, over the last couple of years, he'd forgotten she was there. Only when he was arranging to go back to Ranarici he'd had to think of her again. *Do I leave her in Bryttania and never think of her again, or do I take her back and hope her jinks didn't come to fruition on the seas?*

In the end, his conscience had won. Perhaps fate had won, too, because Ivar had picked her out to go with him. Ivar had lost interest in her worth since Lord Guader's rebuff. And as Ivar rightly pointed out, he didn't need many thralls as they could capture more. So, here she was, on the dock, ready to be loaded onto the ship. He sighed heavily and looked away from her. *Once she is at Ranaricii, I can truly forget about her.* He jumped off the rock and moved nearer to the shore. Once there, he scanned the food, piled high in the carts, as it rolled towards the shore. From his vantage point, he spotted Bard –the one person who didn't look happy to be returning—his gaze narrowed on him. Bard had obviously enjoyed his freedom under Ivar's watch, and wouldn't enjoy going back to his normal position as a farmer, with his wife, back at Ranaricii. He would have to keep an eye on him.

"It's a good day, sire," Gunnar said to Ubba as he neared.

Ubba dragged his gaze from Bard and smiled at his second in command. "Já, it is. I'll be glad once our feet are on the solid land of Ranaricii."

"Me, too, like the rest of the men, no doubt," Gunnar chuckled, for although they were all seafaring folk, the solid earth was more settling for their souls.

Ubba sobered. "Have prayers been given to goddess *Ran* for a smooth crossing?"

"Já," interrupted Asmund. "We have all prayed to the Goddess of the sea for calm waters."

"Good," said Ubba as his gaze sought out Rosfrith. "Good."

As the goods and captives neared the shoreline, Rosfrith watched in wonder at all the fine vessels waiting to be loaded with the items they had brought with them from Jórvík. Not long before, she had spotted Ubba standing high above, presumably keeping a check on progress. He appeared aloof and powerful. Her forehead puckered. She'd always felt his power, but for some reason, away from Ivar and the others, he oozed authority. Her gaze narrowed on him briefly, before she was shoved forward from behind.

Although Ubba was now out of sight, he stayed on her mind. *Do all these vessels belong to him?* She studied the boats, which she'd heard being called *dragonships*. If they did, she had greatly mistaken his wealth and obvious power. She, like the other captives, had assumed Ivar was the leader. She worried her bottom lip, not knowing how she felt about her findings.

Once nearly all the cargo was on his boats, Ubba relaxed. It had been a long trek from Jórvík to the shore, but luckily, they hadn't had encountered any problems. But, then again, he hadn't expected any because most of England was now ruled under their Dane Law.

Suddenly feeling the warmth of the summer day, Ubba strode off the boat towards the shore. Kneeling down, he quickly dunked his head in the cold, refreshing water and shook it. He pushed his fingers through his hair before knotting it back at his neck. He needed that, to awaken and freshen him up before their sea journey.

As he kneeled and quietly said his personal prayer to the god of travel, he watched the captives get shoved onto the boats. It was obvious, by the way their eyes longed for the land, that they didn't want to go. He shrugged, unconcerned. He needed the extra help at Ranaricii, and after all, it was the reason he'd fed and kept them alive.

Earlier on, he'd instructed his boatswain and Gunnar to put all the captives on the boat he was on. He wanted to keep an eye on them, and definitely on Rosfrith. His gaze searched for her and he grunted. Her hair was still unbraided and flowing down her back. He sighed. She wouldn't have that crowning glory for much longer. Suddenly, a frown appeared on his face. *Why should I care that her hair will be cut short?* All thralls had their hair shaved, indicating they were of a lower social class and of no consequence.

He yanked his gaze away from Rosfrith, unsettled by this conflicting thoughts. He would be better not thinking about the Lord's child again, for once they survived the journey and were in Ranaricii, his duty to her was finished. She'd be only a thrall, the same as all the other thralls.

Grunting to himself, he made his way back to the boat.

"Gunnar, place the captives towards the stern," Ubba said as he stepped on board. His eyes narrowed on the group, who were in the process of sitting down. "Make sure they are secured. I don't want anyone going overboard. Once we are out at sea, they can be freed."

Bard stepped forward. "Is that a good idea to free them?"

"Sire," Gunnar corrected, irritated with Bard's lack of respect.

Ubba brushed his gaze over Bard, before inwardly sighing. "Are you questioning me, Bard?" His eyes narrowed on him. He was glad to notice Bard flinch under their icy blast.

"No, sire," he said taking a step away.

"Well, let's get underway then," Ubba said, before turning inwards. "To Ranaricii we go!" A cheer filled the air.

Once the boatswain gave the order, the ship slowly moved away from the shore, only picking up speed when the rowers found their rhythm.

The sea crossing was cold, long, and rough.

It wasn't long after the shore of England had disappeared, Rosfrith swore the wind picked up and the waves doubled in size. Unused to being at sea, anxiously, she scrutinised the Danes. They didn't seem the least bit bothered by the conditions. They'd even climbed a mast to lower a large red sail. She relaxed a little. They wouldn't have opened it if the weather was going to be too bad, but, being tied to one of the masts when the ship sunk wasn't how she wanted to meet her maker.

After a couple of hours of bobbing up and down, Rosfrith felt her stomach clench. It rolled as much as the deck she shakily stood on. Thankfully, they'd been released from their bindings, so she was able to put a hand to her mouth and lean over the side. Within seconds, she was throwing her stomach's meager contents for the fish to eat.

Once she had no more in her, and heaving became too painful, she steadied herself and used the back of her hand to wipe her mouth. She scowled. The Norsemen were laughing at her. It wasn't her fault she didn't possess sea-legs. After gingerly making her way back to the mast, she closed her eyes and prayed for her sickness and the journey to end.

A couple of days later, Rosfrith felt the excitement growing amongst the men. She looked to where they did and saw the land in the distance. Initially, excitement filled her too—they would be on solid ground—but then she remembered, it was not her homeland. There would be no friendly faces waiting to greet her.

A couple of hours later, they neared the shore and were tethered back to the mast. Now they were nearing, if she sat up straight, she could see the area was crammed with people. Her pulse sped up, and her hands became sweaty. She glanced around the vessel and saw the smiles on the Danes' faces. They were obviously happy to be home. She only hoped the people taken from Dunwich and Northumbria would have a good reception.

When they docked and were untethered once again, Rosfrith tried to stretch out her arms and aching muscles, but she didn't have much time. She, along with the others, were pushed forward, off the boat, straight into the chaos on shore. Once there, they were efficiently divided into two groups.

Rosfrith shivered and tugged her threadbare cloak tighter around her—not that she had much spare cloth to wrap. It was too small for her now, it was the last piece of clothing she'd been given by her mother when she was two and ten winters.

"Those," Ubba pointed to one group of captives, "are to be taken to the block after they have been prepared. Let the merchants barter for the slave they want, and bring me the coin after," Ubba said to Asmund. He turned towards the other group. His eyes quickly flicked towards Rosfrith before turning back to Asmund. "These are to be my thralls…" before his words were out of his mouth, Astrid, his bedmate, fused onto his lips. His body immediately responded to her warm, and passionate display. He grabbed the back of her head to hold her still for a deep kiss, while his other snaked around her waist, binding her to his body. *Thor's teeth, I've missed my bedmate!*

Rosfrith watched, shocked by the amorous display. But regardless how she felt, she couldn't take her eyes away. The woman practically wrapped her body around him, and he appeared to be burying her within his body.

Once he managed to break away from Astrid's luscious mouth, Ubba turned his head to look for Asmund. "Sort everything out. I've got things to attend to. I'll be back later," he said before giving Astrid another deep kiss. "Or not," he laughed, as the people around him cheered.

Rosfrith watched Ubba stride away, with the lady still wrapped around him, carrying her as though she weighed nothing. Something stirred within Rosfrith, but she didn't know what.

Rosfrith fought the need to cry when she saw her beautiful hair lying on the ground, being blown into the water. It had been her pride and joy. *Another thing is taken away from me.* She resisted putting her hand up to her scalp because she could see how much had been cut off just by looking at the other thralls around her.

Movement drew her gaze away from her discarded hair. A group of women were coming towards her. Some of them had short hair, like her, and the ones with better clothing had longer hair, hidden under scarves. She growled in an attempt to get rid of the lump of fear that was growing. Cutting off captives hair was evidently another way to belittle them, but she'd have to get used to this life now.

Before Rosfrith had more time to think, hands grabbed at her clothes, attempting to strip her of them. Instinctively, she tried to stop them because she didn't know what was going on. Within moments, her cloak was gone. She looked around. Some of them had already been stripped and were being doused by water. Another humiliation to be standing in the cold, naked amongst the whole town. What alarmed her more was some of the ones nearer the crowds of villagers had more than women's hands on their naked bodies.

Determined not to crumble with embarrassment, or even fear, Rosfrith dropped her arms and stuck out her chin in defiance. She wouldn't physically fight them, then hopefully, the humiliation would be over quicker. She closed her eyes tight and listened to the women around her, understanding every word.

"Rodents, full of fleas and crawlies they will be."

"Don't look as though these can do one day's work, let alone more."

When she felt gentle hands turning her, she opened her eyes and saw an elderly woman speaking to her.

"Turn the other way, girl, so the male villagers don't get an eyeful." Her hands gently guided her.

"Hilde, you're too soft on them!"

"Would you like to be stripped in front of all those men's eyes?" Hilde nodded towards the shore. "I surely wouldn't. Besides, this one is barely an adult. Likely, no man has seen her yet."

One of the women sniggered. "That will soon change."

Hilde scowled at them. "Likely so, but I'll do her this small kindness. She's going to be one of our sire's thralls and it will be no good for us if she is sour."

Rosfrith listened to the women. Her heart softened to the kindly older woman, but she didn't say anything. It would be better if no one knew she spoke their language, yet. It could be to her advantage.

Within minutes, Rosfrith had been stripped, doused, and recovered with a thin shift, an undyed tunic, and an apron, which she learned was called a *hangerock*. Even though it was summer, the clouds covered the sun here, and she shivered as her body celebrated the warmth the clothes gave her.

The same gentle hands which dressed her, encouraged her along the dock towards the village, where a large fire was roaring. When they broke through the crowd, gathered around the fire for warmth and to observe the goings on, Rosfrith noticed the other group of people who had been separated earlier on.

She felt like crying. Unfortunately, their fate wasn't as kind. They still stood naked in the cold air, forcibly lined up. Rosfrith turned away when the first one was yanked forward and branded with a hot iron. The screams of pain and smell of burning flesh made her heave. If she had anything in her stomach, she knew it would have been on the floor. Taking steadying breaths, she wondered when it would be her turn.

"Poor slaves, least your life will be slightly better," Hilde muttered before guiding Rosfrith and the other thralls away from the fire towards the blacksmith.

A couple of hours later, Rosfrith was sitting on a hard platform, which was to be her bed. She glanced around at the rest of the thralls within the longhouse. She squeezed her eyes closed as her hand came up to finger the metal collar the blacksmith had encased around her neck. She felt a tear slip out of the corner of her closed eye.

Her life as a thrall in Ranaricii was about to begin, whether she cried about it or not.

Chapter 11

Winter 871- Ranaricii

As she had done for the last two years, Rosfrith awoke as the winter sun crawled lazily across the horizon, flooding the coastal valley with the early morning light through the light mist. Sighing, she, along with the other thralls, got up from their pallets ready for their daily work of grinding corn and salt, planting, milking, churning, washing, even building walls, herding, peat digging, or Rosfrith's least favourite job, spreading manure. Luckily, today, she was in the longhouse, serving the ones within its thick walls.

Pulling the hem of her tunic up from the floor to stop the snow wetting it, Rosfrith made her way across the courtyard towards the building, eager to get inside its dense walls, which kept it cool in the summer and stopped it freezing in the winter. A rooster, perched high on the roof, crowed the coming of a new day as she reached the entrance.

She stepped inside and stopped, giving her eyes time to adjust to the lack of light from within. Her first job today was to tend to the fire, so it was warm when Ubba and the others awoke from their slumber.

The thought of Ubba made Rosfrith falter for a moment. For some time, she'd been experiencing strange feelings for him—feelings she couldn't quite put her finger on. She received no better treatment than any of the other thralls and, by rights, she should hate him—he'd taken her away from Dunwich and everything and everyone she knew. But, when she saw him, her heart gave a leap and she became fidgety. She sighed and pulled herself together. It must just be down to her age of eight and ten winters.

Rosfrith peered towards the dying fire and located Ubba's form sleeping near it's waning heat. Ubba, as the Chieftain of Ranaricii, had his chamber towards one end of the longhouse, but as he had no wife, he only used it when he was in need of female company.

Rosfrith scowled when she thought of the many nights she'd seen him in the company of bedmate. Mostly, it was the woman called Astrid, but not always. There were many willing women to share his bed. Shaking her murderous thoughts away, she stepped over the sleeping bodies, being careful to take a wide berth of Ubba.

Once she reached the fire, Rosfrith coaxed the embers of yesterday's fire back into life. As it started to splutter, she stood and grabbed the wooden spoon ready to stir the leftover stew for breakfast. She screamed, nearly dropping the spoon into the iron cauldron when a hand clamped around her ankle.

"Mmmm, what have I got here?" a voice, lazy with sleep, asked as he tugged on her leg.

Not wanting to be dragged down onto the man, Rosfrith tried to pull her leg away. But she had no chance with the strength in the hand grabbing her. Reacting instinctively, she used the wooden spoon to hit the offending hand.

"*Thór*'s teeth!"

"What's all the noise?" asked Ubba. He sat up and rubbed his hand through his hair. When he saw an angry looking Bard and an angrier looking Rosfrith, he hid his smile. "What's wrong?"

"That wench wrapped my knuckles," said Bard scowling at Rosfrith.

"You shouldn't have tried to pull me down onto you," she replied angrily, before tempering her voice. It never did her any good to argue—it usually just ended up with punishment if she insulted anyone of the *jarl*. She lowered her gaze and sidestepped away, "I'll get you some bread and buttermilk to break your fast."

Ubba eyed Rosfrith as she moved carefully around Bard. He caught the same determination she usually had shining in her violet eyes, but he noticed something else about her this morning. For some reason, it was the plump mounds pushing against her undyed homespun tunic and her shoulder-length hair that drew his attention. His eyes narrowed on her retreating back when he spotted the material stretched over her hips. *When had she grown into a woman?*

He continued to watch her while she retrieved the bread and buttermilk. He noticed her laugh with one of his older servants, Hilde. Ubba didn't think he'd ever seen Rosfrith smile, let alone laugh. Her face lit up, and dimples appeared in her cheeks. Something inside him stirred. Something he had no mind to explore. He rubbed his beard. It was far too early to analyse these strange, unidentified emotions. *Thor's teeth!* He sometimes wished Sigurd had never mentioned his vision to him—then a part of his mind wouldn't always be attached to her.

He regarded her again, and cursed, suddenly feeling uncomfortable. The tightening in his loin made him look away from her direction. He pushed his hand over his face in an attempt to control his desire. *What just happened? When had she turned from a little girl into a woman?*

When Rosfrith neared Ubba to serve him food, for the first time since they'd been in *Bryttania*, he examined her face properly. She had grown into a striking woman. Pale skin, unusual violet-coloured eyes, framed by long, dark lashes, and a petite nose. *Why haven't I noticed her beauty before now?* He grunted and yanked his gaze away. He knew it was because he always thought of her as a child.

He did his best to ignore her for a while, but he couldn't help but catch glimpses of her. His eyes narrowed when she served Gunnar and he noticed Bard watching, obviously interested in her. His jaw tightened, and he tore his gaze away. Even though he wasn't happy Bard was taking an interest, Rosfrith was evidently a woman, and if she were arousing him, she'd be catching the attention of others. The only thing he could do was to make sure she had garments that fitted her, so her bodily form wasn't so obvious to all that looked. It wasn't good for her to be walking amongst his men like that—it would only serve to cause problems—for him and her.

Unable to help himself, he watched Rosfrith lean towards the fire. A reflection of a flame glinted on her neck brace. His jaw tensed and he tore his gaze away. *Why am I worried about her? She's a thrall. She'd most probably been bedded already*. He looked down at his hands, so he wasn't tempted to watch her again. *Mayhap, I will allow Rosfrith to become a bedmate of one of my men?* He glanced around at the men gathered around the fire. He grunted. He didn't like the thought of any of them touching her.

Unaware Ubba was watching her, or even the attention of the other men, Rosfrith handed out the stale crusty flat loaf, which was baked last week. Hilde handed out the stew, which looked more appetising once the cold surface fat had disappeared.

When she turned to serve Ubba a second portion, she hesitated. He was staring at her. She tried not to blush at his obvious perusal and in her haste to get away, dropped some stew by his feet. "Sorry, sire," she said, flustered. He grunted and waved her away. Rosfrith lowered her head and scuttled away, mortified he was angry with her, and even more so that she was becoming clumsy around him.

Ubba finished breaking his fast just as he felt an arm wrap around his shoulder. He looked up at Astrid, her hair tousled from sleep and a pout on her lips.

"Why did you not come to bed, Ubba?" she asked, sitting next to him, rubbing her hand up and down his arm in a suggestive manner.

Ubba didn't answer. He flicked a glance at the men around the fire, who were obviously interested in their conversation. His eyes narrowed on them. He gave a little grunt when they either looked away or got up and moved away. When he watched them, rather than reply to her suggestion, he heard her small sigh. But he still didn't answer her. He had nothing to say. He hadn't wanted to join her in bed—so hadn't.

"Perchance, you could come back to your *bed-closet*, now?" Astrid purred, into his ear.

Now it was his time to heave a sigh. He didn't know what was wrong with him. Normally he would jump at the chance.

When he'd returned from *Bryttania*, he'd been on a high, jubilant about their successes overseas. He'd thrown himself back into being Chieftain of Ranaricii, and he'd certainly thrown himself back into Astrid and a number of other bedmates. But, now barely two winters later, he was bored and searching for something, but he didn't know what.

Perhaps he was down because, over the last couple of days, he'd received word from his brothers. They had moved on to Wessex, ready for battle, but had found King Alfred very content to pay them good coin to leave. At the moment, Ivar had informed him they were thinking of marching to London for the winter and then moving back into Northumbria the next year.

Last night, he'd briefly contemplated joining them again, another adventure. But then he changed his mind. Perhaps the long, dark winter was playing with his mind? He didn't know, but what he did know was he needed to be alone to understand why he was feeling agitated. Too many things were crowding his head, and he needed to clear it. It had got to the stage where even Astrid didn't please him. Her nagging was starting to interfere with his enjoyment of her.

Later on, after telling his men about his plans, Ubba gathered his warm clothes and packed his sack. Astrid didn't help because she was sulking somewhere. Interrupting his conversation with Gunnar, who would be taking over in his absence, Ubba waved to one of the servants passing him. "Bring me some cheese, salted fish, and bread."

"Já, Lord."

From across the room, Rosfrith watched the exchange. Feigning disinterest, she carried on with her chores until the girl returned with the items. Her brow furrowed. Ubba was packing them into a sack. Her stomach clenched. He was leaving. Grabbing a jug of buttermilk, she moved nearer to overhear what Ubba was saying to Gunnar.

"I'll be gone until the next full moon," Ubba explained to those around him. It wasn't unusual to go off into the wilds for some time on your own, so no one questioned him. He nodded towards his friend. "Gunnar will be in charge while I'm gone. If he is out, it is then Asmund." Ubba had caught the scowl on Bard's face before he'd moved away from the group. Ubba ignored him.

For a while now, Bard had remembered his place, and had caused no problems. But, Ubba was confident Gunnar would sort it out, if Bard forgot again.

Too busy listening to the conversation, Rosfrith jumped out of her skin when warm breath hit the back of her ear. She turned suddenly, stumbling into a solid body. Hands clamp around her arms before she heard a low chuckle.

"Jumpy?"

Stunned, she looked up into Bard's eyes before trying to twist out of his hold. When he gripped tighter, she wanted to knee him where it hurt, but she couldn't afford to upset him. Especially if her sire was going. "A little," she lied as she tore her gaze away, trying not to engage any more conversation. "Excuse me, I must finish serving, *vikingar*." She noticed a smile slowly spread across his lips when he let her go.

Bard leaned closer, enjoying how skittish she was. "I do like a jumpy woman in my bed." He laughed when she scowled at him. *I might have fun taming Ubba's little pet.*

Rosfrith stepped back and quickly moved out of his vicinity. She mentally made a note not to get that close to him again.

When she had finished her morning chores and returned to the hall to serve food, it was obvious Ubba was ready to go after he had eaten. From under her lashes, she scanned the room—unfortunately, her gaze landed on Bard, who was lifting his mug in a salute to Ubba's health. He winked at her. Panic hit Rosfrith clean in the chest. Not thinking, just acting on impulse, she leaned across the table and placed her hand on Ubba's. "Please don't go, sire."

The room went deathly quiet.

Rosfrith withdrew her hand and stood upright when she realised people had stopped eating and were watching them.

Ubba's gaze glanced around the quietened room before narrowing in onto Rosfrith. "What is it to you, wench, if I go?" Ubba inwardly cringed at the tone of his voice, but it wouldn't do letting the others know that he had a soft spot for her.

"Um," she muttered, thinking on her feet. "I mean, there is still snow on the ground, sire. Wouldn't it be better to go once it's thawed?" She hoped no one would detect the tremor in her voice.

A laugh went around the room, making her jump.

"We aren't soft like you Anglo-Saxons!" one of them roared in laughter.

Ubba smiled at the man before he turned his head to address Rosfrith. He had no idea why she thought she could speak so boldly to him, but he understood he'd have to be hard on her. She needed to know her place as a thrall—not only to protect her from others but also in a way, to stop his desire for her growing. "As they said," he used his arm to indicate to the men gathered around the top table. "We Danes are not soft…" His eyes turned icy. "But, mayhap I have been on you?" Ubba ignored her intake of breath and the weary look that appeared in her violet eyes. "You," he stated loudly, "Must remember your place here." He ignored the sniggers. "You did not bring your title with you—you are neither jarl nor bondi, you are not free. You must remember you are my thrall, my servant, to do with what I want."

Rosfrith felt herself pale under his words, but she was determined not to cry at his harsh words.

Ubba carried on, knowing what he would say next would shock her to the core, but it was the only way he could think of protecting her while he was away. Especially now she had shown her feisty nature to all his men. Some of them liked nothing better than breaking the spirit of women. "In fact, when I come back I will give you freely to whichever of my men I wish." He saw terror in her eyes and heard the cheering of the men, but carried on. "*No one* is to touch her when I'm away." He eyed the group, hoping they heeded his words. "For, on my return, I will give her to the one who serves me best." As the chattering and noise increased, Ubba spotted Rosfrith's chin raise. He was impressed at her courage, even though he could tell from the depths of her eyes she was scared. He wasn't going to give her to someone on his return, but he didn't want them to think her fair game when he was away. It was the only thing he could think of doing.

"Sire?" Rosfrith muttered, terrified at what her words had started. *He is a beast, even worse than Bard!*

"Silence." Ubba took his eyes off her and scanned the room. He noticed Hilde, his oldest most trusted thrall. He motioned her forward. "Hilde, why has her hair been allowed to grow?"

"I'm unsure, sire. But, it is winter and as we thralls aren't allowed scarves to protect…"

Ubba cut her off with a wave of his hand. "Regardless, her hair is to be sheared." He hoped if she looked more like a thrall, his men's attention might be diverted from her. "And, Rosfrith, you'll do well to remember your place here. You are no lady here. Do you understand?"

Not looking at him, Rosfrith nodded.

"Answer me. Do you understand?"

This time, she looked directly at him. "Já, sire," she bit back. "I understand my place here."

He sighed. He didn't like the look of hate in her eyes, but it had to be done. "Gunnar?"

"Já, sire?" Gunnar leaned forward to speak to Ubba. He'd been listening and watching what was going on with interest.

"You understood my command? Rosfrith is to be given as a gift to one of my men, *but* only on my return."

Gunnar's eyes narrowed fractionally. His sire was being very forceful with his demands. Normally, when Ubba went off for solitude, he didn't particularly care what went on in his absence—as long as he didn't have to deal with any fallout on his return. "*I* heard you." Gunnar wasn't going to answer for any of the other men because as far as he was concerned, they could do what they liked with her—she was only a servant after all. *They* could decide whether she was worth fighting with their sire for.

"Good," said Ubba. He stood and pushed away from the table. "I'm off." He wanted to get out of the room. Even though he knew he was the cause, he couldn't stand seeing Rosfrith looking so crestfallen. Nor could he stomach the looks Astrid had been given him throughout food. He glanced around at his men, ignoring Astrid and the puzzled look on her face. She knew him well enough to know what just happened was out of character, but he was in no mood to explain things to her. He noticed Rosfrith had taken herself towards a dark corner of the longhouse. "I'll return on the next full moon." He leaned down to grab his furs and sack. "Men," he bowed, "Astrid," he said politely before walking to the door.

Rosfrith watched Ubba leave. The men crowding around him were slapping him on the back. She scowled, anger brewing in her belly. She was just another possession. She snorted. *To think I've been having soft thoughts about him! He is just as much of a lout as all the others.*

When the door shut behind the men, cutting out the noise, cold, and light, Rosfrith closed her eyes, willing her threatening tears away. She crossed her arms, rubbing them to keep away the chill. Once again, she felt truly alone. Ubba, the one person she'd let herself become attached too had also left her to the harsh realities of life. Just like her parents. Just like everyone she knew.

Chapter 12

Ranaricii

Rosfrith placed one filthy hand on her back in an attempt to stretch out the ache, while the other wiped her hair from her brow. In the week since Ubba had left, she'd kept herself busy with any chores needing to be done, even her most hated. Anything to be away from the longhouse and the uneasy feeling she got when she was in there. There were too many eyes that followed her, showing her too much interest that she neither encouraged or desired. A noise made Rosfrith turn quickly, but she relaxed when she realised it was Hilde's voice from behind her in the barn.

"Rosfrith, remember, we must shave your hair today. Ubba will be back soon, and he won't be pleased with me if I haven't done his bidding," Hilde said, shaking her head as she continued to rake up the manure.

Rosfrith gave her a half-hearted smile and nodded. She didn't want her hair shaved—it would be lovely to grow it long once again, but she wasn't a child or a lady anymore, with time to keep her locks in good condition. Her chest tightened, but it was not Hilde's fault the task had to be done. And, with the mood Ubba had left in, she wouldn't chance him coming back early and taking it out on her or Hilde. "All right, let's finish off here before it becomes too dark. I'll wash and then come to your shelter." She eyed the elderly woman who had worked as hard as her all day. "Hilde, you go off now, I'll finish up."

Hilde straightened up with a deep sigh. "If you're sure?"

This time Rosfrith gave a genuine smile. "Of course, I am. You go, and I'll be there shortly."

"I'll need to go to the sire's longhouse first, to stoke the fire as I'm sure the others won't think." Her greying eyes glanced at Rosfrith. She took a step nearer and tempered her voice. "I don't trust Asmund or Bard not to blacken our names to the sire if things aren't in order."

Rosfrith nodded. "What about Gunnar?"

Hilde shrugged. "He's more of a sensible head on him, but..." she patted Rosfrith's arm. "He's still a man. And you, my dear, need to be careful, I've seen the way some of their eyes follow you."

Rosfrith had felt them too, which was why she stayed away from them. In an attempt to lighten the atmosphere, Rosfrith joked. "I don't think I have to worry, stinking of manure."

Hilde's eyes crinkled as she gave a small smile. "Your beauty shines through." She patted Rosfrith's arm. "Finish here, and meet me at my home." She turned and placed her rake against the wall and walked out. Hilde was one of the luckier servants, having been given a small shelter of her own for her and her family. Rosfrith could only hope one day, after being a loyal servant, she too would earn freedoms to make her life a little easier.

Once Rosfrith had finished, she placed her rake next to Hilde's. She sighed, knowing it wouldn't be long before the animals would have to be cleaned out again. There were no crops growing at the moment, because of the snow, but the muck still needed to be piled up ready for the thaw and planting of crops.

She glanced down. Her tunic and hands were a state. The tiny wooden bowl of water in the barn would not cope with the amount of muck on her hem. Sighing heavily, she realised she would have to go to the stream. It wasn't that she didn't like cleaning her clothes or bathing in it, she never felt better than when she was clean, it was the fact that snow lay on the ground and the water was freezing.

As she left the barn, Rosfrith stretched out her aching muscles and scanned around, her eyes adjusting to the light. It wasn't going to be long before night descended and she didn't want Hilde to cut her hair in complete darkness, so made the decision only to have a quick wash down by the stream to get the muck off her hem and skin. She didn't have a spare tunic, so she'd have to ask Hilde to borrow one of her older tunics. Tomorrow, she would then wash her tunic before people got up. Rosfrith hoped if she placed it on the dark stones, it would dry in the winter sun.

From his hidden position, Gunnar quietly watched Rosfrith as she stretched. His eyes narrowed in on the straining material before his puzzled expression smoothed out. She had been troubling him over the last week, and not because she'd made herself scarce in the longhouse. *No, what troubles me is my sire's wishes before he left.*

Rosfrith, although once a lady, was only one of Ubba's thralls. Ubba had many of them, keeping the running of his fortress smooth, and sharing the most attractive ones between his men to keep them happy. But Gunnar had known Ubba since they were knee-high, and there was definitely something unfamiliar in his friend's eyes when he glanced at Rosfrith. It wasn't lust he saw in Ubba—Gunnar had witnessed that in his sire's eyes many times before. This seemed more of a connection. It was much more than Ubba protecting his property.

Gunnar rubbed his beard, keeping his gaze firmly on Rosfrith. His sister, Astrid, would not be pleased if she realised. She'd been the chosen bedmate of Ubba for many years, all in the hope she would become his wife. But, much to her and Gunnar's disappointment, Ubba never took matters further. Yet.

When Rosfrith walked towards him, unaware of his presence, he decided to matters into his own hands—try and work out if Rosfrith had designs on, or feelings for, Ubba.

Rosfrith nearly jumped out of her skin when a hand appeared out of the shadows and grabbed her arm. Trying to shake the grip, she cursed loudly when she pulled her neck.

Gunnar raised his eyebrows at her language. She was obviously spending too much time with the rest of the thralls. Once she'd stopped pulling away from him, and was steady on her feet, he let go and took a step back. "Rosfrith. I didn't mean to startle you."

Rosfrith eyed him warily. He'd never done her any harm before, but that didn't mean *when the cat was away*.

"Where are you off, in such a hurry?"

"To wash, my lord." She grabbed her tunic to indicate the dirt on it. She watched Gunnar's grey eyes narrow. She tensed. He was up to something—it was evident on the emotions flying over his bearded face. Standing a little taller, in an attempt to look less vulnerable, she added, "I need to go. Hilde is expecting me. She needs to cut my hair while it's still light."

"Ahh," said Gunnar reaching out to touch her hair that glanced her shoulders. "Such a shame to cut this off."

Rosfrith stood as still as she could when he pushed some behind her ear. When he took a step forward, she held her breath.

"It's the same colour as the midnight sky," he said, fingering some strands, before his eyes narrowed back onto hers.

Rosfrith hoped he didn't notice her flinch. She didn't want to upset him because she could be brutally punished—but she wished him gone. When his large hand moved to the back of her neck, holding her firmly, fear made her stay where she was.

"Now, let's see why Ubba has taken you under his wing." Gunnar hauled her roughly towards him. He gave her no warning or time to protest, as his lips descended onto hers. Initially, it was never his intention to kiss her, but it was the first time he'd been this near to her. She was beautiful, even under a layer of dirt. Besides, in his reasoning, he was only going to test her, to see if she was loyal to Ubba.

Rosfrith closed her eyes and stayed as rigid as possible while Gunnar's lips explored hers. She felt his hands roam over the back of her body, attempting to mould her into his, but she still stayed emotionless. She was relieved when, as suddenly as it started, Gunnar broke off the kiss. She watched a small smile flicker on his lips.

"Are you a maiden?" Gunnar asked quietly.

Rosfrith felt her cheeks colour.

Even without her uttering a word, he got his answer. His gaze narrowed on her face. "What is Ubba to you?"

Rosfrith spluttered before answering. "My master," she said defiantly. "Didn't you hear him before he left? I am his thrall." She hoped the hurt didn't show in her voice.

Gunnar grunted and yanked his gaze away, trying to find the distance for composure. Truthfully, she'd aroused him, and if she weren't a maiden, they'd be rolling in the hay right now. But, she hadn't been with a man, and Gunnar had the idea that Ubba was saving her for himself, despite his parting words. She wasn't worth the risk of falling out with Ubba, regardless of her appeal.

When Gunnar glanced back at her, her swollen lips and flushed skin nearly had him changing his mind. Her appeal shocked him, so he gathered himself together. "You smell too much like an animal for me, thrall," he said before stepping a safe distance back. He ignored the hurt look flicker across her face. He said what he did more to douse his arousal than upset her. He glanced around. The place was empty, most people already inside in the warmth. "Don't stay out here long," he said as he walked away. "After your hair is sheared, you're needed in the longhouse to serve ale, thrall."

Rosfrith's hands clenched at her sides. She didn't know if she was angry, scared, or humiliated by what just happened. She only knew if it had been anyone other than the acting Chieftain, she wouldn't care, she would have used her knee in his tender parts, just like Hilde had shown her and just like she'd used on many male thralls who thought they could put their hands on her. *They thought wrong.* Once Gunnar had gone around the corner, she started towards the stream, determined to get to Hilde's as soon as possible.

Watching their embrace from another darkened corner was Bard. A slow smile spread across his lips. *So, the serving wench isn't just Ubba's—Gunnar is obviously having some fun, too.* He shifted deeper into the hut when Gunnar, not aware of his presence, passed him. When the noise of footfalls quietened, he stepped forward to watch Rosfrith. *Maybe it's time I get some of the action, too.*

Rosfrith's steps faltered when she spotted Bard lurking by the opening of one of the storerooms. She glanced at him from under her lashes, and continued on her way without acknowledging him or, with any luck, gaining his attention. She took another quick peek, and he seemed too busy with something in his hands to be bothered with her.

When Rosfrith left the buildings and neared the stream, she slowed. The stones and area around, although already slippery with a thin layer of snow, had even slimier moss underneath. The last thing she needed was to end up in the cold water. After rolling the arms of her tunic up, she bent down, leaning forward to wash her hands and arms. The water was frigid, but at least the muck was being removed. Once her arms were clean, she cupped some water to wash her face.

A noise from behind made her stand quickly. Her speed as she turned, together with eyes full of water, made her stumble backward on the stones. She cursed as her soft shoe stepped in the water. It wasn't long before the icy water claimed the bottom of her dirty tunic. Frightened, she stepped out of the water. Rosfrith scanned her surroundings, but she couldn't see anything around.

When her heart returned to its normal beat, her brain registered the cold. She examined the bottom of the sodden tunic. Annoyed, she realised she'd have to take the tunic off so she could wring it out properly. It would be too heavy and cold to walk back to Hilde's otherwise.

She checked around to see if anyone one was in the vicinity. When she was happy there wasn't, she removed her cloak and then reached to take off her *hangerock*, the shorter length woolen apron that was suspended by shoulder straps. Once it was off, Rosfrith folded it and placed them both, well away from the water's edge.

She checked her surroundings again, then bent down to grab the ends of her tunic. She tugged it over her head and took a sharp intake of breath—the air was cold only in a thin shift. Working quickly, she bent down and, keeping away from the water's edge, washed the hem and wrung out her tunic. She was anxious to get to Hilde's because it was getting late.

"Well, well, what do we have here?"

Rosfrith's hands stilled. She closed her eyes hoping she was wrong. *Bard must have followed me.* She silently cursed herself for being so naïve.

"I asked what you were doing, wench."

Rosfrith daren't stand and turn. Staying still, she continued to look out over the water. "Wringing out my tunic, *vikingar*." She cringed when she heard him take a step nearer.

"Stand when you address me, thrall."

Taking a breath, Rosfrith slowly stood before turning. She held her tunic in front of her shift. She didn't miss his eyes inspecting her from head to foot.

"It's a bit cold for that, isn't it?"

She felt nauseous when she became aware of his gaze narrow in on the front of her thin shift. "I am washing the hem of my tunic, *vikingar*. I will put it on now."

"Not on my account." There was a sneer on Bard's lips.

Clutching her tunic close to her breast, she said nothing.

"Anyway," Bard said, looking around, "I think you left one of the gates open in the barn. The animals might escape."

Rosfrith's brow furrowed. "Did I?" She was puzzled because she always double checked all the gates were closed, mainly because she'd been in awful trouble if any of the livestock got out.

Bard's eyebrows rose. "You question me, thrall?"

Rosfrith glanced at him, even more confused. His request implied he was annoyed with her for questioning him, but his tone didn't.

"I'm sorry, *vikingar*. I will check right away."

"See that you do," Bard said, before taking a step to the side and waving her past. "Thrall," he added, his eyes narrowing on her.

Rosfrith grabbed her tunic tight to her chest and hurried past him. It was only when she was halfway to the barn, she remembered her *hangerock* and cloak were lying by the river. She hesitated briefly, but she didn't want to go back down to the river. There was something in his eyes that told her he was trouble. *I'll pick my clothes up tomorrow.*

Once the barn was in sight, Rosfrith felt relieved. Clutching her side, she stopped to take a brief glance around, making sure Bard hadn't followed her. Everywhere was empty. She took in a large steadying breath and continued to the barn. She opened the large door and stepped away from the cold and impending darkness.

Once inside, away from the frigid air, Rosfrith bent over to ease the ache in her side. After she had caught her breath, she tugged on her tunic—to cover herself and to ease the cold. She scanned the barn and walked deeper into its darkness. *All of the pens are secure—just like I thought they were.* A frown creased her forehead. She shivered, unease prickled down her spine. *Why did Bard tell me they were open?* She glanced around the darkened barn, to check she was alone. She blew out a breath, irritated with herself. She's sensed he'd been up to no good, but in her haste to get away, hadn't questioned why. She should have trusted her instincts and gone directly to Hilde's.

She turned to leave, until the crunch of stones from outside the barn stopped her in her tracks. Fear gripped her. She cursed—she hadn't shut the door behind her—anyone could follow her in. She held her breath and waited until the noise disappeared. She let go of her breath slowly, still too spooked to make much noise. She forced her clenched hands open and sighed with relief. She swivelled back towards the animals, glad that none of them had picked up on her tension. When she was satisfied all was normal, she walked back across the barn, determined to get to Hilde, as, no doubt she'd be wondering where she was.

Halfway across, she stopped. She felt her body heat, and her heart sank. Bard stood in front of the doorway—a smile on his face, her *hangerock* and cloak in his hands. *This isn't good.*

"Forgotten something?" Bard said, before he turned and shut the barn door.

Rosfrith cursed as she watched her only exit close. When he brushed past her, deeper into the barn, she lowered her eyes, refusing to look at him. She didn't turn around, and in the silence, she tried to work out what to do. She glanced up and checked the closed door. She knew, despite the apparent ease Bard had closed the door himself, she wouldn't be able to open it before he reached her.

"Wench, I said, did you forget something? Turn around and face me."

"Já, *vikingar*," she said, before turning to face him. Nervously, she stretched out her hand for him to give them to her. She hoped he didn't detect her hand shaking.

Bard didn't move. "What, no thanks?"

"Thank you," she stuttered out.

Bard tutted and turned his head to the side, taking his gaze off her. He pursed his lips, making a show of his irritation. "I've made an effort to return these to you, and I get a half-hearted, thank you?" He suddenly turned to look at her, his gaze narrowing dangerously.

Rosfrith felt her heart pound, but calmly answered, "I'm sorry. Thank you."

After a moment, his features softened and a smile flickered on his lips. "That's better, now come and get them." He extended his arm.

Rosfrith paused, uncertain. She knew although she was reluctant to near him—she didn't trust him—she'd have to take them. The moment she stepped towards him, deeper into the barn, Rosfrith knew her instincts about him had been correct. His hand grabbed her wrist in a tight circle and he pulled her into his hard chest. His yank had her breath sailing out of her lungs. As soon as she was near, he forced her hand behind her back, while his other arm snaked around her waist, completely bonding her to him. He turned and pushed her against one of the barn's wooden supports. The slam against the pillar hurt her head and emptied what air she had left in her lungs. Dread prickled down her spine when his breath made contact with her ear.

"Now, let's see if you can thank me properly, wench," he whispered before his head lowered to her neck and nipped her skin painfully.

Fear raked its claws across her body, as goose bumps covered her. She tensed, refusing to yield, struggling against him, but he wouldn't budge an inch. In response to her protests, he leaned on her more, forcing her tight against the wooden pillar, while he carried on his assault. Every muscle in her body bunched, trying to break herself free. She wiggled and pushed her hand against his chest, to get some distance, but he didn't move. The only thing she could do was move her head sideward, in an attempt to avoid his searching lips. But, his hand moved from her waist to grab her chin, holding her in place for his plunder. While she fought to keep her lips together, his knee forced its way between her legs.

Rosfrith whimpered. It was no wonder women feared men, they were so strong and brutal. Fight as she might, she knew was no physical match for Bard. He painfully pulled down on her chin, eventually parting her lips. As her lips parted in protest, Bard's tongue pillaged her mouth, and his hand released to clutch painfully at her hair, keeping her still. She didn't want this, so she struggled widely. *I'm not going to make it easy for him.*

When his grip firmed on her, Rosfrith couldn't stop releasing a gasp of pain in her throat. His hold was so tight, she would be left with bruises. His searching tongue made her gag, but he didn't stop, grinding his mouth against her lips. Under his brutal assault, she felt her lips spilt, and tasted blood. Her eyes started to mist with tears. It didn't take her long to realise her struggles aroused Bard. She would have to use her brain, not her strength, for she was no match. Forcing herself to relax, she let his mouth plunder.

Sensing what he thought was Rosfrith's surrender, Bard let go of her wrist and moved his hand to cover one of her breasts.

Rosfrith could have wept with the pain of blood returning to her tingling hand, but instead, she knew this was her window. Desire had made him lose his advantage. Using her free hand, she searched for the rake she knew was hanging on the other side of the pillar.

Once she'd found it, she swung it around and hit the back of his head. She knew it wasn't a strong blow, but as she hoped, the surprise had him releasing his hold on her. He stepped back and then let go so suddenly, she stumbled back onto the pillar and slammed her head. She had no time to think of the pain, as she used her hand to brace herself from falling. For a moment, she watched him rub his head and look around the barn, trying to work out what had happened.

Rosfrith knew she didn't have much time, so she stabbed him the area she knew would hurt. She watched him double over in pain. He cursed and when he half-straightened, she saw something violent flashed across his eyes before they narrowed into slits.

"You, wench," he said through gritted teeth. "I'll kill you!"

The sound of his angry voice brought her to her senses. Without looking back, she ran towards the door. With a super-human strength, she didn't know she possessed, she hurried to open it, leaving Bard behind.

Rosfrith watched from a hidden spot, as not long after, Bard exited the barn. He looked both ways, a scowl marring his face. She backed away when he started to throw barrels and carts over randomly, looking for her.

Desperately, she tried to think where she could go. Going back to the longhouse she shared would be too obvious, and she might put the others there at risk, so that was out. She couldn't go to Hilde's because she'd told him that's where she was headed. Instead, she decided to hide in the shadows until inspiration took hold.

After staying put for a while, and avoiding the late-night stragglers, Rosfrith doubled back to the barn. Bard wouldn't expect her to go back there.

Once she slipped inside, she pushed the door shut. She found her discarded cloak and *hangerhock* and searched for a quiet, dark area, away from any moonlight, which entered through the gaps. Rosfrith sat and wrapped her arms around her bent legs. She hugged them tightly in an attempt to stop the shaking which had begun to take over her body. *What am I going to do?* She knew she wasn't safe in Ranaricii anymore. She closed her eyes tight in the vain attempt to stem her tears. When she took in a sobering, shaky breath, Rosfrith realised there was no way she was going to be able to hold back them back.

Disorientated, Rosfrith awoke to sunlight, which was trying to cut through the gaps in the barn. She rubbed her eyes and then realised she wasn't in her bed. She was on straw in the barn. When her sleep cleared, and her brain caught up, the whole awful situation came back to her. Panicked again, she wondered how on earth she had slept? She should have been running, not crying and sleeping!

Standing quickly, she scanned around, trying to gather her thoughts. Now her tears were spent, she had to think of her options. She knew she still couldn't go to Hilde or her longhouse because Bard would easily find her, and Rosfrith wouldn't be surprised if he beat her to death—he had, after all, threatened to kill her when she'd hit him. If he did take it upon himself to murder her, all Bard would have to do was pay Ubba some coin for damaging his property and that would be it, she thought bitterly.

She thought for a while, trying to keep her emotions in check. Her only option was trying to get someone to listen to her side of the story. She had no idea where Ubba had gone, so she couldn't plead to him. She closed her eyes. *Although, will he take my word against one of his loyal men?* She liked to think he would, but, as he'd told her before he'd left, she was only a thrall. She shook her head. Ubba wasn't an option.

Her only real hope in the whole mess was Gunnar. He was in charge, and despite their run in the other day when he'd kissed her, he always seemed a fair man. He would know from her actions she wasn't an easy woman. *Mayhap if I can talk to him, he could calm Bard down?* She took a deep breath, trying to slow her heartbeat down now her decision was made. She would go and find Gunnar, and hopefully, he wouldn't want any trouble while Ubba was away.

As quietly as she could, Rosfrith cracked open the barn door, just enough to see outside. It was still early. The sun was only just lighting the sky, highlighting the snow and frost on the floor. Rosfrith hoped most people were still tucked under their furs. The fewer people who saw her making her way to Gunnar's longhouse, the better. She went the long way around, to avoid the main longhouse because Bard slept in there. She hoped he'd consumed enough ale in his anger to keep him sleeping for most of the day.

Moving within the morning shadows, little by little, Rosfrith made her way until Gunnar's building was in sight. She sighed deeply. Now all she had to do was find a way to speak to him. As she hovered in a darkened corner, Gunnar's door opened. Her breath hitched. Bard was exiting the longhouse! He was talking to Gunnar in an aroused way, and Rosfrith realised her opportunity to explain might have already passed.

Panicking about what her next move would be, instinct took hold, and she decided to flee.

Chapter 13

Escape

Rosfrith was out of breath but kept running. She couldn't stop, fearing Bard would be following her. Keeping the image of his enraged face clearly in her mind gave her the incentive to push on. Fear propelled her, on through the deeper snow when she could barely break through.

Once the initial fear of being followed passed, she bent over, trying to take in air. Its cold stung her lungs, but she inhaled deeply. She needed it in order to push on. She spared a glance back towards Ranaricii and cursed heavily. In her haste to flee, she'd left a trail in the snow. *How silly could I be?* Bard would easily track her. But, there was nothing she could do now, so she scanned the area, trying to work out what to do.

Far beyond where she stood was a hut perched halfway up one of the mountain ridges. *Mayhap I can seek shelter there?* She hesitated, knowing the cabin would be too obvious. But, she would need shelter when the night winds and predators arrived. She made a decision. She would head for it. Besides, its height advantage might afford her a view of Bard, if he was coming for her. She didn't have a lot of time to think her decision through, but if she were right, she'd be able to reach it before dark. She felt pain in her feet and looked down at her sodden leather shoes. She needed to get up there before the cold of the night would freeze her, taking away any choices she might have had.

She pushed forward. The way ahead parted into two valleys. To the left, a stream followed the valley's floor. To the right, a forest pathed the way. She shuddered. Neither option appealed. She gave the dark forest another glance, and decided that she'd more likely find something more dangerous than Bard within its thick interior. Besides, the water would help mask her scent from the dogs. So, she pushed on, down towards the stream.

When the pathway constricted towards the frigid water, afraid of falling and breaking a bone, Rosfrith tempered her speed. It didn't seem as though Bard was following yet, so she had a little time to slow and regain some of her breath. It felt as though she had run forever. Tired, hopelessness washed over her. *Maybe I should have let Bard take what he wanted rather than risking my life to protect my virtue?* Pulling herself together, because she knew thinking like that would be no good, she huffed out a breath, which turned white in the air. *No, he will never touch me again.* She cleared her mind in order to concentrate. Rosfrith neared the stream carefully, one snow-covered, slippery stone after another. When the snow thinned, she picked up speed. She slipped and her foot hit the water. Cursing, she pulled it out—her shoes hadn't been treated with fish oil to make them waterproof. While she shook it, she scanned around and quickly realised she would have to walk through the water, regardless of her cold feet. It was the only thing that would mask her scent if Bard brought dogs with him.

She pulled up her hem and entered the shallow water. Painstakingly slow, Rosfrith made her way over the slippery rocks under foot, only stopping briefly to wet her dry mouth when fear had dried it. The stitch in her side had started to ease into a small jab, and her breathing levelled for a while—until the excited sound of dogs reached her ears. She froze as despair threatened to take over. *Bard is on his way and he is bringing the dogs!* She could never outrun the dogs.

Rosfrith closed her eyes and took in a breath. She tried to control the sickness and fear threatening her. When the barking grew louder, instinct kicked in. *No, Bard won't win.* She'd survived this long on her own in a foreign land, and she'd survive now.

She opened her eyes, ready to continue. And stopped. Some large animal was by the stream. From the distance, she couldn't make out what it was, but there was no way she could go that way now. If it was a bear who had emerged from hibernation early, he would be too dangerous to encounter. Making a decision, she turned away from the stream, and climbed the slope. Fear boosted her on, and even though she tripped on the moss-covered stones, and skidded on the snow-covered ones, she made quick time.

Once at the top, she stood to catch her breath. Her hand squeezed her side to relieve the ache, which had returned. Her eyes narrowed. *How can I get across the snow without my tracks being obvious?* The barking of the dogs made her turn sharply and she cursed. She had no choice.

Rosfrith ran as fast as her wet tunic and snow would allow, not stopping until she reached the edge of the dark forest. She hesitated and peered into its darkness, made all the darker by the brightness of the snow on which she stood. Her instincts told her not to enter. Bears, wolves and all manner of dangerous things inhabited the woods, but when the hounds' excited barks reached her on the wind, her choice was gone

Her head whipped around and she spotted the dogs and men in the distance. Her pulse quickened. They were running at speed. Her heart tightened in fear, before kick-starting with a thud against her ribs. She needed to move into the forest—fast. She hurtled into and through the thick foliage, her heavy, wet tunic snagging on the branches, slowing her progress. But she pushed along as best she could, the sound of dogs making her hurry.

Exhausted after the hours of running, Rosfrith lost concentration and tripped over an exposed root. She landed heavily on her knees and hands. She stifled the scream in her throat, afraid to expose her whereabouts to the braying pack on her trail. Still on her all fours, she momentarily closed her eyes against the sting in her palms. *Mayhap I should give up? Mayhap I should wait here on the ground to let destiny take its course?* Despite her daily praying, God had seemingly abandoned her in this heathen land. *Maybe it is time to abandon my beliefs, morals and even, my life?* Then she remembered Bard face and her stomach lurched. *No way is he going to get his filthy hands on me!* She still remembered the state he'd left the servants in her home in Dunwich. *I'd rather freeze to death, alone in the forest, than endure what he wanted!*

Like her mother.

With renewed determination, she pushed herself up and dusted herself down. Looking around, she chose her next route towards where she thought the start of the mountain was. With a determined oath, she set off again.

Hiding behind a tree, Ubba stilled, and held his bow and arrow taut in his arms. It wasn't his weapon of choice, but he'd mastered it easily enough. It was better than his sword or an axe for hunting. His icy blue eyes narrowed in concentration before he swore under his breath. *Why are the hounds from the village making so much noise? They are making my prey skittish.* It was soon sunset and his prey should arrive.

Rolling his shoulder as much as his stance would allow, he turned his gaze back onto his target—on where he was anticipating his elk or deer would make its appearance. All had been tranquil in the forest, apart from an occasional insect breaking the water surface of the partially frozen pond. Previously, a white fox had taken a drink from its waters, until the barking dogs had made it disappear.

The lowering sunlight broke through the branches of the trees where Ubba patiently hid. He ignored the pain in his feet, cold from walking through the snow earlier, and the ache in his arms. He shifted the slightest bit to keep his gaze in the shadows. He was nearly invisible to the eye, his Viking clothing blending into the background. *Now I have to watch and wait, and hope those damned barking beasts don't frighten my dinner away.*

When the shadows grew longer, and no prey had appeared, Ubba cursed quietly to himself. He was running out of time. If he did indeed slay something, he would have little light left to dress it and return to the safety of the hut before it was dark. His brow furrowed while he debated his options.

Hearing a noise, his gaze flittered past the trees towards the pond. His acute hearing picked up on the sounds of birds and a rustling. He afforded himself a small smile. A deer or elk, or some type of prey, was on its way after all. His fingers circled the leather grip on the bow, and he drew the string taut once again, raising it to eye level. This time determined to get his prize.

He waited patiently, listening to the approaching noise. His forehead puckered slightly. It wasn't the normal timid footfall of a stag. *But mayhap the persistent barking of the dogs have spooked it into a panic, and it is less surefooted than usual?* The prey would be wary and harder to kill while panicked, but Ubba was confident enough in his hunting skills not to worry.

His eyes narrowed against the fading light, and he strained to see into the shadows of the woods from where the sound came from. He made out the snap of twigs as the animal slowed, cautiously approaching the water.

Steadying his arms, he waited to catch a glimpse of its hide, ready for his shot. The split instant before he released his grip, he realised it wasn't a beast, but a human! It was too late to stop his arrow, the only thing he could do was to defer his deadly aim downwards. He prayed to Odin that he hit the ground instead.

It seemed like an eternity, but in no time at all, he heard a piercing scream.

Fear pounded through him. He turned quickly and grabbed his axe and belongings. He scrambled out of the forest towards the pond, hoping he hadn't killed the human.

Within no time at all, Ubba was upon the body lying on the floor. The person wasn't screaming anymore, it was deathly quiet. He glanced around before he squatted down next to the figure. When he reached and turned the body over, a curse laced the air when the hood fell away. It was Rosfrith, his thrall—the girl he'd sworn to protect, the girl he'd possibly killed. "Thor's teeth!" he shouted, before snorting. *Maybe the gods are playing tricks on me for thinking of her too often?* For only last night, he'd dreamed of Rosfrith in his bed, not on the floor, dead!

He quickly searched to find where he might have struck her. Ubba was glad when he saw his arrow embedded in the hard ground. *Hopefully, I didn't find my intended target?* He glanced down towards her feet and saw a tear in her tunic. Flipping the hem of her dress up, he saw red on her shoes. He *had* hit her. He prayed to *Eir*, the Goddess of Healing, for help.

Bending down on one knee, he placed one arm under her knees and one under her neck. In one fluid movement, he was standing, and effortlessly carrying her back to the cabin.

When he arrived, Ubba used his foot to push open the wooden door. Luckily, he'd prepared the cabin for a late return—the fire was glowing, and his furs were already placed on the floor for him to sleep.

Pushing the door shut, and the cold weather out, Ubba carried Rosfrith to the corner of the cabin, to his furs. Bending, he gently laid her down. As soon as she was settled, he stood and threw off his outer layers off, before bending once again, gathering her upper body into the crook of his arm. He tapped her face lightly. Ubba breathed a sigh of relief when she started to come around. "Rosfrith, it's me, Ubba, your sire."

Confusion clouded her violet eyes when they opened. "Sire?"

"Já," he said, still holding her in his bent arm. He held her faltering gaze, praying she didn't pass out again.

"Sire?" she murmured softly, again.

"Unfortunately, I've shot you with an arrow. I need to look at it," Ubba told her. His eyes narrowed to inspect her. She didn't look as though she was listening to his words. She had a far-away look in her eyes. "*Thor's teeth.* Rosfrith, I need to look at your wound." He positioned his mouth nearer to her ear in order for her to hear him properly.

Her fuzzy mind took a while to catch up to what was happening. She wasn't thinking, only feeling. Her heart faltered, as the fanning warmth of his breath fluttered gently over her face towards her ear. She couldn't hear his words, could barely breathe. When his hand moved down her body to gather her hem, Rosfrith could barely contain her whimper of suppressed delight.

Her quiet moan, deep in her throat, forced Ubba to stop. His gaze returned to her face, confusion marring his features. When he noticed her raise her lips towards him and close her eyes, he realised what she was doing—of how the situation might appear to her in her half-sleep state. He tensed, the muscle in his jaw flexing. "Snap out of it, Rosfrith. I need to look at your wound."

The harshness of his voice, snapped her back into reality, shattering the intimacy of the moment. Her eyelids flung open, as she tried to decipher what was going on. Mortified at her mistake, and feeling the blood rush to her face, she tried to get out of his embrace but pain sliced through her thigh, stopping her in her tracks.

"Still," he commanded. "I need to tend to your wound."

"The one you made," Rosfrith shouted weakly, trying in vain to move away from him.

Not letting her go, Ubba sighed. He tempered his voice, realising the whole situation *was* his fault. "Já, I did, but stay still. I need to lift your tunic to take a look."

After a long silence, a battle of wills, Rosfrith realised she was defying her sire, which wasn't allowed. Feeling faint and tired, she nodded her consent. She watched Ubba turn towards her feet, and lift the hem of her tunic.

Once she'd given her nod of consent, he ignored her frightened eyes, which had started to mist with tears. He wasn't going to hurt her—well, no more than he'd already done. Ubba felt her pale flesh tense under the initial touch of his cold hand. He paused briefly for her to relax. Once she had, he continued to inspect the wound, not daring to look at the shapely leg in his hand.

Once he was finished, he gently placed her leg back onto the furs. He stood and walked over the other side of the room to gather some cloth. He tore it into strips and dipped some of them into warm water, which was in the pot over the fire.

While Ubba was busy, Rosfrith watched his every move. She was glad of the silence, she had time to think about how to explain her appearance in the forest. He was bound to ask. As a thrall, she was not free to roam wherever she wanted. When he returned, Ubba kneeled by her, and Rosfrith felt her nerves jangle.

"I'm going to wash it, Rosfrith." He put one hand under her knee. He noticed her unsteady inward breath. He ignored her and carried on, using his other hand to gently sponge around the wound, carefully wiping away the warm, sticky blood to see the extent of the damage his arrow had made.

Once the warm trickle of water had finished, Rosfrith could feel Ubba prodding the wound, presumably to check if there was anything left in it. It throbbed and burned. But it wasn't just her wound affecting her breathing. His nearness had an unwanted effect on her, too. She gritted her teeth, hoping he'd put her skittishness down to the wound he'd caused her. It embarrassed her that she could feel every one of his probing fingers spread over her thigh, inspecting the wound. His flesh seemed to burn her.

"There is nothing in it, thank the gods, but it's a nasty gash. I'll clean it properly, and then bind it," he said before he placed her leg down and stood over her.

Rosfrith glanced up at him. He was huge, towering over her. She felt like that small child again, scared to her bones by the beasts. Feeling exposed, especially as his eyes wandered over her legs, Rosfrith shuffled to pull her hem back down. She heard him snort, but unsure what it meant, said nothing.

"You'll need to stay still while I do it," was the only comment he made before walking over to the fire.

Later, Rosfrith watched as Ubba bent towards the fire, restocking the logs, and stoking its embers back into life. Even though she felt faint, it was her duty as his thrall to tend to the fire, not her sire's. "I'll do that, sire."

Ubba turned towards Rosfrith, glad to hear her speak. From the time he'd cleaned her wound, she had been too quiet. To be honest, he'd been quiet, too, trying to untangle all of the emotions churning in his head—guilt for what he'd done, respect for her bravery, annoyance that she was here in the first place, and, the one that was most on his mind, attraction. It wasn't unusual to be attracted to the opposite sex, whether a free lady or a thrall, but usually he'd ignore it or did something about it. Either way, he moved on. For some reason with Rosfrith, he still had that old niggling feeling about protecting her, just like in Dunwich. It conflicted greatly with his desire for her.

He glanced at her and noticed her face pale when she attempted to move. A scowl appeared on his face, and his voice hardened. "You, stay where you are. I will tend to things until your wound heals. Get some sleep. It's late." He was glad when she stopped moving and closed her eyes. He noticed her face screw with pain, but he tore his gaze away from her suffering.

Ubba rose very early the next day, glad Rosfrith had slept most of the night, despite her thrashing around at times – with pain or dreams, Ubba was unsure.

After he had attended the fire, he grabbed a biscuit and ale and sat watching her sleeping form. His brow creased as he thought in the silence. *Why was she wandering through the forest during the cold evening?* If he thought about it, her clothes were disheveled, and her whole demeanor was wrong. He huffed. There were questions his thrall would need to answer.

When Rosfrith awoke and he'd given her some liquid to quench her thirst, he couldn't wait any longer. "Why are you so far from the longhouse, from Ranaricii, Rosfrith?"

Rosfrith noticed his piercing blue eyes had narrowed on her. Fidgeting under his glare, she wiggled deeper into the woven blanket he had placed around her. *How can I tell him about Bard?* She couldn't—he was one of his loyal men, and she, after all, was just his thrall. "Um, um. I got lost?" She caught Ubba let out a snort and turn his gaze away before he started poking the fire. It was obvious he didn't believe her, but it didn't seem as though he was going to question her further. Yet.

After a long silence, Ubba asked, "Do you feel hungry enough to eat?"

Rosfrith placed a hand on her stomach. She hadn't eaten since before mucking out the barns, but she feared if she placed anything in her stomach, it wouldn't stay, so she lied. "No."

Ubba turned to look at her. Regardless of what she felt, she needed to eat to keep her strength up. Her wound would need all her energy to heal, and there wasn't much spare flesh on her body to help that happen. "You will eat—," he softened his tone when he saw her become distressed, "—it will help you recover quickly."

Rosfrith lowered her gaze to the floor. "Já, sire." She just hoped she didn't embarrass herself by throwing it back up.

"I prepared some *skause* the other day. It's elk. The broth will be good for you." He said before grabbing the pot to put onto the fire.

While he reheated the broth, Rosfrith relaxed back into the furs. Tiredness overwhelmed her. It didn't matter that she'd slept the night, her body told her she needed more. Within no time, she was fast asleep again.

The change in Rosfrith's breathing indicated to Ubba she'd fallen to sleep before he had time to feed her. He put the bowl down and swivelled around on his feet to look at her. This time, with the light of the day creeping through the cabin, he noticed that asleep, she looked like the small innocent child he'd taken from East Angles. He sighed heavily. He knew better. Since the last time he'd seen her in his longhouse, and noticing she had grown into a woman, Rosfrith had been on his mind too much for comfort. It had confused him more than he cared to admit.

When he'd protected Rosfrith from his brothers and their men, all those years ago, and brought her over to Ranaricii, he'd thought he'd done enough to ease his conscious. After all, it wasn't his fault her father had been a liar and her mother had chosen to leave her. He'd repaid his debt to his conscious. To be honest, she hadn't even entered his mind for a number of years—she was just his property. But, when he'd seen her the other morning, he'd noticed her as a woman for the first time. He couldn't deny that his interest had stirred. And not in an innocent way. Normally, it wouldn't be a problem. If a thrall took his fancy, they would couple. But, for some reason, he didn't wish to. Something was stopping him taking her and being done with it. Confused, he turned away to tend to the stew and tried to think about just looking after her. The broth would take a while to heat through, and sleep was more important to her now.

As Ubba finished eating his stew, the barking of dogs, which he had heard yesterday, got nearer. He placed his pot down. Curious, he walked towards the door, reaching for his weapon. He glanced at Rosfrith and noticed her stir in her slumber. She didn't awake. He opened the door and braced himself to go outside to find out who was coming. He closed the door behind him, to conserve the heat within the walls and to protect Rosfrith.

Squinting into the distance, he tried to check if the advancing men were friend or foe. When the dogs neared—much faster than the men trailing behind them—Ubba relaxed a fraction. He knew the dogs well enough—they were from Ranaricii. He quietly observed them as they sniffed around the area—they were following a scent. He wondered what scent had come so near to the cabin. His gaze narrowed on them before flicking back to the following men. *Something was wrong*. On alert, his muscles tensed.

Within minutes, the dogs were at his feet and started to howl at the door. A crease marred his forehead. Their howling indicated they'd found what they were looking for. It only took him a second to figure it out. An unease flowed down his spine. He quietened the dogs down, patting them on their heads, and waited patiently for the men to come.

Ubba noticed them slow down and turn to each other when they detected him standing next to the cabin. He was too far away to know what they said to each other, but he had an idea. Turning, he placed his axe down. He didn't want to look threatening, but it was within easy grabbing distance—should he need it.

"Bard, Eirik, Rabbi, Daan," Ubba nodded to his men.

"Ubba," Bard said slowly

Ubba noticed his gaze searching behind him, towards the cabin. "Is there trouble in Ranaricii?" He watched as Bard quickly tore his gaze away and glanced at the men flanking him.

"Um, nay, Sire. We are–," he took a step forward, "—out hunting for bear."

Ubba noticed the questioning looks off the men, but the look Bard gave them served to silence them. "'Tis a little early. The snow hasn't melted yet; the bears will be sleeping." Ubba levelled a hard look at Bard. He knew he was pointing out the obvious mistake, but neither were silly. They knew the dogs previous howling indicated that their prey had been found. They had found Rosfrith. He widened his stance, hoping Bard would not choose to disrespect him in front of the other men. *His men.*

"Já." Bard smiled. "We are practicing, that's all, Sire. It is such a clear morning."

Ubba noticed the furtive glances between Daan, Rabbi, and Eirik. They appeared uncomfortable with the lies in front of their Chieftain—unlike Bard. When he was back in Ranaricii, Ubba knew he had no choice anymore—Bard would have to be dealt with. "Good." He wanted to close the conversation down, wanted the men gone, but he knew he had to act as normal as possible. "Have you enough food to get back to Ranaricii? I have some *skause* and sourdough here, if you need." He paused, before adding, "But, by the looks of your sacks, you have plenty to get on with." He noticed Bard's cheek twitch.

"No, Lord. We are fine," Bard said between gritted teeth. "We will be going, leave you to your…" Bard flicked a glance at the cabin once again. "Your *skause.*"

Ubba nodded and relaxed his stance slightly, now that they were going.

As they turned to leave, Ubba noticed Bard turn, a smirk on his lips. He moved a step nearer his axe.

"Oh, by the way, sire. Have you seen anyone around these parts?"

"No." Ubba noticed the three other men turn towards him too.

"No one, at all?"

Ubba's gaze narrowed on Bard, urging him to dare question him. "No."

Bard changed his tactics. "We found a lot of blood down by the lake when we sheltered for the night. Did you make a kill, Lord?"

Ubba hoped the men didn't notice him tense. "Já, but it got away."

"Did it now?" Bard shrugged as though he didn't care—but they both knew otherwise. "We'll see you back at Ranaricii, then, sire."

"Já, *you* will, Bard." Ubba was glad Bard flinched. He'd obviously realised he'd stepped over the mark. But regardless of any remorse, he would be dealt with for his insolence.

When Ubba was sure they were gone and wouldn't be returning, he turned and opened the door. Taking a deep breath, he walked in. Something had happened between Bard and Rosfrith. He'd find out.

While questions filled his mind, Ubba tended the fire. His gaze whipped around to seek Rosfrith when he heard movement. She was pushing herself up. Even in the darkness of the cabin, he noticed her face pale and her eyes glaze. "Don't move. I'll help." He strode over and knelt next to her, putting an arm around her shoulders and bolstering the furs. Once she reclined back down and a little colour had returned to her face, he couldn't put it off any longer. "Bard was just here."

"Oh," Rosfrith whispered, as her gaze bolted towards the door.

Ubba's gaze narrowed. "He's gone." He scanned her reaction on her face before he brought his piercing gaze back to hers. "I need to know what happened, Rosfrith. I cannot go back to Ranaricii unarmed with the facts."

"Um," she said, lowering her eyes.

Ubba held her chin tight when she tried to pull away. "Now. Tell me," he demanded.

The intensity of his gaze was piercing. Unable to pull away, she looked down at his lips. Her tears threatened because he was angry with her. *Mayhap Bard had lied to him?* She didn't want to say anything, but he was her sire, and he'd asked her outright. Unsure of what to do, her tears began to gather and spill.

Ubba flinched when wetness touched his hands. His instincts told him to comfort her, but he couldn't, he needed to know the facts. Without them, he couldn't help her. His voice became stern. "Tell me, Rosfrith. Was it Bard who put those bruises on your skin?" He felt her chin tremble under his fingers before she nodded. His fingers appeared so large and rough holding her delicate chin, he yanked them away, not wanting to touch her. He needed to distance himself from her.

Rosfrith watched as Ubba stood and walked towards the fire. His back was still facing her when he said, "Did he hurt you?"

"Já," she said with a shaky voice.

Ubba's gut tightened. He took in a breath before he turned from the fire towards her. He held her gaze for a while, his blue eyes looking deep into hers. "Did he rape you?" When she shook her head, his breath came out in a short blast. That was one blessing. "Are those bruises on your body from Bard?"

"Most of them," she answered truthfully. "But some are from my fleeing."

He turned away from her to stoke the fire while he tried to control his rage—his rage at Bard for hurting her; his rage at himself for not seeing it coming; his rage at not being there to stop it; and his rage for caring.

Later in the day, after bouts of sleeping and eating, Ubba knelt down next to Rosfrith. "I need to tend to your wound."

She hesitated and noticed his eyebrow lift slightly. "All right, sire." She lifted her tunic herself. It seemed less intimate. She felt his fingers spread, as he tenderly examined her wound. The gentle probing of his fingers around the wound's edge made Rosfrith wince.

"Does it hurt?"

"Já, but it will be fine now, sire."

"While we are in this cabin, you can dispense with my title, Rosfrith."

"But what would I call you?" Rosfrith asked tentatively, taken aback by his request.

"Ubba."

"If that is what you ask of me, sire—" She hesitated when his eyebrows flicked upwards. "I mean, Ubba," she said, rolling his name on her tongue. It felt too unfamiliar saying it.

He sighed as though the weight of the world was on his shoulders. "It is, but only here, Rosfrith. Not in Ranaricii."

She nodded, understanding his dilemma. As his thrall, she would never be permitted to call him Ubba.

Rosfrith watched as he efficiently changed her dressings, a calmness on his face. While his attention was firmly on her wound, Rosfrith took the opportunity to study him. Surprisingly, he hadn't aged much since she'd first seen him at Dunwich. He had more lines near the corner of his blue eyes, telling of his outdoor life, but they added to his rugged handsomeness. His long hair was still the same dark blond, with no hint of grey. His shoulders, under his tunic, were strong, yet the hands that were touching her were gentle. She sighed as a strange, warm feeling worked its way through her, pooling low in her stomach. *Já, he was a strong and handsome man.* She felt her pulse quicken.

Ubba glanced up at her. "Is that all right, Ros...?" His hands stilled and his gaze narrowed on her, trying to work out why she was flushed.

Embarrassed at being caught studying him, she turned away. "Um, já, thank you." She felt her mouth dry and leaned forward, to push her tunic back down. She felt too exposed. Ubba didn't protest, just watched her, before he stood and turned away. She ignored the snort he gave.

"Would you like something to drink before I finish up?" he asked without turning.

Rosfrith shook her head, not confident her voice wouldn't betray her emotions.

He turned to look at her when she failed to answer. He opened his mouth to speak, but changed his mind, giving a quick shake of his head. He made his way towards the corner of the room to retrieve clean bandages.

Rosfrith watched his broad back and panicked. She brought her shaky hand to her forehead, trying to think. *I can't let him that close again. He might guess that I'm attracted to him.* She closed her eyes, trying to compose herself.

Once Ubba had torn another strip, he returned towards Rosfrith. He hesitated in his stride when he noticed her hold her hand up to stop him. She appeared frightened. "What is wrong?"

She didn't answer.

He blew out his cheeks, then released them. "Rosfrith, what is wrong?" he started to walk over, but he noticed her flinch away. He rubbed his beard with confusion. He'd cleaned and changed her bandages on many of occasions, why was she scared of him now? He was only helping her. He tried again. "Rosfrith?"

"'Tis all right, sire. I will tend to my wound from now on," Rosfrith said, more firmly than she had intended, but her emotions were playing havoc.

"What?" He regarded her, a puzzled expression on his face. "Why? Have I not done a good job? And why are you now calling me sire?"

She dragged her gaze from looking at the floor towards the flames of the fire. She stayed quiet, only shrugging her shoulders.

He let out an impatient breath. He didn't know what he'd done wrong. He looked around for inspiration and found none. His hand clenched the bandage and he looked at it. He was only helping her. *Women and their unfathomable moods. She is turning out as unpredictable as Astrid.* "As you wish." His posture became rigid and the look he gave her didn't hide his impatience. "If you like, Rosfrith. I'm not going to argue with you." He threw the bandages near her. He needed to get out. "I'm going to get more firewood."

When the door slammed shut behind him, Rosfrith collapsed back onto the furs. Her chin trembled. That had not gone to plan—but it was for the best.

Rosfrith felt agitated as she moved around the small cabin. She tripped on a wooden stool and when she righted it, sat on it. She felt hot and light-headed, so she flapped her hands in front of her face, in an attempt to cool down and push back the tears, which she felt forming. For the last couple of days, since she'd told Ubba she'd look after her wound, the atmosphere was frosty between them. Her mind was stressed—she hadn't even slept during the night although she longed to. The hard ground had been covered with plenty of furs, but it hadn't provided any comfort for her aching muscles and throbbing wound. She took in a deep breath. Her mood could be as simple as being overtired—although not back to normal, she'd taken on some of the tasks in the cabin so Ubba could go out hunting. *Maybe it's all too much for me? The wound and being forced to live so close to Ubba—when I'm attracted to him.*

It was quiet in the cabin and although she'd barely completed any of her work, she hobbled over to the furs, deciding to take a rest. Her leg was giving her trouble, but she daren't tell Ubba. She hadn't even told him that she'd used the last bandage a couple of days ago. She didn't want to bother him to ask for more because he was barely grunting at her questions at the moment, let alone making conversation.

Exhausted, she settled down and slept soundly through the afternoon, only waking to the sound of Ubba cutting up meat. She wiped the sleep from her eyes and started to push herself up to sit. She gasped sharply at the pain in her thigh. It stabbed at her like a hot knife.

Ubba turned quickly at her gasp, his gaze narrowed in on her. "Is your wound bothering you more than before?"

She shook her head. "It's only because I've been still. It's stiff, that's all," she lied, biting her lip to stop any further protests. It was more painful than before, but she didn't want him to check on it. For her own sanity, she needed to keep him away, so she deliberately changed the conversation. "What have you caught?"

"An elk."

The thought of eating anything turned her stomach, but wanting to get rid of the strained atmosphere between them, she smiled. "Wonderful."

"It's large enough to keep us fed until you can walk back to Ranaricii," he added in a monotone voice, not looking at her.

Rosfrith felt fear claw at her stomach at the mention of Ranaricii – she didn't want to return and bump into Bard, regardless whether Ubba had assured her he wasn't a concern.

The afternoon passed slowly, with Ubba cutting up the elk, and Rosfrith falling in and out of sleep. She jumped when his hand shook her shoulder.

"Food is nearly ready."

"I'm not particularly hungry, sire."

Ubba's gaze sliced to hers. "I don't care. You are to eat to keep yourself strong." He turned back towards the fire when she nodded.

Rosfrith rubbed her hands up and down her arms but stopped when it felt like little needles pricked her skin. Despite the warmth of the blanket and fire, Rosfrith started to shiver. She glanced towards Ubba, who was busily preparing the food, but her mind and her body felt heavy. It was strange, while she shivered, rivulets of perspiration ran down her neck into the hollow between her breasts. She shook her head to clear her muggy thoughts, but stopped quickly, the movement making her dizzy.

"Are you all right?" A frown marred Ubba features when he turned and noticed she had become pale.

"Já," she managed to squeak out, her parched throat and heavy tongue made talking difficult.

He stood and slowly walked over to her, his narrowed gaze inspecting her. He wasn't happy. Her pallor had changed and had an unnatural shine.

"Sire—water..." was all Rosfrith muttered before she shut her eyes and surrendered to the blackness that beckoned her.

"Rosfrith!" Ubba shouted in panic when he felt a sudden coldness hit his core. He made his way over. He bent and pulled her into his arm. "Rosfrith!" He grabbed her chin to wake her, but she didn't respond to his calling. When her head rolled back in his arm, he swore profusely. He gently cradled her in the nook of his arm, afraid to hurt her. He noticed his hand visibly shake when he touched her forehead. Her skin was hot and faintly damp. *She is burning up with a fever!* He swivelled and tugged her tunic up, to check on her wound. He cursed again. The smell told him what was wrong.

He lay her back down, carefully, and turned his attention to her thigh. He wiped his clammy hands before he removed the bandaging. Her wound was red, hot, and obviously infected. He cursed again, annoyed he'd left her to tend to it herself. He should have dealt with cleaning it, despite her protests—he knew the signs of an infection, he'd witnessed it many times after battles. Or at least he should have taken her back to Ranaricii to get it tended to. He rolled his tight shoulders. His selfish actions of keeping her near could cost her her life

He sighed deeply and rubbed his face. There was no point thinking about that now. He knew what he had to do—he was glad she was unconscious. He stood and grabbed a pot, intending to get some snow to melt. Once it boiled, and his blade heated, he would have to mar her beautiful skin. He was not looking forward to it.

Later, Ubba stood and wiped the sweat from his face with the back of his hand. Blood smeared over it. He covered his mouth with his hand and glanced out through the open door, ajar in an attempt to cool Rosfrith's fever. All was quiet outside, mirroring the scene inside—at last. It hadn't been so peaceful when he'd had to burn and cut out her infection. She had screamed and struggled, but she never came out of her comatose state.

After taking in a couple more calming breaths, he looked at Rosfrith. She was sleeping. He shut his eyes for a moment, trying to regain his composure. Ubba released a small snort when he noticed his hands were still trembling. He'd killed and dressed many beasts, including men, but the sight of Rosfrith's wounded thigh, churned his stomach. Before he could think about it any longer, a moan had his eyes flinging open.

He strode over to her and placed his hand on her forehead. *She is hotter than before.* He let out a deep sigh. He scanned around, wondering how best to help her. A rabbit, almost invisible against the snow, drew his attention towards the doorway. He had an idea. He'd have to keep her infected wound dry, but he could cool the rest of her down.

With her eyes closed, Rosfrith dreamed. One minute, she was in a beautiful dream world, where a wonderful coolness bathed her burning body, and she felt light and free. The next minute, she was in a place where only pain and heat existed, where a force pushed against her, stopping her retreat. Try as she might, twisting and turning, she couldn't get out of either.

A couple of hours later, as night was drawing in, Ubba kicked the door open with his foot. In his arms, Rosfrith lay, lifeless. He gently placed her onto the skins, which he had placed away from the fire, so she didn't overheat. He pulled a thin cloth over her to cover her nakedness. He turned and grabbed the water bowl. Dipping in a cloth, he returned to wet her lips. "Drink," he urged, knowing she could barely hear him, but he carried on regardless.

When he'd made her as comfortable as possible, he slumped back against a wall and pressed the heels of his hands against his eyes. Fear gripped his gut. In the quietness of the twilight, he made out her breathing—too fast and unsteady. Perspiration still clung to her skin, even without her clothing, and Ubba knew enough about infections to know she might not survive.

He hoped she did.

Over the next couple of days, Ubba dutifully carried Rosfrith to the two pools, which were up the snowy mountain. One was a natural hot spring, too hot for Rosfrith at the moment. The other, a small bowl of tepid defrosted snow, warmed by its proximity to the hot spring. Each time Ubba took Rosfrith there, he carefully bathed her; her head against his shoulder, her back along his chest. When he felt the fire within her cool, he returned to the cabin to clean her wound with warm water.

In her semi-conscious haze, Rosfrith was aware of being carried into cold water. She wanted to protest about the chill, but she was vaguely aware she felt safe there. Besides, for a while, the intense heat and pain would dim enough to let her doze. Through her dreams and hallucinations, she was aware of a strong arm curled around her waist, keeping her close, while water dripped over her head and face, cooling her.

Time stood still for Rosfrith—night and day were the same—but time was important for Ubba. Each day meant more chance of Rosfrith's survival.

He smiled to himself at the absurdity of it all. If anyone saw him in the pool, talking randomly to a naked sleeping woman, they would think he had lost the plot! He had no idea if Rosfrith knew what was going on, but she must be aware of something. Even in her disorientated state, Rosfrith had protested about him seeing her naked. He knew that getting her temperature down was more important than her modesty, although he would confess not minding the view.

When Rosfrith suddenly thrashed in her sleep, she woke Ubba. He slept next to her, in easy reach, now her fever had dimmed. He got up on his elbow, and looked down on her, moving a hair from her forehead. "Sleep, Rosfrith. Your fever has broken. Your body needs the rest."

She wasn't aware of much, apart from his voice. She felt calm—she wasn't alone—so she closed her eyes and relaxed against his body. For once, she was glad of the warmth of his skin—his touch no longer burned hers.

"How long have a been sleeping?" Rosfrith enquired when she felt strong enough to speak.

"About five days."

Rosfrith was shocked.

"Are you hungry, now?" Ubba smiled at her.

"A little," she said, moving to get more comfortable. Her strength faded and she sat back. She was obviously weaker than she thought.

"Good, I have some good bone broth for you." He turned to get a small bowl.

Rosfrith watched him, she had no strength to protest to having food or for him serving her. She felt overwhelmed by his kindness, and was glad he wasn't angry with her anymore.

"Once you have your strength back, we'll go back to Ranaricii," said Ubba.

Rosfrith's mood deflated. She was glad his back was to her, so he couldn't see the disappointment on her face. "All right, when?" she managed to say calmly.

He swivelled around on his feet, before stretching and passing her a bowl of stew. "Within the next couple of days." He shrugged, keeping his gaze towards the floor. "I need to gather provisions first."

A frown rippled over Rosfrith's forehead. His mood had changed with her again—he appeared down and wasn't making eye contact with her. She watched as he stood and walked around the small area. "Why do you need provisions if we are heading to Ranaricii?"

"Because this cabin needs to be ready, in case someone needs it in an emergency. Firewood must be left," he turned around to face her but wished he hadn't. He was struggling with his feelings for her. While she had been ill, he'd cared and looked after her—something he'd never done for anyone before. Apart from the times he panicked he would lose her, he'd enjoyed the time. But now she was getting better, he was missing the closeness. He couldn't allow it to continue—she affected him too much.

Rubbing his beard, he flicked a glance at her then tore his gaze away. She looked too tempting, sitting crossed-legged, on the furs. *His furs*—the ones he'd laid on with her. "Amongst other things," he mumbled, losing his train of thought. He shook his head, trying to gain some composure. This was silly—expected from an unworldly youth, not from a grown man. They had to go back to Ranaricii, but the thought wasn't bringing him any joy. He wanted to stay, locked away, with her.

"Then I will help you," said Rosfrith, her voice sounding unsure.

He didn't want her to help, he wanted to do things for her, but within a couple of days, they would be back to reality. She would once again be his thrall. *It would be best if I remembered that.* He tried to put his feelings aside, becoming firmer than he intended. "Of course, you will, Rosfrith. You're my thrall, after all," he said, his voice gaining a hard edge. "And remember, I am no longer Ubba, but sire." He felt his chest squeeze, but he couldn't tell her.

Rosfrith could feel herself physically recoil. "Have I done something wrong?"

When Ubba's icy gaze landed on her, she flinched, not realising his anger was aimed at himself. Her heart hammered against her chest. When he said nothing, she knew she was being emotionally nudged aside by him. And it hurt. She needed to flee the suffocating cabin, its atmosphere now oppressive. She stood, glad her shaky legs were keeping her upright. "Excuse me, sire," she hated the use of his formal title, but he'd made it clear their social boundaries were back. "I need to leave."

"No. Stay and rest. I will leave," Ubba said firmly, before turning to leave.

Over the next couple of days, Rosfrith's physical strength slowly returned, although her mental strength felt at its weakest. Ubba barely talked to her, that was, if he was around. He spent much of his days hunting. If they happened to be in the same vicinity, they both went about their daily tasks without hardly a word spoken amongst them. He did enquire once about her wound, but she supposed he was thinking about how she would manage the walk back down the mountain to Ranaricii, rather than caring for her. *I might as well be invisible.*

Throwing down the rabbit by the dying fire, Ubba waited while his eyes adjusted to the darkness. That was strange, Rosfrith usually had the fire roaring at this time, ready to make food. He glanced around, expecting her to be near her furs, trying not to speak to him. He couldn't blame her. He had been awful to her. But it was the best for the both of them. His brow furrowed. *Where is she?* She wasn't in the cabin, but she couldn't have gone far, her cloak was there. He felt his heart speed up as he tensed. He didn't like her wandering around without him. He'd seen a bear while hunting. It seemed some of the hungrier ones were coming out of their dens already.

Ubba turned and grabbed his axe. As he stepped outside of the hut, he looked down. He rubbed his beard as a smile grew on his face. Rosfrith would be in trouble if she were being hunted—her footsteps in the snow were so obvious. Suddenly, a chill went through him, and he sobered. He remembered Bard. He had been hunting her. Grunting, he shut the door and followed her steps.

While Rosfrith washed in the warm water of the hot spring, her body became alert. Ubba was nearing. Her back was towards the spot where he would eventually emerge, so she closed her eyes. *Should I retrieve my clothes now, or stay where I am?* She chose to stay and felt her pulse quicken.

Ubba quietly made his way towards the spring. He'd spotted Rosfrith in the water and briefly debated whether to turn around. But, he couldn't stop himself walking towards her. From the shadows, he watched her bathe. His nerve endings tingled with the force of his attraction to her, but he rolled his large shoulders in an attempt to dismiss those feelings. He had come to apologise for his foul behaviour, that was all. He stepped out of the shadows. "I'm sorry, Rosfrith," said Ubba. He reached the stones surrounding the spring.

Rosfrith squeezed her eyes tight. Now he was so near, her emotions became off balance again. Oh, she knew she liked him, loved him even, whatever her experience of love was, but, to him, she was his possession. One he could rightly use, and then discard. She would have no say in the matter. *Can I cope with that? To love someone, only to lose them again?*

"I've been a fool the last couple of days, but I shouldn't have taken it out on you." He waited for her to turn to look at him, but when she didn't, he continued. "You've done nothing wrong. It's just..." Ubba stopped and glanced into the direction of Ranaricii. "It's just..." he let out a large puff. This was harder to admit than he thought. "It's just, I've started to have feelings for you."

Rosfrith's chest squeezed. He did feel something for her—it wasn't just her fantasy.

"But when we arrive back to Ranaricii, you will have to forget about this place, and become my thrall once again."

Even with his final words, her decision was made. Whether she regretted at some later point, it didn't matter. She slowly stood up out of the water, her back still to him. She took in a steadying breath and gradually turned around until she was completely exposed to him.

Ubba stayed silent. Not that he could say anything. He watched her intently, trying to work out what she was doing. Although his face betrayed no emotion, his insides were churning.

Does she realise how difficult it is for me not to reach out and touch her? Does she know what she's doing to me? Whether she remembered or not, she'd been naked in his arms on many occasions, but she'd been lifeless. Now the glow on her skin and the faint smile on her lips made her breath-taking.

"Would you join me, Ubba?" Hoping he didn't notice her arm shake, Rosfrith held out her hand.

He wanted to say that he was pleased she'd used his name, but all he managed to do was gulp when she nodded at him.

"I would like you to," she whispered.

There was an eerie silence between them.

Before he moved a muscle, Ubba's gaze made a thorough appraisal of her assets.

She resisted the urge to cross her arms, to protect her modesty. After all, she was offering her body to him, it would be silly to act coy. She noticed the tension within him, but only because his hands were flexing by his sides. "Come to me, Ubba."

He didn't need any other encouragement. Hastily stripping his clothing off, Ubba almost ran into the spring, stopping short when he reached her. Once again, he couldn't move. She overwhelmed him.

While he stood, his hand wavering, as though it didn't know what to do, Rosfrith's heart pounded, so hard she thought it would burst. "Touch me, Ubba."

A lazy smile spread on his lips when he got his senses back. He moved forward, the water rippling around his thighs. Reaching out, he gently took her hand—it was so small next to his. He could feel her tremor through it. *So, she isn't as sure about this as she seems.* That made him feel better—at least both of them were unsure. He rubbed his thumb along the sensitive skin of her wrist, then bent and sensually kissed the center of her open palm.

She watched as he placed a kiss on her hand, her pulse kicking up a gear. Her breath caught when he glanced up at her. His piercing blue eyes probed her soul, asking her so many questions. She smiled and nodded and within seconds, he claimed her mouth— tentatively at first, as though he might break her, but before long, it was possession he sought.

Moving towards the edge of the water, he gathered her into his arms, arching her backward with his kiss. When he felt the rock he'd been aiming for, touch the back of his thigh, without breaking the kiss, he sat and pulled her astride him. Carefully breaking the kiss, he moved his hands to cup the sides of her head. "Rosfrith, are you a maiden?" He asked gently.

She nodded, biting her bottom lip with concern. She noticed him let out a short puff of air. *Is he displeased with me?*

He gave a small smile. "All right, Rosfrith. It's going against everything I want right now, but we are going to have to take things slowly. I'll try not to hurt you."

She gave a little nod, not entirely sure what he meant, and was glad when he started kissing her again.

Later on, when the cooling air made shivers over their skin, Ubba carried Rosfrith back to the cabin, as though she didn't weigh anything. When his hard body pressed her down into the furs, it felt utterly right to them both.

Chapter 14

Back to Ranaricii

Much to Rosfrith's alarm, a welcoming committee waited for them to descend into the village. Rosfrith knew they were there to welcome their sire back, not her, but the side glances and nods didn't go unnoticed by her, regardless of how discreet they thought they were being.

"Welcome back, Ubba," Gunnar said, a genuine smile on his face. He leaned in to whisper into Ubba's ear. "You can take your seat back as soon as possible. Ruling is not as easy as it looks." He laughed as he straightened.

"I'm glad someone realises that," Ubba chuckled, knowing his friend would have found it easy. He glanced around the gathering crowd, nodding and greeting as he went. Out of the corner of his eye, he caught a couple of women whispering. He glanced in the direction they were looking. He sighed. Regardless of him being their Chieftain, there would be gossip.

He walked over to Rosfrith, who at the moment, looked as though she hoped the earth would open and swallow her. "Look who I found on the way down the mountain," he said as he raised her hand that he'd grabbed. "My wandering thrall."

A couple of the people standing around gave a little snigger, not understanding what was going on.

Ubba drew her to his side, ignoring her reluctance. He noticed Bard quietly standing to the side, obviously not happy his Chieftain was back, even less that Rosfrith was with him. Ubba directed his voice in Bard's direction. "I'm keeping her close." He let her remove her hand when she tugged it. "I want to know how she survived up there—on her own." He added, knowing full well people wouldn't believe him, but they would never question him.

He looked directly at Bard and narrowed his eyes. He was glad when Bard lowered his. While in the cabin, he had decided to send him back to *Bryttania* to fight with his brothers so he'd be out of the way. He'd tell him later, without the crowd.

Rosfrith watched the silent exchange between the two men and didn't know if to be thrilled or more scared that Bard would get his revenge somehow. When she watched Ubba stride over to Bard, she was unsure what to do.

"Bard."

"Lord," said Bard.

"You and I will meet later on for a talk," said Ubba.

Bard nodded and glanced over Ubba's shoulder.

He turned to find out what caught Bard's attention. He hoped it wasn't Rosfrith—but it wasn't, it was Astrid.

"Welcome back, Ubba," Astrid purred. She pulled Ubba's face towards her lips.

Ubba's instinct was to pull away, but when he heard the cheer of those around him, those who'd expect him to bed Astrid on his return, he let her kiss him. He didn't want to make a scene and didn't know what to do to protect Rosfrith yet.

"Come," Astrid said, pulling him towards the main longhouse. "I've missed you," she said with a knowing smile.

Much to her disdain, Rosfrith could feel her face redden. She growled in her throat. She felt embarrassed, ridiculous even. How silly of her to expect any more of Ubba. He hadn't promised her anything, in fact, he had told her everything would go back to normal once they returned. Pursing her lips, she took a step back, and turned, unable to watch the two of them anymore.

Once Ubba had managed to untangle himself from Astrid, he glanced around to find Rosfrith. He didn't know what he was going to say, but he wanted her to know he hadn't forgotten her over a kiss from Astrid. A frown crossed his face for the briefest of moments. He was disappointed to observe Rosfrith walking away. He let out a defeated breath. He knew he had said that when they returned, she'd become just his thrall once again. *Mayhap it is what she really wants?*

Ubba watched Bard walk into the longhouse and hesitate. He'd obviously expected people to be milling around, as usual, but Ubba had made sure it was empty. He didn't want anyone overhearing their conversation. "Bard." He nodded from his chair and indicated for Bard to sit on the low bench in front of him. He didn't fail to notice Bard's hesitation before doing what he asked. "We need to talk."

"About what, Sire?"

Ubba noticed the rolling of his shoulders, but Bard was doing a good job of seemingly not to care. He would soon, when he changed the course of his comfortable life. "Rosfrith," Ubba stated and noticed his body tense.

"What of the thrall?"

Ubba didn't fail to notice him drag the last word out. "You are to stay away from her," he stated flatly.

Bard stayed quiet for a while before a sly smile grew on his lips. "Why, Sire? Have you taken a fancy to a bit of rough?"

Anger and something he didn't quite recognise sped through Ubba. "Enough," he said. "I don't need to explain anything to you. She is *my* property, and you are threatening it. Stay. Away."

Bard's eyes narrowed. "As you wish, Lord," he muttered through gritted teeth.

Ubba knew by Bard's demeanour that he wouldn't appreciate being reprimanded over a thrall. He would go after Rosfrith one way or another. He sighed before standing. "I have made myself clear, Bard. If *anything* happens to Rosfrith, whether from an accident," he narrowed his gaze, his blue eyes becoming icy, "or by you, *you* will be held accountable. You and your wife." He waved his hand in dismissal, wanting Bard to go before he blurted out why he wanted to protect Rosfrith. *She is mine and mine only.* Now he just had to find a time to tell her.

Rosfrith sighed heavily while she poked the longhouse fire back to life. She scowled at the flames as they spluttered to life. *Life? What has mine become? The same as before.*

She glanced around the darkened longhouse, it was unusually quiet for this time in the evening, but it suited her dark mood. She'd been in gloomy disposition since arriving back from the mountain and her time spent with Ubba. He'd obviously meant it when he said things would go back to normal when they returned from the mountain back to Ranaricii. It definitely had—she'd gone back to her chores, along with the other thralls, and she'd hardly seen Ubba, even though all her work had been centered around the longhouse. He appeared to be doing everything to avoid her. She would crumble if she let herself, but she wasn't going to.

The only thing that made her feel better was when Bard sailed away on a ship, back to *Bryttania.* The look he'd given her when she had gone down to the docks to check that he was really departing, was murderous. She hoped he wouldn't live to return. A shiver flitted over her.

"Anything wrong, Rosfrith, are you cold?" Hilde's voice broke her thoughts.

She smiled at her only friend when Hilde regarded her with a somewhat wary expression. With the mood she'd been in lately, she was probably waiting for her to snap at her. "Já," she lied. "A little."

During a particularly low time, Rosfrith had told Hilde of her coupling with Ubba. But Hilde had dismissed their act as normal. Although she had tried to tell Hilde about her feelings, her friend dismissed them, too, telling her, quite abruptly, that she should not expect reciprocal emotions from their sire—it was just the way of life for chieftains to couple with the thralls, and think nothing of it. They were purely possessions. Those few words of experience had been enough to crumble Rosfrith's heart, but she carried on. She had to.

Once the last person was fed, Hilde, Rosfrith, and another couple of servants tidied up. She felt a small dig in her ribs and noticed it was Hilde's elbow.

"We haven't seen the Lord, tonight," Hilde whispered. "Nor that woman, Astrid."

Rosfrith's gaze followed Hilde's and cut to the bed-closet at the end. Her heart constricted. She knew where he was. And with whom.

"Do you mind?"

"Of course, I don't mind. Why should I?" Rosfrith said to Hilde trying not to sound defensive. She did mind—very much. All of a sudden, she wanted to be out of the longhouse, even mucking out the animals instead.

Hilde shrugged. "I was just wondering, that's all."

As much as she loved Hilde, and knew she was trying to help, Rosfrith did not want to acknowledge what was happening in *that* room. She swallowed her irritation and changed the conversation to a less personal one. "Will you rinse out the bowls, or shall I?"

Hilde let out a short huff. "We will," she said, catching the attention of another couple of women. "You sweep, Rosfrith. With your sour mood, you need to be on your own."

She bit down her reply, choosing to pick up the brush instead. She watched Hilde and the others leave, their arms full. She sighed deeply, wondering whether to call her back because she was now stuck in the longhouse - somewhere where she didn't want to be.

Knowing it was better to leave it, she put all her pent-up tension into vigorous brushing. Finally, she started to relax. It wasn't Hilde's fault that she'd been a fool, she'd apologise later for her surly behaviour.

When she glanced up from the floor, she realised she had unconsciously made her way near Ubba's chamber. She cursed her stupidity. She'd been so wound up before, she hadn't realised what she was doing, but now she was near, she could hear the sounds of coupling from within. She felt a burning sensation in her chest and stomach. She clenched her jaw as she struggled with the sensation of hurt and fury.

Unable to take anymore, she grabbed the brush tightly in her hands and moved far from the sire's room. She fought her tears. She knew she was jealous of Astrid and angry that Ubba had aroused her desire when she'd been defenseless. But, she was also angry at herself. In her heart, she'd wanted Ubba *and* given herself willingly. It might hurt her feelings that she was *only* a thrall to him, but it had been her own choice. Not caring if the longhouse floor was clean enough, Rosfrith left as soon as she could.

As soon as he'd finished, Ubba rolled off Astrid and silently cursed. He used his arm to shield his eyes, attempting to feign sleep, so she wouldn't feel the need to talk. His plan to forget Rosfrith had back-fired. He'd deliberately missed food this eve, choosing to spend the evening with Astrid instead. He'd hoped his previous desire for her would be rekindled. Despite how he'd been treating her since returning from the mountain, she'd been overjoyed at his offer. But, the time spent together had done nothing to awaken his desire. All he had done was think of Rosfrith and why she didn't want to be with him.

He tried many times to talk to her, but each time, she'd been just out of reach, or there were too many people around. He'd wanted to tell her how he missed her, and that she didn't have to fear Bard anymore, as he'd sent him to *Bryttania*—but he hadn't even had a chance to speak to her about that. The mischievous god, *Loki*, was obviously playing tricks with his life.

"Ubba?"

He didn't answer and caught Astrid huff in annoyance, but he didn't move. If he did give her indication he was awake, she'd expect him to talk. And he didn't want to talk—not to Astrid. All she wanted was to chat about him marrying her—the wedding she thought she was entitled to. He wasn't going to marry her—he'd never even asked her!

He inhaled deeply and turned, pulling a fur with him. He was tired and angry with himself. *Thor's teeth. What possessed me to allow Astrid back into my bed?* He'd been wrong to take her back, but once Rosfrith had walked away, he let his physical needs rule his behaviour. He knew it was the biggest mistake of his life. Tomorrow, he would explain to Astrid what was going on in his head—he owed her that—but for now, if she wanted to share his bed, she'd have to talk to his back because he certainly didn't want to hold her close to him. When she quietened, in a mood or because she fell asleep, he did not know, but he knew when he dropped into slumber, he would only dream of embracing one woman. *Rosfrith*. She had managed to burn herself into his thoughts—day and night.

It was no good denying it anymore. He didn't want Astrid, he wanted Rosfrith.

#

"Hilde, out," Ubba said the moment he stepped into the barn.

Hilde glanced at Rosfrith, unsure of whether to leave her. When Rosfrith nodded, she breathed a sigh of relief. She wanted to protect her friend, and even though Ubba was a good sire, ultimately, she still had to do as she was told. "Sire." She nodded at Ubba as she sidestepped him to get out of the barn.

Rosfrith gripped the rake and levelled a look at him. She was angry, and she didn't attempt to conceal it. She didn't care if he was her sire, time had allowed her shame to burn within her. She had long given up praying to God, but some deeply rooted customs about virtue had apparently stayed with her.

He took a step nearer. "How are you, Rosfrith?" His gaze lingered on her face for a fraction of a second, before it lowered, down her body.

If anger wasn't pumping through her, she would have moved to shield herself from his scrutiny. *How dare he seek me out as though he hasn't hurt me!*

A smile lit his face. "I think it might be better if you put that down," he laughed nodding to the rake in her hands before his face sobered. "We need to talk. *I* need to talk."

She huffed and threw it down onto the hay. It wouldn't do her any good to keep it—she might end up striking him with it.

Glad that she'd thrown the rake, for he didn't put it past her to use it—if the look on her face told him anything—he took a step towards her. He left enough distance, so she felt comfortable, but he knew she was within easy reaching distance. "I would like you in my *bed-closet*." When he saw fury shoot across her face, he realised he had worded that incorrectly. He stepped forward to close the distance, she took a step back, growling at him.

"No way, sire!" she shouted, tears threatening to spill.

He shook his head. "What I meant to say is, will you share my bed with me, Rosfrith?"

"What, with Astrid?" she shot back, not concerned if she sounded catty—she felt it.

He shook his head. "No, not with Astrid." Frustrated that nothing was coming out right, he reached forward and grabbed her hand. He hauled her forward and crushed her against his chest, hoping that actions would speak louder than words.

As her feet left the floor, it enraged her how easily his strength could subdue her. He'd hurt her, more than anyone before, yet he wanted her to forget. She twisted in his arms as his hand slid up her spine to force her closer.

"Rosfrith, be still. I mean you no harm."

She stilled. "You just want another coupling?" she spat out, knowing her voice sounded bitter.

His eyes narrowed. "No, Rosfrith. Despite what you think, you were never someone to pound my frustrations on. I wanted you." He let out a snort as he looked down at her lips. "I want you. I still want you."

Even though he was her sire, she couldn't let it be that easy for him, so she growled again. "What I want, Rosfrith." He bent, and his breath tickled her ear. "Is... you."

She cursed when she noticed the desire for her in his voice. She had wanted to block that out, but his endearments, whispered in her ear, were starting to thaw her.

"If I place you down on your feet, will you promise to listen?" he asked.

She nodded, needing to get away from his embrace so she could think. As soon as her feet hit the ground, she took a step back. "I'm listening."

"My actions," he pushed his hand over his face, "since we arrived back to Ranaricii have been wrong, I admit it to you. I want to correct them."

"How?" she whispered.

"I realise that I need you, Rosfrith. Mayhap our fates have always been entwined? I never understood why I had the urge to look after you, even when you were a child in Dunwich. I've always felt connected," he laughed. "Even when Sigurd told me you were trouble."

"Sigurd told you I was trouble?" she asked, confused.

"Já," he waved his hand, "He mentioned it in passing." He took a tentative step forward. When she didn't move, he leaned forward and kissed her forehead when it puckered. He was glad she didn't mind.

"Did he?"

Ubba laughed and straightened. "Já, he did. And I can't wait to find out how much trouble you will be," Ubba jested.

When a smile flickered on her lips, he became bolder. "Can I kiss you, Rosfrith? I've wanted to for so long." When she nodded, he circled her in his arms. He couldn't disguise his desire and took her mouth in a hard, savage kiss. *Rosfrith is mine, be damned what is right.*

The desire and heat emanating from Ubba thrilled her. It was what she needed at this moment—a show of how much he wanted her. A yearning to match his kiss broke free within her. She matched his kiss with the same force. As a moan left her throat, the painful feelings faded from her thoughts.

When they both passed the edge of consent, he pushed her up against a wooden beam, frantically grabbing at the hem of her tunic. Then, for the first time since they'd been alone together in the cabin, his name trembled from her lips.

Ubba's mouth fused to hers again while he drove himself, and Rosfrith, until there was only a blinding heat, clambering for release.

Once they stilled, their mouths still mating, Ubba realised he was trembling. No woman had ever done that to him before. He broke off the kiss, placing his forehead against hers, trying to catch his breath. "I want you, Rosfrith. In my bed. In my life."

Her voice hitched. "As your bedmate?" She still didn't know how she felt about that yet, even though they had laid together again.

Ubba searched deep into her eyes and slowly smiled. Lifting a hand, he brushed a stray hair behind her ear. "No, sweet, Rosfrith. As the mother of my children."

Tears began to gather and spill out of Rosfrith's eyes. "You mean it?"

"Of course, I do. I only ever speak the truth to you," he replied.

Overjoyed, she played with his hair, her arms back around his neck, pulling him nearer. She whispered into his ear. "Will I still have to call you sire?" she laughed.

"Only if you've been naughty," he muttered, his voice thick with longing.

When she threw back her head in laughter, he bent to nibble the pulse throbbing in her neck. He growled when his access was limited. "We'll need to get that necklace off, later. Come, let's find somewhere more comfortable," Ubba whispered. "My chamber. I want you there, forever."

Astrid stood in the shadows of the barn, listening to Ubba's declaration. She had followed him in to talk to him. She'd wanted to last night, but he'd fallen asleep. When she'd seen him walk into the barn, she had hoped that after their talk, they'd enjoy a tryst in the hay. She scowled. She hadn't expected this scene to greet her.

Astrid's face screwed up and her lips thinned as she attempted to remember their conversations when he had returned. *Did he mention the thrall at all?* She shook her head. It was no use, she couldn't remember—she'd been too pleased to see welcome him home to question what had happened whilst he was away. She let out a short, irritated breath, being mindful not to disturb them. *Perhaps I should have questioned why she'd returned with him, instead of focusing on getting him into bed?*

She glanced at them again. It was evident they were indeed lovers. She waited for the hurt and anger to ride through her because this wasn't the time or place to make a scene. She'd confront him later, or just make him remember why he loved her, not anyone else.

Stuck in her hiding spot, she stood quietly, unable to tear her gaze away. Bleakness filled her heart, but when she noticed the tender kisses Ubba placed down Rosfrith's neck, anger took its place. *She* was a lady of the jarl, not some dirty thrall. *How dare he?* Chieftain or not, he needed to remember he had been bonded with her for years. Even her brother, Gunnar, had reassured her Ubba would propose marriage. She'd already planned the wedding feast in her mind.

Tearing her gaze away, she realised she had a choice to make. Confront him and perhaps lose him? Or decide that this hiccup meant nothing? Like most chieftains, he could be merely indulging in a fling before settling down with her. Settling on the latter, she decided not to panic, but unable to leave, she carried on watching, her temper quietly simmering at the slight.

When she'd seen as much as her stomach could handle, she took a tentative step back. But, as she pulled her gaze away, she froze. Her gaze narrowed and she leaned forward to study Ubba's face. *He loved her!*

Astrid turned away from their coupling, covering her mouth while she heaved. Nothing came up. She'd lost its contents earlier on. Once her nausea subsided, she straightened and glanced at them again anxious to see if they were still oblivious to her presence. They hadn't noticed her. She alternated between relief and anger until her lip curled with a half-smile. She placed a hand on her growing stomach. *It's not important what they are up to, now. Ubba and the thrall will pay in time. In a matter of months, Ubba will have to marry me.*

#

Thank you for reading my book. I hope you enjoyed it as much as I enjoyed writing it. Find out what happens to Rosfrith and Ubba, in the follow-on books – Viking: Deception and Vikings: Revenge.

If you enjoyed 'Vikings: Taken' a review on Amazon or Goodreads would be very much appreciated.

https://www.amazon.co.uk/-/e/B00AS0256Y
https://www.amazon.com/-/e/B00AS0256Y

Thank you

Ceri Bladen

#

Here is a snippet of one of my books - 'Twe12ve'. It is a modern romance, with Norse gods!

Prologue

Brian's tired eyes narrowed. He grimaced at the torrential rain that pounded his car's windscreen. Even on full power, the wipers fought a losing battle to remove the water, while Brian fought another losing battle against the condensation that obstructed his view.

For a brief second, he dared to let go of the steering wheel to clean the windscreen. He tilted sideways to reach for the napkin in the seat beside him. He cursed as he fingered the half-eaten breakfast McMuffin that his heartburn wouldn't allow him to finish. He licked the sauce off his fingers and eventually grabbed a paper napkin.

Leaning forward, he wiped an area big enough to look through, but as he did, he realised this just wasn't going to be his day. Ketchup smeared across the glass. He exhaled loudly with frustration and threw the napkin onto the floor. It silently joined the other debris that he kept meaning to remove from the car.

Brian drove on slowly, with the spray from the vehicle in front adding to his lack of vision. He grabbed the steering wheel a little tighter because he hated driving in storms. To be honest, at that moment, he was on a fast track to hating life.

Squinting, Brian bent over the wheel in an attempt to work out exactly where he was. Suddenly, he realised that he was near a junction - and the lights were red. Praying that he wouldn't aqua glide into another car, because *that* would really make his day, he slammed his foot on the brakes. Luckily, he didn't collide with anything, and once he'd come to a stop and could breathe again, he wiped his clammy brow with his hand.

He sat back and took a deep breath in the hope of relaxing. But, try as he might, he couldn't. With his fingers tapping impatiently on the wheel, Brian attempted to block out the summer storm and the uncomfortable lack of air inside the car. There was no point worrying that he couldn't breathe, it was *his* fault. He should have taken the time to get the air conditioning fixed. If he had, not only would it have taken away the humidity of the storm, more importantly, it might have stopped his wife nagging him about it, too.

Rolling his shoulders, Brian attempted to dislodge the uneasy feeling he'd had since he'd dragged himself out of bed this morning. It unsettled him. Although he couldn't put his finger on the reason, he thought it could be to do with the fact that he'd spent last night in the spare room. He blew out a short breath and sulked for a while until honking from the vehicle behind him made him jump. Startled, Brian pushed down on the accelerator and moved quickly away from the lights; so quickly that his tyres struggled to search for traction on the waterlogged road. Once he'd made it through the traffic lights, and the annoyed driver had passed, beeping him, he slowed down.

When his heart finally resumed its regular beat, and he could think clearly, Brian made a mental note to ring his wife when he arrived at work. Looking back in the cold light of day, he realised that he'd been a prize jerk last night - coming home drunk *and* obnoxious. It wasn't even the weekend, only Tuesday.

Lena, his wife, had been fuming with him because their dinner had burned *and* he'd missed the final episode of a series they were watching together. After her initial verbal tirade, the only time she'd spoken to him was to tell him to use the spare room! At the time, he hadn't cared because he'd silently laid all the blame at her feet, not his drunken ones, but now, well, he could see *he* was at fault.

Realising he was coming to another junction, and seeing the red blur of traffic lights, he slowed, gradually this time. He let out a breath in frustration. It just wasn't his day - even the lights were against him.

While Brian waited, pressure built in his skull. He pressed the heel of his hand into his eyes and wished his thumping headache and heartburn would go away.

Was karma repaying him for his actions last night?

He snorted. He didn't believe in karma, but if he did, he was sure that it had a lot more in store for him than bad weather and a headache.

Suddenly feeling deflated, he tried to shake his negative thoughts away. Whatever mood he was in, he wasn't going to get out of it by sulking. It didn't matter how much stress he and his wife were under, he needed to do something about it. He knew deep down that for the last four years he hadn't been dealing with their situation appropriately. *He* had no choice, but Lena had given up all her family and friends for him. Drinking and emotionally pushing her away was cruel - it made him the biggest loser around.

Determined to make amends, he gripped the steering wheel tighter. It was time to show Lena how much he appreciated her commitment. Before he went home tonight, he'd get her some flowers and hopefully, that action would allow him access to some bedroom attention, too. He grinned.

Now, that would be nice.

Brian flicked a glance at the lights and noticed, at last, the rain had lessened enough for him to crack the window open. He bent and reached for the winder, desperate to let in some fresh air. As his window slowly lowered, he looked at the car that waited next to him. It was sleek and black, with blacked-out windows. Its engine purred.

Brian bristled as his irritation grew once again. His fingers tapped the steering wheel. For all the effort he put into work in his menial job, he'd never be able to afford one of those.

Again.

When thoughts of his old life entered his head, he grimaced, bitterly remembering how life could play cruel games - giving with one hand, taking with another. But, he understood it was no use hankering for the past, and for all their previous luxuries. He had to remember that the most important thing was that he was much safer now, and Lena, too. He mustn't forget that.

Not being able to help himself, Brian sneaked another sidewards glance at the car. Okay, he could admit he was jealous. It didn't matter that he was trying to forget his past, he never would, and it irritated the hell out of him that *his* red Ford looked like a rust bucket compared to that!

Unable to look away, his interest increased when he attempted to work out the brand of the car. He hadn't seen one like it before. Brian shifted in his seat, craning his neck to see if it had a maker's badge. He couldn't see any; in fact, it didn't seem to have any marks.

Strange. He shrugged. *It could be one of those prototype cars.*

Losing interest, Brian glanced at the wet road and checked on the lights. A frown added some more wrinkles to his brow. For some reason, the lights were taking ages to change today.

A quiet whirring made Brian glance at the car again. He watched as the black windows lowered. He let out a short breath in irritation; they had electric windows, not manual like his.

Get ready for some bragging.

Brian forced a small smile in readiness, knowing the 'look at my car' routine; he'd done it often enough. His smile faltered when he saw four men, all dressed identically in dark grey suits, white shirts, and black ties, looking directly at him.

Uncomfortable, Brian touched the pager the police had given him. He lifted his other hand briefly to acknowledge them. They gave no response. Quickly pulling his hand back from the half-wave, he resisted the urge to wind his windows up. He was bugged. They could have acknowledged him, not made him feel silly!

A pathetic sounding horn from the car behind pulled Brian out of his negative thoughts. He looked at the light, which was now green. Sighing with relief, he changed into gear and pushed down on the accelerator, eager to get away and into work for a much-needed coffee.

The black car pulled off effortlessly and passed him.

Brian barely resisted the urge to flick the bird. The little 'boy racer' in him urged him to put his foot down and try and keep up with them, but the adult in him knew his car had no chance. Instead, he followed it for a while before it turned off the main road.

Brian drove on before becoming bored with his company and the silence. He reached over to put the radio on. Crackling, it picked up a signal and '3 am' by Eminem boomed out. Singing along, Brian forgot his previous agitation. *So what if they had a better car, or that four males wanted to dress the same?* He smiled to himself. *Perhaps they belonged to some strange cult?*

When the song finished, the radio crackled again. He gave it a tap. The stormy weather was obviously playing havoc with the signal. He fiddled with the notch until 'Four Days' by The Counting Crows eventually blasted out.

Happy with the choice, Brian turned his attention back to the road.

With only seconds to register what was in front of him, he crossed his arms in front of his face. The last thing he saw, before his head smashed against the steamy windscreen, was the sleek black car.

A woman ready to give up...

Mountain lion shifter Marisa wants only to be put down. Madness taunts her every day. Her tormented past won't let her go—until grizzly bear shifter Riley and his young children shake up her world. They give her something to live for, if only she can escape her brutal history.

A bear shifter haunted by tragedy...

After the horrific loss of his mate years ago, solitary back country ranger Riley raised his cubs alone. Raging sorrow is no place for a daddy bear to stay stuck, though—especially not after he meets Marisa. Because the damaged yet riveting woman is the only one who can finally heal his shattered heart.

A shifter town faced with dangerous outsiders.

But when Marisa's ruthless past hunts her down, neither Riley's fierce vigilance nor her own wary instincts are enough to protect her. The wild spirit of an entire town filled with untamed shifter magic must come together to safeguard them all—and to show two devastated souls they need one another to become whole.

The sickening crack of a rifle shot split open the night, its echo booming through the sky.

"*Mama!*" The agonized little shriek sliced through Riley's head.

"No!" He sat bolt upright in bed. Leaping out of it in one move, heart walloping in his chest, he landed on his feet with a heavy thud.

Gasping for breath, coated in sweat, he looked around wild-eyed. His bear slammed around inside his head, snarling, fully alert and ready to defend his home.

Silence greeted him. Soft, peaceful quiet.

Riley blinked as awareness slowly surfaced. He was safe in his room, surrounded by the pre-dawn dim. The stillness. The calm. Through the slightly open window, a cold winter breeze whispered. For several long seconds, he stayed motionless, listening for any sounds of danger. He heard only his own harsh breathing.

Finally, he swiped his hand over his eyes, hard, clenching his teeth over a groan.

A nightmare.

A nightmare about something he had never actually heard or seen. A nightmare he hadn't had for a long time. For many years, it had haunted him daily before it faded to a less insistent horror. But the past few months had brought it back with alarming frequency and intensity.

After another long moment in which he thoroughly steadied his breathing, he turned to a chest of drawers against the far wall and yanked one open with unnecessary force. Shoving his hand in and coming out with a pair of loose black workout pants, he pulled them on.

Feet still bare, he padded quietly out into the hallway, heading down to Finn and Laney's rooms. His ears still rang with both the gunshot and the growled cry of his own voice. Afraid he'd actually yelled out loud, he wanted to be sure he hadn't woken his children.

Carefully opening the door to Finn's room and tucking his head around it to look in, relief instantly blanketed him as he saw his son. Finn had kicked off most of his covers, as usual. He was sprawled on the bed, face-down with his head turned to one side, looking like some sort of giant starfish. His quiet, even breathing filled the room in the cadence of peaceful sleep. Smiling faintly, Riley gently closed the door and went to Laney's room.

His daughter was securely snuggled under her comforter, sleeping on her side with one arm flung out, both legs scissored forward at the hips as if she were sleeping mid-stretch. Her face in the early morning light, peaceful as she very gently snored, looked so much like her mother's that Riley's jaw tightened. His heart exploded with love for both his children as it did each time he saw them like this: vulnerable. Targeted for death by some people in this world simply for being different.

Merely because they were shifters, just like their murdered mother.

Soundlessly shutting his daughter's door, Riley exhaled a slow breath as he went downstairs, shoving away the ancient fears. He needed to focus on the here and now. Right now, he needed to work out. Right now, he needed to break a sweat. Right now, he needed to get himself back into balance.

The workout room at the back of the cabin he and his children called home, the small but impressive place he had built by hand years ago, wasn't a gym in the traditional sense. It held only a large mat and was bordered by the floor-to-ceiling window on the east end that looked out over the San Juan Mountains into which the cabin nestled deeply.

Not bothering to turn on the light since the sun would be fully up not too long from now, and also because Riley's eyesight was much sharper than any pure human's, he walked to the center of the mat and stood for

3

many seconds with his head bowed, his arms down along his sides, his bare feet firmly planted. He took a long, deep breath, trying to inhale peace and balance and certainty. Then, he exhaled a long breath out, expelling the rage and unsettled feeling the nightmare had left him with. Again and again he practiced his breathing, focusing solely on his body, on this moment.

His bear whispered inside him, just as present and just as soothed by Riley's actions. It was a serenity Riley had worked on for years now. It was a tentative one, held together only by relentless practice and grasping at hope.

"If you don't do something, your bear's going to rip you apart, Ri." The long-ago wisdom of his best friend, Joe, whispered in his mind. "Find something before that happens."

He had. It had taken a long time and a lot of painful figuring out, but finally he'd settled on something that seemed to help. He'd taken up aikido in the hopes it would help settle the seemingly endless rage and grief over his mate, the mother of his cubs, the only woman he had ever loved, having been ripped from their lives. It took the edge off the restlessness, the rage, so he kept it up for years. Not only for his sake, but for that of his children. They deserved to have a father who wasn't completely driven by grief.

They deserved to have a father who wouldn't also be ripped away from them simply because he couldn't hold it together.

For his bear's sake, he kept his job as a backcountry ranger in the mountains. It gave him a lot of alone time roaming through the wild lands, often in his animal form. That time was pure necessity for his soundness of mind, and it grew more essential with each passing day.

His practice, his job, and the daily needs of his two children often seemed to be the only things keeping Riley Walker on this side of sanity, and he damn well knew it.

"Good job, boss," he murmured to himself. "Good job, bear."

Quietly, he snorted. Good thing no one was around to hear him talking to himself. It was a kind of dumb little mantra, but he liked to say it to himself, out loud, every day.

He needed the reminder he was doing okay.

The past haunted him still, to the point he privately was afraid he'd never truly shake it. Secretly, he hated it— the constant belief no one except his immediate clan could really be trusted. He wanted to trust more than just his family, more than just those in town he knew well. Yet his instinctive suspicion of strangers remained a deep-rooted uneasiness he couldn't dispel no matter how hard he tried. He'd finally given up, accepting he would always be suspicious of those he didn't know.

Keeping his bear on this side of sanity, though—that was harder. Much harder. The giant creature he shared his body and soul with got more aggressive with each passing year, no matter what Riley did to keep a leash on that side of himself. The aikido helped, the meditation helped, the long runs in the mountains helped. But his bear was a hairsbreadth away from being totally uncontrolled. Every day, he had to work to not lose that last bit of lucid connection with his animal.

One of these days, that control would finally sever.

Riley didn't know what the fuck he would do then. Shifters with out-of-control animals had to be put down. They were far too dangerous to the human world. To the shifter world. But he could never allow that. Not when he was a father. Not while he had two children who were like his own heart walking around outside his body.

They'd lost one parent. He'd vowed on that terrible day they would never lose another.

Not today, bear, he thought grimly to himself. *Not today.*

His bear simply rumbled inside him, content at the moment with Riley's deep breathing practice and centered mind. Riley shoved away all thoughts and focused on the moment. The physical here and now.

After he finished long minutes of deep, deliberate breathing, he opened his eyes. The sound of the nightmare gunshot had finally faded away from his head, thank fuck. With relentless intensity, he began his daily aikido practice, moving from stance to stance, he and his bear flowing together through the moves. In this way, they were completely connected. Briefly, but it was there.

Thirty minutes later, covered in a sheen of sweat,

he finished. Walking over to a set of cupboards against the wall, he pulled out a towel and wiped his face and neck with it. The sun had just risen, pretty orange and pink dawn colors gently flooding in through the east-facing window. Riley walked over to it, absently rubbing the towel over his sweaty head. He cocked his ears for any noise, but the house was still peacefully silent.

Being a Saturday morning, his children would easily sleep for at least another hour and a half. Since the mountains were still in the depths of winter, Finn and Laney were soundly caught by the instinctive hibernation habits that made bear shifter children exceptionally deep sleepers in the long, cold months. He snorted quietly. His kids also were like any others their age on the teetering cusp between childhood and teenagerhood. They were big fans of sleep in general.

Next to the window, he watched the sunrise with sincere appreciation for its beauty. It slowly illuminated the woods outside the window, which were still patched with snow. The landscape showed few signs of life, which tended to come late here at this high mountain altitude.

As he mentally went through his plans for the coming day, Riley suddenly froze.

In a corner of the woods visible through the window, his eyes tracked deliberate movement.

Automatically stiffening, he quickly relaxed when he

recognized his brother Quentin's mate, Abby. In her wolf form, she trotted by on her morning run.

Movement behind her froze him again. When he realized what it was, he felt his face go blank as his mind suddenly churned. His bear snorted and growled deep inside him, the balance he'd gained through practice sloughing off at Riley's newly ruffled thoughts.

A female mountain lion followed like a whispered shadow behind Abby, her huge paws probably moving soundlessly over the forest floor, her movements controlled and wary. Riley sucked in a breath.

Marisa. The shifter who had dragged all the trouble here a few weeks ago. The sexy, broken, bizarrely intriguing woman he'd been unable to stop thinking about despite his utter confusion at *why*.

He watched her, his body utterly still. Humans tended to be number one on Riley's hate list, but some shifters ended up there too. He didn't know Marisa well enough to hate her, but he knew she came from bad, broken stock. That alone was enough to put her on his suspicious to-be-watched list.

Outcast shifters weren't to be trusted any more than unknown humans were.

He didn't care that she was here at the Silvertip Lodge, protected by the Silvertip clan, which was Riley's family, and particularly mothered over by Abby. None of that meant he had to trust her.

She supposedly had been an innocent pawn in

everything that had gone down less than two weeks ago, had been used and abused by the shifters she'd fallen in with merely due to the circumstances of her birth. Outcast shifters sometimes had children and raised them in the lawless life they knew. But that didn't mean she wasn't possibly faking her plight somewhat or that there wasn't actually some sort of secret plan for her to worm her way in here and pave the way for another attack. She came from the sort of shifters who were always looking for a way to grift or outright threaten anyone they came across. Upstanding citizens of the shifter world they were not.

Even so, Riley couldn't help it. The woman was flat out fascinating to him, both as her mountain lion and as a woman. As a human, she was really pretty, although she never smiled and generally looked both troubled and wary. Her prettiness could be a cover for damaged and duplicitous or cruel and evil. Riley had absolutely nothing to base it on, nothing logical anyway, as Abby had tartly pointed out to him several times.

"Seriously, Riley," his brother's mate would say, her eyes narrowed at him in warning, "you need to be nicer to her. She doesn't deserve to have you glaring at her all the time."

Softly, he humphed to himself. He shouldn't have to have a reason to doubt and distrust. He knew better than many here that this was a world of exceptional danger. Sticking to their own was the safest course.

Marisa was definitely not part of Riley's clan. She didn't belong here. She was an outsider.

Then why, damn it, did he find her so damned interesting?

His jaw tightened as he recalled how he first met her: in the massive fight to help save his brother Cortez's mate Haley during what everyone now called the bridge battle. Marisa had howled in a lion's hair-raising screech of despair when the man she'd loved had been killed. Riley had been ready to fight her, to meet the challenge he was sure she would offer in the face of her lover's death.

Instead, she just gave up then and there, collapsing into her human form and breaking down into terrible sobs that wrenched at his heart despite the bloodlust that had come with the fight to protect his family, his clan, and all the residents of the town.

Then, she had looked up at him. Her desperate whisper still haunted him. "Kill me. Please, just kill me."

Shocked, he'd refused. What the hell had happened to her, living with crazy outcast shifters, that she wanted to die? He couldn't tell if her animal was out of control, but if it was, she'd likely hide it from everyone as much as she could. Just as he did.

He still sometimes thought of how small and broken, how vulnerable, she'd looked when Abby and a few others had gathered her up and led her away, her stumbling bare feet leaving bright red bloody tracks on the snow. He couldn't imagine ever killing someone so haunted. So clearly in need of protection. So damned beautiful despite the anguish marking her features.

As if she could hear his distrustful thoughts, could sense his memories, Marisa abruptly turned her tawny gold head toward his cabin as she padded by.

She looked right at him where he stood in the window. Her gait faltered slightly, but she didn't slow as she trotted after Abby, who hadn't noticed him. He stared, caught by the beautiful lion's smooth, if guarded, stride. Marisa gazed back at him with her golden eyes, keeping him in her sights until just before she disappeared into the woods. At the last moment, she raised her lip in a snarl at him. A warning.

Don't watch me. Don't look at me. Leave me alone.

Riley snorted to himself after she disappeared, then turned his back to stride out of the room with newly angry steps. Fine by him. He didn't want anything to do with her. Broken, fucked up outcast. Submissive lion girl, wanting to die, chickening out of everything.

He snarled. All she'd done in the week or so she'd been here was ask every strong shifter she came across to put her down. Beg them, even. She was giving up. Giving up on life.

That was something Riley couldn't accept, wouldn't ever accept. His mate had died fighting for her life. Fighting for their cubs' lives. Fierce to the end. She *never* would have given up.

Angered to his bones about Marisa just wanting to

die, and even more angry that he gave a shit about it, Riley avoided her as much as he could. Yeah, he had no problem leaving her alone. She was damaged. Hell, she was fucking defective.

His neck immediately prickled at those thoughts. *Bullshit.* He growled under his breath, earlier relaxation completely evaporated. *Fuuuck.* It was a false thought, thinking he could easily leave her alone. Worse, trying to believe she was broken so badly she was beyond any fixing. Something told him she wasn't really that far gone. Not yet.

His jaw clenched even harder as the incessant question, the one he'd been doing his best to ignore since the moment he'd first seen her, roiled through his mind yet again with explosive force.

If he didn't give a damn about the outcast Marisa, why was he utterly fascinated by the defensive, snarling lion girl who wanted only to be put down?

2

———

Marisa sat where she could see everybody. She quietly observed the high-spirited activity around her, taking in every detail with a hard-won practice she'd birthed long ago from plain necessity. Every doorway, every window was within her line of sight as the bustle of shifters in here decorated the barn for some sort of event coming up. What was it again? She frowned and forced herself to focus on the right here, right now. Oh, right. Valentine's Day.

She huffed quietly to herself. Valentine's Day seemed like a clever way for businesses such as this fancy lodge just for shifters to entice money made up of hope and starry eyes from people desperate for something they thought was love.

Love didn't exist. Love was a bullshit concept made

up by those who just wanted something they could use to control others.

"Marisa!"

Without moving her head, she shifted her gaze to the tentatively smiling woman who called her name. Abby. Wolf shifter, friendly, protective. Just as watchful as Marisa, but Marisa suspected Abby's watchfulness didn't come from the same reasons hers did. Abby was happy. She had a good life. She'd probably always had a good life. Marisa didn't understand it, but she also found she didn't care because it didn't matter. Abby had the sort of life Marisa never would. *Not worth the ripped bedsheets you were born on,* the old taunt jeered at her.

Breathe. She listened to herself and took a deep breath, then another. Then she laughed, so deep inside herself only bad kitty could hear it. It was pretty damned ironic that the one simple mantra she'd used to survive her whole life was the one thing she wanted to stop forever: breathing.

Too bad none of the shifters here would answer her plea to end it. They all must be cowards.

Abby beckoned at her hopefully. "We could use an extra hand setting up. But only if you want to." Her voice was inviting but not pushy.

Even so, Marisa shook her head immediately. *No way.*

Abby's expression was understanding, if slightly disappointed. "Okay. If you change your mind, everything's over there." She gestured at the not-insignificant number of boxes and bags filled with decorations that the others were putting up around the inside of the barn.

Marisa huffed again to herself as she let her gaze sweep the building. They were decorating the place to look like candy hearts had thrown up all over it. It seemed a shame to embarrass a really nice barn this way. Well. Not just a really nice barn, but one she would bet was the fanciest in the entire state of Colorado. The stalls didn't house horses, but chairs and tables and lights and a whole lot more decorations. The floor was swept clean with no signs any equine had ever stepped a single hoof in here. Heated with fancy glowing lamps affixed to the ceilings, built from large granite blocks and heavy, carefully constructed wood, the barn screamed elegance and money.

It intimidated the shit out of her.

Not that she'd let any of them know it. But it made her feel...small. Really small, and really poor. The whole place did. She'd never in her whole life imagined something as fancy as the Silvertip Lodge could exist outside some glossy magazine in the supermarket checkout aisle. And the grocery stores she'd always shopped at never carried those kinds of magazines, anyway. Marisa Tully didn't shop at nice places and never had.

In fact, not only was this the fanciest barn she'd ever seen, this was the third fanciest place she had ever seen in her life, period. The first two fanciest she'd only seen a few weeks ago. Number one was the lodge itself, a beautiful retreat open only to shifters who came from all over the country and even the world. They came here to vacation where they could safely let their animals roam around on the private, guarded property without fear of being glimpsed by humans. The sight of the stunning main lodge building had stopped her short when Abby had gently helped her to it after the bridge battle. She'd instantly felt outclassed by the shifters who lived and worked there, the powerful Silvertip grizzly bear shifter clan that had taken her in.

Taken her prisoner was more like it, but she'd sure never thought a prison could be this nice. Or, she grudgingly admitted to herself, that prison guards could be this nice too. Even if they did refuse to put her down.

The second most beautiful, deluxe place she'd ever seen was the cabin the clan was letting her stay in while she was here. She had shyly said something to Abby about how elegant it was. Abby, bustling around getting it sorted for her the day they'd tucked her into it, had laughingly said it was a decent enough cabin, but she wished they could have put her up someplace even better. She hadn't said it unkindly or rudely. It was just matter of fact to her.

Marisa hadn't answered. There was no point in letting these shifters know she was trailer trash who'd never been anywhere better than a Denny's in her entire

16

lifetime. If she did, they would judge her. Being judged sucked. No thanks.

But still. They were nice to her. A little wary, but nice.

She looked at Abby again, at the others so cheerfully putting up ridiculous red hearts and pink and silver streamers all over this beautiful, stupid-rich barn. Wrinkling her brow, she tried to remember their names.

Pix, the small woman who improbably enough was a dragon shifter. The tall, huge, stern-faced man who was her mate, a bear shifter. His name was...Barrett? No. Beckett. There was also Jessie, a pretty blonde with a really adorable little boy named Grant. Jessie's mate, Shane, wasn't here. He worked weekends at the lodge and was out fixing the lights in a building or something like that.

Marisa's face softened as she gazed at their little boy, who toddled all over the barn on his sturdy little bear shifter legs, covered head to toe in rainbow glitter from a bag he'd gleefully explored before any of the adults had thought to check what was inside. Children, she always liked.

The lines in her forehead intensified as she watched them all. They were just so damned freaking nice. Each one of them, even though they didn't have to be. Not to someone like her. As an outcast shifter with no clan to call her own, no group of shifters having her back anymore since the screwed-up bunch she'd been involved with had been either killed, captured, or fled after the bridge battle, she had no right to be treated well by the shifters here. The same shifters who'd been attacked by the outcasts. But that didn't seem to matter. Every single one of them had just been plain kind to her so far, with varying degrees of friendliness. Some of them looked at her oddly now and then. Occasionally worse.

She knew it was because they all thought she was insane. That she was from bad blood. They also all knew by now she wanted to be put down. She'd been asking anyone who seemed strong enough to do it. No one would. Nefarious, that stupid name the leader of the outcast group had called himself, had told her she was worthless. But even he wouldn't put her down. He'd had a use for her. Using her, like everyone else in her life ever had except Derek.

No. At the thought of her brother, she shied away. She couldn't think about him. He was going crazy just as surely as she was. He'd escaped from the bridge battle, but the same madness he fought might have taken him by now. *Dead and gone, dead and gone.*

She closed her eyes for a second and dragged in a harsh breath. Nothing good ever happened. And if it did, it never lasted.

Inside, she felt dead and broken and knew it would never end. Beautiful lodge or not, spacious little beautiful cabin of her own or not, it wasn't real for her and never would be. She wasn't the kind of person who got to have nice things and never had been.

A faint growl vibrated the back of her throat. She swallowed it down hard and opened her eyes. Her cat, the big tawny beast living inside her, was getting restless. She needed to go out soon for another run to settle the creature. Abby had taken her on a run just this morning, like she'd done every day since Marisa had been here, but it hadn't been calming. No, it had been unsettling. Nerve-ruffling.

All because of *him*.

Riley Walker. Enormous grizzly bear shifter, his coat a startling black with a silvery hump, he was also a really attractive guy in his human form. Okay, fine. A really sexy guy. But she didn't trust any guys, especially not the sexy ones. They were usually the worst of all.

He'd stared at her from the upstairs window of what must be his house as they'd jogged past just after dawn. She had felt his gaze on her, tickling at her skin. The faint sensation of something riffling through her fur, like a breeze that blew her sideways, had turned her head toward the sleek, clearly hand-built log cabin tucked into the trees up by the lodge.

Looking down at her from the window, his face was unreadable. But his eyes—oh, his eyes. Dark, flat, and cold just like they'd been that day on the bridge, they'd stared back at her. Like they were bullets and she was the target. Something in him *wanted* something from her, though hell if she knew what.

She'd automatically curled up her lip at him as she passed, warning him away. *I'm a big, bad mountain lion, boy. Don't you mess with me.*

Yeah, right. Like a huge grizzly bear would ever be scared of a kitty. But maybe he should be. Marisa's mountain lion was a crazy wildcat, a terrible beast, a brute of a killer on huge silent paws.

He'd kept staring at her until she and Abby jogged out of sight, his expression impassive. Like he had secrets as dark as hers. What secrets could he have? He was just a huge grizzly shifter with glacially cold eyes who had refused to kill her on the bridge when Justin had been killed. Justin, that stomach-curdling piece of garbage who'd tried to ruin her life in so many awful ways. She knew they all thought she'd screamed with agony when he was killed because she loved him.

They were wrong.

She'd screamed because she thought his death might release her. It didn't. She'd still been there, still trapped, still broken. It had hurt so badly, knowing the horrible truth that her nightmare would never end, that she'd just stayed crumpled on the ground in shocked despair until Abby and the others took her here to the lodge. Trying to save her.

But they couldn't save her. No one could.

So Riley also thought she was broken. Fine. She

didn't care—except that with him, she did care. Dammit. Big jerk, big giant sexy shifter. It *did* matter what he thought of her. Her cat grew even more restless inside. Why? Why did she care? She didn't know him at all, and she didn't want him thinking he knew her.

As if her idiot mouth was disconnected from her rational side, Marisa suddenly called out to Abby, turning her head to look at the wolf shifter. "What's the matter with Riley? Why is he so...dark?"

The room went abruptly, awkwardly silent.

Oh, crap. Every single adult shifter in there, the five or six who'd been chattering and laughing as they worked, just froze for a minute, though at least none of them turned around to stare at her. Marisa kicked herself. Freaking great. Now they would think she was even more crazy, even more fucked up.

Suddenly, she panicked. Maybe they would think she had designs on Riley, that she was some sort of danger to him. She knew some of them *had* to think she was bad, no matter how nice they were to her face. She'd been running with a pack of outcast shifters, after all.

Outcast shifter, outcast pack, crazy girl who wanted to die. That had to be a recipe for disaster to such a freaking good clan like this one.

Abby, also frozen in the midst of taping a giant pink heart with the words WILL U BE MINE emblazoned on it to the metal bars over the side of one of the stalls, her back still to Marisa, answered in a casual if somewhat tight voice. "He lost someone important to him a long time ago. It was very hard."

Without thinking, Marisa blurted, "And he still hasn't gotten over it?" God, that wasn't fair. She'd had to get over so much, so many things, almost right as they happened. She'd never had a choice not to.

With a sudden fierceness that startled her, she deeply, desperately envied Riley's luxury in still being able to live in whatever hurt he had, to know his people loved him, that they let him live in pain and they understood it. That they still supported him, even if his eyes were scary black and dead. No one had ever given a shit about her. She could tell everyone here gave a lot of shits about Riley and his pain, whatever it was.

Riley's dark, angry voice shot out like a whip crack right behind her, startling her so badly she almost fell off the chair. "None of your damned business, lion girl. You don't get to judge me. You don't even know me. But I know you, and you're pretty fucking broken. So broken you don't even want to live anymore. So who are you to be asking questions about other people's lives?"

Marisa stumbled to her feet, nearly tangling with the chair as she whirled around to look at him. Shock warred over her skin, which goosebumped up with the suddenness of his appearance. She'd been so deep in her thoughts, so mad about the crap deal she'd been handed in this life, that for a second she'd stopped keeping an eye on all the doors into the barn and missed Riley's quiet entrance.

And oh, daaamn. Damn it, damn it. Like a kid eyeing a favorite piece of candy, Marisa just gaped at him, as usual. She couldn't help it.

Damned sexy man. Sexy, sexy man. Even bad kitty got quiet when she saw him, watching him out of Marisa's eyes with a stillness she never seemed to have otherwise.

Riley was huge. Muscles draped over more muscles, his entire body like a honed machine ready to attack at any moment if needed. His golden-brown hair couldn't cover the darkness inside him, which bled out of him like a fury. His face, even hard with anger as it was now, was strong and drop-dead gorgeous, and she was unable to take her eyes off him. Oh, he was hot. So stupid man hot, the kind of hot that had women falling over their feet when they looked at him. Women like her, being an idiot. She wasn't an idiot. Her cat wasn't an idiot.

A growl rumbled deep inside her chest, threatening to work its way loose. Bad kitty trying to get out. Struggling, Marisa pushed her down. *No.* Not now. She ground her teeth and turned her stare at Riley into a glare to match her rising growl, to deflect the mountain lion trying to scramble out of her.

Now she was angry too. Good. Anger was good. It kept her alert and wary. He was so freaking gorgeous, and her hormones wouldn't let her forget it. Even clad in jeans and a long-sleeved button-up work shirt, very rugged hiking boots on his feet, she could tell he was ripped. His biceps pushed hard at his sleeves, and his thigh muscles strained against his jeans.

But what really got her was the heaviness in his voice. The darkness. Worse yet, she heard something that made a shiver rise along her spine, that made her cat yowl with sympathy—*sympathy?*—somewhere in the back of her head.

Broken.

It hit her so hard the breath almost whooshed out of her in a gasp. That was it. *That* was what she'd been sensing about him this past week, the thing she hadn't been able to understand. The reason she was so stupidly fascinated by him, sexy man muscles or no.

Riley Walker was broken and desperate, and his bear was barely in control.

He was hiding it under cold rage, the blank eyes that didn't share anything about him with anyone who cared to look. Marisa cast a wild glance over at Abby, who was staring at them both with alarm, and the others, who'd now turned around too. Couldn't they sense his animal was in trouble? Riley's bear was not only a beast but a savage one barely leashed.

Her cat was clawing at her to get out, to get at him.

Marisa blinked. Wait.

No. Not to get *at* him. Not to attack him or guard

herself against him. But to—to run up and rub herself against him?

She couldn't stop the confusion rippling over her face. What the hell? Bad kitty never wanted to rub up against anyone like she was a trained house cat. Never. Especially not big, dominant male shifters. She just wanted to brawl with them and show them what she was made of. She was made of vicious claws and deadly swipes and fire and brimstone spitting out of her howling mouth.

Marisa's mountain lion was just as out of control as Riley's bear. That was why she had to be put down. That, and other things Marisa didn't want to think about anymore.

"What are you glaring at, kitty cat?" Riley's voice was a challenge, the seesawing battle under it to keep his bear in check apparent to Marisa's ears. But she caught something else in there as well.

Curiosity and surprise.

Well, that made two of them.

She opened her mouth to make a retort, something, anything. Before she could say a word, the barn doors smacked open in a flurry of noise. Two kids tumbled in, laughing and shrieking with delight as they tossed snowballs at one another.

"Hey, now!" Abby said, but her tone was light. Not stern at all. "Shut the door, you wild hooligans. Don't get snow on any of the decorations." A smile busted through her voice, pure love radiating through it.

Marisa felt sudden tightness in her throat as an old memory ricocheted through her mind like a really unwelcome cannonball. *Shut the fucking door, you stupid little girl. You'd better not let any of that rain get inside here and ruin the floor. Worthless bitch.*

The room started to haze out.

Breathe.

She breathed, blinked hard, made herself focus. Focus on what? Ah. She pounced, latching her attention onto the two children. Finn and Laney. Despite herself, she softened, caught by them, feeling suddenly wistful. Kids were cute. Fun. She liked kids, always had.

The minute she'd met these two, a pair of nearly twelve-year-old twins, she'd naturally loved them like they were part of her own family, like they were a niece and nephew she adored. They'd gravitated toward her too, instantly liking her back. They showed her all around the Silvertip Lodge that was their home. Oh, they were so sweet. Silly, playful, and they didn't worry she might be a danger. She was no danger. Not to them. Never. Even bad kitty seemed to like them.

But that didn't matter. Grabbing the inside of her lip with her teeth, she worried at it. Marisa would never have children. There was a hundred percent chance she'd screw them up beyond repair. Being raised by bad seeds meant children came out as bad seeds too. She'd never inflict that sort of terrible future on a child. Especially not now.

"Dad!" Finn's voice launched across the barn, pure childlike joy in it. "Catch it if you can!"

He lobbed a snowball directly at Riley. Turning swiftly so she wouldn't miss it, Marisa witnessed the thing wash over Riley's face that always startled her, coming from the man with dead, cold eyes: softness. As he raised up a fast hand to deflect the snowball, a genuine smile suddenly crinkled up his expression, making him look less monster-like than she could have imagined. In fact, he looked positively *pleasant*.

Riley Walker, the shifter with the uncontrolled bear and some sort of dark anger everyone knew about and allowed to exist, was a loving father. It never failed to surprise her. Did his clan know he harbored a raging, angry, violent beast inside him? Did his children?

Before her perplexed mind could follow those strands, Laney caught sight of her and made a beeline straight over, a giant smile lighting up her cute little face. Oh, that girl would be a knockout when she was older. She needed someone to make sure she knew how to handle it.

"Marisa! We made tornados in a bottle at school yesterday! It was so cool! I know how to do them now. Finn and me will show you." She raced over, sliding to a stop just before Marisa. She stood there and beamed, keeping herself maybe a foot away. They'd learned unasked-for hugs were something Marisa couldn't tolerate. Not even from them, much as she wanted to.

"Finn and I," Riley automatically corrected. His face also automatically turned into a frown as he looked at Marisa. With a powerful will, she ignored it.

"What's a tornado in—" Marisa managed before Finn turned and also bounced over, his happy grin as big as his sister's.

"Marisa, we have to show you, it's so cool! Dad, can we show her? Please?" Finn used his best begging voice, as did Laney, both of them giving their father pleading looks.

Marisa felt her cat balance quietly inside her, watching with the calm she never had except around these two children, as she waited for Riley's answer.

3

Riley just barely managed to keep his mouth closed as his cubs surrounded Marisa like she was the best thing since barbecue. Fuuuck, the woman was so pretty. Why was she so pretty? Why did he have to notice it? But damn. She was.

That little crop of dark red hair with glimmers of gold strands. Those green eyes, almost blue-green, like the pine needles at the height of summer, with sliding shadows in them that said she was hiding big, dark stuff behind their prettiness. Her small body, a compact package, in good shape but thin. Too thin. Those outcast assholes hadn't kept her well fed. That, or she couldn't hunt very well.

He studied her more as she interacted with Laney and Finn, a genuine smile ghosting over her sharp little face as they turned back to bombarding her with details about their school day when he didn't reply to their question right away. Oh, no. Kitty-cat could hunt. Her mountain lion was a lethal hunter. He could tell by the wiry muscles in her arms that showed through the dark gray long-sleeved tee shirt she wore, the controlled energy of her body, the way her eyes tracked everything in the room. Keeping watch. Making sure nothing escaped her gaze.

Yes, she was a good hunter. But the outcasts hadn't let her hunt enough to feed herself. Riley felt a growl working its way up his chest. Didn't matter if he didn't want to trust her. Didn't matter if she came from outcasts. Shifters shouldn't let any of their group go hungry. Ever.

He sensed something a little sad about how she acted around his children. He always sensed that about her, the weary sadness. Something haunted her. Unexpectedly, he wondered if she had younger siblings or cubs of her own. The thought of her having cubs of her own brought a rumble into his chest.

Was she mated?

That thought made his bear inexplicably irritable and restless.

He got irritated at himself. This was ridiculous. He didn't need to worry about the history of some lion shifter girl who wanted to be put down. He opened his fucking dumbass mouth and said, "Are your hands broken too? You're not much help just sitting there. Fine way to pay back how kind my clan has been to you."

"Riley," Abby warned in a low, shocked tone. Anger simmered under her voice.

Fuck. Even for him, that was out of line. His bear snarled inside him, feeling dark and heavy. Shit, shit, shit. He needed to get out of here. Now.

"Abby." Riley glanced at his brother's mate, using sheer force of will to keep his voice even. "Can the cubs stay here and help you for a while? I have to go out on patrol. I'll be back in time for dinner tonight."

Out of the corner of his eye, he saw Marisa startle slightly. Odd.

"Of course," Abby said. Her voice was neutral too. She didn't know why he'd popped off, but she was accepting his request as a half-assed apology.

Too bad she wasn't the one he needed to apologize to.

Abby glanced at the cubs, softness crossing over her face as usual. Everyone loved his children. "I can tell there are two young shifters in here who have a lot of energy to blow off right now. I can use all their help I can get."

"We can help lots, Aunt Abby! Rawr!" Finn made a mock growl.

"Behave, hooligans," Riley warned. But he flashed a fast grin at his two mischievous kids before giving them an appropriately stern look. They both giggled, nodded, and zoomed toward Grant, who grinned a drooly little-kid grin at them. He loved them as much as they adored him. Tugging him along, they found a box and started

31

pulling out whatever the hell decorations were in there for the lodge's latest guest event. He couldn't keep track of that stuff since he didn't officially work here.

He turned for the door, aware Marisa still stared at him. An apology tripped on the edge of his tongue, but if he said it now, in front of everyone else here—shit. He had to escape before he made things way worse. He was being an asshole, and he didn't even know exactly why. She might be a stranger, but that was no excuse to be a total shit to her. Or to be a bad role model to his kids.

Whatever the fuck was wrong with him, he didn't dare open his mouth again right now. Who knew what the hell else might fall out of it with his bear snarling around inside him?

As he passed by Marisa, closer than he wanted but he had no choice in order to leave, she pushed out a whisper only he could hear. "You just lied to them."

What the fuck? Riley stopped dead, pinning her with a glare. His vow not to speak again went out the window. "Who the hell do you think you—" he began, but she shook her head, hard.

"I don't know why I said that," she said, still in a whisper. "But it's true." Her eyes were beginning to glow, an indication her mountain lion was close to the surface.

This close to her, Riley couldn't help but notice something else that pissed him off.

She smelled good. So good. Like jasmine and fresh raspberries and those sweet little oranges Riley kept around the cabin because the cubs liked to snack on them. She smelled...edible. *Edible.* What the hell?

Head spinning with confusion, he opened his mouth to say something harsh again. Mean. Anything to keep her away from him. To keep her at arm's length—hell, at football field's length—away from him. Instead, the idiot words "Are you wearing perfume?" came out instead, like he was some kind of prize fool.

Her brow wrinkled up. After a long pause, she shook her head. "No."

She studied his face. She was really looking at him. Right at him. Most days he saw her, she seemed to sort of ghost out and stare through folks rather than meet their gaze directly.

For a long second, they just looked at each other. Riley's pulse banged so loudly in his ears he couldn't hear any other noise in the room. Then, something even more crazy just busted right out. "Well, you smell good."

The words came out easy. Real. True.

She kept staring, her expression curious but otherwise unreadable. Just as he finally turned, and this time really did stride out of the room, head still banging as if he'd just been shoved face first down a roller coaster track, he heard her soft, bewildered whisper behind him.

"Thank you, Riley," she added even more softly, like his name was just floating on her tongue.

A weird little ripple of feeling shivered through him, tingling at his skin as he strode fast and hard away. His bear roared in his mind. Also bewildered. Also utterly fascinated.

Fascinated by the sexy, complex, sad little lion girl he couldn't seem to shove away, no matter how damned hard he tried.

Marisa's head whirled. Everything else around her was normal. The others were all back to laughing and goofing with one another while they worked hard putting up the decorations. She blinked, wondering if the short interaction with Riley had been a dream. But no. His cubs were here. Diligently putting streamers up on the bars of the stalls, following Abby's directions. Everyone was so happy. So giggly. It was so...homey.

She suddenly felt suffocated. She needed fresh air. Any air. Her cat was clawing at her from the inside, pushing. Growling. Hissing and snarling, trying desperately to take over Marisa's body. To knock the human out of the way so she could burst out and do whatever it was a mountain lion did.

Breathe. Breathe. Breathe!

Sucking in a long, desperate breath through her nose,

Marisa glanced over at Abby. But the sudden, crazy desperation still clutched her, making her feel dizzy. Panicky. Should she ask permission to leave? No. She wasn't a prisoner. Right? Abby had told her she was a guest. She wasn't under lock and key. Nobody watched her every move.

Okay, some of them did. Some of them definitely didn't trust her. She could feel it, even though they were nice. Polite. But that was nothing new. Distrust was something she was used to. Distrust was something she understood.

She felt staticky. Like she was about to become unglued. Taking another deep breath, feeling it whistle into her chest, she shot a quick glance over the room one more time. No one was looking at her. No one noticed her.

Turning, she quickly and quietly hustled out of the barn doors that had just closed behind Riley. A friendly burst of laughter behind her, some dumb joke about a fisherman and a crane and some sort of smelly bait that one of the guys was telling the room, made her chest ache for second. Why? The feeling was familiar but at the same time unknown. Clenching her jaw hard, Marisa pushed her way out the door, shoved it closed it behind her, and went out into the hush of the cold day.

Instantly, her cat settled. Angry, big mountain lion. Such a huge animal inside her. Not as huge as Riley's bear, though. His bear was enormous. Beautiful. She frowned. Could she say his bear was beautiful? Was that the right way to talk about his bear, a guy's bear? An enormous, strong, raging bear that was out of control.

Marisa's frown smoothed out as she moved faster and faster away from the barn, toward the woods. Yes, she could say that about him. Riley was big and sexy, and *he thought she smelled good* and his bear was beautiful. She could think that.

Pausing, she turned around to look at the barn. At the lodge beyond it. Oh, that lodge was gorgeous. This place was beautiful. Gorgeous, and so...quiet? What was a good word? Her head felt scattered. Serene. Yes. The Silvertip Lodge was serene.

Snow piled in huge white drifts everywhere from the recent storm. Pathways were neatly cleared, the road had been plowed, but everything else lay under a deep blanket of clean white. Fairytale beautiful. It was absolutely, breathtakingly fairytale beautiful here. Like nothing else in her life ever had been.

Looking at it all, feeling the quiet hush everywhere around her, the peace of a place well protected, safe, Marisa let herself dream for a just a second. Dream that this was her home. That she was safe here. Welcomed. That she belonged here, that she could fit in.

Her cat clawed at her. A sharp yowl rattled through her head, sent the beginnings of a growl rumbling up her chest. Right. Not for her. This place wasn't her home. Sooner or later, everything would just get worse. Just like it always did for her. Her home was nowhere and never could be.

Inside, the animal claiming part ownership over her being screamed. She had to run. Now that she was outside, she had to get out and run. Her steps moved into a trot, then faster, as she fled the stifling closeness of the others back in the barn. Their genuine happiness.

She was almost to the tree line, her cat surging inside her, ready to leap free through the snowy landscape, when she saw a flash of movement ahead. Her quick steps skidding to a halt, she peered into the trees with each shifter-enhanced sense she possessed. Her heart beat uncomfortably fast in her chest as her breath snarled in her throat. Tensed, half ready to go leaping back toward the barn, she suddenly relaxed.

Riley. Up ahead of her, moving through the quiet forest with purpose.

Marisa hesitated. She didn't want to see anyone else. She didn't want to see *him* right now, that was certain. But her cat yammered and pushed at her, still eager to sweep out of her and run.

He had said she smelled good. Watching as his back disappeared into the snowy woods, chewing on the instinct to stay by herself and the other, overpowering instinct to keep going forward, she finally relented to her cat. As always.

On quick, silent feet, feeling herself already in the heightened state of awareness that meant the mountain lion part of her hovered just beneath the surface, watching out of her eyes and hearing out of her ears, Marisa pressed forward. Tentatively, then more quickly, she gained on him. He moved so gracefully for such a big man. His steps were nearly as quiet as hers. She hesitated slightly. Again, not wanting to startle him.

But just as she drew breath to call his name, he abruptly stopped, whipping around to face her.

"Are you following me?" Gone was the puzzled softness that had been in his voice as he whispered those startling words—*you smell good*—to her earlier. Cold tension spread through his words now.

Apparently, this had not been a good idea. Warily, she ventured, "No. I need to go on a run. I didn't know where you were. This just seemed the quickest way to get away from all of the...buildings."

His left eye twitched slightly at her. He grunted. "Buildings? The *others* is what I think you meant to say. Right?"

It was cold today. So cold. Not a single dripping sound of melting snow could be heard. The fairytale beauty of the lodge extended out here into a pretty winter wonderland Marisa knew full well was untouched by ugly things. The hush here at the edge of the woods felt bizarrely safe. Like a refuge that would never, ever let her down.

She finally shrugged at his probing look. "Them too, I

guess. Everyone's really nice, but I just felt—I had to get outside. That's all."

She sounded so calm. So normal. Weirdly, she felt both tense and relaxed around him at the same time.

The silence deepened. Marisa studied the huge bear shifter as he stared back at her. The skin on his face was smooth, as it seemed to be most days. For work, she guessed. Even so, she could see the faint shadow of stubble playing over his cheeks, his chin. She figured he probably had to shave twice a day. From observing the ones in the outcast group, she knew male bear shifters' facial hair grew very quickly.

His eyes were shuttered as ever, although she could see the hints of his animal glowing in them. Deep inside them. His short cropped golden-brown hair was uncovered by a hat, just as his hands, hanging casually at his sides but with a hint of tension she could sense, were also bare. It was, she thought somewhere in the back of her head as she stared at him staring right back at her, one of the benefits to being a shifter. Walking around on a winter day like this and not worrying about freezing was a definite plus.

How the minuses outweighed the little perks, though. So much so.

Her mouth opened before she could censor it, like it had earlier, back in the barn. "Why did you say that to me? I smell good. Did you mean it?"

Riley flinched backward, an unreadable expression

finally shifting over what had been his stock still face. He swallowed, and her eyes traced the bob of his Adam's apple down to where his neck disappeared beneath the gray uniform shirt he wore. When he spoke, she jerked her eyes back up to his.

"I don't tell lies, Marisa. I don't know why I said that to you, except that it was the truth." His words came out softer than before but still cold. Perplexed. As if he was wrestling with himself.

Another funny silence held them for a long moment. Finally, she jerked a shoulder in a dismissive shrug. She didn't care. Right? "Okay. I'm going on a run. My mountain lion is, I mean," she added unnecessarily. Somewhere inside her, a part of her that apparently still cared what she looked like to others kicked herself.

"I need to be alone right now. I really didn't mean to disturb you. I just want to run." Babble babble. He didn't need to know this. He didn't need to know anything about her.

His eyes still bored into hers, the expression on his face that she couldn't read seeming darker and darker.

Why was she still talking? *Shut up,* she ordered herself. But she couldn't. Mouth open, stupid words blurting out. "I feel really out of place. Everyone makes me nervous. I don't belong here."

Riley's face turned suddenly hard, thunderclouds moving behind his eyes. Whoa. His bear was pushing against him the same way Marisa's cat always, always pushed against her.

"You're right." His voice snapped out, so harsh and sudden she flinched. "You don't belong here. This isn't your home, and I don't know why you're still here."

Unexpected hurt thwacked her chest at his words. Her cat yowled inside, the sound of it scattering painful shadows through her head. *Breathe.*

Then—*snarl. He,* the angry bear guy, was yelling at *her?*

Her chest heaved with the sudden furious need to explode words out at him. "I know I don't belong here." Her voice lashed out, loud and sharp in the quiet forest. "I know this isn't my home. I don't belong here because I don't belong anywhere. I never have."

Unstoppable, her voice kept rising. "I don't know why I'm still here either. I don't have any secrets about the outcasts to share with all of you. I have nothing against any of you, and there's no way in hell I'm ever going back to them." Damn it, she couldn't stop talking. The words surged over her control, spilling out like she was crazy. Ha-ha, crazy Marisa. What else was new?

"I don't belong anywhere and never will, do you understand me? My animal is out of control. I can't handle her. That's why I want to be put down, Riley. *I cannot control her.*" She took a step toward him, feeling an overwhelming need to force him to understand the importance of her next words. "Your bear's out of control too. Isn't it? Can't you understand me, then? Can't you see why I need to be put down?"

His face wasn't blank now. He was caught somewhere between shock and horror. Maybe even disgust. Gasping air stuttered in her chest as she finally managed to shut up.

Slowly, staring at her like she was an alien life form, he shook his head. "No. I don't understand that. I don't understand not wanting to fight for your life at all costs, no matter how fucking sad and broken you think you are. What the hell is wrong with you, Marisa?"

Suddenly, he was shouting at her. "Why do you want to be put down? Why do you want to *die?*"

She almost doubled over, the word seeming to slam into her gut like a fist punch. Her cat screamed in her mind as a growl bubbled out of her throat, followed by another, then another.

"No," she moaned, shaking her head. "Please, no. Not like this," she whispered. When it happened like this, it hurt. It hurt so badly she would scream. A scream that sounded like it was out of a horror movie.

She didn't want him to see her like this. She didn't know why, but she just didn't. Without another word, she turned and hurtled into the forest.

"Marisa!" His voice called after her, alarmed. Maybe even regretful? She didn't turn around. She couldn't. The cat was in control.

A scream ripped out of her throat, followed by

another. Awful. Awful, horrifying sounds. Screeching, yowling, raging. So loud she was sure it could be heard at the barn.

She didn't even have time to shuck off her clothes. The cat forced her way out, exploding through Marisa's skin in a fury of golden fur and deadly claws and the bloodcurdling shriek of her kind.

She bolted away, deep into the forest, leaving everything behind her. Fleeing the man who still called that name, *Marisa,* over and over behind her. Barreling into the silent, snowy mountains, letting them swallow her up whole.

5

R iley stood in the quiet of the snow-blanketed trees, his heart thumping erratically as he watched Marisa bound away from him on four legs.

What the hell had just happened? Her outburst seemed to come from nowhere. So had his. As he thought that, something tickled at him. An uncomfortable something that felt like...shame.

He had no right to lay into her the way he did. His bear rumbled inside him, moving with the forceful darkness that always made Riley stiffen.

She was right. His bear *was* out of control, no matter how much meditation or aikido and deep breathing he did. But how the hell had she known? He kept it so well hidden from everyone. He huffed, his breath showing white in the chill air. That was probably why. She didn't know him like everyone else here did. She didn't have preconceived notions of what he was supposed to be like, how he was supposed to act.

Who he was supposed to be.

Riley ground his jaw for a long moment, staring after the spot where she had disappeared. The mountains would take her, give her enormous space to run. To breathe. To simply be. That, he understood. That was why he was out here too.

Swearing, he turned and began to walk northward. A voice behind him drew him up short.

"Riley! Hold up."

Riley blew out a breath before turning around. Quentin. He had his big brother voice on. Ah, shit. Since their parents had left on their crazy yearlong second honeymoon, leaving Quentin officially in charge of the lodge as well as all his brothers who lived here, it had been interesting, to say the least.

But the concerned look on Quentin's face quelled his annoyance. Quentin strode up to him, peering past him. "Is she out here? Did you see her?"

Instantly, Riley bristled.

"See who?" He bit the words off, giving his brother a challenging look.

Quentin snapped his gaze from the woods to Riley, his brows lowering at the tone in Riley's voice. Tersely, he said, "Abby said Marisa was helping decorate the barn for the dance, but then suddenly she was just gone. She said you," he jabbed a finger at Riley, "specifically asked her to keep an eye on your cubs, so she didn't come out here herself to find her."

Now it was Riley's turn to give his brother a searching gaze. Something in Quentin's tone was off. Slowly, he said, "Abby sent you out here to look for her. Because Abby's worried about her. Right?" Riley held his brother with a look.

Quentin's gaze narrowed slightly as he nodded. "Exactly."

"Bullshit." Riley brought his fist into the palm of his other hand, making a slamming sound that was loud in the stillness of the day. His bear roiled inside him. He needed to get out there into the woods soon himself. "You just want to know where she went. Where she is. Who she might be talking to. Because you still don't trust her."

Just as quickly, Quentin shoved the words back at him. "Neither do you. So why are you calling me out on it?"

They stood for a few seconds, half glaring at one another, Riley's bear roaring inside him with some strange sort of urgency. A need to go out there and follow her. Which was crazy. Riley had work to do. Keeping tabs on Marisa the crazy shifter wasn't part of it.

Quentin didn't back down an inch from the glare match. There was a reason their parents had left him in charge of everything, Riley had to grudgingly admit. Quentin was sharp and paid attention to everything. Which was usually a pain in the ass.

47

Finally, his brother shrugged. "You know I don't trust her. I don't know what her endgame is. Abby's convinced she's found another poor lost soul to rescue, but I'm still not sure about that. Those outcasts were a little too organized for my taste."

Riley couldn't argue. The bridge battle had been not only well organized, but highly orchestrated. The outcasts they'd managed to catch and toss in the holding cells designed to contain shifters in the basement of the town jail still weren't talking. Most of them were halfway to insane anyway, but the way they'd clammed up made everyone here uneasy. Riley didn't like it, and he knew Quentin didn't either.

Quentin jerked his chin at the woods. "So. Are you going after her? I saw her, Riley. And I heard the two of you yelling from half a mile away. I think the entire lodge could hear her when she was shifting." He grimaced in sympathy. "Sounded like it was a bad one."

Riley clamped his lips over his teeth for a moment, the echo of Marisa's agonized screams still ringing in his ears. When the shift was that bad, things definitely were not good between the human side and the animal side. That was obvious to anyone as far as Marisa was concerned, though. Any shifter who wanted to die as badly as she apparently did sure as hell didn't have a good relationship with her animal.

At the reminder of her bizarre quest, he felt the anger

at her desire to be put down slip over him again. But this time, another feeling joined it.

Sympathy.

Or maybe empathy was the right word. Ah, fuck him. He sure as hell didn't want to die, no way, but he and his bear were struggling, and he knew it. She'd been right. He did understand her. For some reason that made no sense no matter which way he looked at it, he thought maybe he understood her in a way no one else in the world did. And that was the fucking saddest thing he'd thought in a long time.

Forcing himself to take a long, deep breath before he answered, he realized from the shaky control inside him that he'd have to do another aikido session before bed tonight if he wanted to hang on to anything even remotely called centered. Or sane.

"She didn't want anyone to go after her. She wanted to be alone. I don't think she's going anywhere. She... wasn't in control of that shift." He felt his eye twitch as he thought of her horrific shift. "Her cat took over. Trust me, if she's still in cahoots with the outcasts, then they all must be crazy. Because that girl is a complete lunatic."

He ground that last sentence out, trying to sound casual. Forcing it over the suddenly deep snarls of his bear. Knowing it was partially true while at the same time it was a huge lie. Marisa had some sort of big issues, that was for sure. She was messed up. That was a definite.

But something in her was worth saving, and her cat knew it. Hell, he knew it.

His bear rumbled in him. Dark, angry, and fuming with something Riley couldn't figure out but knew was about to burst out whether he wanted it to or not.

Damn it. He had to shift, now.

"Gotta go. I'll tell you if I see her," he managed to toss out at his brother's skeptical face before he turned and slammed into the woods, fast.

Away from his brother. Away from the lodge. Away from Marisa.

The truth was hitting him hard. Knocking him on his blind, dumb ass.

Marisa wasn't a lunatic.

Marisa was in despair.

The howls as she'd shifted were filled with it. He'd recognize the feeling anywhere. He just had to admit it. Despair and Riley knew each other way too well.

Marisa didn't really want to die. She was running. Hiding. She wanted to give up from a pain that was so bad it was destroying her from the inside.

Riley knew that pain as well as anything in this world. It was still trying to eat him, but he fought it every day.

And fuck him if he wasn't going to convince that lion girl to do the same thing.

R iley grunted as he struggled to lift his end of the box. "You're killing me, human," he growled at the man straining at the other end of it. "What do you think this is, the flyweight division of weightlifting? Pretend you've got the strength of more than a fucking butterfly."

His boss and best friend Joe snorted a laugh as he also strained to lift his end. "Well, I'm not blessed with super shifter strength over here. Doing the best I can, bear," he drawled out.

A snarl lifted Riley's lip. "Whatever. We must both be wimps. Who knew fucking paperwork would weigh this much?"

Joe groaned in reply as the two of them finally managed to heave the overly large, overly heavy box up onto one of the sturdy shelves in the storage room at the back of the national forest ranger office. Panting slightly, he swore, "Filling this big of a box up to the brim was possibly the dumbest thing you and I've ever done. Let's never tell anyone about this."

Struggling to hold back the sharp retort that Joe had been the one to fill the box, Riley managed a tight nod. "Agreed."

He got a sharp look in return. Riley ignored it. He'd been behaving like an ass all day long. What else was new?

They walked in silence back down the hallway to the front office. The budget was so tight these days the state had said they could no longer afford a full-time receptionist. Their regular one now worked only part-time. Between Riley and Joe, they covered the desk and the phones the rest of the hours. It was bureaucratic idiocy, having two outdoor-trained guys working the phones and answering emails, but someone had to do it.

Riley's bear grumbled inside him. Yeah. Among all the other things, this was one of the reasons he knew he'd been struggling more and more to keep a handle on his wild side. Sitting at the damn desk answering phones and emails didn't do much to keep him or his bear happy. He'd taken the job as a free labor seasonal ranger the first summer after he graduated high school, earning his way up to a paid position by that fall. He'd done it because he loved being outside; he loved wandering through the backcountry. Even back then, when he was still young and stupid and didn't know what he wanted from life, he was a big fan of keeping the forest in his mountains properly managed and open for people to do what they wanted, within reason. People and other shifters.

A growl rippled its way up his throat, muttered out on his angry breath. Frowning, Riley didn't even try to hide it. Joe knew him well enough to not be afraid of his bear's snorts and snarls when they came shuddering up through Riley's human form. He knew they were never directed toward him.

Marisa had been missing since her gut-ripping change yesterday. Her tawny backside and long, black-tipped tail had been the last he or anyone else had seen of her. Beautiful, messed up, scared woman. The thought of her out there alone all night and now most of the day, even in her shifted shape, was making him crazy.

He wasn't her friend. He didn't know her or where she came from. But the pain in her that had screamed at him in echo of his own had made him worry about her. He'd been unable to get her out of his mind, picturing her snatched up again by the remaining outcasts or slunk off to another set of local shifters to ask a big, strong alpha to put her down.

Worst of all, he kept picturing her getting her wish and being put to death by someone who didn't understand her. Someone who didn't care.

He snarled again, just barely under his breath. *He* didn't care about her. Even if he wanted to help her find her way out of whatever lost hell she existed in, he didn't care about her. He couldn't.

He couldn't care about a woman ever again.

His bear snarled, but not in accordance. In angry response, instead. One that said Riley was lying to himself. Again.

"Fuck me," he growled out loud.

Joe immediately deadpanned, "Thanks, but no thanks. Natalie would kill me. After I killed myself."

Riley rounded on his friend so suddenly Joe stopped right in his tracks. "Not funny. Don't ever joke about something like that." Riley's voice was darkness itself.

"What the fuck is up with you?" Joe finally snapped back, though he kept his body language relaxed and didn't offer any other challenge. He knew shifters very well.

Roaring his frustration to the uncaring hallway walls, Riley stalked toward the front of the building. "I'm being an ass, and I need to stop it," he gritted out. Joe knew him. He knew whatever was up Riley's butt, it wasn't anything to do with Joe.

They stopped in the front office. By habit, both stood still for a second, each side-eyeing the other. Joe shrugged, but the sudden glimmer of a half grin tugged at his mouth. "You need to stop being an ass? Then fucking beat me to the chair, you lazy fuckin' bear."

Yeah, a good friend who knew how to not take Riley's shit personally. He snarled back, though he let his own grin roll over his face, "It's on, you slow-footed human."

They each lunged for the rolling chair that sat behind the desk. Riley just managed to slam himself into it before Joe knocked into him and the chair both, sending all three sprawling to the ground in a sudden lurch of curses. Pinned under the chair with carpet fibers up his nose, Riley started laughing. He laughed until he roared, then he laughed some more. Joe laughed with him, shaking his head.

"Pair of idiots," Joe said, which set them both off again for a few minutes.

Riley laughed until his sides ached. Good. This shit was cathartic. He'd taught himself long ago that laughter could be the perfect way to chill the hell out. He'd needed it.

As they finally hauled themselves up off the floor and Riley set the chair back on its wheels, he shook his head. "Thanks, asshole."

"Anytime, asshole," Joe returned good-naturedly.

That was all that needed to be said. The atmosphere returned to more normal.

"One of these days, we're going to break our necks doing this," Riley added.

Joe snorted, rubbing the stubble on his chin as a less playful look dropped over his face. "At least we're trying to make this bullshit somewhat fun."

Riley made a disparaging sound in the back of his

throat. Joe was right. They'd each been so reluctant to start sitting at the front desk that they'd taken to making a stupid game out of it. Some days, at an unspoken signal, they'd each race for the rolling office chair at the front desk. Whoever got to it first and managed to sit his ass down in it was actually the one who got to *not* be saddled with desk duty the rest of the week.

Dumb, but it broke up the monotony. And, Riley thought in silent appreciation of his best friend understanding him, it made for a good way for him to knock off behaving like a jerk, stomping around all growly and irritable.

Even though Riley was faster than Joe due to his shifter reflexes, it actually ended up going half and half. Most of the time that was because Joe would take to outwitting him or flat out playing dirty by knocking Riley off balance or shoving something in his way to trip him. Today had just been a flat out run. "Sorry." Riley clapped Joe on the back. "I actually really need this right now. Bear's been going fucking nuts."

Riley and Joe had known one another since before they could toddle or talk. Joe's human mother had grown up in an equally close friendship with Riley's mother, Elodie, and they passed the friendship tradition down to their two sons, who'd been born within weeks of one another. Since Joe had grown up here in Deep Hollow, as had his parents and grandparents before him, he knew as much about shifters as any human could.

But he would never fully understand all the intricacies of being one. Riley often found himself sharing more with Joe than he did with anyone else, even his own clan. But not everything. Joe knew Riley worked hard to keep his bear from giving in to too much wild restlessness, but even he didn't know how touch and go it had been lately.

The only one on the face of the planet who knew that was Marisa.

Wherever she was. Damn, he was worried about her. Grown-ass woman or not, kickass mountain lion shifter or not, he was worried. He could admit it. Pretty, sexy, locked-down, confused, confusing woman. His bear hummed inside him just picturing her.

Joe cackled softly. "What the hell look is that on your face, bear? What were you just thinking about? Your face just got mushier than Natalie's does when she watches her favorite soap opera." Joe's stay-at-home wife, Natalie, who homeschooled their two children while also running a thriving Etsy business, had only one vice in the world, as Joe liked to say. That was her soap operas she enjoyed zoning out to every day while she ate lunch and the kids napped.

Had his face gone all soft and mushy? Interesting.

Riley headed back down the hall to the lockers where he and Joe kept extra uniform sets and began changing back into his street clothes. They were officially closed for the day, and he was ready to get out of here. To maybe go look for Marisa. "What look? I never get a mushy face.

Shut your pie hole. You're imagining things." He tried to keep his tone light, but Joe wasn't buying it.

"Wait a second," Joe's voice drawled again, the way it always did when he was noticing something. "Could this have anything to do with a certain outcast shifter who's been staying with you all up at the lodge since the bridge battle? Mountain lion, right?"

Riley snapped his head around to pin a look on Joe midway through yanking off his uniform jacket. "What the hell are you talking about, human?"

Joe settled his hands on his hips and shook his head, a wide grin slowly unfolding on his face. "Thought so. Everly was talking to Jessie this morning, who told her you and that mountain lion shifter had some sort of spat. Apparently, or so she said, the energy between you guys was kind of wild."

Riley kept his jaw tight as he thought of what an ass he'd been to Marisa yesterday. In front of the others, too.

"So Everly told Natalie about it, who texted me about it later." Joe shrugged. "It was news to me. I was just waiting to see if you were gonna say something about her."

Everly was a local shifter whose family ran Deep Hollow's most popular watering hole, The Tank, which was just a few doors away from the Mountain Muffin bakery where Jessie worked. Apparently, they liked to flap gossipy lips to one another. Nothing stayed secret for long in this small shifter town.

58

Riley swallowed a groan. Thinking about Marisa must have made his face go soft and stupid. Enough so Joe would have noticed and finally felt like calling him on it. Not looking at his friend as he yanked off his work shirt and pulled on one of his own, he said casually, "Yeah. So what?"

He couldn't fool his best friend, and he hadn't really thought he would. "Oh, hell no. Don't pretend to get all secretive with me, Riley Walker. I can read you like an open book."

Silence beat for several moments before Riley finally turned and looked at Joe. Joe was giving him the beady-eyed look Riley knew well. The one that said, *We've been best friends practically since the womb. Even though I'm human and you're a shifter, I know you better than anyone, even your own family. Cut the shit and get real.*

Yeah, of course there eventually had been women after Riley's mate had been killed. Years later. But just casual, one-night-stand women to scratch his natural itch. One and done, and he moved on.

Marisa, though.... She was different, and Joe could sense it.

Riley exhaled a long sigh. "Her name's Marisa. Mountain lion shifter. She was with the outcasts, we took her back after the bridge battle because she was hurt and just—"

He couldn't bring himself to say it. Brows lowered, concern edging into his voice, Joe finished for him,

"Because she's crazy and is asking every strong shifter this town has to put her down? Because she's a nutcase?"

Even though there was no censure in Joe's voice, only simple curiosity as he recited what everyone in town already knew by now, Riley felt a sudden protective rage flare up. His bear rumbled in him and his eyes must have started to glow, because Joe's eyebrows raised. As Joe slowly unfolded his arms from in front of him, letting his hands fall to his sides with palms up in a "peace" gesture, he looked away instead of directly at his friend. Never in his life would Riley hurt Joe or any of the humans in town he knew and trusted. But Joe understood shifter etiquette well enough he knew how to behave around them when their animals got agitated.

Shifter etiquette said looking one right in the eyes at the wrong moment could be seen as a challenge. That was something a human would never win.

Riley sucked in a long draw of air, let it out, and pulled in another long, deep draw of calming breath inside him. He was impressed with how steady his voice was when he answered, "I know what everyone says. And honestly, I thought it was true at first too. But she's not crazy, Joe."

Joe stole a look at him and kept eye contact, slowly nodding.

"She's not crazy." Riley heard the conviction in his own voice. "Those outcasts did a fucking job on her, and she's just—she's been hurt bad somehow. I mean, on the inside. Something messed her up, and from what she told me, she also had a pretty crappy childhood." A frown darkened his face. He wanted to hurt anyone who had ever hurt her. Even her own family. "But she's not crazy. In fact, she's pretty damned interesting, and the twins love her. And—fuck it," he exploded. His fist slapped into his other hand.

He'd been such a shit to her because he liked her, and that was terrifying as hell. It was time for him to just man the fuck up and admit it out loud. "Fine. I like her. I really like her, and so does my bear."

Another long silence stretched between them as Joe digested Riley's admission. Finally, he murmured, "Well, okay then. That's pretty huge." He shrugged almost casually, turning to change into his own street clothes, but the deep meaning of his words lingered, almost vibrating in the air.

Joe knew as well as anyone that after the trauma Riley had suffered when his mate had been murdered, his bear had been shut down for years. For a shifter's animal to like someone new, to actually be interested in them, was a big deal in the shifter world after something as devastating as the loss of a mate.

"But." Riley paused. He looked at the backside of the desk shoved into the locker room. The fake trim was peeling off and it had wobbly legs. They really needed to get it replaced, but there wasn't money for that, either.

"She took off as her cat yesterday. After we had our...
whatever the hell you called it. Spat."

Joe cocked a brow at him. "And why'd you have
that?"

Riley growled. "Fine. I've been a dick to her. A pretty
shitty one to her yesterday."

"Because you like her, and it freaks you the hell out."

There was a long pause of heavy silence as Riley
looked at Joe, and Joe simply looked back at him, straight
on. Not backing down an inch this time, even though
Riley knew his eyes had to be reflecting his bear. But Joe
wasn't challenging Riley. Just looking right at his truth
and daring Riley to own it.

Finally, he gave a stiff nod. "Yeah. No one else
knows."

Now Joe guffawed. "Hell if they don't. Open book,
my friend." His tone softened. "Everyone would understand why. Hell, if anything ever happened to Natalie, I
don't think I could ever look at another woman again
without feeling sick to my stomach."

Riley frowned down at his work shoes, shoving them
each off with the opposite foot. He lightly kicked them
into the bottom of his open locker.

"But it's okay to really like another woman, Ri. Grace
wouldn't mind." Joe's voice was soft but firm. "She'd have
hated to see how much you've suffered."

At his mate's name, Riley nodded, eyes still on his
feet, working his jaw from side to side. Joe was right. It

would have hurt her to see the angry, closed-off man he'd become after she died. Emotions roiled through him at her memory, as always. But the emotions were just the old anger that he'd yet to catch her killers.

He would honor Grace's memory forever, keep it alive for the cubs' sakes, but she was gone. He'd truly accepted that several years ago.

Now it was Marisa's face he saw in his mind. Her face, her enticing scent, her agonized cry as she shifted.

And all he wanted to do was keep her from experiencing any more pain.

"Yeah," was all he finally said. He looked up at Joe. "Marisa is—well, I'm not sure what she means to me, exactly. What I do know for sure is she's not crazy. And she hasn't come back since she ran off. I don't know where her head is right now, but I don't think she's in a good space to be out there alone."

"She's a mountain lion. I'm thinking that means she's pretty good at taking care of herself."

"Yeah." Riley's voice was soft. "She's a lot more badass than she seems to think she is. But still. She needs someone to remind her of that."

His phone buzzed. Grabbing it up, expecting to see a text from either of his cubs, his heart stuttered at the words there from Abby instead.

Marisa came back. We're all meeting for dinner in town. You and the cubs want to join us?

Casual, simple words exploded his world into something bright and excited. "She's back," was all he could manage. "She's okay." Even he could hear the relief that shot through his voice.

Joe nodded then grinned. "So. What are you gonna do now?"

Riley knew his face was smiling, but he couldn't seem to stop it. "Tell my hooligan children we're eating in town with their favorite mountain lion shifter. Then, as soon as I see her, I'm apologizing to her for being a jerk."

Joe's eyebrows raised as his grin got bigger, but he didn't say anything more than, "Sounds like a good plan, bear. Have a good time. And hey, don't be a stranger at our place. Bring that lion lady over some time. I'm sure Natalie would like to meet her. I might need to meet her too," he said casually as he turned and sauntered back down the hall, whistling lightly under his breath. "Gotta see who's interesting enough to finally start making you not be an asshole half the time anymore."

Riley reached down, grabbed one of his dirty socks, and chucked it right at Joe's back, hitting it dead on. Joe yelped and threw him the finger over his shoulder. But he still sauntered away without looking back, whistling, and, Riley was sure, still grinning big.

He grunted to himself as he yanked off his work pants and pulled on his jeans, but a grin had crept onto his face too. Joe was a good friend. Only good friends could understand. "Good job, boss," he murmured his daily mantra like a prayer, for once saying it not just to himself, but to his actual boss too. "Good job, bear."

Then he hustled out the door, determined to get to Marisa and apologize. Determined to tell her she didn't need to run anymore from whatever was hurting her.

Determined to be honest with her about the fact that he really fucking liked her, that she definitely smelled damned good, and that there was no way in hell he was going to let her be put down.

Because she deserved to live.

Abby and Quentin argued above Marisa's head as she sat on the plush leather couch and examined the painting that hung on the wall. Set in snowy woods that looked like the forest around the lodge, a dark storm brewing overhead as fat snowflakes wafted down, the painting depicted a bunch of different shifter types running in the woods—grizzly bears, black bears, big gray timber wolves, red foxes, mountain lions like her bad kitty, panthers, bobcats. In the skies above flew bald eagles, golden eagles, hawks. Two dragons swooped in the far upper right corner of the painting, one black, the other silvery gray.

She stared at the dragon shifters in the painting, transfixed. She'd met exactly one dragon shifter ever. Pix. Pix was nothing like she'd thought a dragon shifter would be. She was small, smart, funny, and could hold her liquor and crack a side-splitting joke. She was down to earth and friendly, not a snooty rich person like Justin and Nefarious and the other outcasts had said dragons were like.

Marisa had realized over time that a lot of what they had told her was complete bullshit. That shouldn't have surprised her. What should have surprised her was how long she'd allowed herself to believe it.

Just like all the shifters she had met so far at the Silvertip Lodge, not a single one of them had matched up to her assumptions of what they'd be like.

ASS-umptions, girl. Finger pointing at her, angry drunk face shouting down at her. *When ya ASS-ume somethin', you make an ASS outta U and ME. Got it, girlie? Dumb bitch, how the hell could you have come from me?*

A vision of Derek, trying to protect her while their monstrous parents raged and spat and yelled and hit, flashed into her mind. He'd always tried to protect her, even when they were little. Then she unwillingly pictured him as his mountain lion, as crazed and enraged as hers was. As confused and lost, and still stuck with the insane, totally fucked up Nefarious Desperados. Being forced to fight for them, just like Marisa had.

The only family she'd ever had—she'd ever loved—and she couldn't do a damn thing for him right now. If he was even still alive.

Suddenly feeling like her throat might close up,

feeling as if she might suffocate on memories alone, Marisa sucked in air. *Breathe. Breathe.*

Riley. Safe. Strong. Just as protective. She grabbed onto the remembered image of his face, his scent. Big bruin, huge humped shoulders, silvery cast to his dark fur. Gorgeous man, dark, shuttered eyes, hidden smile that for some crazy reason lit her up from within. Why? She still didn't know.

Riley. The mystery, the conundrum that twisted her brain up into unsettled, intriguing ideas each time she thought about him.

Riley, not at all what she'd pictured normal, non-outcast bear shifters to be like.

Not at all what she'd ever thought a man could be like.

"Abby." Marisa startled at the sound. Quentin, sounding defeated. Bear shifter, businesslike, definitely a little suspicious of Marisa. She'd sensed it from the moment she'd met him, even though he too was polite to her. Abby's mate. Also Riley's oldest brother. He and Riley looked alike. Same with Cortez. There was another brother, she couldn't remember his name. He had dark hair and eyes. He didn't look like them, but Abby had told her they all took after their father except that one, who'd gotten their mother's hair and eyes. And there was yet another brother, one who'd moved far away and rarely came home anymore. Such a big family. Boisterous bear clan.

Derek's face popped into her head again. She and her brother looked alike. So alike they could be twins, though they weren't. Marisa squeezed the insides of her mouth together, her teeth stopping just short of biting her cheeks, until the image of his face went away. Too hard to think about. Too painful.

Quentin said, "I do not want to interrogate her. This is not actually the Spanish Inquisition, as you keep insisting."

Abby, standing in front of the couch with her arms crossed as if she were guarding Marisa, cocked her head at her mate. "Oh, no? Then why did you call her in here to ask her a million questions about them? About the shifters she probably never wants to think about again, let alone talk to you about?"

Marisa stayed focused on the painting. Little cubs tumbling around, bears and wolves and foxes, playing together in the snow. Was that a—a monkey up in one of the pine trees? She squinted. It was kind of orange. An orangutan? Weren't they sort of orange? She used to call Derek an orangutan after they'd seen a TV show about monkeys and other ape-like creatures. He sure acted like one sometimes while they'd grown up. Dumb, dumb, sweet little brother she loved.

She flinched. No. Not going there. *Breathe. Just breathe.*

Quentin thrust a hand through his hair and glanced at Marisa. She flipped her eyes to his, expressionless, then

69

looked back at the painting. It was a lot more interesting than his and Abby's conversation. She could lose herself in it. Just drift into it. The painting reminded her of the snowy mountains her cat had run in for hours yesterday. So many hours. It lulled her. Felt so good, so free, so easy. Just running and not thinking about anything at all.

Stay here. Stay here, she ordered herself. With an internal shake, she dragged her gaze away from the painting and back to Quentin. He opened his mouth again, expression still troubled, but Abby cut him off with the sternest look on her face Marisa had yet seen.

"Enough, love. Look at her." Abby gestured at Marisa, although her eyes didn't leave her mate's. "She's exhausted from being out in the mountains overnight. She was alone the whole time. Just let it go for now. She needs to get back into this body."

Abby's eyes finally moved to Marisa, a thoughtful look moving over her features as she said those odd words. *She needs to get back into this body.* Marisa thought she caught worry in her expression, but Abby smoothed out her face and quirked her lips into a smile. "We're all heading into town to grab some food. And you're coming."

Marisa automatically started to shake her head, but that firm look came back onto Abby's face as she held up a finger. "No. This time you don't get to bow out of it. You're not a prisoner here, Marisa," she added softly. "What you are, at least what I'm thinking of you as, is a

70

friend. A friend we're all just barely getting to know. We want to know you better. I was really worried about you." She smiled gently. "Everyone would love for you to be there. Truly."

A friend. Marisa frowned. Was that what she was? Did she even know what such a thing was anymore?

You ain't got no friends, you common little whore. Words hissed at her on a regular basis as she grew up. *Boys like you cuz you spread your legs for all of 'em. Girls pretend to like you, but they just want to get to know your trampy little secrets so they can get close to them boys too. And then they all gonna dump you in the end, because they know you ain't nothin' but trash, Marisa Tully. Never have been, never will be any more 'n that.*

"Marisa?" Abby's voice. Concerned now.

Marisa blinked, looked up at Abby. Abby stared at her, smile wiped away, a frown etched in her forehead. Her eyes glowed faintly with her wolf. Marisa's cat rattled somewhere inside her. Deep inside. Always there, no matter what she did. *Breathe.*

"Okay. Yes. I'd like to go with you all." Her words surprised her even as she said them.

Abby relaxed, though her look lingered for a moment. Then she shot another stern warning gaze at her mate before she beckoned toward the door. "Come on. You can ride with me and my big bully of a mate over there."

"I'm no such thing." Quentin's protest was good-natured.

71

"Don't let his mean bully ways get to you." Abby's voice began to loosen now with a hint of laughter. "He's been in charge of running everything since his folks left on their honeymoon last year. You may have noticed all his brothers are more than a handful. He says it's like trying to herd cats. In other words—"

"—it's a task filled with deep frustration and sometimes a blue streak of cussing when they push me bad enough." Quentin finished Abby's sentence. "My beautiful mate is right, as always. Sorry, Marisa. I did push you. But I take the safety of the clan very seriously. After what happened at the bridge battle, I've been on alert." His sincere voice dropped softly to Marisa's ears as he slung an arm around his mate, tugging her through the doorway as she in turn tugged at Marisa's hand to follow them.

She regarded his back for a thoughtful moment, though she let Abby pull her along. Like Riley, Quentin didn't trust her yet. But he trusted his mate, and Abby trusted her. Marisa wasn't sure why Abby seemed to like her so much. Why she thought of Marisa as a friend. But it felt strangely good.

Maybe what she needed was just that. A friend.

8

B undled into the truck, Marisa watched the wintry landscape flow by as they drove down into the little town of Deep Hollow. She hadn't spent much time there and hadn't been back since the bridge battle. Her chest tightened when she thought about that, but nothing else happened. She didn't shut it out; she didn't feel like passing out. She felt...nothing, really. But not in a bad way. Instead, what she felt seemed to be mild anticipation for the evening ahead. Okay, that was cool.

Abby was right, she was exhausted, but not so much she didn't feel like being a little social. She actually was looking forward to being around the others after being out in the mountains all night as bad kitty. As usual, she couldn't remember anything about that. That might be for the best though.

Abby chatted the whole way there. Although it was

casual, Marisa sensed the other woman's need to keep the mood light.

She blinked when the truck slowed to a stop and parked. They were on a street in Deep Hollow's cute little downtown in front of a storefront that smelled good. Really good. Her mouth suddenly watered. Climbing out of the truck behind Abby, she looked at the carved wooden sign above the doorway.

Uncertainly, she read the name. "We Got Whatchu Want?"

Abby made a little "mm-hmm" noise in her throat. "They have just about everything you might want to order. Everyone just calls it Whatchu Want. A lot of people around here have a sense of humor. Some of the store names are pretty generic, like the Deep Hollow Market. But some people decided to spice things up. The more you hang out in town, the more you'll notice it." Abby didn't quite look at Marisa as she said that, but Marisa got the point.

The more she hung out in town implied she would want to spend time here. Which would imply she was still alive. Her face twitched involuntarily, but she felt nothing upset inside. No reaction, no urge to find the strongest shifter around her and beg to be put down. Even bad kitty stayed quiet.

It was just because she was hungry. That was all.

Without rising to Abby's bait, kindly as she probably meant it, Marisa followed Quentin and Abby inside. The place was small but lively. As her eyes quickly adjusted to the light within, she saw booths, barstools along a counter, even a little dance floor off to one side. The scents of hamburgers, hot dogs, steak, pizza, salad, potatoes, and numerous sugary sorts of desserts like pies and cakes instantly hit her sensitive nose. She swallowed hard.

She knew her cat had hunted yesterday because when she'd woken up in the woods, naked and slightly shivering, she found blood on her chin, her hands, washed down her stomach. And she felt full. But that had been at least twelve hours ago, and she hadn't had a bite since. One thing shifters needed a lot of was food.

Sudden loud chaos interrupted her hungry thoughts.

"Quentin! We saved the big booth over here." A tall, dark-haired man waved at them from the back corner. Marisa hunted for his name again. He was the Walker brother she'd only met once because he'd been out of town working until just a few days ago. Abby, who had hung back slightly to make sure Marisa made it inside, seemed to sense her internal struggle.

"Slade. He's in the middle of the clan, age wise. This time of year isn't usually fire season, but with the weather being as warm and dry as it has been in a lot of parts of the country the last couple years, he and his crew have been working even into the winters."

At Marisa's quizzical look, Abby added, "He's a wildland firefighter. The first crew to go in to fight fires on foot, on the ground. They're called hotshots." She snorted then, but her tone was affectionate. "Slade definitely thinks he's a hotshot."

"I can hear you, you know! But you can call me a hotshot regardless of my job. I've got no need to be shy about my abilities." Slade wagged his eyebrows at them, drawing a groan from Quentin. This must be a well-rehearsed speech.

Following Abby to the booth where Jessie and Grant also sat, casting a glance toward the delicious sizzling smells coming from the grill tucked back in the kitchen, Marisa listened as Quentin and Slade started ribbing one another over who was the hottest hotshot on Slade's crew. Before they got to the booth, she finally tentatively ventured the question that had been hanging onto the edges of her mind. "Will the others be here too?"

Abby gave her a speculative look. "By the others, do you mean the other wild Walker brothers? I'm betting at least Riley will be."

Marisa wasn't sure exactly what she felt when she heard his name out loud. Her cat twined through her mind, sinuous but quiet.

"If you mean Cortez and Haley," Abby went on, "I don't think so. Cortez had a long work day today, and I think he's still out with clients. Haley is probably working on her deadline."

Marisa didn't reply. Her stomach tightened. Quietly, slowing her steps just before they got to the booth

Quentin had already reached and slid into next to his brother, Marisa felt flatness drape itself over her again. Familiar worry. Apparently, she wasn't free of that quite yet. "Is it really because they're working? Or is it because they don't want to see me?" *Because I'm the reason the outcasts came to town,* she couldn't bring herself to say. Even though it was the truth.

This time Abby stopped short, turning to face her. Firmly, she shook her head. "Absolutely not. Nothing that happened was your fault. They don't think that at all. No one here does."

Marisa punched out her next words even though they tried to stick in her throat. "How can you be sure it wasn't my fault?"

Forehead crinkling with distress, Abby sighed. "Because they were a part of your history that's done now. The outcasts. Right?" Abby searched her eyes, her wolf starting to glow in her own.

Marisa stayed silent for a long moment, fighting to stay present as ugly memories swarmed up, threatening to swallow her like they always did. Before she could answer, a bustle of eager voices at the door roared in like a tumbling tidal wave of excitement and chatter.

"Marisa!"

She barely had time to turn around before Laney and Finn rushed in, bringing a blast of cold air with them along with the scent of pine trees and fur and wildness. They must have been in their bear shapes not long before they got here. She couldn't help the usual funny little billow of what might be happiness at seeing them. Such cute kids. Sweet, precious, playful cubs.

They skidded up to her, both careful not to touch her, and began babbling a million miles a minute. They'd done this, that, and the other at school today, and they'd missed seeing her, and where had she been, and could they maybe sometime this week show her one of their favorite spots on the mountain, their dad said they could, oh, and could they sit next to her to eat?

They were so excited to see her. It made her catch her breath, made her want to smile, made her almost want to hug them close to her. Almost. But she wasn't quite ready for that. She settled for nodding in answer, which launched another zoom of chatter from them.

Abby laughed and shushed them. "Give her a second to answer, you two rascals. Where is your father anyway?" Abby's voice was light, but Marisa could feel her quick glance.

"He's coming in a minute," Finn answered casually. Suddenly distracted by something else in the room, he jabbed his sister in the side. "There's Willow and Laurel! I'm saying hi."

"Ouch! Don't poke me. Hi, Laurel!"

With a solemn look, Laney assured Marisa, "We're just going to go say hi to them; we'll be right back. Save us seats."

Before she could reply, they scampered off toward two girls over in the corner. She caught bear shifter scent from both of them. Their eyes on her were quizzical, but their smiles were friendly enough as they tentatively waved at her before Laney and Finn descended on their booth and the four of them fell into an instant animated conversation.

Abby laughed as she slipped into the booth next to Quentin and patted the cushion seat next to her. "They're like little hurricanes. Hard to catch your breath around them."

"I love it. They're so happy, so normal." The words popped out of Marisa's mouth before she could censor them. She sucked in a breath. How easily it had come out, but no one else at the table seemed to notice.

Of course. For them, lively, excitable, chattering kids were the norm. Kids just allowed to be kids, to be silly and fun and free and not worried every second they might get slapped, or punched, or kicked.

No one here was like Marisa. Not a single one of them could understand where she'd come from or how she'd lived.

She waited for the inevitable little kick of pain, of long-dashed hopes that now existed just as misery, to spring up as usual. But nothing happened. She felt her forehead wrinkle up as she waited for it. Even bad kitty still stayed quiet within her, seeming as expectant and surprised as she was.

It didn't hurt. It didn't bother her. In fact, what she felt was better than that.

She *craved* it. What they had. What all these shifters here, the ones who lived up at Silvertip Lodge, the ones who lived down here in Deep Hollow, all seemed to have and take for granted as being their due in life.

Just simple, easy, regular life. Nothing grander than that, but definitely nothing worse.

A normal, happy life.

She wanted to have that too, so strongly it startled her with its intensity.

"Hey." A pair of fingers snapped right in front of her face. She shied back, hard. "You sitting down or what?"

The other brother, Slade, was looking at her like she was a science experiment in danger of blowing up any second. Abby and Quentin also stared at her, Quentin with a resigned sort of quiet and Abby with that gentle concern Marisa was growing to like.

She liked it because it meant someone cared about her. She'd never had that before in her life.

Another startlement hit her as she realized something else. She'd gone away for a moment, and they'd noticed it. But she hadn't actually left in her head. She'd been here. Which meant she hadn't really gone away. She'd just been thinking, but she'd stayed present. Aware of the right here, right now.

That was a first. A first ever, since...the thing.

Abby broke the silence. "Come on, sit next to me.

The twins will probably get all wrapped up with the Bain girls. I think Finn has a bit of a crush on Willow, and Laney and Laurel have been best buddies since before they started to crawl."

The smells of food rolled over Marisa again. Someone cranked up a goofy old western song on the jukebox, abruptly filling the room with twangy music. Slade and Quentin groaned in unison. Marisa felt something weird happen to her cheeks as she settled into the booth next to Abby. They hurt, sort of.

"Marisa." Abby's voice, lighter than before. "Did I see you almost smile?"

Was that what it was? She'd nearly forgotten what it felt like.

"Menu." Slade pushed a crinkly piece of paper at her. "We're getting a few baskets of wings and fries to start with. Tradition. Then everything else."

"What else do they have?" Marisa peered down at the menu.

"Well, tell us Whatchu Want and they got it!" Slade busted up into a big laugh, joined by Quentin and then Abby. Playful, silly laughter.

She felt it again. That funny little stretch over her cheeks.

"Aha!" Abby crowed. "Another almost smile! See? Being with us is a good thing, Marisa."

Marisa let the stretchy feeling stay on her face. Yes. It was a good thing. Her mountain lion was quiet inside her, settled. She wasn't feeling panicky or claustrophobic like she had yesterday in the barn. The big run had probably helped.

But it wasn't just that. It was also being here with these shifters. They were friendly, relaxed, playful. They seemed to like her. They seemed to accept her, even with her past as an outcast.

They seemed to want her here.

That was something Marisa had never in her life truly felt. Not being wanted for who she was, at any rate.

She relaxed more and more as Quentin and Slade goofed around in the booth, as Abby and Jessie chatted comfortably, as little Grant was swept up by those two friends of Riley's cubs, Willow and Laurel, and smothered in hugs and kisses and giggles by all four of them as they headed over to the small area that was a kid play zone with plastic balls and such.

She let the mouthwatering smells of anything she wanted to order waft over from the grill and make her belly rumble with anticipation.

She let the sounds of chatter and laughter and normal, chill shifters and humans around her wash over her in a soothing bubble of sound.

She surreptitiously tapped her toe a tiny bit to the rhythm of the country song as it still blared out from the jukebox.

She let herself feel...*something*. Something, not nothing. Something that seemed to be good.

Then Slade and Quentin, who appeared much more relaxed and laid back right now than she'd yet seen him, gave each other a look. As if on unspoken cue, they threw back their heads and in unison began bellowing out the words to the song. They knew it perfectly.

Now it was Abby's and Jessie's turn to groan, especially when Jessie's mate, Shane, strolled over from where he'd deposited more quarters into the jukebox, also bellowing out the words to the old song at the top of his lungs.

"Uh," Marisa murmured, staring at the three big, burly bear shifters belting out the old-timey country song without a care in the world. "Does this happen often?"

Jessie rolled her eyes, although the expression on her face as she watched her mate was indulgent, filled with such a deep wave of love that Marisa felt the weirdest little squeeze somewhere in the middle of her chest. "All the time. This is exactly what they love to do when we get together. And just wait. They haven't even started drinking yet. Things get totally ridiculous then."

"Welcome to the Silvertip clan, Marisa," Abby added, also shaking her head at her mate where he sat next to her, still roaring out the song with his brother. "Whether they're brawling or enjoying life, there's never a dull moment around here."

Never a dull moment. But not in a bad way. Not in a scary, unpredictable way. Okay, the bridge battle hadn't been very fun. But this? This kind of fun and silliness was...wonderful. The outcasts hadn't been like this at all. Their ideas of fun had usually involved a great deal of *not fun* for someone else.

Marisa's face still hurt from the stretchy feeling that gripped her mouth. But she liked this. A lot. This was comfortable.

For the first time since being here, she understood what it was like to just be a part of these shifters. To almost be one of them.

The front door opened again. Still caught in her smile, which she could feel getting bigger and bigger on her face as now Abby and Jessie joined in with the singing, rolling their eyes as they gave in to the goofy high spirits of their mates, Marisa felt herself automatically pulled in the direction of the door.

Her breath caught in her throat as Riley's enticing scent and the sight of his big body filled the doorway. He almost unerringly saw his children and went straight to them, nearly getting bowled over as the two jumped up and raced over to fling their arms around him in quick hugs as he dropped a kiss each on top of their heads. She thought maybe very soon they'd be getting too old to allow him to do that anymore in public without squirming away in embarrassment. But for now, they still loved it, and she sensed he was going to take every opportunity to do it he could.

Watching them together, the three of them, the little family unit of father and two children, did a strange thing to her chest again. It squeezed it together in something she intimately recognized as pain. Something she intimately recognized as the bruising knowledge that never in her life had she had that herself. Familiar. Sad. Ugly. Old, old news.

But more importantly, more excitingly, her chest also expanded at the sight. Her heart beat hard as she watched them. It felt so big and happy she caught her breath again.

It made her happy just to watch Riley with his cubs.

What did that even mean?

Riley looked up and just as unerringly, his gaze found hers. He squeezed his children once more and released them to go pelting back to their table with their friends and that darned adorable little Grant bear baby. Then, making her heart beat harder and louder, Riley's eyes locked on hers as he strode directly toward her.

R iley barely heard his brothers hollering out that damned country song Slade always like to play every time he was in town and they hung out here at Whatchu Want. The sounds of his children giggling with their friends faded behind him, along with the light bustle of the few other patrons in the restaurant which he knew would soon expand as they neared the dinner hour.

His only focus was the pretty lion girl sitting in the booth with his clan, her eyes locked on his as he strode right up to her.

Ignoring Abby's and Quentin's glances, even as they still belted out the song, he bent down and asked Marisa, "Mind if I sit here? My kids told me you were saving seats for them, but Laney courageously said they would give them up so I could sit here with you instead."

A small sound escaped Marisa's pretty mouth before

her eyes widened and she clamped her lips shut again, looking startled. Behind her, Abby broke away from the song and leaned forward to say over the sounds of the boisterous singing clan, "That's a record. First you've been smiling, now nearly laughter? I knew there was some happy in you somewhere."

Abby's grin was big as she said it, and her tone was deeply affectionate. She threw the quickest glance at Riley before turning back to start singing again with the rest of his ridiculous family. Her little look said, *She's doing well. If you make it worse, I will kill you with my bare hands.*

Got it.

Marisa's eyes were still wide. She looked at Riley, but her lips were twitching. She nodded at him to sit down, scooting over a tiny bit so he could slide in next to her. He did, squishing into the booth close enough that his thigh was pressed along hers, their hips touching, and their arms would mash into each other when they ate if he didn't put an arm on the back of the booth behind her head.

He badly wanted to do that. But he'd learned just like his children had that for whatever reason, Marisa didn't tolerate uninvited touch. He didn't like thinking about what that might mean. What might have happened to her in the past. Instead, he twisted in the booth seat so he could look at her. She looked back at him, the corners of her mouth just turning up.

Damn. Lion girl was more than pretty. She verged on beautiful. Not just because she was smiling. Hell, he hated that kind of shit. Telling a woman to smile just to make her pretty. No, Marisa was beautiful because of something else.

Because she looked genuinely happy in this moment.

The shock tingled through him as he realized it was the first time he'd seen anything other than either sorrow or blank nothingness on her face since she'd been here.

Well, except for yesterday when she'd rightfully lost it and yelled at him. Still looking at her, he spoke quietly enough so the crazy singing clan couldn't hear him, because this was for Marisa's ears alone.

"Sorry about yesterday. I was a dick to you. The kind of things I said to you, only an absolute ass would say. I could tell you why I said them, but it's not an excuse because there is no excuse. So, I'm sorry, Marisa." He leaned the slightest bit toward her to enunciate his words, though not enough to seem intimidating. "I won't do it again. Ever."

The way he emphasized that last word, *ever,* took the smile off her face again. But not in an unhappy way. She stared at him intently, her eyes moving back and forth between his. She was trying to read him. Trying to see into him. He sat there and just let her look.

His bear was so quiet right now, so calm. His bear was always calm when he was around his family, when he knew exactly where his children were and they were safe, but this was different.

His bear was calm and quiet and focused right now because of Marisa. Because she sat right here, next to him. Also safe.

"Okay." The word was so quiet, so quick, he would have missed it if he hadn't been looking right at her.

"Okay?"

She huffed out the tiniest breath of air, her lips starting to twitch up again. "Okay, thank you. I mean... I accept your apology? I just mean... Okay." She floundered, slipping a lip between her teeth and very lightly nibbling on it.

Hoo, damn. That made his dick pay sudden attention. He swallowed, shifting in his seat.

Then, more quietly, she pulled up one shoulder in a shrug. "I don't have much experience with apologies, Riley. In fact, I have no experience with them. I don't really know what you do when someone says they're sorry to you."

Riley felt something dark and hot flash through him. Anger. "Has no one ever apologized to you for anything before? Ever?"

She shook her head, seeming suddenly tense at his tension. He forced himself to take in a breath, blow it out. He wasn't angry at her, but the sudden flash of it made her afraid. The thought of that suddenly enraged him.

He forced it down so he didn't make the situation even worse.

"You deserve *I'm sorrys* from people who do you wrong, Marisa. Everyone does. I can tell you've had a lot of wrong done to you. Haven't you." He didn't bother making his last statement a question.

Before she could answer, a plastic container of thick, crispy fries was suddenly slid across the booth table, spinning to a stop right in front of the two of them. The waitress jerked her chin at Riley and said, "You, ya big lug. You're having the rest of your usual, aren't ya?" The chirpy voice of the server, Casey, spoke just as the country song ended and the rest of the table whooped and howled. She rolled her eyes and shook her head at them, but grinned. Then she gave Marisa a curious glance. "What can I get for you, darlin'?"

Marisa seemed nonplussed at the energetic ball of woman. "I haven't really looked at the menu yet, I'm sorry. Oh." She gave Riley a quick glance before looking more firmly back at the waitress. "I mean, I'm not sorry. I mean...oh, just bring me whatever his usual is. I'm starving."

The waitress, who actually was co-owner of the place, raised her eyebrows but just nodded, sizing up Marisa. Scenting her. Then she leaned forward and said in a low voice, "Gotcha. I'm always starving after big shift too." Smiling broadly, she added in normal tones, "Welcome to town, darlin'. I'll get you guys hooked up with more food in a jif." She turned to the rest of the table to take their order.

Marisa stared after the woman. "Do the locals know about shifters?" she asked Riley, her voice so low it was almost just a breath. Her voice would have been drowned out anyway. Another honky-tonk song had started up on the jukebox, probably thanks to Slade doing his usual jamming in of quarters into the machine.

Riley kept looking at her as he talked. He decided he really liked looking at her. "We've mostly got shifters in town, but we do have a lot of humans who live here. The ones who grew up here know about us. Tourists, though," he added, giving a quick glance around the still sparsely filled room, though the door kept opening as more people began to come in, "they don't know. The human ones, that is. Casey's a shifter too. She knows all of us, and I'm sure she could smell your cat. You know how it is after a shift."

He gave a quick glance at his kids, as was his habit when he was around them, to just constantly check and make sure they were still there, were still okay. When Marisa didn't answer, he glanced back at her. She was looking at him, a slight crease marring her forehead.

"I'm not sure what you mean?" Genuine puzzlement filled her voice.

He regarded her for a long second before answering. Her dark rust-colored hair, a few golden strands lashing through it here and there, framed her face, stopping just short of her shoulders. Pretty eyes, oh, that pretty green he had to damn well admit slayed him every time he looked at her, fixed on his. Her cat still moved deep inside them, a reminder she had a wild, virtually uncontrolled animal in her. Just like he did. Being this close to her, her scent filling him, was going to his head.

But her words didn't make sense. How could she not understand him? Was being an outcast that lacking in knowledge of how shifters worked?

"After a big shift," he prompted, watching closely to study her reaction. "How it still clings to us, the scent. Kind of like the memory of being in our wild forms is still hanging onto us, and other shifters can tell." He tried to keep the puzzlement out of his voice as he spoke, but he knew he couldn't keep it out of his face.

She flushed slightly, finally moving her eyes down to stare at something fascinating on the tabletop. "Oh. Right. That. Sure, I knew what you meant. I just wasn't paying attention."

Shit. He didn't want to make her uncomfortable. But he also didn't want to shy away from things. He glanced briefly at the rest of the booth. Shane had joined them, settling in beside Jessie. They were all laughing like the lunatics they were at some videos on Slade's phone. None of them paid any attention to Riley and Marisa.

Good. He loved his clan, even when they drove him insane, but he wanted this moment with her to stay as private as it could be. That she was sitting here at all, talking this openly with him in the midst of all the chaotic noise and laughter around them, was some sort of miracle.

"Sorry." He grabbed her attention with that word. Said it again to be sure she understood he meant it. "Sorry. I know being an outcast isn't like being in a regular shifter community, and maybe I made an assumption."

For some reason, she flinched at that. But she kept listening.

"By regular shifter community, I mean in a clan, like bears, or in a pack, like wolves." His eyes probed hers at that, searching for comprehension. Nothing. Well, again, that wasn't too weird. Outcasts were almost never made up of single-species groups. They tended to be a mish-mash of shifter types. And mountain lions didn't even have groups, like a bear clan or a wolf pack. They usually had their family unit and that was it. Not to mention her family's outcast status could have prevented her from understanding some of the shifter world basics. He really needed to remember that.

Carefully, he kept trying. "Or even a whole shifter community like Deep Hollow." The buzz of the room around them filled the air with all of that. Community, connection, easy space. He was used to it. Grew up with it. The more he spent time with Marisa, the more he realized it was completely foreign to her.

What the fuck had growing up outcast done to her?

Frowning, he tapped his fingers on the squeaky vinyl of the booth. "Marisa, I admit I don't know much about outcasts. I just mean maybe you didn't get to experience a lot of the same things I did. But what I don't mean to do is to imply the way you grew up wasn't normal."

Her eyes snapped up to his, fast. This time, something like fear washed over her face. She spoke quickly. "No, that's true. Things were very different for me growing up. Nothing at all like the way you grew up. Or anyone else here." She gestured slightly at the rest of the table. "That's part of why I popped off at you yesterday, Riley. I don't really know how to...*be* in a group of regular shifters. I'm sorry."

His frown deepened. She kept apologizing for things that weren't her fault. "You didn't pop off on me, lion girl. You were speaking your truth. And that's always okay." The words left his lips almost as a whisper. It was like no one else was even here at the table with them, like they were suddenly in a little bubble of just the two of them talking.

"I was never allowed to speak my truth." Her gaze seemed far away. "Not growing up, and not with the Nefarious Desperados."

Riley peeled his lip back in distaste. "Nefarious Desperados? What is that, some sort of wack biker gang?"

She snorted a tiny noise that might almost have been a laugh, except that it was edged by anger. "Just the dumb name of the outcast group. The leader of the group called himself Nefarious. He liked to say he was one nefarious motherfucker in charge of a bunch of desperados." Her look darkened. "But he was just a huge jerk. A dangerous one who was cruel to all of us." Another look flitted over her face. One that seemed like she was having an unhappy memory. She looked up at Riley, her gaze searching his. Suddenly serious. "I'm glad I'm not with them anymore. I'd rather be here."

The last sentence fell out like an unexpected admission. Her eyes widened and she inhaled once, sharp. But she didn't take it back.

Very carefully, not wanting to startle her off, Riley said, "I'm glad you're here too."

He meant it.

They stayed quiet for a few moments. The laughter of their booth-mates and the growing number of diners in the restaurant provided a cheerful if loud backdrop to the moment.

Finally, Riley took a breath. He wanted to steer the conversation back to what they'd been talking about. "So about you popping off on me. Look. I was an ass to you, I said things I shouldn't have, and when I thought you were following me, I was even more of an ass. But," he said, watching her really carefully, talking even more carefully so he didn't make her shy away, "I think since you've been here, you've been holding things in. Not really talking about where you came from or anything that happened to you when you were with the outcasts. I think you just needed to let it out, and I gave you that opportunity. And that's why you popped off on me."

He ran out of words. Breathing kind of fast, almost nervous, his stomach filled with a weird little tension, he waited for her to respond. He wasn't usually this open with anyone except the cubs. And they were still kids, so he still shielded most of his pain and insecurities from them.

She searched his face for a long time, seeming as caught up in the quiet moment between them as he was. Finally, she offered a tentative smile that didn't quite lift her lips. "You know people really well, don't you? You understand things in a way I don't think anyone I've ever met really does. Why is that?"

Riley grabbed some fries, doused them in ketchup, and shoved them in his mouth to chew and swallow before he answered. "I started getting into meditation and a type of martial arts practice called aikido many years ago. Needed to do it to help me with bunch of stuff in my life. On the way, I learned an awful lot about why people sometimes do what they do and what's really going on. I'm not perfect at it, hell no. Witness: being a jackass to you yesterday."

He waved it off as she opened her mouth again, the words *I'm sorry* beginning to slip out of her pretty pink lips before he stopped her with a savage shake of his head. "Stop saying that. You don't have to apologize for everything. Like I said, I think others need to start apologizing to you more often. And you need to accept that, Marisa. Because you're worth it."

There was a lull at the table. Without thinking, he reached out his big hand to cover hers where it lay cradled in her lap. Just slipped his hand over hers, wanting to comfort her. Natural. She startled under it, fingers tensing.

Shit. She didn't like being crowded. Or touched without being asked. That she was sitting here, scrunched in this close to others, to him, was more than he'd seen her do yet. He started to pull his hand back, twitching his body away from hers as much as he could in the tiny space he had on the edge of the squeaky booth seat.

Then she shocked the hell out of him.

"Don't. Come back." She turned her palm up under his, catching at his hand, and twined her fingers over the back of it, stroking his knuckles, tracing the outlines of old scars. "What are these from?"

Her voice was light, almost breathy, but not in a silly, vapid girl way. In a way that said this moment was like the both of them held a tiny little hummingbird egg together, so small and fragile they could crush it without meaning to. She kept her gaze on her fingers, on his scars, but held onto his hand.

She didn't let go. Or ask him to.

Riley thought the air trapped in his lungs was making him lightheaded. He pushed it out, breathed in again, then turned it into words. "Those are from old fights. From a way of trying to forget what happened a long time ago. A way to make it better." He shrugged, studying the old scars as well. "Didn't work. Just left me those reminders. Every time I look at them, I remember."

Green eyes, shadowed, looked up at him though her fingers still traced the scars. "Remember what?" Her voice was slightly hoarse. Like it was hard for her to ask.

That, Riley understood. Some things were fucking brutal to remember, and he strongly suspected she knew that from a hard place of memories herself.

Before he could answer, her eyes flicked past him in the direction of where he could hear Laney and Finn playing a massive game of tickle with Grant and the Bain girls. Her hand pressed his for a long moment. Firm, like she was trying to etch the feel of his hand in hers.

Looking back at him, she guessed. "Their mom. Right? Something happened to her."

His bear rumbled. Knowing his eyes were probably just starting to glow, Riley kept his gaze locked on Marisa's, away from anywhere else in the room. "What do you know about it?"

Marisa shook her head. "Nothing. No one's ever said anything about her, and your kids haven't mentioned anything to me, either. But...she's not here. And you— you're so angry, Riley. I can sense it, deep down."

Her voice whispered so low he could barely catch it.

But it was an obvious truth, and it hung between them

Riley slowly took in another long breath through his nose, letting it fill him. He exhaled just as slowly, willing his heart to stop banging so hard. But when he spoke, it wasn't anywhere as difficult as he'd thought it would be to say it out loud, which he hadn't done in years since everyone here knew all about it. "Their mother died years ago. The twins were only two."

Marisa's face was impassive, but her eyes began to glow too. "What happened to her?"

The words flowed out quick and simple like they meant nothing, even though they meant everything that his life had become. "She was killed. Murdered."

Marisa barely sucked in a quiet breath, but her hand clenched on his so hard it almost hurt. "I—was it outcasts? Did they do it? Is that why you were so suspicious of me? Why Quentin was too?"

He eased his hand back over hers, now the one stroking her. Her hand was so small in his. Small, but strong. It fit into his just right. He felt the crazy urge to protect her. To keep her from awful truths in the world. But he knew, without knowing the details, that Marisa was already aware just how awful this world could be.

"No." He said the words fast, not breaking eye contact. Holding her in this small but enormous space as he told her the reason behind his out-of-control bear. His reason for needing to fight every day to stay sane and focused. His reason for being cold and cruel whenever anyone new, even a shifter like herself, appeared in his home.

"It was shifter hunters. Humans who know about us and hunt us for fun. They somehow found out about her. They stalked her and the cubs one day when they were all out playing in the mountains in their animal forms. She managed to hide the cubs and led the hunters away from them."

His voice was calm as he spoke. So calm it felt like it wasn't even him talking. "They shot her dead and left her body for me to find hours later. The cubs don't have nightmares about it anymore. But I do, and I wasn't even there when they murdered my mate. Shifter hunters took her from us like she was only an animal, some dumb creature they could use for sport. But they knew full well she was human, and a mother, and they shot her dead anyway."

Whiteness dropped so fast over Marisa's face it was like seeing a color screen suddenly turn to black and white. She began breathing in gasps, like she was about to hyperventilate or pass out. Alarmed, Riley stopped talking, but she suddenly shoved at him, yanking her hand out of his.

"Let me out. Please," she whispered in a ragged, panic-stricken tone. The sound of it was so desperate he somehow leapt backward out of the booth, almost landing on his ass in the aisle.

She moved out of the booth fast and bolted down the hallway toward the bathrooms, looking like a terrified rabbit fleeing imminent death—not like a mountain lion shifter as strong as he knew she was deep down.

"Riley!" Abby's voice was a few octaves higher than usual. The entire table went quiet. Luckily no one else in Whatchu Want had noticed, since it now was packed with diners and the volume was significantly up. "What happened? Is she going to be sick? I knew that shift was a bad one." She fretted, looking like she was about to get up and follow. Then, she suddenly lowered her brow and cast a fierce look at him. "Or was it you again? What did you say to her now?"

Quentin, Slade, and Shane all suddenly glared at Riley. Despite what any of them might have thought about an outcast plopped into their midst, none of them saw any reason to disrespect a woman.

"Nothing like that!" Riley looked wild-eyed at them, then back down the hall where Marisa had disappeared into the ladies' room. He wanted to follow, but something told him she needed a second to herself. Maybe a lot of seconds. There was nowhere else to go down the hallway except the bathrooms, so she was safely tucked away back there for a few minutes.

"I just—never mind." He swung his head back around to plant an equally fierce glare on his family. "You know what? She and I were having a private conversation, and it's none of your business."

Shane snorted, pulling Jessie close to him. "Nothing in this family is private."

"Yeah, well, this is," Riley snapped back. "I'm going to go hang out with my kids for a minute. They know better than to pry into shit that isn't their concern," he added with a pointed look in turn at the five of his damned nosy adult kin sitting at the booth.

Then he stalked over to where his kids played with their friends, casting only one glance toward the hallway Marisa had fled down. Not following her made his entire body shudder with the effort, but he forced himself to leave her alone for just a few minutes.

Whatever demons haunted the sexy lion girl, telling her about his own family's brutal history had just triggered them into overdrive. If she was like him, she needed some time to pull her shit together and not let her cat get the better of her.

Much as it half destroyed him to do it, right now he had to let her face whatever hellacious demons tormented her on her own.

But if she didn't come back in five minutes or less, he was going to head straight to her and help her fight them.

She wouldn't need to fight alone ever again.

Marisa burst into the thankfully empty bathroom. She raced to a stall, yanked the door back, and hovered over the porcelain bowl, ready for the dry heaves she could feel building inside her to turn into actual puking.

After a few minutes of waiting in dread for what turned out to be nothing, she realized the only reason she wasn't going to hurl was because there was nothing in her to come up. Whatever bad kitty had eaten yesterday had already been absorbed into her system, and the only thing she'd eaten since then were the few fries the waitress had brought. Apparently, they weren't ready to leave.

Small victories.

Wiping a hand across her mouth anyway, she backed out of the stall and turned to the sink to splash water on her face. The sight of herself in the mirror shocked her to a stop. She was whiter than a ghost. Whiter than the polar bear shifter who'd been a reluctant member of the outcasts, the only one Marisa could even vaguely call a greatly watered-down version of a friend.

Her face looked like hell, but it was her eyes that startled her the most. Her cat was blazing inside them. Raging, glowing out so fiercely any human who looked at her right now would either scream and run or fall to the ground in a flat out faint.

Good thing no one else was in here with her. She needed to calm down. She needed to get hold of herself. Of her inner animal.

"Hush, you," she croaked to the mirror, gazing back at the wild, angry eyes. "Simmer down," she whispered at the shadow of her bad kitty she could see sliding around in them.

Closing her eyes to block out the sight of her own pasty expression, the inner wildness that seeped out, threatening to cause her to lose control, she turned on the taps to splash icy cold water all over her face and throat. Gasping as the water rolled down under the front of her shirt and ran into her bra, she made herself be relentless. She tossed water onto her face, scrubbed at it with her hands, pressed her shaking fingers against her eyes to push away the wild glow.

The panic, the sorrow, the rage in them.

Shifter hunters.

The words curdled her blood. Shifter hunters were

sick, awful humans who hunted shifters, but not just for fun, as Riley thought.

They hunted shifters for cold hard cash.

Some people, random humans, maybe even the government, had somehow found out shifters existed. They tracked them down to capture or kill. Killing them wasn't usual. Capturing them to turn them over to secret agencies that put them into cages in horrific labs and studied them was much more common. Shifter hunters got way bigger bounties for bringing living shifters to the labs. They still got paid for dead ones, but live shifters were the real prize.

Funnily enough, living shifters had been the reason her parents had finally met their ends.

Thinking about her parents curdled Marisa's blood even more. Secrets, so many secrets. Secrets she hadn't yet told anyone here. She hadn't been lying to Riley when she said she didn't know anything about the outcasts. That she kept no outcast secrets from him or his clan. That was true. The outcasts had wanted her for one reason, and that was to breed. They told her very little about any of their plans, dumb and poorly thought out as those usually were. Clever, the outcasts were not.

No, she wasn't keeping outcast secrets from Riley and the wonderful, kind, fun and funny Silvertip shifters.

But the secrets she did keep would get her shoved out from them anyway, now that Riley had told her about his mate. Now she knew the reason behind his haunted expression, the reason for his angry vigilance. He despised outcasts as much as he did shifter hunters, as did the entire Silvertip clan, and they would make an outcast of her again if they found out the truth.

Which was yet another reason she needed to be put down. She *had* to be put down.

Didn't matter that Riley was sexy and said she smelled good and held her hand and thought she was worthy of respect. That she was worthy of apologies.

Didn't matter that his kids, his cubs, were darling angels who made the bitter knots all tangled up inside her loosen just a smidgen more each time they smiled at her or wanted to tell her all about their day.

Didn't matter that Abby might be thinking of her as a friend, that they all took her to this goofy restaurant in the little shifter town that was their home and made her smile for the first time in forever.

None of that would matter at all once they discovered her real secrets. Her horrible, ugly, dark secrets that she'd thought had nothing to do with anything here but now had everything to do with all of it.

Pulling harsh paper towels out of the clunky old-school dispenser on the wall, she rubbed them over her face, savagely wiping away the water with their appropriately rough texture. Wadding them into a crude ball, she slammed them into the waste bin as she left the bathroom, steeling herself for the next thing.

The thing where she said thank you to the Silvertip

clan, but now it was time for her to go. The thing where she stepped into the growing dark outside and tried to figure out where to run next.

The thing where she said goodbye to Riley and to his beautiful children and left them behind.

Taking a deep breath, she pulled open the door—and almost smacked right into someone. Marisa gulped and stepped back, despite bad kitty trying to send a hiss up her throat.

Haley. Mate of Cortez, Riley's brother. Ex of Justin, who had deliberately ruined Haley's life, in part because Marisa had turned him into a shifter. Haley, whose marriage had been destroyed because of Marisa.

Haley stared at Marisa like she was an alien who made no sense at all. "Hi," she said, looking at her very carefully. Like she wasn't sure if Marisa might not try to bite her. Or, more likely, because Marisa looked like crap right now. "Can we talk?"

Marisa didn't answer. She was trying to not let bad kitty come snarling out. The mountain lion in her felt tense and defensive. Ready to tear through Marisa's fragile hold on her and bust out with claws extended.

Breathe, damn it. Just freaking *breathe* and stay present.

She jerked her head in a nod and stepped out into the hallway. Glancing quickly out at the dining area, she looked for Riley but couldn't see him. That he hadn't followed her to the bathroom, hadn't stood outside waiting to hear if she was okay, should have hurt a bit, but it didn't. Riley had known she needed a moment. He might not have known why, but he'd recognized her need for space the same way she was sure his fearsome grizzly bear needed space a lot of the time too.

She was going to have to leave him, run somewhere else, find another shifter group that had someone strong and ruthless enough to put her down, and *that* truth hurt. Knowing she had to leave him and his cubs, when just a few days ago it wouldn't have mattered, hurt.

Bad kitty liked Riley. Marisa liked Riley. Riley seemed to like her. She understood none of it, but it was all true.

The hiss still willfully caught in her throat threatened to turn into a choked cry of crazy pain.

Being a shifter fucking sucked. Especially being a truly fucked-up shifter.

She took a breath, fortifying herself. Squaring herself by planting her feet firmly on the floor, Marisa raised her head to look at Haley, who was taller. "Okay." Her voice wavered but held steady. "Lay it on me."

Haley blinked. "Uh, lay what on you?" She sounded genuinely puzzled.

Crinkling up her brow, Marisa kept pushing bad kitty back to where she could just let Marisa be for a moment. "Everything. We haven't talked since—that day," she awkwardly stumbled over the memory of the terrible bridge battle. "But now's a good time." She glanced again down the hallway, calculating whether she could reach the front door before Riley or his kids saw her leave.

No. She couldn't leave without seeing them again. Or without having this conversation with Haley.

"So," she returned her attention to the confused blonde woman, "go ahead and let me have it. How much you hate me because of Justin. Because of what I did to him. And because of what that did to you," she finished in a low voice.

Haley's expression abruptly cleared. "Oh. Marisa," she cocked her head to the side, a small frown creeping on her face now, "do you think I'm angry at you?"

Marisa looked cautiously at the other woman. Funny, because she was the one who'd really been the other woman in the situation between her and Haley, although naturally she hadn't known, since as it turned out Justin was a lying sack of lying liar. "Aren't you?"

Haley leaned back against the wall of the hallway, crossed her arms over her chest, and studied Marisa for a long moment. It was seriously uncomfortable. Marisa managed not to squirm. Still somewhat struggling to keep in bad kitty's hisses helped with that.

Finally, Haley murmured, "I had a feeling he did it to you too. What he did to me. The games, the manipulation. Being a total psychopath, especially at the end. I never hated you, Marisa. Well," she corrected herself, rolling her eyes skyward for a second, "in the very beginning, I did. When he told me about your existence, that he was leaving me for you, yeah, I hated you. But I had no idea who you were back then. I didn't know about any of this."

Haley waved a hand between the two of them. Now it was Marisa's turn to stare at her, confused. "This...what?"

"Being shifters. I knew they existed because of my friend Pix, but I had no idea that's what happened to Justin. I just thought you were human, like me. I had no idea you were a shifter and that you had turned him."

That ugly truth thumped into the air between them, heavy and raw. Marisa didn't answer at first. Clattering sounds, sizzling noises, and busy voices from the kitchen floated out, mingling with the swell of conversation from the dining room with the thumping new song on the jukebox that finally wasn't country. She found herself wondering if the table she'd fled would be singing to this one too. Finally, she said in a low voice, "I didn't do it by choice. I was forced to."

To her surprise, a faint smile turned up Haley's lips as she shrugged. "I know. That didn't bother me. Well, it did because I really started to think about what that would've meant for you."

"For me?"

Golden strands of Haley's hair bounced on her shoulders as she nodded. "Yeah. Cortez told me a lot about being a shifter after he turned me that day." A sudden smile burst over her face, lighting her up with a palpable joy.

What would that feel like? Joy at being turned? There had been no joy when Marisa was forced to turn Justin.

"Just being a shifter myself now, knowing what it was like when I asked Cortez to turn me, made me understand a little bit about how awful it must have been for you, turning Justin and losing him in the battle. Oh," Haley swiftly changed topics. "I wanted to apologize to you for not talking to you sooner. I do have a deadline for my book"—Haley was an author, which was amazing to Marisa, who could barely read, let alone fathom writing a book all by herself—"but that wasn't the only reason." She heaved a sigh. "I'm just a big chickenshit. True story. But I really am sorry. I should have come and talked to you sooner."

Apologies. Actual, genuine apologies, to *her*. First Riley, now Haley. Marisa felt rocked by the amazingness of these things. Two people apologizing to her the same day when no one ever had apologized to her in her entire life. Was this some sort of record or what?

She turned back to what Haley had said. Suddenly, she needed to correct it. "That's not all true, by the way. It wasn't awful for me when Justin died. Well, it was," she amended. But she couldn't tell Haley exactly why. That was one of the dark secrets she still needed to keep close. "I didn't love him, Haley. Not once, not ever.

You're right, he was a psychopath. A monster. And he became an even worse one after I turned him." Something hot bubbled in her throat now. Not a hiss. "I have to apologize to you." The words pushed out, thick with the heat of tears that fought against bad kitty's subsiding hisses. "When I turned him, it made him worse. Because we weren't mates. There was no bond between us. Not even attraction, not really. And apparently if you turn someone without it being because you love them, it makes your animal go crazy."

She whispered those last words. Partially because the tears were clinging to her throat, partially because it was a horrible admission. A terrible, terrible truth.

"I'm the reason he went totally insane and tried to turn you so you'd be forced to join the outcasts too, Haley. I'm sorry."

Haley's mouth had opened somewhere during Marisa's rapid speech, but not like she was shocked. More like she was trying to say something. But instead of speaking, she suddenly moved forward and pulled Marisa in for a hug. A tight, clutch-y, girlfriend-y type of hug.

Marisa did hiss this time, shock ricocheting through her. She struggled for half a second then stopped. Haley had already let go, stepped back. Back against the wall, watching Marisa with a solemn face.

"I'm not sorry I did that. I know you don't like being touched without warning. Abby told us all."

Abby was nice. So nice. Leaving her would hurt too.

"But," Haley watched her so closely now Marisa was halfway sure the other woman was trying to read her mind, "I think that's not true anymore."

"What's not true?" Marisa's whisper was too low for a normal human to hear, but Haley and her super sensitive hearing could pick up on her words no matter what.

"That you don't crave closeness with other shifters. I think the outcasts messed you up. All shifters enjoy touch. Cortez told me that, and he was right. Because they need to be close to one another, they need to know the others are there for them. I think the outcasts tried to ruin that for you. But it didn't work. And you needed a hug. And I gave you one, and I hope you don't hate me for it. Because when I was really sad, I needed hugs too. So I'm not sorry, because I can tell it didn't bother you as much as you were afraid it would."

Marisa's mouth would have hung open, but she was keeping herself tucked up, tucked into herself, like she usually did to stay safe. She found herself saying, "It wasn't terrible. It was really thoughtful of you. Thank you," she whispered.

Her mountain lion flitted through her, hisses and growls muted. But still there. She tugged at Marisa. Tugged at her to go.

Haley turned to head back into the dining room. Then she stopped quick and turned back to Marisa. "Don't leave. You're wanted here. I can tell Riley likes you. And his kids seem to adore you. And you're not the enemy. Stay."

"How—why would I be leaving?" Marisa held her breath, waiting for Haley's answer.

Haley sighed. "Because you think you're not wanted. But that's not true. Don't leave them. Don't leave us, Marisa." Her expression was suddenly fierce. "You are wanted here. And if you need a new home, I think this is a really great place to make that happen. It's working out really well for me so far," she added, that little smile lighting up her face again.

That look meant she was thinking about Cortez, her mate, the one who'd turned her because she wanted it. She'd loved him so much, she wanted to become a shifter too. That was love. At least, Marisa thought so. She'd never had love before, or seen it be a healthy, good thing between two people. Her parents had been...monsters.

Her cat paced and muttered inside her, sending shivers of nervousness skittering through her.

"Maybe we could be friends too," Haley offered shyly. "Pix is my bestie, and Abby and Jessie are awesome, but there's always room for another friend. Always," she said firmly. "Especially someone as nice as I suspect you are under that mask you like to wear. And I can tell you're good for Riley. And his kids." Her tone turned solemn again. "Don't leave yet, Marisa. Please." She held out her hand, as if to take Marisa's and lead her back into the dining area.

Don't leave. The words hung between them again, but this time not heavy. Not ugly.

Hopeful. Kind. Welcoming.

Bad kitty hissed. No. This was too much. Too scary.

Haley's eyes widened, started to glow as her bear shot protectively to the forefront. But she inhaled, clearly trying to keep herself steady. Her hand stayed stretched out. Still welcoming.

No one's your friend, you dumb little bitch. No one gives a shit about anyone else, least of all you.

No! Bad kitty hissed and scratched, forcing her way out. Pushing, clawing, demanding to take over. To take charge.

To run and hide. To flee to safety.

Oh, shit.

"I can't." She started to hiss. A cat's low, fierce growl. "She won't let me."

Gasping, feeling the change start to come over her without her permission, just like always, Marisa whirled in a panic, pelting down the hallway toward the front door of the restaurant. She barely heard the beat of the jukebox music, barely noticed those she shoved out of her way in her frantic need to escape before it was too late.

I don't want to leave yet, the words whispered in her skull as she raced around the outside of the building, seeking and finding an alley behind it, dark and hidden from anyone's gaze, her cat already beginning to rage out of her, her bones shrieking with pain as they shifted. *I'm sorry, Riley,* was her last coherent thought before bad kitty leapt out of her, swallowing up Marisa and hurtling away on four paws.

Running, running, fleeing everything here. Taking her to the mountains, into the quiet dark and cold. To leave the world that made no damned sense and would never, ever be safe.

"Are you sure you checked all of the back fifty behind the barn?" Riley heard the hard edge to his voice as he snapped at Abby, but he didn't care. Marisa had been gone for three hours now. Yes, she'd come back yesterday, but this time felt different.

Too different. Bad different.

His bear raged and thundered around inside him, desperately wanting to shift back into that form. Riley held on with every last scrap of will he had. He knew he stank of huge, angry bruin, since he'd just run the entire eleven miles from outside Whatchu Want directly through the forested wilds back here to the lodge searching for Marisa. Following her nervous scent.

Why was she nervous?

The look on her face after he told her what happened to his mate, and then what Haley had told him about her brief conversation with Marisa in the hallway at the restaurant, how Marisa had bolted out of there, clearly about to shift and totally unable to stop it—ahh, fuck. It all told him that this time, things were different. Marisa's pain, whatever the hell had happened to her to break her spirit and make her want to die, had really come roaring up for her. Trying to control her. Whatever reasons she had for wanting to be put down, they were real to her.

After she disappeared from the restaurant, he'd instantly known something was really wrong. Half frantic already, trying to hold his shit together in public as well as in front of Finn and Laney, he'd asked Slade if he would keep the twins with him while the rest of them went to search for Marisa. Riley and Abby had decided to shift in the dark behind the restaurant to follow her scent. Quentin had wanted to come too, but Abby had gently said he might frighten her. So far, the people she seemed to know best here were Abby and—she said with a knowing look at him—Riley. Marisa trusted them.

Marisa trusted him. He didn't know why she did, but it made him feel somehow essential.

He'd held on to that thought as he and Abby had bounded through the dark, following Marisa's trail. She'd veered in a beeline straight toward the lonely heart of the mountains then abruptly circled back to the lodge. They'd lost her scent on the lodge property, however, since her scent already lingered everywhere up there merely from the time she'd spent there so far. Had she stayed here? Left again? The only reason he hadn't thundered back over the entire open mountain range was because Quentin, Shane, Jessie, Haley, and Cortez had gotten to the lodge in their cars by the time he arrived in a panic. They were positive Marisa was here somewhere.

He was beyond distraught about her. Deep down, he was terrified.

Abby's voice was calm when she answered him now, laying a quelling hand on Quentin, who had turned on Riley with the protective anger of a bear whose mate was being disrespected. "She's not in the back fifty acres behind the barn. Her scent definitely circled back around to the front, so I don't think she's far from the main part of the property. Oh," she suddenly said, surprise brightening her voice as she looked at him. Then she turned to look at the others gathered there, milling about in concern as everyone tried to figure out which way to go next. "Has anyone checked her cabin?"

With a moan that was partly anger at himself and partly relieved hope, Riley whirled, rocketing the several hundred yards toward Marisa's cabin, the others on his heels. As he tore up to it, he suddenly skidded to a halt. Relief swept him as his eyes, accustomed to the darkness that had fallen, fought against the bright snap of the porch light to see her sitting there. She sat at the top of the stoop, leaning against the railing as if too exhausted to sit up straight.

Behind him, he heard Abby draw a sharp breath of relief. She murmured, "Be gentle."

Always. He would always be gentle with Marisa.

Riley slowly walked up to her, keeping his eyes locked on her face. She seemed listless, but when she raised her eyes to his, he could see the bright flare of her cat in there. Emotions paraded across her face, clear as a beacon. Uncertainty. Fear. Despair, ugly, painful despair that was beginning to break him. Witnessing the suffering she was going through was nearly as painful as the worst experience he'd had in his life.

He thought he knew what that might mean, but now wasn't the time to think about that. Now, he just wanted to be sure she wouldn't run again.

"I couldn't go without saying goodbye." Her breath heaved when she spoke, as if she held back tears, the only brightness in her eyes coming from the glow of her cat. "She let me come back here."

Without asking, he knew she meant her mountain lion.

"I need to leave, Riley." She looked at him, really looked at him, her eyes catching his and sending a stab through his chest at her vulnerability. She glanced past him to the others, back to him. Her gaze moving back and forth between Riley and them, speaking to all of them, she whispered, "You've all been so nice to me. You took me in, even though you knew nothing about me except I came from them." She didn't need to say the word *outcasts.* "But I can't stay."

She stood up, the breath still heaving in her chest. Riley abruptly realized how hard it was for her to say all of this. He longed so badly to go to her, to comfort her, but again something told him to just wait and let her speak. She needed to say whatever it was she was about to say.

"My mountain lion is out of control. I can't control her. So I left the restaurant. Haley," she said softly, looking toward Haley, or at least Riley assumed she must be since he wouldn't take his gaze off her face, "you were right. You could see it. I've been trying so hard to not let everyone know, because I know how dangerous it is for shifters to know another one's animal is out of control. That's part of why I've been asking you all to put me down." Her eyes moved back to Riley's, their color as dark as the trees shadowed by the night around them. "I know you think you can help me. But you can't. No one can."

Abby finally said, "Yes, we can, Marisa. Just let us—"

Marisa shook her head violently, her dark red hair stringy around her face. "You don't understand. I can't tell you all of it because it's too awful." Her tone was so gutted it stabbed at Riley. He felt his bear raging inside him, but not with the need to break free and just go rampaging through the woods looking for the unknown meaning behind her pain.

No.

His bear wanted to go to Marisa.

To comfort her.

To protect her.

Abruptly, Marisa went down to the bottom of the steps, now standing just a few feet away from Riley. He towered over her, suddenly realizing how genuinely small she was. Beautiful woman. Tortured woman. Her soul was splintering apart right in front of him, and he felt helpless to stop it. She looked at him, her face half terrified and half certain. Audibly swallowing, the light from her cat's eyes glowing even brighter, her face rippling with the struggle to hold back the wildcat, she shuddered, forcing out the next words.

"My family, my parents..." She stopped. Swallowed noisily before she went on. "They were shifter hunters."

A gasp. It sounded like Jessie. Then a growl that could have been anyone's.

Riley flinched in shock at the words but he stayed rooted to the spot, listening. His body felt cold.

Unwavering, Marisa went on. "I was born to humans. I was human."

Another gasp from behind him. Riley didn't look away from Marisa.

Her voice caught on itself now. Scratchy, thick with emotion. "They hunted your kind. They said you were monsters. Monsters." She shook her head. "They were the monsters. And then—then."

Her voice broke, and Riley almost went toward her. But she snapped her gaze at him, her cat fierce in her expression, warning him away. Protecting herself even as she gave herself up. Every centimeter of his body trembled as he ruthlessly forced himself to stand still. To simply keep listening to what she had to say.

Keeping her eyes right on his, their brilliant light glowing in the dark, she went on in a flat tone. "Outcasts who knew what my parents were captured me and my brother one day. Nefarious's group. He bit and turned us right in front of our parents, not that they would have cared anyway." Even though her voice stayed flat, the sheer pain of those words scratched the air like a dagger. "Then he had his outcasts kill them while we were in our first change, and I was glad to see them dead. They never loved me or Derek. They hated us for existing."

Her voice was soft, almost far away. But she kept looking at Riley. Making sure he heard her.

"The outcasts took us to live with them. Nefarious wanted us to be like them. He wanted some sort of army of crazy shifters he could control. Because he knew what would happen to us since we were turned against our will."

The night was so silent, so deep, it felt like a living presence. Riley's head felt like it might explode, then it compressed, then it expanded again. His chest heaved like Marisa's, everything inside wanting to punch out. To smash something.

In a soft but relentless voice, she went on. "He knew we would go crazy eventually. That we would not be able to control our animals, that we'd give in to the worst base instincts. But since he made us, he'd be able to control us. He wanted that. He said he could use that for his own ends. That's why he made us turn more humans. Like Justin." She finally moved her gaze away from Riley, looking behind him. He didn't need to turn to know she looked at Haley. He could feel the horror rising from the others, all the hair on the back of his neck prickling at how charged their energy was.

Marisa looked back at Riley. Her words stayed calm, so calm they were expressionless. "I can't control my cat. I'm going crazy because she was forced into me, and it wasn't my choice. I'm dangerous, Riley. I was already from bad stock, and now I'm actually dangerous. And I'm so sorry about your mate," she whispered, dark sorrow finally flickering in her eyes. "My parents didn't kill her, but it could have been them just as easily. I know they turned in or killed others."

His bear churned inside him, clawing to get out. Riley knew his eyes glowed as bright as Marisa's.

She screamed suddenly, the noise a horrifying blend of woman and wildcat. He jerked at the sound, heard snow crunch behind him as the others must have all reacted too. "I'm begging you, please, put me down. Please." Her voice was a ragged cry now, shoved out in pure desperation. "I'm not worth saving."

She abruptly flung herself onto the cold snow, exposing her throat to the night air and the horrified eyes of everyone surrounding her.

Waiting to be killed.

Quentin stepped forward, his eyes as bright as everyone else's.

Roaring, Riley leapt in between Marisa and his brother. Ready to defend her. "Don't you touch her," he snarled, his voice so low it rumbled through him.

Quentin threw his hands up, slowly shaking his head. "Riley. Peace. I wanted to make sure *you* weren't going to do anything you'd regret later."

Riley snarled at his brother. Low, long, serious. So serious that everyone else got major glowing eyes as well, and Jessie, who'd only very recently been turned into a bear shifter by Shane, looked nervous, even though her own bear clearly moved under her skin and in her eyes.

Voice still snarling, Riley said, "I've got this. Back off."

Without looking at them again, he dropped to his knees in the snow beside Marisa. The ice-skimmed cold seeped through his jeans, but he didn't give a shit. He could hear her heart beating so loud it practically thumped through her shirt. Her eyes were closed, her breath making little white puffs into the cold night air that he could see in the gleam the porch light cast out. Gently, he reached out to touch her shoulder. She stiffened, breath speeding up, her eyes still closed.

Then she wrecked him completely by arching her neck back more and exposing it for a kill strike.

A groan born of mixed rage at everyone in her life who'd made her feel worthless and the pain he understood burned up his throat, sounding out into the dark as a sharp keen. "Marisa." His voice cracked. "No one is putting you down. Least of all me."

Her eyes opened, but she stared at the sky above them. "My parents were the same kind of monsters who murdered your mate. Who murdered Finn and Laney's *mom*." Her voice broke on that word, sending slivers into Riley's heart too at the old, never forgotten sorrow. "And then there's me." She finally moved her gaze to look at him, though she still lay crumpled on the snow, neck gleaming under the soft yellow glow from the cabin porch light.

"I wasn't born a shifter, Riley. That was forced onto me, forced into me. My cat is crazy. I don't remember anything when I'm her, when I'm out there as her." Her voice heaved. "I'm just going to get crazier until I really do snap. I won't be responsible for hurting anyone here. I couldn't handle that. She's in control, and I'm not."

Silence stretched for a long, tense moment. Then another quiet plea. "Put me down."

The last three words were a whisper, one that crawled out of her throat.

Riley clenched his hand on her shoulder, feeling how bony it still was. "No," he said softly. "It's not true."

"W-what?" Her brow furrowed slightly. Her breathing slowed somewhat.

His voice trembled with the effort to not shout the words so she would understand. "Marisa, you're not going crazy. Your cat isn't in control. Or if she is, she's on your side."

Now she finally moved her head, turning it so her fragile neck no longer jutted up as an offer for something no one here would take. Hair and snow clung to one cheek as she looked at him. "I don't understand."

Even though his voice stayed low, soft, Riley put every bit of conviction and strength he had into his words. "I would never judge you for the sins of your parents. You are good people, Marisa Tully. You are a good person."

He watched her eyes staring at him, unblinking. But her lower lip trembled.

"And your cat isn't crazy. Neither are you."

"How do you know?" Her whisper was so low it almost melted into the snow.

"Because," he slid his hand down her arm to gently grip just above her elbow, ready to help pull her up, "she came back here, didn't she? Because she knew you couldn't leave without saying goodbye. She let you come back. You are your cat, and you remembered to come back."

The lip tremble turned into a shake, then an earthquake as her whole face crumpled in on itself. Then, the floodgates opened and tears began sliding down her cheeks, running down her chin. Faster and faster, and she didn't even try to stop them. He pulled her up, unresisting, until she was on her feet. Small, thin, impossibly beautiful woman. Leaning into him, now her shoulders shaking. She was getting the front of his shirt wet. His bear roared. The need to protect her, to keep her safe while she finally let go and cried it all out, overwhelmed him. He had to get her inside where she could feel safe. With him.

Finally he glanced back at where everyone else still stood, collectively almost holding their breath as the scene played out. Shane looked solemnly at Marisa now sobbing into Riley's chest, pulling Jessie close to him in some sort of protective response to seeing another woman bawling. Haley, also snuggled into Cortez, looked like she might cry too. Abby, oddly enough, seemed pleased, although her eyes mirrored the shock Riley knew everyone there felt.

He looked at Quentin. His brother still had some doubt on his face. Riley gave him a hard stare. Quentin grunted under his breath, one side of his mouth tucking up in an accepting half-smile. Nodding once at Riley, he then turned to his mate and simply said, "Looks like he's got things handled here."

Abby nodded, hair gleaming under the first shafts of moonlight rising from the east. "And Slade's got the cubs for the night. He texted me to say whatever's going on, he's got them as long as Riley needs. Everyone will be fine. Let's leave these two alone. Let me know if she needs anything in the morning," she added to Riley as she turned to Quentin, tucking her arm through his as they strolled away.

Riley watched his clan members as they left. Trusting him to not only take care of Marisa, but that he'd keep them safe too from whatever demons lurked in her past.

Deep inside, uneasiness whispered that Marisa's past wasn't done with them yet. For now, though, all he could focus on was keeping his beautiful lion girl safe and sound. Brushing a kiss over her hair, he murmured, "I've got you. I've got you, you're safe with me. Come on." He gently walked her into the cabin, knowing with every fiber of his being that even if he didn't know exactly why, everything had just changed for good.

Marisa was his to keep safe from now on. After the cubs, she was the most important thing in the world. He would do anything to protect his sexy lion girl.

No matter what dangers might still wait for them.

12

Marisa barely felt the steps up to her cabin under her feet as Riley opened the door and guided them inside. Her entire body felt detached from her, as if it were a puppet she controlled but couldn't feel. The tears were unstoppable. They poured out of her as if she'd had an ocean locked inside, one that finally had broken free of its dams. It was terrifying but so necessary all at once.

She let the tears come since she was helpless to halt them anyway. Riley's big, protective arms were wrapped around her tight, but not so tight she didn't have the space to howl out her pain. He just held her close, held her safe.

Safer than she'd ever felt in her life.

Completely unrestrained, she let herself bawl in earnest. Crying it all out seemed to be the only thing she was capable of at the moment. The relief of finally having told everyone the truth of her life was immense. The tears were like a final cleanse, clearing out all the hurts, the doubts, the old wounds. Washing away the primal fear that she was broken beyond repair and unfixable.

Riley held her close as she sobbed, his mouth dropping small kisses on her head, his arms strong and sure around her as the two of them stood in the middle of the cabin's small living room. His strong, hard body, the one that seemed like it could take on a thousand enemies and win, protected her from the world. But at the same time, his strength allowed her to fall apart.

This was a true release, and he was giving it to her. Even through her tears, Marisa felt enormous gratitude that he was a strong enough man to let her cry and not try to stop it until she was ready.

Slowly, so slowly, the heaving sobs eventually dwindled. It felt like she'd cried it all out, emptying a lifetime's worth of pain. The tears finally ebbed to a stop, though her heart still felt raw. But she also felt...light. So light, as if the heavy burdens she'd carried for so long had finally been lifted.

It felt like a precious miracle.

Marisa felt mixed rumbling in her chest. Suddenly more aware, she pushed back.

No. No growling, not now. She wasn't letting bad kitty out. She wouldn't let out a snarl, or aggravated hissing, or the incessant demand to change so she could flee again across the empty mountains. She wouldn't—

Wait. Wait, wait, wait. Marisa stopped short. She almost held her breath as she listened to her own body.

This was different. She couldn't identify the rumbling in her chest, but it wasn't a growl.

Riley whispered a laugh over her head, his warm breath stirring her hair. "Are you purring?" His voice was a low, comforting rumble by her ear. She could hear the smile in it.

Abruptly, she was fully back in her body. Lifting both hands, she splayed her fingers out, pressing her palms over her chest. Low, faint, but steady. There. "Is that what that is?" She could hear the wonder in her own voice.

Bad kitty knew how to *purr?*

Riley briefly nuzzled the top of her head, which made the rumbling in her chest intensify. "I think so, pretty kitty. Pretty lion girl." He stepped back and very gently took her shoulders, turned her so she faced him. "Beautiful lion *woman.* Strong, sexy woman. Yes, that's your cat purring." A big smile curved up both sides of his mouth.

She stared back at him, still feeling the vibrations beneath her hands, looking closely at him as she tried to figure out what was different about his face. It hit her. "Your eyes. They're really blue, aren't they?"

He chuckled again, those amazing eyes still drinking her up. "Always have been."

She shook her head, finally taking away one hand to

reach forward. Tentatively, she touched the stubble on his cheek. Oh, sexy man. "No, they haven't. I'd swear they were blacker than night the first, I don't know, dozen times I ever saw you."

He blew out a sigh, glancing around her cabin. "Yeah. I know. I get really dark when I'm angry. When—" He paused, seeming to search for the right words. His glance came back, settled on her again. "When I thought about what had happened to my family. Every time I thought about it, I had to work so hard to leash my bear that it took all my energy. I know that made me grim. Mean, sometimes."

He huffed a breath again, leaning into her palm where it rested on his cheek. "It scared me when I began to realize I was so enraged over what they had done that I was losing control over my bear. Over everything. Even over my own happiness," he said, as if he'd just realized it. "Huh. I never really thought about it that way. But it's true. The only thing that kept me grounded was finding something to balance, which was the aikido and the cubs. I've kept my shit together for them. They're never losing another parent."

He said it so fiercely, she could see his bear rumbling deep in the shadows of his eyes.

But they stayed that sexy, clear blue.

She nodded. This moment suddenly felt both strained but light, heavy but gentle. "What was her name?"

133

"Grace." The way he said the name spoke volumes, but she didn't hear the deep sorrow of someone clinging to something long gone.

She just heard him honoring his dead mate, as a good man should.

"And you found the ones who killed her?" Her stark words were calm, but her cat stopped purring. She seemed, instead, suddenly wary.

There was a long beat. As she watched, fascinated, his eyes definitely darkened again. The stormy sky blue went closer to navy. By the way he clenched his jaw, she knew he fought to keep himself on an even keel. After another moment, his eyes slowly started shading into the lighter blue. Then he shook his head. "No. They're still out there. That's part of why I didn't trust you at first, Marisa. Knowing they're out there has made me not trust strangers. Mostly humans, but unknown shifters, too. And," his voice hardened again, "we know some outcasts have worked with shifter hunters before, to get them to take out enemies."

Shock and anger lashed through her at that terrible piece of news. Shifters, even if they were outcasts, working *with* shifter hunters? Against their own kind? The thought was enraging.

He nodded, then shoved up one shoulder in a regretful half shrug, keeping his eyes locked on hers. "Yeah. So partially because we knew that, Quentin didn't want to trust you either. He's suspicious of everything anyway. But he said Abby was so convinced you had just been used, that you were caught up in something you wanted no part of, that he wouldn't let me do anything. Like interrogate you."

Her voice suddenly threatened to stick in her mouth, but she managed to shove out the words . "Would you have? Interrogated me?"

He shook his head, slowly but firmly. "No. I wanted to, but I couldn't. My bear was so interested in you. I was so interested in you. I knew you weren't bad. You weren't really one of them, Marisa, and I knew it deep down. I tried to make myself believe you were, so I tried to push you away. I was an ass to you. Because I was scared shit-less. I was so terrified of what it might mean I wouldn't even let myself think it." His hand reached up hold hers where it still cupped his face. "I'm not scared anymore. Are you?"

Marisa felt her breath speed up. "No. I could never be afraid of you, Riley. But," she added quickly. She had to ask. "Are you—is she—Grace, I mean. Is she—"

She didn't have to finish her stumbling sentence for him to understand. His hand in hers tightened, fingers stroking the back of it, eliciting tingles that ran down her arm, through her body. "She'll always be the mother of my cubs. We will never forget her. One day I will avenge her." The shade that rippled through his voice when he said that made a long, low shiver skitter down Marisa's back. Her cat growled in support.

"But," his voice softened again. "Although they were wonderful years, and I've mourned her for a long time, she's gone. I truly let go of her a long time ago. It's what she would have wanted me to do. I had to anyway, if I was going to be an even halfway decent father to Finn and Laney. Part of her will always be in my heart, Marisa. She deserves that. However," he murmured, pausing for a long moment. Eyes still locked on hers, he turned his face until the inside of her hand covered his mouth. Pressing his lips against it, he kissed her palm so slowly, so tenderly, that the breath started rattling in and out of her chest, her entire body heating so fast she felt lightheaded.

Moving his head back, his own breath coming quicker, he studied her face with a new expression on his. One filled with a sweet, rich hunger. "However, I haven't been able to stop thinking about you from the first second I saw you. You are not weak, Marisa. You are not unworthy. You are worthy of every joy and amazing thing in this world, do you hear me? And," he growled, his eyes a sexily ravenous blue that threatened to devour her willing body, "you are so fucking sexy I can't deny this anymore."

He crashed his lips onto hers, meeting her more than willing mouth, kissing her so hard and fast their teeth scraped together as she molded herself to his body. Riley groaned, pressing his hands against her ass then lightly squeezing it. She gasped against his mouth, closing her eyes, shamelessly pushing herself against him.

Yes. This. All of this. All of him. This was what she wanted, and needed.

Riley murmured something into her lips, the sound a rumble of excitement that curled and danced along her nerves. She felt delicious goosebumps tickle up and down her body as she arched fully into his kiss.

Never in her life had anything felt like this. All the times she'd tried to find something with some random guy that resembled love, anything that could take her away from the ugly realities of her life for even a few moments, disappeared into a forgotten haze.

Because this was incredible. Spectacular. Filling up her heart and soul in a way she knew was realer than real.

"Marisa," he groaned against her mouth. The sound of it held such deep longing, such pure worship, that she felt its echoes in her heart. "Now. Need you now."

"Yes," she whispered back.

Without warning, her hoisted her up in his arms, drawing a small gasp of surprise from her. But she quickly melted against him, wrapping her arms around his broad shoulders, nibbling at his neck, his cheekbone, as he strode toward her bedroom. Gently, he set her down on the bed. Carefully, he stepped back, never taking his eyes from hers.

Marisa's breath hitched in her throat. They weren't even naked, they'd done nothing yet but kiss, but just having Riley look at her this way sent trembles racing all over her body. His eyes, shadowed with pure desire, wouldn't let hers go. She felt the heat spreading throughout her, lighting a delicious fire in her veins. The sensation flickered beneath her skin, the moment so charged with erotic electricity she thought she might explode.

From a torrent of tears to being totally turned on. She almost giggled at the inane thought, until Riley started to unbutton his shirt. Then she just stopped thinking. Her breath seized again, catching in her throat as she watched him take off his shirt.

Then his pants.

Under which he wore nothing at all.

Her eyes widened and she almost forgot to breathe.

Oh, holy... The man was ripped. Nothing but pure muscle. Muscles slid from his shoulders all the way to his forearms, plated across his flat stomach, surged down his legs.

And between his legs. Oh, holy everything. Her lips parted. Riley was big everywhere. Definitely.

Marisa dragged her eyes back up to his, which looked at hers with that burning desire. His mouth curved up in a smile at her dropped-open mouth, but when he spoke, his voice was solemn. Respectful. "May I undress you, Marisa?"

Sweet, kind, thoughtful man. She was about to rip her own clothes off, and here he was, asking her permission like a gentleman. Not sure her voice would work, she just nodded. He padded toward the bed. Completely at ease in his body. Completely unafraid to share all of himself with her.

Marisa found her voice. "Riley. Fast. Take them off fast. I want to feel your skin next to mine."

A sound that was half growl, half groan sounded in his throat. "Slow," he gritted out. "Have to go slow, or I might not be able to give you the attention you deserve."

Oh, that was sexy. So very, very sexy.

At the edge of the bed, he paused. Carefully, gently, he reached out a hand to touch her feet, then slowly unlaced her shoe. She almost laughed. She'd forgotten she still had shoes on. Was this sexy? This couldn't be sexy. Suddenly embarrassed, she started to sit up, reaching for her shoes herself. But he shook his head. "Let me. They're just shoes." He added in a whisper, "You deserve to be worshiped, Marisa."

Worshiped. Marisa's head spun at the simple word that rocked her world. No one had ever worshiped her before.

As promised, Riley undressed her slowly. So slowly but so deliberately, with small touches on her bare skin after he removed each piece of clothing, that she was panting when he was done. Each graze of his thumb over her sensitive flesh, each breath as he kissed her stomach, her legs, her arms, set her pulse rocketing.

She thought she might pop like a cork from all the exquisite tension inside her. Her breath vibrated in her throat as gasps tumbled from her lips.

"So beautiful," Riley murmured, staring down at her like she was the most incredible thing he'd ever seen. "Let me see all of you now."

With fingers as light as air, he pulled off the last wisp of her clothes, leaving her completely exposed to his heavy-lidded gaze. His breaths, she noted, were coming as quickly as hers. A light moan of appreciation was more suggestion than sound as he gently stroked her everywhere, exploring each curve, each hollow, every inch of her body.

"Riley," she said, his name falling out in a gasp. "I need you."

"Yes." His voice was a deep growl filled with desire. Then he reached for her, sliding his body over hers, the expression on his face as purely worshipful as he'd promised.

But to her surprise, he moved off to her side, then onto his back. Hands still gentle but with just as much urgency as she felt, he rolled her on top of him. "Want you up here," he murmured. "Want you to go at your pace. You lead this, beautiful woman."

Marisa gulped at the raw need in his voice. His body trembled beneath hers. She realized with a jolt that he wanted her as badly as she wanted him, but he was holding back.

For her. So she could for once in her life feel in control of something.

Her heart burst wide open, flooding her with a world-rocking depth of connection and wonder. Oh, this man.

Every nerve in her body felt alight from the way he'd been touching her as he undressed her. His thick, heavy dick pressed hard between them, stoking the flames higher. She let a pleased smile slide over her face, then slipped her hand between them to take the heavy warmth into her hand. Squeezing it, feeling it pulse against her fingers, she grinned even more as Riley's control loosened. He made a garbled sound, his eyes darkening with passion rather than the fury she'd sensed in him for so long now.

"Ah, babe," he muttered, straining against her, his hands smoothing along her back, sliding over her ass, pressing her into him. "You feel so good, Marisa. So damned good."

"So do you," she whispered back. She was ready for him. More than that, she wanted him with a deep ache. She needed to feel him inside her, filling her completely. Claiming her as his.

Jaw flexing, breath still rattling in his throat, he gritted out, "Your move." His eyes held hers as his fingers kneaded the backs of her thighs, curved up over the dimple where they met her ass.

"Mmm," she answered. This was fun. This was powerful.

This was sexier than anything she'd ever done in her

life, because it was with Riley. Riley, who made her heart crack open. Riley, who *had* her heart.

She lifted herself above him, positioning. A sweet, taut silence stretched out between them, filled with a deepness and meaning she wasn't entirely sure she understood.

Her cat purred in her chest.

No. She understood exactly what it meant.

This was Riley, her Riley, and she was joining him in every way that was most essential right now.

Slowly, she lowered herself onto him, inching her way down his girth, gasping right along with him at how perfect it felt. He fit her like they'd been made for one another.

Finally, she was seated all the way down on his thick, sexy dick, feeling it pulse just the slightest bit inside her. Like he was ready to burst, right on the edge already, but still holding back for her. Letting her lead the way, even if it was half killing him.

"Babe," he groaned, and she started to find her rhythm with him.

Slowly up, then back down. Up, then back down. Her slick heat grew even slicker, even hotter, as she rode him, rocking up and down, her hands tightly clutching his shoulders. His hands settled on her waist, fingers splayed down over her ass, pressing her down and pulling her up in rhythm to her movements. In time with her tempo, matching her stroke for stroke, gasp for gasp, kiss for kiss when she reached for his mouth with hers.

The sweet tension rose, sending splinters of lightning crackling through her. Riley's face tensed, his breath slicing in and out. "Marisa," he growled. "Marisa!"

The wild, strong sound of his voice leaped through her, making the lightning explode. She cried out as everything shattered beautifully within her, keeping her eyes locked on his as he followed her, his hips pumping into hers and then abruptly stilling as a savage cry of joy burst out of his throat, echoed by hers.

Together, they rode the spiral of pleasure up and up, clinging to one another, eyes still locked on one another, their gasping voices echoing throughout the cabin.

Together. Exactly the way she'd never in her life known she would ever find but knew in her soul was meant to be.

Together now and forever, with Riley.

13

———————

Marisa started stretching before she came fully awake. It felt so luxurious, so incredibly good to be in her body. She purred, letting it rumble through her in a swell of contented happiness. Opening her eyes, she blinked at the view outside her bedroom window, which was as charming as ever. Taking a deep inhale, Riley's scent washed over her, strong in the room. Smiling, she turned over, but he wasn't in the bed with her. But another scent hit her nose.

Coffee? Ohhh, yes. A steaming cup sat on the little wooden bedside table just by her head. Thoughtful, thoughtful man. She grabbed it as she sat up, cradling the deliciously hot mug between her hands as she took long, slow sips of the ridiculously strong stuff. So good.

Blinking, she came more awake. Riley was here with her, in her cabin, and he'd gotten up early enough to make her a cup of coffee and left it sitting by her bed. She realized the smell of it must have woken her up. Her face felt funny. What was that again? Oh, yeah.

A smile. A smile stretched her face so wide it was making her cheeks hurt. Delicious, fun hurt.

Putting the coffee down for a moment, she got out of the bed. The first thing she saw was Riley's shirt crumpled at the foot of it. Her cheeks hurt even more as she grinned wide, grabbing his shirt and pulling it to her face to inhale deeply. Pausing only for a moment, she slipped it on over her head. A little giggle almost escaped. The sleeves hung well past her hands and the tails of the shirt brushed the backs of her knees. Rolling up the sleeves, she grabbed the hot coffee and quietly slipped out of the room, wondering what he was doing.

Before she even left the bedroom, which connected right onto the main living room of the cabin, she stopped. Oh. Oh, my. Her jaw slowly fell open in pure appreciation as she stared at the scene before her. Still cradling the mug between her hands, she leaned her shoulder against the door jamb and watched Riley—sexy, surprising, stunning Riley—as he went through some sort of workout routine in front of the main picture glass window. He was completely naked, his body such a glorious specimen of spectacularly fit maleness that she just stayed there and soaked it up.

She admired the rippling muscles in his back as he stretched his arms out, bending at the knees into some

145

sort of pose. Right. He did some sort of martial arts practice. She couldn't remember what it was called. It was stunning to watch though. His entire body was a honed machine, pure muscles from his heels to his fingertips. All the years patrolling as a ranger in the mountains as his bear and doing this practice clearly had kept him incredibly fit. Driven in large part by the need to protect his cubs and his clan from the horrors of the world that both he and she knew only too well were real.

Those horrors were more at bay today, though. She felt...centered. Focused. Clear. More clear than she'd felt in a long time.

Only a few sips remained in her mug when he finally lowered his arms to his sides and turned. His face was already curved into a grin. "Did you enjoy watching?"

She let it spill out of her. A laugh. A real laugh, one of sheer enjoyment. "Yes. How long have you known I was standing here?"

"When you got out of bed. Cats aren't the only ones with extraordinary senses." He held a hand out to her. "Do you want to try a pose or two?"

She set the mug on the floor and went straight to him, padding soundlessly over the large dark blue throw rug to the beautiful coppery-golden wood floor by the window. "Yes. What's it called again?"

"Aikido. Here. First off, put your hands just so."

He moved her hands together in a defensive pose. Feeling his big hand curved over the back of hers raised soft little tingles up and down her arm. She smiled like a lucky cat with cream.

"I can see you smiling," he murmured, though he didn't stop from efficiently moving her hands, then her legs, into the proper placement.

"I like it when you touch me," she returned simply.

"Mmm." The heat from his body warmed the space around them. "Now," he said, sounding businesslike but still warm. "Move your body like this to meet any aggressive action from an attacker."

Step by step, Riley took Marisa through an entire sequence. The moves were simple, but as they practiced, she began to move faster, feeling the workout as she progressed. Five minutes, then ten, passed in a pleasant stretching of her muscles.

Fifteen minutes later she was breathing fairly hard. "Okay, this is definitely work. How much longer should I hold it?"

"Five, four, three," he murmured, watching her intently. Her thighs felt like they were about to give out, but she held steady. "Two, one. Well done. Good morning," he whispered, catching her by the waist and pulling her to him.

She eagerly let herself melt into him, her own "Good morning" muffled into his lips as they kissed for a long time. Kissing him was a good thing. A very good thing.

Finally, he pulled back, the look in his eyes sparking

more desire in her body. But he said, "Do you want to go out to eat?"

She nodded, starting to turn to go back to the bedroom to grab some of the clothes Jessie had managed to find for her. But Riley gently caught her arm. She looked at him with a question in her eyes. He gently tipped his head toward the day outside. "I mean, really out to eat. In the woods. As beautiful bad kitty and big scary bear."

She couldn't muffle the snort of laughter that escaped her. Trying to stifle it only made it worse. Riley was already grinning, laughing along with her. "See? Not so big and bad and scary if we just let them be what they are. Which is us."

Marisa cast one doubtful glance out the window, suddenly nervous. "What if she forgets and tries to leave again?" Her cat snarled lightly, deep inside.

Riley reached for the door, opened it, held it as he gestured for her to go out before him. What a gentleman. "Your cat is not going to get lost or leave again, Marisa. She knows exactly where she is."

Yes. She did.

He followed her out into the bright early morning. Leaping past her where she still hesitated on the porch, he shifted in his bear halfway through his flying jump over the four steps leading up to her porch. Jaw dropped so low she thought her chin might hit her knees, Marisa stared at the enormous black bruin with the huge silvery hump that exploded out of Riley, landing on enormous paws with a thunderous smack before turning around to wait for her. His eyes weren't inky black like she'd seen them the first time in the bridge battle. They were instead a warm, soft brown.

He stood there quietly. Patient. Waiting for her. Not pushing.

Marisa shivered lightly as the breeze picked up, though she was always warmer in human form after she'd been turned than she ever had before. But she wasn't shivering at the cold. She shivered in anticipation of what her cat might do. What it might be like today, this shift. After everything that had happened, after all the awful, bone-cracking shifts before—she was nervous now.

She didn't have to be.

It was easy. So easy. She flowed from one form to the other, surprised it wasn't painful, as it always had been before. Not today. Today, it was so fast. So simple. So effortless.

As if she and bad kitty were one. As if they were each beginning to know they had to work together.

Shaking herself from the ends of her whiskers to the tip of her heavy tail, Marisa cocked her furry ears at Riley. So big, so protective, her bear. She knew without a doubt he would do anything to keep her safe.

She also knew without a doubt that she was more than capable of keeping herself safe. Letting her mouth stretch open, she let out a playful yowl. *Come play. Let's go. Follow me!*

Whirling on her powerful haunches, she shot into the woods. From the ground shaking behind her, she knew Riley followed her in an instant, propelling his enormous body along with a grace and ease that would have taken her breath away if she wasn't using it to run flat out into the woods, joy sparking through her limbs.

This was what she was meant to do. Run. Explore. Play. With shifters like Riley. Those who accepted her. Those who valued her for herself.

Those who maybe loved and accepted her, no matter what.

That thought had her sliding through the snow to a stop in a tiny grove several hundred yards away from the cabin. She could faintly hear vehicles in the distance at the lodge, but the forest had swallowed them up with its beautiful pine trees, stretching their snow-laced green branches up to the clear morning sky.

One last thing. One last thing she had to let go of. To express.

The one last thing remaining between her lion self and her human self, blocking their future as one seamless being.

The biggest shame. The biggest sorrow.

Turning to face Riley, who had skidded to a perplexed halt behind her, his huge shape leaving a wide track in the snow, she dropped to her belly and crawled toward him. Keeping her eyes on his, but not like a predator.

Asking from both her souls to be forgiven.

Riley watched as she came closer, whuffling with concern as she stayed on her belly. When she reached his feet, he anxiously put his head down, nudging at her with his huge snout. Trying to make her stand up on all fours. Which she couldn't, not yet. Not until he understood. Carefully, finally averting her eyes but not in the submissive way she had yesterday when she had begged to be put down, she rolled onto her back, exposing her belly.

Riley huffed with alarm, pushing at her, trying to get her to stand up. He wasn't accepting her display of submissiveness around him. She could tell she worried him with this display.

This was not submission, however. This was begging again, but this time for forgiveness.

She let out the tiniest mewling sound, then another. Soft, kittenish noises fell out of her mouth like the sort a mother cat would use to call her babies. Riley nudged her again and again, very gently stroking her belly with his face, still upset. He used the side of his massive snout to nuzzle her gently behind her neck, eventually licking the top of her head. She stayed there, staying still, mingled shame and hope holding her down.

Finally, he gave up. He didn't back away from her, staring at her with annoyance or exasperation. She could tell he didn't quite understand, but, amazingly, it didn't matter to him. He snuggled next to her, very delicately stretching his enormous forearm to reach over her, hugging her sleek feline body beside his massive one. She pressed into him, their powerful heartbeats knocking together, eventually beating with the same rhythm, the same rate, the same cadence of connection.

Beating together like two hearts that wanted to be one.

Slowly, listening only to the quiet drips as the warmth of the day fought against the coldness of the snow, Marisa let herself relax. Inch by inch, she nestled against the giant bruin with her. Joy pulsed through her, pushing aside the shame. The sadness. Riley rumbled next to her, purring in the odd way that bears did when they were happy. Slowly, gently, even more easily than before, Marisa let herself slip back into her human form, the laughter already bubbling out of her lips. Riley followed a heartbeat later. She sat up and bounced to her feet, whirling to talk to him. He still stared at her with those smoky blue eyes, confused but matching her smile with his. Laughter, real laughter, just flowed out of her, as free and easy as anything ever.

She felt an enormous smile reach across her face as she spoke. "There wasn't anything to forgive her for. Ever. It wasn't her fault. It wasn't mine. You're right. I'm worthy of having her, and she's worthy of having me. She's not a bad kitty, she's a *badass* kitty." Marisa pressed her hand once again to her chest as she had yesterday, feeling the purrs rattle through her so hard they shook her frame from pure joy. From pure relief.

Riley shook his head, his smile still there but mystified. "Whatever happened to you, beautiful, strong lion woman, I don't know what it was. I'm just glad to see you so damned happy."

Marisa grabbed his hand, pressing it into her chest so he could also feel the purring. Right onto her boobs, actually. He wagged his eyebrows at her, gently tweaking his fingers over her perky nipples, and she laughed.

Then she told him the last big thing.

"Riley, when I was turned, I was pregnant."

His smile abruptly dropped, and his hands stilled, although he kept them firmly on her breasts. Not looking away from her, he nodded, waiting for her to finish. Giving her space to tell her story.

"I was searching for the kind of love I'd never gotten from my crappy parents. I looked for it everywhere. With every crappy guy I could find. I didn't mean anything to any of them, because I didn't know what I really needed. I chose them blindly. Stupidly."

She kept her voice steady. Riley kept his eyes firmly on hers. Just listening. Not judging. Good man. Sexy, strong, real, marvelous man.

"The last one got me pregnant. Finding out about that was terrifying and awful." She breathed in slow and long at the memory. "I had no idea how I'd take care of a child. I could barely take care of myself. Of course, I told

153

the guy. Even though he was just a one-night thing, he still deserved to know. He jetted right away, of course. It was what I'd expected."

She paused to check Riley's face. Serious but intent. Listening carefully. It warmed her in places she hadn't realized until right then were cold.

"I didn't tell my parents. That would have been useless. Derek and I were living away from their house by then, renting a little place on the other side of town and doing our best to make life work with the shitty jobs we had. He completely freaked out when I told him, of course. But he's my brother, and he and I have had each other's backs since always. After he was done freaking out, he swore he would do his best to be the best uncle he could, even though I told him it wasn't his responsibility to help. But he's my true family. He wasn't about to abandon me."

Her voice finally wavered, tears swimming up as she thought about how hard Derek had tried to protect her when they were with the outcasts, even while dealing with his own raging inner animal and getting the shit beaten out of him by the others every time he tried to protect her. Blowing out a hard breath to clear the tears, she went on.

"I was about four months along when the outcasts found us. When I was bitten and had the mountain lion forced into me." Her voice cracked again at the terrifying memory.

Riley murmured under his breath, the sound full of compassion. But he didn't say a word. He simply let her speak.

Marisa steadied herself for this next part. The hardest part. "When my cat was forced into me, the result was that I lost the baby I was carrying."

Riley made a soft noise, but he stayed steady. He stayed there.

He stayed with her.

Her voice whispered softly as she said the next words. "She blamed herself for it. She was full of shame about it. Shame and so much pain. Ohhh." Marisa's eyes suddenly drowned in water as she felt the pain deep inside her cat. "It would have been her kit too." The stark realization of that hit her hard.

She shook her head. She'd thought the mountain lion inside her was such a monster, such a bad kitty. But she'd just been as damaged by Marisa, by being shoved into her, by that unwanted transition for both of them making Marisa lose the tiny life inside her. Knowing her cat had grieved as deeply as she did, maybe even more, made her heart shiver in sympathy. In empathy.

"You know," she said slowly, feeling out the words as they came out of her mouth, thinking the thoughts out loud, "all of that was stuff I already felt myself, my whole life. Shame, and pain, and just hating myself. Because that's just what I'd been taught. To never value myself. Wow," she whispered. The enormity of it sledgehammered her as her eyes still trembled with tears.

She kept talking. Saying this felt like a cleansing wash she hadn't known she needed, even beyond the tears yesterday. "Combined together, we were a giant mess of shame and rage and pain. So that's why she always wanted to run. To flee. And I let her because I had no idea how to stop her. I had no idea how to live with a freaking wild animal inside me. And I just now realized it."

"Babe," he whispered, his fingers so gentle, now tucking around behind her back, holding her securely as she told him her story.

"She was running because she didn't want to be put down. She knew she wasn't a lost cause. Neither was I. She knew she didn't really want to die, and neither did I. Neither did I, Riley."

She looked at him as that truth swept her. "So she's been running. Since I've been begging to be put down. She knew I wasn't going crazy. Somehow, she knew. But how did she know?" Marisa whispered the last part, heart stuttering in her chest. Hopeful.

She knew. She knew before he said it out loud.

Riley's hands tightened on her back, pulling her closer to him, although they still had eye contact. "Because," he said, his voice strong but cracking just a bit from some huge emotion, "she knew from the beginning that you and I are mates."

Mates. The word seemed to shimmer on the air. Full of promise and hope and the potential for something like joy.

A wondering smile played on his face as he kept going. "She was shoved into you from force, from anger and hatred and fear, and that's why most humans who have an animal forced into them will eventually go crazy, go feral, be put down or just die otherwise, probably from fighting. But she had found her mate, so she was fighting to live so you would know it too."

Mates. Riley was her mate. A wild, expansive happiness bubbled up inside her, lightening her entire body.

"I never thought I could have a mate again." Stormy blue eyes, holding hers, looking at her with wonder. "Not just because I was blocked off by sorrow and rage, but I literally thought I'd only ever have one."

He moved his hands down to hers, catching them and bringing them up between their chests.

"But here you are. Here you are, Marisa. My mate. My beautiful, badass, warrior mate." The smile that filled his face told her he was feeling a happiness he'd never thought he'd experience again either. "My mate who has found balance with her mountain lion."

She purred. "Yes. Kiss me," she added impulsively. "Kiss me, mate."

He did just that, pulling her in close to him, holding her tight and firm. Telling her with his body he'd never let her go. That she'd be safe always.

157

As they eventually shifted back to their animals and walked back to her cabin, side by side, she felt almost complete. Only two things were missing now. Her brother, and Riley's need to still find justice from the hunters who'd taken his cubs' mother from them.

Marisa vowed to herself then and there that she would help her mate fight all the battles he needed to. Because she was indeed a warrior, and this time, she'd never forget it.

14

As quietly as she could, Marisa whispered, "I'm trapped. I don't think I can move. Do they always do this?"

Riley looked at her, a funny smile appearing on his face. "Happens all the time. They pretend they're so grown up, but not yet. Not quite yet."

The heavy, warm weights on either side of Marisa each made little snoring sounds. She melted again for about the seventeenth time that evening. Laney's head lolled against her shoulder, the pre-teen fast asleep. On Marisa's other side, Finn was curled up, tucked beside her like it was the most natural thing in the world. They'd made it almost to the end of the movie, but before the credits rolled, she'd been able to tell by the even cadence of their breathing they'd both fallen asleep on her.

It was so precious, it about busted her heart wide

open. Her mountain lion had been purring for five minutes now, deeply content.

Riley grinned again at the expression that must be on her face. "Pretty stinking cute, isn't it?"

She nodded, totally blissed out.

Riley's gaze softened even more as he kept looking at her. "You look really comfortable there. Like you fit here. They adore you."

Marisa's cat purred. Gently stroking each child on the head or arm where her hands would reach, Marisa felt a positively dopey smile creep onto her face. "It's mutual."

She felt Riley's gaze burning on her for another moment. When he spoke again, his voice was even more quiet, but sure. "You would be an amazing mother, Marisa. The cubs love you. And I know you love them. You're a natural. But I don't want you to think that's what I'm asking from you."

She snapped her head up. The smile still played around his mouth, but his eyes were serious. She wrinkled her forehead at him. "I don't. I know you're better than that. You like me for who I am." A teeny, tiny remembered ugly whisper, *Nobody likes you for nothing except when you puttin' out, girlie,* prompted her to add, "Don't you?"

She didn't like that she needed the reassurance all of a sudden. But she knew she couldn't be expected to fix everything overnight.

One step at a time, kitty-cat. One step at a time.

Riley's face darkened even as he nodded. "Absolutely. You know I do. I know it'll take you a while to trust anyone. But I'll always be here for you, and I'll always tell you the truth."

The needed reassurance made a more relaxed feeling blossom in her chest. "I know. I am trying. I just need to make sure every now and then."

His smile wrapped around her, hugging her even though he sat in his dark brown leather recliner instead of on the couch with her and the twins.

Because she did, in fact, feel very sure around him, here in his home, pure mischief made her add, "I was actually worried you only like me because I have dangerous bad kitty claws and a super sexy booty." Then she wagged her eyebrows at him to let him know she was teasing him.

Riley muffled his loud burst of laughter when Finn mumbled in his sleep against Marisa's shoulder. But the simple pleasure of laughing at her silliness stayed in his face, showing in the wrinkles around his eyes, the way his mouth, oh, that sexy mouth, wouldn't stop smiling at her. "Your dangerous kitty claws are very impressive. And your super sexy booty—oh, yeah. That's something I very much appreciate."

His voice dropped a notch as he said that, his appreciation abruptly evident in his expression. Marisa swallowed at the instant heat that crowded the room. She managed to croak out, "Well, okay then." Even though everything had been so comfortable this evening, eating hamburgers with him and the twins, playing a board game with them—a board game, so old-fashioned, so fun —she'd been so hyperaware of him the whole time, every passing glance or casual brush of his arm against hers had sent little thrills throughout her body.

Sweet silence held them as the movie they'd watched with the twins ended and the streaming service on the TV suggested about five others to watch. Casting around for something to distract her from Riley's knowing smile, Marisa looked around the house. Coming here had been such a treat. Riley and the twins had driven to her cabin to pick her up, even though she was only several hundred yards away from his place.

Finn had leapt out of the car and run up her little walkway so he could proudly walk her all the way out to the car. He even held the door open for her to climb in. Her heart melted a thousand times over at the adorable boy trying to be such a protective little man, even though his sister had been yelling things out the window at him like, "You have to hold her arm by the elbow! And watch where you're walking so you don't take her through a patch of ice!"

When they'd arrived at their home, she'd felt outclassed again for just a moment. Oh, what a beautiful place they had. But then she reminded herself that she belonged here, that they wanted her here. Slowly, she'd relaxed. This was the first time she'd been in Riley's home. From the outside, the place was nice but snug. The inside, however, was much more spacious than it seemed and perfectly put together. Finn and Laney had proudly shown her around, explaining with great seriousness how their daddy had built it by hand, long ago before they were born, with their mama's help. With the guileless sweetness of children, they had showed her the photos of their mother, which were scattered around the house but not overwhelmingly so. There was no shrine to her, no enormous framed portrait. Other than a few regular-sized photos, Marisa couldn't get a sense that she'd ever even been here. Then again, she thought as she once again gently stroked Laney's soft hair, brushed the back of her index finger over Finn's impossibly soft cheek, she had died when they were only two. Almost ten years ago.

Quietly looking up at Riley, she asked, "Do they remember her?"

She watched him carefully, afraid of upsetting the cozy balance of the evening. But he remained relaxed where he sat, watching her and the twins with an expression she couldn't completely read, although he wasn't upset.

"Not really. I've asked them now and then over the years to tell me if they can remember her presence. Remember her holding them, or even remember what she smelled like. But they were so young. They don't have solid memories, no. More like just impressions, from what they tell me. They asked me a lot of questions about her when they were younger, and I told them everything I could remember about her. And Laney knows how much she looks like her mother."

Marisa nodded. When she'd first seen the photo of Grace, her eyes had widened at the resemblance.

"It's terrible what happened, and it always will be. But aside from that, they are so lucky with how they grew up, Riley." Although she kept her voice soft, she watched him closely to make sure he understood what she was saying. "She loved them unconditionally, and clearly you did too. Everyone here does. They're so safe, so loved. There's a real community here, not to mention all sorts of friends in town. You grew up here..."

She gestured around the cabin then softly jerked her head toward the outside to indicate the entire lodge. "I know you've been scared for their safety their whole lives, and that is so understandable. That's a horrible thing, and I know you'll always be worried for them until you catch the ones who did it."

His face didn't change, although the corners of his eyes tightened. She went on, still picking her words carefully but being utterly truthful with each one. "Your home is officially one of the fanciest places I've ever seen in my life."

"Fanciest?" His brows raised. "It's a nice place, this home. I'm proud of it, and I should be. But I do my best not to be fancy. I definitely don't want to raise two spoiled brats."

Marisa shook her head. In the back corner of the living room, the fire crackled from the fresh pieces of wood Riley had thrown on earlier. "These two are definitely not spoiled brats. But I don't think you understand where I came from. Riley, honestly, I know none of you here seem to think this is a big deal. The lodge, all your little cabins here. It's all just home to you." She couldn't keep the genuine awe out of her voice. "But I keep thinking this place is like a fairytale. Look. Here's another ugly truth about me for you to hear."

She looked him square in the face. "I'm genuine, literal trailer trash. I grew up in a trailer park. There were a couple nice people there, but not my family. I didn't even make it past eighth grade. The only reason I didn't get knocked up when I was a teenager was because Derek knew how the boys liked to be with the girls, and he was the one who sat me down and told me how to be careful. For a little brother, he raised me much better than our parents did."

She bit off a sigh. She didn't want to sound sorry for herself. But she did want Riley to know everything about her. He knew the worst of her secrets. She wanted him to understand what she had come from and why she still needed to run from it. Because it didn't define her anymore.

"I've never seen money like this in my life," she

admitted flat out, looking straight at him. "I know your place here is fancy, the little cabin I'm in is in fancy, and Quentin and Abby's place is super fancy too. I have to tell you, everything up here is just so much *more* than I've ever known in my entire life. The trailer I grew up in, and then the place Derek and I moved into together until we could figure out our own shit. We had the crappiest little apartment you've ever seen in your life." She kept her voice low so she wouldn't wake the cubs, although she glanced down at them every now and then to make sure they were still sleeping.

"I don't want to judge you because you come from money. I don't want you to judge me because I don't. I just want you to know everything about me."

Riley waited a beat. When she stayed silent, he nodded. "Fair enough. But I don't come from money, pretty kitty. Me and my brothers were not all that much older than the cubs when our parents, who had very little to their name, finally managed to scrape up enough to put a down payment on a ramshackle miner's cabin and all this land up here that no one else wanted. They managed to get it for a song, but it was still a really expensive song for them. The whole lodge, Marisa? Everything up here? We built it all. We built all of it by hand." Quiet pride slipped through his voice. "Oh, sure, later on, you know, we hired crews and stuff to help out. But we built a cabin that all five of us and my parents lived in by hand. My point is, I come from hardworking stock, so I do know what it's like to not have anything. I know how lucky I am, and the cubs are," he added softly.

He uncrossed one long leg from where he had rested it across the opposite knee and stood up, heading toward Marisa and the cubs. Smiling down at his children with the indulgent, incredulous smile of love that often passed his face when he looked at them, he said, "We're lucky because we always had massive amounts of love."

Then he looked at Marisa, gently reached his fingers to tip her chin up to his. His thumb stroking the side of her cheek, making her shiver and smile, he added in a serious whisper, "And from now on, so do you."

Marisa wondered if she could explode from the joy that burst through her as he said that. He bent down to scoop Finn up into his arms, who woke up enough to mumble something about being able to walk on his own. Riley murmured at him, "Whatever, kiddo. Get back to dreaming," as he turned toward the curved stairway leading to the upper floor. Whispering to Marisa, "Hang on, I'll come back down for Laney. She's too big for you to carry," he easily carried his son up the stairs.

Marisa listen to the creak of the stairs and the noise the floorboards made overhead as Riley walked down the hallway to take his son to his bedroom. Leaning down, she dropped a kiss on Laney's head. She waited quietly until he came back down the stairs, just stroking Laney's hair and listening to the young girl breathe as she slept. Her cat purred so hard she could hear it. When Riley returned and gently lifted Laney up from the couch, she yawned and snuggled against her father. Smiling, he murmured, "It's a wonder they still let me do this sometimes at their age." He glanced at Marisa, eyes wondering. "They really like you. They completely relax around you. You make them feel safe, Marisa. Be right back," he said before turning to take Laney upstairs.

Marisa snuggled into the couch, turning so she could face the fireplace on the opposite side of the large room. The cubs were a little old to be sleepily carried to bed by their father, but she suspected it happened more often than they would probably admit. Growing up without a mother had probably made them crave the closeness and protection of their remaining parent more than most children. Her cat's purr intensified, the vibration by now familiar and comforting. It wasn't her place to take over as the cubs' mother—but if it was her place to be in all of their lives, she would never say no to that.

Moments later, Riley came back downstairs. He went straight to the couch and settled in beside Marisa, positioning himself until he held her on his lap with her tucked safely in his arms. Safety. That seemed to be the theme tonight.

"What will you do with them if you ever find them?" She didn't have to say *the shifter hunters* for him to immediately understand.

Slight tension swept through his body, but his voice was still calm and quiet when he answered. "Debatable.

Years ago, I instantly would have said I'd rip them limb to limb. Now, I'm not so sure. Even though they're human, knowing about shifters and turning shifters in to human government agencies that are killing them makes them eligible to be thrown into shifter prison. That would definitely not be a pleasant experience for any human." His voice held such dark certainty that Marisa's skin goosebumped.

"Have you ever seen one? A shifter prison?"

Riley shook his head, resting his chin on top of her head and stroking her hands where they were clasped in front of her. "No, but Slade has. Don't ask why. It's not my story to tell, and we don't talk about it very often. But anyway, he said they're pretty rotten places, and he has no desire to see one ever again. He also said some shifter hunters he saw there were definitely going to have a pretty nasty time of it for the rest of their lives. So, sometimes I think it might be better for them to end up there when I finally catch them."

They stayed silent for a few more moments. Warmth and a slight tingle suffused Marisa as she sat there. She knew she wouldn't stay tonight, not with the cubs here. Even though they adored her, and it was mutual, she wasn't quite ready for them to see her coming out of their father's room in the morning. But she would enjoy snuggling with Riley on the couch until he drove her back to her cabin later.

"Do you have any idea where they are?"

The silence went on so long Marisa twisted her head to look at Riley face to face. His expression made her heart stumble. After a long moment, he shrugged. "Maybe. I caught their scent not that long ago."

Marisa shot up straight. His eyes were still blue, but the darkness in them made her shudder. He held her gaze as he went on. "One of the many reasons I wasn't sure about trusting you when you showed up during the bridge battle was because not long before it, I scented them nearby. One, at least. I know there were a few shifter hunters that went after Grace and the cubs back then, but only one was responsible for her death. His scent was all over the scene when I found her body."

Marisa's heart constricted as he said that even though his voice stayed calm. "He's the one I've hunted all these years. I picked up his scent not that far from Deep Hollow about a month ago. I told Quentin, so we could try to track it as best we could. But there are so many shifters around here, all the guests, and their scents are all over too. It was murky. I let everyone know. We were on really high alert. It was pretty stupid of him to return here. After what he did, he had to know that I and every other shifter here would kill him on sight if he was ever caught back in this area. But it was only the one time."

Riley frowned reflexively, clearly caught in the memory. "He might have just been scoping out the area again, then realized it was too hot for him to be able go after any of the shifters around here so he left. Who knows."

He blew out a hard sigh then suddenly reached forward, gently putting his hand on Marisa's cheek. He traced one of her eyebrows with his finger, drifted his fingers over her jawline. Despite the heaviness of the conversation, she leaned into his hand and smiled at him. "That feels good." She let her purr rattle audibly into the room.

Riley turned his hand, tucking his fingers behind her head and pulling her toward him while he leaned forward as well. "I'm so glad you're still here, beautiful woman. You stay in our lives." His lips ghosted over hers, sending more chills and a thrilling desire through her. Pulling back slightly, he murmured, still looking into her eyes, "But I won't ever be able to sleep comfortably at night until I know we're all safe. I will find them, Marisa. I will avenge her death." His voice chilled the room.

And I, she thought to herself, feeling badass kitty growl deep inside her, *will find my brother and avenge what's been done to both of us.* But she didn't say it out loud. She knew Riley would stand beside her, always, but like his vengeance for his mate's death, this was her battle to fight. She refused to drag any of the Silvertips into more trouble.

Now that she and her cat were one, she could handle anything.

He kissed her deeply again, the soft noises of their

lips touching making Marisa murmur and moan against his mouth. Finally, he pulled back reluctantly. She sighed as well and leaned her forehead against his.

"I should go," she said just as reluctantly.

He nodded. "When you come over tomorrow night, there's something I want to show you."

"And what exactly would that be?" She could hear the suggestiveness in her voice.

His groan echoed in his chest, spilling out into a growl of need. "Oh, definitely some of that. The twins are spending tomorrow night at Slade's house. He loves the crap out of them and tries to spend a lot of time with them every time he's in town. So, we'll have the place all to ourselves, my beautiful lion woman." His voice was more than a suggestive tease. It was an erotic promise that made her thinking jumble up and her breath come quickly.

"But there really is something cool I want to say is happening tomorrow night. And then I might show you a little bit more."

Marisa leaned into his kiss, losing herself in the moment. Eventually, she whispered back, "Deal, mate."

15

Marisa stood beside Riley on the porch, his arms strong and warm around her waist as he gazed steadfast after the disappearing furry rumps of Finn and Laney. Their rumbled snorts of of excitement drifted back on the still air as they bounced through the snow toward the welcoming lights of the cabin Marisa could see about a quarter mile away. Her eyes, which thanks to her cat had better vision in human form than she'd ever experienced in her life before she'd been turned, caught a shadow moving in front of the light of the faraway cabin. Slade, waiting on his porch for the twins to reach him.

She sighed as she snuggled in closer to Riley. "How wonderful for everyone here to have family right around, have everyone watching out for the kids here. It's safe. So..." she struggled for the right word.

Riley's large hand squeezed her hip, his fingers

working slow circles on her upper thigh that sent the delicious thrill tripping through her. "So wonderful? Warm? Welcoming?" A smile teased his voice.

Marisa felt the smile tip up her mouth as she bumped her leg against his. "Yes. All of those things. You sound like a brochure advertising the wonders of the Silvertip Lodge."

His laugh vibrated through her. "Pretty much. Those are words that are actually used on some of the brochures and the website. Abby's been partially in charge of guest relations ever since she and Quentin got together, and though the lodge was pretty damned amazing before she got here, she's brought even more to the place. Quentin is a lucky dog that someone as cool as Abby decided his sorry ass was worth something."

A grin still rippled through his voice as he made fun of his older brother. Then it dropped into seriousness. Brushing a kiss across the top of Marisa's head, he murmured in the low rumble that sent more delicious chills shivering through her, "But not half as lucky as I am."

Marisa nestled her head into his chest, feeling his strong and steady heartbeat beneath her ear. A tumble of more shadows flickered across the lights of Slade's cabin. "Is that them? Did they make it there?"

She felt Riley's phone vibrate in his pocket where it pressed against her leg. He reached down, pulled it out, and swiped his thumb across the screen which glowed softly. Glancing down at it, he nodded. "Safe and sound. Now, beautiful woman," he said, brushing another kiss across the top of her head before glancing toward the eastern sky. "We need to hustle so you can see what I want you to see. Come on." He grabbed her hand and headed down the steps, gently pulling her along with him.

She let her fingers squeeze into his, feeling the smile that still busted wide open across her face as they crunched down into the snow and headed away from his home, angling left through the trees. There was no path—the last edges of twilight made everything dim—but she could see well enough with her enhanced vision. Her cat's reassuring purr rumbled through her. Marisa sank into it, feeling the amazing world, being one with her mountain lion as she tried to keep up with Riley's long strides. "You know my legs are shorter than yours. We in a race?"

His hand tightened on hers. "Sort of. I don't want you to miss this. It'll be pretty cool."

"Where are we going?" Anticipation and excitement zinged through her as they hurried through the woods, the only sound their booted feet crunching on what must be a path beneath them that had been walked before.

"Up ahead. Almost there."

Riley led her out of the trees to the edge of the meadow that sloped down to the east. A faint glow edged the tops of the pines that ringed the far end of it. Marisa looked at it, puzzled. "It's not Deep Hollow, is it? There's nothing in that direction. Unless there's a hidden city I don't know about?"

In reply, Riley pulled her in front of him until her back was nestled into his chest. She let out a little sound of appreciation, pressing into his huge, warm bulk, her rear nudging right against the bulge in his jeans. His breath whistled in as he wrapped his arms around her, his hands crossed protectively over her belly, fingers splaying over her hips. "Not too much of that just yet, pretty lion girl. Need to see this before you make me lose my concentration."

Marisa sighed, holding still but keeping herself pressed into his comforting warmth and strength. She could be all about making him lose his concentration. It was definitely a fun thing to do. In fact—

The rounded edge of something glowing a burnished gold suddenly tipped above the eastern edge of the trees. Marisa gasped in delight. "The moon!" Even as they watched, it slowly rose above the trees, impossibly huge and glowing.

Riley's breath whispered over her hair. "Super moon tonight, babe. It's actually called the Super Snow Moon because it's during the cold snowy season. Even just a regular moonrise is always incredible up here. But super moons are ten times as cool. I wanted to watch it with you." He nibbled at her ear. "I wanted to see your reaction to it."

The impossibly bright light bathed the entire meadow as they watched the moon rise all the way up above the trees. "It's so big," Marisa murmured, riveted as the huge globe slowly sailed upward in the sky.

"Definitely is," Riley murmured back, pressing his hips against her backside, the large bulge of his cock pressed against her ass. With a cheeky grin, she wiggled her butt against it. He groaned.

"Okay, I can't tease you anymore until we're back at the house. Otherwise, I'll just toss you down in the snow right here." The deliciously rough scrape of his voice made goosebumps pop up all over her body.

"Mmm," was all she said in reply.

But the grin stayed on her face. Sexy, sexy man. She could get so used to having him in her life like this.

In fact, she wanted that without question.

They watched together as the moon rose fully above the trees, spreading the reflected sunlight all around, creating the nighttime winter wonderland that even a human could see well enough in to navigate. The incredible beauty and peacefulness of the scene filled something in Marisa. She hadn't even recognized the feeling as loneliness until right that moment. "Your home is so beautiful." Tentatively, she added, "I really like it. I love it more every day that I get to live here too."

He groaned, tightening his arms around her, huge sexy man, giving her such shelter. Such safety. "I want this to be your home forever, Marisa. It feels right, having you here."

She nodded against his chest. "It feels right to me too." She kept her voice a hushed whisper in the magical wonderland beauty of the moment. Her cat rumbled with purrs inside her, twining through Marisa's mind with equal serenity. Happiness.

After several more moments watching in silent appreciation as the moon rose, Riley finally pulled himself away from her, though he slid his hand down to grab hers once more. Marisa was blissfully aware of every heartbeat, of the palpable energy rising between them. They turned and went back to the little path in the woods, now so brightly lit up that individual pine needles were clearly visible on the trees as they walked back. The serene hush of the place encircled them, cradling Marisa in a cocoon of warmth and delight. Pure, sheer contentment.

Home. Could it be?

Her cat purred, softly whispering through her with that deep connection that also felt better with each passing moment.

Yes. Yes, it could be home.

A deeper tingle of excitement flitted within her as well. Riley's hip kept bumping hers as they walked back, the warmth and promise of that contact making her entire body buzz. Still in silence, they reached his house, walked up the few stairs to the front door, then went inside.

Gently, Riley let the door shut, wrapping them in the safety and quietness of his home. Together.

Watching each other, still wordless, they shucked their clothes right inside the doorway, leaving them dropped on the floor right there. Marisa stood naked in front of him, her breath beginning to come faster as his eyes drank her in. Their beautiful blue shade darkened with appreciation as the expression on his face turned to one of mingled intense lust and longing and elation all at once.

"Here," was the only word he said, reaching for her as hungrily as she went to him. Their lips met in a tangled kiss of deep need, the quiet magic of the night shimmering through them both. He ran his big hands down her naked back, pausing over the bumps of her spine, stroking his fingers over her bony hips. He whispered into her mouth, "Gotta feed you more, woman. Need more of you to hold onto."

Just the sound of his voice sent a deep ache straight between Marisa's legs, the feeling of heavy, delicious fullness shivering with an urgent, insatiable need for him to be there.

"Riley." His name was a throaty murmur, so deep it felt like it vibrated through her body. His own breath came sharp and fast as he looked at her. "Inside me. Now. Please."

He didn't waste another second. Reaching his arms below her ass, he lifted her up to his waist, where she wrapped her legs around him. She nibbled on his neck, drawing out a groan as he strode with his long legs up the stairs and down the hallway to his bedroom. She shamelessly rubbed herself against his waist, knowing she was leaving her wetness on him. Marking him as hers.

"Ahhh, babe." His voice shuddered with desire. "Can't wait. Going to give you what you're needing the second I get you on my bed."

She moaned in response, nipping at his neck, pressing her hands into the back of his head, frantically rubbing herself on his belly like a shameless cat in heat. Badass kitty purred deep inside her, urging her on to the overpowering need to have this man claim her. To claim him back.

He walked into his bedroom, still holding her tight against him, and went straight to his bed. As he gently set her down, he went with her onto the bed, her legs still wrapped around his waist. Keeping the bulk of his weight off her by propping himself up on his elbows, he curved his hands around the back of her head, fingers tangling in her hair, looking into her eyes. The sweet, excited arousal she saw in them matched her own, making her breath rush faster. He butterflied his lips against hers again and again until she was panting.

"More," she said in a breathy, demanding whisper.

She felt his chuckle vibrate in his chest. "As you wish,

babe," he whispered before crashing his lips onto hers, kissing her senseless with every ounce of his being.

His tongue quested in her mouth, danced with her tongue, his lips sucking and stroking and pressing against hers until she wondered if it was possible to have an orgasm just from kissing. Tremors and sizzles zipped all over her body, making her shake with pure longing.

He ran his fingers down her side, stroking every inch of skin along the way, making her gasp into his mouth. He didn't relinquish her mouth, still kissing her with a wild, fierce desire he'd held back the other night. They'd been so tender with one another then, careful and gentle.

Not this time.

This time, he wanted to own her. And she was definitely, one hundred percent okay with that.

She pulled her hand away from his back and found his where it still stroked down the length of her body. Insistently, she pushed his hand down, trying to shove it between their bodies, trying to push his hand right on to her flaming pussy, which felt like it was going to explode if it didn't get touched soon.

Riley pulled his head back just enough to murmur at her, his eyes brimming with the presence of his wild side, "So it's like that, huh?" A thrill ringed his words.

She panted in response. She couldn't find words. Sexy, sexy man. Her man. She wanted him. Needed him. Wanted every inch of him on this gorgeous, full snow moon night.

His fingers quested in, smoothed themselves over her mound, dipped into the heated spot between her legs that need to be touched right fucking now or she felt like she might pass out. He stroked his fingers into the warmth and wetness, dragging a cry out of her as he dragged his fingers through.

A savage, delighted grin raced across his face. "As you wish, my beautiful lion woman." And in a heartbeat, he pulled his hand away, pulled his hips back, and thrust into her.

Marisa cried out at the welcome invasion, the thrill of having him fill her. Legs still wrapped around him, she put her arms around him once more, feeling his broad back beneath her palms. "Mine," she growled, meeting his thrusts with her own. She knew her cat had to be glowing out of her eyes as brightly as his bear glowed out of his. "You are mine, and I want this, Riley," she said, her eyes searching his.

He gently thrust in, making her gasp. Then he slowly pulled out, making her protest in an inarticulate babble. Thrusting back in, he said quietly, "Are you sure?"

She nodded and pulled his head down to hers again. "Yes," she hummed against his mouth.

He thrust into her again and again, so hard they both slid across the bed. It was wild, fierce, perfect. Marisa could feel the fire sweeping over her already, knew she would shatter with just one more thrust.

Abruptly pulling her head away, she reached for his neck and bit him.

Claiming her man.

Her mate.

Riley roared, once again slamming into her, his eyes a swirling hue of gold and blue as his orgasm thundered over him, leaving his powerful, sweet warmth inside her just as she exploded around him. In the midst of his shuddering and shaking, he growled, "Mine," then turned and sank his teeth into her shoulder.

Marisa screamed in sheer bliss as another orgasm shattered over her on top of the first one, her entire body a paroxysm of joy as her mate claimed her back.

The two of them, spiraling together, joined together forever. She had no fear. Joy was theirs to have.

Throbbing waves shivered and shattered over them both as they clung to one another, gasping and sweating as the tremors slowly ebbed away. She felt her pulse bang so hard in her ears, she wondered if Riley could hear it. His heart thundered in his chest against hers, the rhythm matching her racing pulse, their mingled gasps of air.

Eventually, slowly, the sensations gently slipped away, leaving Marisa boneless in Riley's arms. She sank into the bed, murmuring wordless little sounds into his face and neck, still clutching him tight with her arms and legs until she finally had to relax them too, her entire body spent with the power of what had just happened.

Claimed. Claimed one another. As mates. For as

short a time she'd been a shifter, she knew exactly what the bites meant.

The smile that rippled onto her face spread through her entire body like a wonderful aftershock of her orgasms.

Riley had claimed her as his mate, and she had claimed him. It felt like the best thing that had ever happened to her. She didn't even have to think about the few highlights in her life to know that was the truth.

Sighing out a murmur of pure bliss, she let herself melt into the bed, still holding him close.

Long moments later, Riley gently turned to the side so his weight wasn't completely on her, then gently slipped out of her. He turned her so he could pull her against him, her back nestled against the heat of his broad chest. He held her close, tight, his hands still gently worshiping her body with little strokes.

Big, sexy, strong man. Huge, powerful, gentle bear.

No longer broken. No longer hurting.

Maybe he wasn't healed all the way, just like she probably wasn't either. She knew one thing for a fact, though. With Riley at her side and she at his, they could do anything they set out to accomplish.

Right as Marisa teetered at the edge of sleep, she heard his voice whisper against her ear. "You, beautiful lion woman, strong, amazing lion woman, are the best people. I love you, Marisa Tully. Mate," he added, latching a kiss onto her neck as he said that glorious word, *mate*.

She exhaled in bliss, pressing back against him, then she whispered out her truth as well. "I love you, Riley Walker. My mate. Best bear ever," she added in sleepy jumble.

His soft chuckle soothed her as she drifted into sleep, safe in his arms.

Riley groaned as something woke him up. Too early. Damned work day. No sweet Marisa in his bed, either. It was a work morning as well as a school morning. A smile drifted over his face as he thought about a few nights ago, when they'd claimed one another as mates. The memory made his entire body rumble with happiness. He missed her presence, although they'd decided they would tell the cubs very soon.

As he turned his head, paper crinkled beneath his cheek. His eyes snapped open as he jerked his head away from his pillow. What the—? A torn piece of yellow notebook paper, crumpled where he'd apparently been sleeping on it, nestled just at the edge of his pillow. Taking a quick swipe at his face to knuckle the sleep out of it, he grabbed at the paper and stared at it. His blood ran cold at the words.

I went to find Derek. I know they've got him nearby. I scented him last night. It was faint but he's out there. He's my family, Riley. I have to do what I can to save him. Now that I know my mountain lion a lot better, and she knows me, I have a really good chance at getting him out of there. You saved me, and now I can save him. I didn't tell you because I don't want to drag all of you into it. This is my battle to fight. I promise I'll be careful. And I promise you, I'm coming back to you and the cubs.

I love you.

Marisa <3

A tiny drawn heart followed her name. His own heart, which had leapt into his throat, felt a tug as he saw that, even as he was already leaping out of the bed.

Damn it. Beautiful, bold, foolish woman. Now that she was finally in touch with her cat, she probably felt invincible. He'd seen it in other turned shifters, though those had always been turned by choice. Once they realized how powerful their animal side was, they often did really stupid things in the beginning.

Like charge off on their own, convinced they could single-handedly take down a pack of ruthless, honorless outcasts.

Swearing under his breath, he pulled clothes on as quickly as possible. Tossing a quick glance at the time on his phone, he strode out of his room, already calling out, "Finn! Laney! Let's get moving. Your ride to school will be leaving pretty soon." Jessie always took the cubs into town with her to drop them off at school on the mornings she worked at the Mountain Muffin.

To his surprise, Laney's cheerful, wide-awake voice answered him from the kitchen. "We're way ahead of you."

"Yeah, Dad," Finn chimed in, also from the kitchen. "We even made you coffee because you're the one who's running late today."

A chorus of giggles followed that statement. Despite his slowly blossoming panic, he couldn't stop a quick grin of pride. He loved those two children more than anything on earth, and each time they displayed another action that showed they were growing up more every single day, he loved it, as much as he knew it meant that one day they would be out on their own.

He was even more impressed when he went to the kitchen and saw they were both already dressed. Raising his eyebrows, he reached for the mug of coffee. "You guys did great," he said simply, knowing the simple praise would mean more to them than his being effusive. "Good coffee. Listen, you two. I have to run you over to Aunt Jessie's right now, unless you want to wait for her here. Something happened, and I've got to go help out."

Laney immediately looked worried, which led to Finn instantly putting a protective hand on her shoulder. He was so watchful over her, even though she was older than him. Watching the familiar interaction, it hit him Marisa must have the same relationship with her brother.

"What's wrong?" Finn asked, watching his father with careful eyes.

Much as he wanted to protect his children from everything in the world, he also never lied to them. "Marisa left to do something that can be very, very dangerous for her. She went alone." Riley blew out a hard breath just thinking about it. "Actually, she went to see if she can help her brother. He's in trouble."

Seeming to sense the deep fear in him, Laney sat up. "Marisa's family? We need to help her!"

She scrambled over Finn to rush outside, despite Riley's sharp, "Hold up! Laney! Finn!" Naturally, they didn't listen. When it came to Marisa, they'd apparently already decided they'd do anything for her.

Finn managed to bolt out the door first, but Riley heard him lurch to a stop outside. A breath later, his controlled but nervous, "Daddy?" assaulted Riley's ears. Laney gasped from where she was on Finn's heels.

Finn never called him Daddy anymore. Riley was Dad now. Only when Finn was scared did he revert to Daddy. Without even thinking, Riley lunged outside, ready to protect his children from whatever was there.

A man stood at the bottom of the stairs, haggard, ragged, and wild-eyed. Shifter. A crazy look in his eyes and desperation on his face told Riley one thing. Whoever he was, he was close to being unhinged.

Riley snatched Finn by the shoulder and shoved his son behind him, a growl building in his throat and spilling out. This wasn't a guest of the lodge. He definitely wasn't a healthy shifter. "Who the hell are you?"

Before the man could answer, Laney's shocked whisper came from behind him. "Daddy, he looks like Marisa."

It hit Riley the second she said that. Yes. This man looked like the male version of Marisa, although even thinner and bearing the marks of many skirmishes. Even so, something was deeply, dangerously off about him. Riley stayed rooted to the spot, aware his bear lurked just below the surface, ready to leap out of him to protect his home and his children from the stranger.

Even if the man was Marisa's brother.

"Tell me your name," Riley demanded, his tone thoroughly menacing.

The man swallowed and closed his eyes for a second, clearly fighting with himself. When he opened them again, humanity stared back at Riley. "My name is Derek. I'm looking for my sister. Please," he said, the shudder in his voice evident along with immense concern. "I need to know what you did with her. She's completely innocent. Whatever it was, please, just let her go or tell me what you did with her."

Startled, Riley snapped, "Why would we have done anything with her?"

The man's look skittered behind Riley, where he was sure Finn and Laney peered around his legs, then back to Riley's face. "Because they told me you would either turn her in to a shifter prison, or you would get rid of her. You'd kill her. And," the man swallowed, the sound audible in the still morning, "I know she was hurting, and she didn't want to go on anyway. Tell me you all didn't give in to her wanting to be put down. Please."

Riley examined the man closely as they stood staring at one another. He was taller than Marisa and had sandy reddish hair and the same green eyes. His facial structure was similar to hers, although a scraggly, tangled, dirty beard covered the lower half of his face. An obvious bruise decorated his cheekbone just beneath his left eye, but the worst part of his injuries was what lay behind his eyes.

Riley knew this man, Marisa's brother, might have no chance at a future. His animal was much more in control than the human side, feral madness having sunk its grip deep into him.

"How can I trust you?" Riley was completely motionless. In full predator mode. His voice flattened even more as he continued. "How do I know you're not in league with the outcasts and just want to find her so you can drag her back to them?"

The man took a step closer. Instantly, Riley growled at him, letting his bear flare fully into his eyes. He reached back to shove Laney and Finn more firmly behind him. But the man stopped, bringing up his hands and shaking his head. "I can't make you believe me. All I can do is tell you Marisa is the only reason I made it in

191

this life. She's always been there for me. I did my best to protect her from that group of psychotic shitheads. Sorry," he said, his glance flickering to the cubs before going back to Riley.

Riley didn't let the tension leave his body, but he decided to take it as a good sign Derek cared enough to watch his language around children. Not that it mattered since those two had already heard every bad word under the sun, from him if not from kids at school, but it was a decent gesture.

Just like something Marisa would do.

"If you do have her, please, let her go." Derek's jaw trembled as he spoke, fighting against the giant, unwanted creature inside him. "Take me to her so I can try to help her get out of here before it's too late."

Every hair on Riley's body prickled at those words. "What you mean, too late?" His words slammed like little bombs into the still air. He felt one of the cubs shiver behind him, though neither one of them moved otherwise.

"They're coming for her. For her, and for all of you. They're angry because of that fight with you all. You killed half of them, then did who the hell knows what with the rest of them, including my sister. The worst one of all got away. He's completely insane," Marisa's brother said, his voice strangely calm as he said it. "Beyond insane, so much so he doesn't care anymore about what he does. I don't even know how he's still in control of his cat, but he is. Even though he's a monster."

Monsters, Marisa had called them. She'd called her own parents monsters. The outcasts were worse than monsters though. They were utterly deranged killers, and every last one of them needed to be ended.

"He and the rest of the psychos he's found will kill every last shifter here." The man's eyes went to the twins again. "Including kids. They don't care about anything decent. A group of insane shifters is a terrible idea. No one can control them, not even Nefarious." His lip curled in derision as he said that name, although a flash of fear billowed over his face as well.

Nefarious. The same one Marisa feared and hated so much. The bastard who'd turned her without her permission. The one she apparently thought she could take on now that she and her cat were one. Riley's bear surged inside him. The hell with that. He'd vowed to himself she wouldn't have to battle alone anymore. He meant it.

Derek looked back at Riley, the struggle evident in his gaunt face. "She's the only thing in the world I've ever cared about. If she's here, I need to get her away. Please. You don't know what kind of crappy life she's already had." His breath went ragged. "I want my sister to find some peace. She deserves that."

He stopped talking then and just looked to Riley. Pleading. Despite clearly being a very dangerous, unhinged shifter, he was begging for help for his sister, unashamed that he cared about her.

He was the real deal.

Riley made his decision in a split second. "I believe you. You look just like her, and she told me all about you. That you're the reason *she* survived this life. But she's not here." Riley heard his voice trying to waver. He forced it down with a choking ferocity.

Behind him, Laney whimpered in nervousness. Then she whispered, "Daddy, we have to go find her." He felt her peek around his leg. "She's our friend," she told Derek in a solemn voice.

Derek blinked at her, his eyes shifting back and forth from human green to glowing golden cat and back again. But he nodded. "Mine too."

Riley breathed hard, working to control his own bear. But they were in sync about this. Finding Marisa was the priority. "She left me a note. She took off this morning. To go and try to find you. To save you. I don't know where she went, Derek." The man jerked at the sound of his name, but he nodded. "But even though she's damned amazing, she's no match for an entire group of crazy, raging outcasts."

Derek's eyes turned bright yellow. A snarl gripped his face. He started to turn away, muttering, "She can't do that. Have to go back and get her—"

"Wait!" Riley's snap stopped the man, who turned to look at him, eyes still an inhuman bright gold. "You're not going alone. I'm coming with you, and so are my clan. And we need you to take us to wherever those parasites are hiding to get the drop on them. Marisa is part of this clan now," he added. "She's a part of my family. She's my mate, do you understand me?"

Saying it aloud made him feel powerful. Strong.

Loved.

Finn clutched his leg harder. "Marisa's your mate, Dad?"

Riley glanced down at his children. Both their faces shone with excitement.

"Yes," he said, unable to stop his smile despite the urgency of the moment. "She is."

"Good," Laney said with a decisive nod. She sounded very grown up all of a sudden. "We love her. And I can tell you do too, Daddy."

Riley's heart exploded with love. He looked at Derek again. "She's my mate, and she's part of this clan."

Derek stared at him for another long second. He finally nodded sharply. What might have been a smile flickered over his expression. "Yes. It means she'll be okay. Thank you," he whispered. "She's good people."

Riley nodded back. "Damn straight she is. You are too. You're her family, and she loves you, which means we're all in this together. We're coming with you to meet the enemy. And to get her before she does anything stupid," he added, feeling his bear thudding around inside him, straining to shift and go find Marisa.

Go find his harebrained, stunning, powerful mate. The woman who had his heart and then some.

Derek turned fully around and took a cautious step toward Riley. Shutting his eyes for a moment, breath shuddering in and out, he swayed where he stood before opening his eyes again. They'd returned to their normal green. "If that's true, if she's safe here with you all, then I need you to do me a really big favor after everything is over."

"Which is?" Riley eyed him warily, even though he was already reaching for his phone to call Quentin and tell him to get ready for another battle.

"Which is when I'm finally lost, that you take care of me so she doesn't have to. So that I don't hurt her or anyone she cares about."

Riley tightened his jaw. He knew exactly what the man was asking, even if he couched it in vague terms so the cubs might not understand his meaning.

Derek knew he was going mad, and he wanted Riley to put him down before it got to the point of no return.

No way in hell would he do that to Marisa's kin.

Derek wouldn't relent, however.

"Promise me. For Marisa's sake." He nodded at the cubs, who'd moved out from behind Riley when they sensed from their father the stranger wasn't a threat. "For their sake. You know exactly what's happening to me. If she found you, then she's gonna be okay." Derek's voice shook, from both emotion and the force Riley could see he was trying to wield over his mountain lion. "If you care about her, you'll do it."

Riley still didn't answer, but he finally jerked out a tight nod. "I'll do what I have to," he said, refusing to commit more than that. Then, he swung his phone up to his face to call his clan and sound the alarm.

They were going into battle again. This time, they were the ones who would have the element of surprise.

This time, he vowed, he would end the outcasts for all the suffering they had brought to Marisa and her brother.

For good.

17

M arisa's tail lashed once against the snow. Then a second time. A silent threat. Her entire body quivered with readiness. Ready to rip and rend with her claws, to rain down destruction upon her enemies.

Rigid force of will was all that held her in place as she waited for her prey.

From her perch high up the giant pine tree, balanced on a branch bigger than her body, she had an excellent view of the trail leading in and out of the little hovel the Nefarious Desperados used to call home. When she'd arrived earlier, cautiously inching up, using her powerful sense of smell as hard as she could, she hadn't really expected to find them. As she guessed, they were no longer staying there. They and some of the captured outcasts of the bridge battle would've rolled over and given up everything, including their location, for a chance to not be sent to shifter prison. These outcasts had no kind of honor.

After spending a year in their company, Marisa knew them very well. They'd originally chosen these falling-down little shacks to live in because one of them had excellent little hiding spots in the basement. They'd also dug out holes scattered throughout the surrounding woods to cache the stolen goods they liked to fence in order to get money.

Not everyone in the group had known about those caches. Derek had known because he managed to get himself in with the higher-ups. Mainly the asshole Nefarious, who hadn't been captured. He was the smartest one, which wasn't really saying very much. He was the only one who knew all the secrets, though he'd shared bits of information with the few he'd tapped as his captains, as he liked to call them. While the Nefarious Desperados had abandoned this ramshackle, frankly disgusting little collection of ancient, abandoned settler cabins and nasty old trailers that had been left to rot by previous owners, they likely wouldn't abandon its little hidey-holes. She'd caught their faint scents, saw their tracks. She thought if she waited long enough, at least one of them would come back.

She was right.

Her sharp hearing caught the sound of voices down

the trail. Lowering herself even closer to the branch, fiercely trying to meld into it, she held every inch of her magnificent feline body still. How had she thought her cat was a terrible thing? Badass kitty was amazing. She was strong, she was deadly claws and fiery screams, she was tenacity and power Marisa had never known in her human life.

Now, working as one with this side of her, she was going to kill the bastards who still held her brother.

She would take pleasure in killing Nefarious, the particularly nasty, insane psycho who'd been the one to turn both Derek and her into monsters.

A monster of a cat she now appreciated with every inch of her being. But that didn't mean she wasn't going to make him pay for doing it against her will.

The murmur of male voices grew louder. She hardly breathed, her sight fixed on the end of the path. There. Two men came into view, striding along the path with empty backpacks strapped on. Good.

She'd done the numbers in her head after the bridge battle and figured out there probably were about fifteen of the original outcasts that got away. Much as she knew she made one hell of a formidable warrior, she had to be very cautious about taking on all fifteen at once.

But just two of them, in their human forms? Easy peasy. She'd drop one of them with a swift clock to the head then force the other one to show her where they were keeping Derek. And even if one turned into his animal, she felt confident in herself.

After all, she was one hell of a badass kitty.

She recognized both of them. They weren't the top dogs of the pathetic outcast group, but they certainly weren't friends of hers. Easy pickings. She waited, silent as a shadow. Foolishly oblivious, the two men continue to loudly stomp down the path, their conversation as they neared her revealing a crude appreciation for females of any species, preferably if they were doing exactly what either of these two men told them to do.

Marisa's lip curled almost of its own volition, but she stayed utterly still.

Closer.

Closer.

She hunkered so low into the branch it seemed as if she could've had pine sap running in her veins. Snow-tipped needles of the fir tree shoved into her hip and her ribs as she waited, soundless. Almost not breathing.

They were right below her.

"So then this dumb fucking cunt says to me—augh!"

Marisa dropped out of the tree like a stone tossed into water. Halfway down she opened her mouth to roar out a hair-raising screech that had the men screeching in return as they yanked their heads back to look up, eyes wide in sudden terror.

Too late.

Marisa plowed into them, smacking directly down

onto one, whacking him sharply on the back of his head with a giant paw. He instantly went limp and fell onto the snowy trail, unconscious. The other man had been knocked off his feet but was quickly scrambling to them, trying to scuttle away like a crab.

Gotcha now, you sick jerk. Badass kitty hissed. Long, low, and dangerous.

Marisa crouched then launched at him, paws spread, claws outstretched, her yowling mouth open in a rictus of terrifying doom.

Even though the guy was also a shifter, not to mention halfway to insane, she'd managed to surprise the shit out of him. Clearly, he was a coward at heart. He shrieked in terror, whatever animal that claimed him instinctively leaping into his eyes with a glow that came too late.

Marisa landed on top of him, smacking them into the ground with a strength that knocked the air out of him. As he floundered beneath her, frantically trying to fill his suddenly empty lungs, she bent her head and opened her jaws directly over his throat. Daring him to do more than try to take a breath. He struggled beneath her but didn't fight her. He simply tried to breathe.

As soon as he caught his breath and lay gasping like a floundering fish beneath her, otherwise not moving, Marisa backed off and shifted to human. Standing naked in the snow, completely uncaring that his eyes immediately went to her breasts—like her, he too had recently been human, so the casual nudity of shifters could still make him leer—Marisa's amazing, powerful badass kitty stretched a horrifying smile across her face.

Hissing through her teeth, she snarled, "Show me where they are. I'm here to get my brother."

18

R iley edged over the top of the hill, keeping his movements slow so he wouldn't be spotted. But Derek beckoned to him, gazing fixedly down below. "They don't pay attention. Most of them are too far gone to be aware of anything but what the sainted leader tells them to do." Cold bitterness ringed his words, the first time Riley had heard anything aside from worry about his sister or a generalized shaky grasp on the moment. "The only ones that might pay attention are the ones that were born shifters. But they're too damn cocky in their own assholeness to really care much either."

Riley pulled up next to Derek, conscious of Quentin, Abby, and Slade moving up on his other side. Behind him and also spread out far to the other sides, he was aware of the many others who also crept silently through the woods to peer down at the stronghold of the outcasts. Cortez, Haley, Shane, and Jessie were flanked just a few feet off to the right, also tense with anticipation. After Jessie had taken the cubs to school and called in "sick" to work, she'd met everyone else out here. Her bear was eager to rumble.

Slade huffed quietly, folding his arms in front of him as he stood rooted to the ground, also staring down. "That's it? That's the rest of the Nefarious Desperados?" His tone dripped scorn. "They're not even remotely keeping an eye out. Clueless idiots." He spat in disgust. Slade always itched for a good fight, but he liked it if the opposite side could at least put up a decent struggle in return. He was a regular on the shifter fight circuit when he wasn't working. It was his way to blow off steam, as well as battle the demons of his own past. Any fight that started up, Slade was sure to happily wade into, fists or claws flying.

On the other side of Marisa's brother, one of the local wolf shifters said, "I think we've got plenty on our side to take them all out. Quentin?" He glanced at the de facto leader of the Silvertips.

Riley caught the slight shake of his brother's head out of the corner of his eye. "This is Riley's rodeo today. We're all here as backup for him. And to protect our clan and our town." The steely note in his voice said nothing good would happen for the outcast shifters below.

Riley felt a quick wave of appreciation at his brother's deferring the situation to him. Most of the shifters around here looked up to Quentin because he was a natural leader and in charge of the Silvertip Lodge and all its security concerns. But as always, Quentin was also a shrewd manager of his brothers. He wasn't about to step on Riley's toes. Since Marisa was somewhere out here too, Riley's bear wouldn't let anyone else take charge anyway.

"Hell yeah, we've got enough to take them out." Riley half turned to survey the significant number of shifters that accompanied them. They numbered thirty or forty. He'd sounded the call to his family and then placed several texts to certain friends in town who were always up for a throw down, not to mention completely outraged after the surprise attack of the bridge battle several weeks ago. None of them much liked outcasts. Shifters of all different stripes waited for his signal to attack.

His only slight regret was that Pix and Beckett were out of town visiting her family, which meant they didn't have a dragon shifter on their side at the moment. The only other dragon shifter in town was a total loner who never got involved in anything. Riley didn't even have the guy's phone number. But he also knew there wasn't a dragon shifter among the outcasts. Not to mention, as Derek had said, three quarters of them were mad as hatters. That made them dangerous, yes, but it also made them disorganized.

With the crew of healthy, strong shifters assembled here, they should be able to quickly take control of the situation.

And find Marisa, hopefully before she did anything brash like put herself in more danger.

Abby's voice, sharp with the notes of her wolf just below the surface, murmured, "All right, Riley. Give the rundown again."

He bared his teeth in a savage grin. He quickly detailed the idea he'd come up with: sending certain shifter types in flanking movements that would take the outcasts by surprise. It was much smarter than simply barreling down the hill.

As he quickly, quietly went through each maneuver, Slade happily cracked his knuckles. "Damn straight. I'm ready for a hell of a throw down. But hey, bro. Where's your woman? We don't want her to get caught in the crossfire."

Haley, who also stood with arms folded as she stared down into the little valley below, snorted. "That girl has a kickass mountain lion in her. You don't have to worry about her. She can hold her own."

Jessie chimed in, "Especially now that she's got some focus." She glanced at Riley, a wild grin sliding across her face. She clearly was more than ready to shift into her bear and get down to brawling with the outcasts. "She might be impetuous, but she's no fool."

Cortez made an approving sound. "I agree. Good

woman you've got there, Ri. Glad she's with us." His tone held deep meaning. He and everyone else had sensed the deep change in Marisa within the past few days. They'd sensed her renewed desire to live. To be happy. She was one of them now. Family. Clan.

A Silvertip, ready to fight to protect them all.

"Okay. Everyone ready?" Riley glanced from side to side, looking at his family and friends, all ranged out like a well-oiled battle team. It wasn't as if full-on battles were really common around here, but shifters did skirmish now and then. Everyone was always up for a good brawl to help settle their animals.

He glanced off to the side, looking at the unknown but very welcome presence of other shifters. There had been some guests at the lodge who volunteered to come along once they got wind of what was going on. Nobody anywhere liked outcasts. Most guests at the lodge were there just to relax, but they were shifters too. Many enjoyed a fight as much as the next one.

This particular one should be damned epic.

"Let's do it," Riley said, letting his bear ripple through him to start the change.

Quentin's low, urgent "Hold on" abruptly halted him in his tracks, making irritated pain shudder through him. "Riley, look. She's down there. Marisa's already there with them."

Heart thundering, Riley looked. Sure enough, his

beautiful mate strode from the woods right into the small outcast encampment, her mountain lion an impressive specimen of deadly beauty. She moved on her huge, silent paws behind the man who clearly was one of the outcasts as he walked slowly toward the others.

Swearing, Riley held still for a moment to watch her. Brave, stunning lion. She prowled fearlessly right into the outcast camp, seeming completely unafraid of being there. She was in control, almost swaggering as she followed the man into the group. Her head swung around, slowly eyeing each outcast shifter that stood there, sizing up each one, then dismissing him or her just as quickly with a disdainful turn of her head that said exactly what she thought of them. Every movement of her body was controlled. Smooth. Powerful. Riley thought his chest might explode with the swell of pride and admiration at seeing her like this.

Marisa owned her space like the badass queen she was. A stunning, powerful, unstoppable queen.

The stunning woman he'd been meant to meet. The honor of which was all his.

He let himself marvel at her for another split second. Then, it was time to rally behind her. He snarled, "Everyone, go!"

With a roar, he let his bear fully take over and leapt down the hill toward his mate.

Marisa's head snapped around at the sound of his

voice. Her jaws opened wide as she let loose an echoing scream, ferocious joy and determination ringing through it. Then, she swung her powerful head back around, screaming at all the outcasts before her.

Screaming that their end was near.

Oh, hell yeah. His beautiful queen was in charge, and shit was going to go down.

Riley surged forward, the thundering sound of everyone all around him booming through the forest. He roared, a cry that was answered by his clan, his family, his friends. Marisa's wild screeching rang through the air again and again, a sound of fierce joy and focused rage. His beautiful mate was ready to seek her vengeance.

Utter chaos had burst through the outcasts the second they realized they were under attack. They all shifted, revealing themselves to be mostly mountain lions, with just a few bears and wolves mixed in. Riley growled as he came ever closer. Their leader had clearly had a plan when he created his army of insane shifters.

He noted one of the outcasts stayed in human form, darting back into the small building that apparently housed them. He felt a snarl curl his lip. Coward. Although, he mused, the analytical side of his head spinning even as he still slammed down the hill toward them, that could be a recently turned one—one who was not far gone enough yet to thoroughly relish being taken over by his feral side.

A large body suddenly slammed into him from the side. It knocked him off balance, drawing another fearsome roar from his mouth. Swinging his head, he rose to his hind legs as the mountain lion that had attacked him bared its teeth and tried to leap on his back as cats did so they could grab their opponent by the back of the neck and hopefully break it.

Riley let out another roar. That would be the last thing this cat ever tried.

He met the crazed shifter head on, battling its outstretched claws of doom with his gigantic, equally lethal paws. Slamming the cat into the ground, he rolled and tumbled with the creature for several long seconds that felt like days. Getting one good look at the cat's eyes for a moment, he saw nothing but sheer madness. Madness that could never be fixed. Screaming, the cat tried again to get to Riley's neck and plunge its teeth into it.

Roaring, Riley rose to his hind legs then pitched downward. Swiftly, he broke the mountain lion's neck. Quick, clean, merciful.

There was no time to stop. Whirling, he searched for Marisa. There, fighting another mountain lion, her paws and teeth slashing and biting like a furious whirlwind.

Most damned beautiful thing he'd ever seen. This was the woman he'd known she was deep inside.

Ready to always fight. To never give up.

His woman.

His mate.

Roaring out his challenge, he waded into the fray, determined to end every single one of the outcasts that had tried to destroy Marisa's life and attack his clan. This time, there would be no prisoners.

19

The second Marisa heard Riley's challenging roar, shock followed by an enormous thrill raced through her entire body as she snapped her head around toward the sound of his voice. Luckily, his fierce cry, echoed from the throats of dozens more shifters as they pounded down the snowy, forested slope toward the outcasts, also startled the man she'd forced to lead her back here. He froze in horror at the sudden wave of shifters bellowing toward them, giving her enough time to swing her head back and keep him in her line of sight before he did anything dumb.

There. A split second after he startled, he looked at her with a fierce, lunatic glare as his animal burst out of him. Another mountain lion, of course. Nefarious had made sure most of them were mountain lions. She hadn't yet spotted him, but she couldn't think about him right now. This cat right here was already lunging toward her.

She was prepared. Letting another savage scream rip out of her throat, one designed to terrify, she met his launch head-on by flinging herself right at him. The sudden move gave her the bare edge of advantage she needed. They met with a tremendous thwack in midair, both howling like demons as they fought one another for all they were worth. This one knew how to fight. Nefarious had made sure all of the outcasts knew how to fight.

Marisa screeched again in a surge of powerful disdain. She knew how to fight pretty damned well too.

She danced as one with her cat, the enormous joy at finally feeling completely at home in this body making her an unstoppable force. She parried every strike from the other cat, answering with her own swift claws. Focused on this fight, she let a part of her remain constantly on the alert for Riley's voice again.

There. She heard a triumphant roar from him. He must have dispatched an enemy.

Snarling with renewed vigor, she whirled to try to get on the back of this cat, to plunge her jaws into his neck and break it. But he anticipated the move. They grappled before she suddenly lost her grip. Rolling and tumbling, she fought for her life. Despite his own ceaseless desire to fight and win, Marisa was much better than any outcast. Unlike all of them who had either been turned by force or shunned by their original animal group—or simply raised in an unhealthy manner—she now was at one with herself and her new adoptive clan.

None of the outcasts would ever dominate her again.

With another raging howl, she finished it, snapping the other cat's neck. She only killed him because he'd so fiercely tried to kill her. She would no longer hesitate to save her own skin.

Marisa Tully was a warrior, and she wanted to live. She had everything to live for now, and she would never let it be taken away from her again.

Whipping around, she hissed and growled, daring any other enemy to come forth. Another outcast, this one a large wolf, obliged by plunging toward her, his muzzle already covered in blood. Shoving down the fear that he'd injured Riley or one of her other new friends, she focused on the battle.

You've got this, she encouraged herself. *You are strong, you are quick, you want to live.* That was the voice she would listen to from now on. She would never let the ugly voices from her childhood rule her again.

Another lunge, and she and the wolf met in midair, slamming together with huge force. Snarling, clawing, biting, and scratching, shrieking with each victorious swipe, every cell in Marisa's body was on fire with thirsty, savage elation at this battle. She'd never in her life thought of herself as a fighter, but her cat was a brawler through and through. And it wasn't uncontrolled. It wasn't something she would not remember later.

Marisa's cat was a brawler, a fighter, willing to stick up for all that was important to her, because deep down, Marisa always had been a fighter too. She simply hadn't realized it until Riley had helped blossom that truth within her.

Long moments later, she had another triumphant win. She didn't have to kill the wolf, though. Battered and bleeding, he finally gave up, turning to drag himself off, limping into the woods and fleeing the scene entirely. Fine. She wasn't sure what exactly the rules were with escaping outcasts, so she didn't follow him. She needed to stay here and help defend her friends.

She also needed to find Nefarious and take him out for good. Where was that bastard? Could he be such a coward that he had fled? She'd definitely scented him when she arrived with the other shifters. He was here somewhere.

A sudden triumphant cat shriek snagged her attention. Derek?

Snapping her head around, she searched for the source of the sound. *Yes.* Her brother, the only other rock in her life until she'd met Riley. There he was, standing victorious over the body of another mountain lion, shrieking his fierce rage at the world, at taking on the enemies who had for so long subjugated him just as they had her. She howled joyfully in return, answering him, drawing his attention to her. He turned to look at her, and she pounded toward him, needing to reassure herself he was all right. As she dove toward him, brawling shifters on all sides howled and battled and shrieked.

She'd almost reached Derek when off to the side the unexpected movement of a human shape snagged her attention. Nefarious. Confused, she stumbled. Why was he still human? He slowly moved toward her, rage in his eyes.

She let her lip curl, letting rage drip from the snarls that rattled out of her throat. She would show him rage. She didn't care if he was stupid enough to come to a shifter fight in human form. She knew he could shift at any moment, so she felt no compunction about facing him down like this.

She slowly prowled toward him, aware from her peripheral vision that Derek did the same. Nefarious waited for them with the most unholy grin on his face. She knew he'd also been a turned human, although he always said he'd wanted to be turned. That was how he'd held onto sanity far longer than any of the others. It was the only way he'd been able to maintain control over the group, although he was the one who had turned most of them so he would also always have that control.

As she prowled toward him, deadly intent in her every step, she wondered in the back of her mind why he wasn't shifting. Maybe he had finally snapped as well?

It didn't matter. He was a monster through and through, and she was finally taking her vengeance on him.

Behind her, there was a sudden shocked roar that boomed over all the fighting shifters with such horror and strength that for a split second everyone paused. *Riley.* A roar of such rage that the terrible sound of it sent more shock shivering through Marisa's entire body from whiskers to tail. His roars sounded again and again, coming closer.

She couldn't look at him, though. She had to keep her eyes on Nefarious. His nasty grin had spread over his whole face, his flat, dead eyes gleaming with some sort of excitement she couldn't understand.

Nearing him, still aware that Derek did the same, Marisa crouched lower to the ground. Ready to spring.

Her heart almost burst out of her chest when Riley's human voice suddenly sounded from behind her.

"*You.* How is this possible?" Shaking fury shuddered through his words.

No! He needed to shift back into his bear. He wasn't safe in this battle as a human. Marisa snarled in warning, never taking her eyes off Nefarious. Protective growls falling ceaselessly from her throat, she moved in front of Riley, shielding him from Nefarious, from all the shifted ones still fighting all around them.

Then Nefarious spoke in the oily tones she'd grown to hate over the year that she'd known him. "Well, well, well. Finally drew out the shadow that's been hunting me all these years. Guess you're a little angry with me still, huh?"

Marisa shook herself, confused. Derek had stopped on the other side of her, controlled snarls still falling out of his mouth too. He was taking the lead, but she could see the struggle in him. He wanted to leap right at Nefarious, tear him apart. She looked at him. *Stay with me, Derek,* she thought to herself hard, sending him that thought with her body language. Imperceptibly, she saw him nod. He was doing his best to hang onto his sanity.

Riley pushed up next to her, standing at her shoulder, his entire body rigid with a horrified rage she still did not understand.

Until he spoke, and her blood chilled at his words.

"You're the one calling yourself Nefarious? How can you be a shifter? I don't understand." Riley's voice was colder than the mountains, colder than the air, icier than the streams that ran through the forest. "How can a shifter also be a shifter hunter who murders his own kind for gain?"

Riley's voice rattled with growls, with shock, with horror. With pure rage. "You took my cubs' mother from them. You took my former mate from me."

Marisa's entire body felt suddenly drenched in frozen shock. Horrified snarls bled out of her throat, again and again.

No. She'd known Nefarious had been turned from being human, but he never once mentioned he'd been a shifter hunter in his previous life.

219

Nefarious was the shifter hunter who had murdered Riley's first mate.

Marisa howl-shrieked with rage as the realization tore through her, but she still managed to keep herself utterly still.

This was Riley's personal battle now. He had come to support her. Now, she had to support him.

The grin that crawled onto Nefarious's face was pure, cold evil. "You know, after I brought in enough shifters, I realized that becoming a shifter actually would be pretty damn fun. And since I knew how shifter hunters work, I knew I could always avoid them. And hell, it was never the money that turned me on so much as the thrill of the chase."

His grin became bigger, more wild, more insane. "Humans are weak and wimpy compared to shifters. I sometimes talked to the shifters I pulled in, got to understand more from the government agencies I turned them into. I came to understand how shifters could be turned. How you can make a band of crazy turned shifters." His eyes gleamed with madness, but one that was still controlled. "How you can have a fuck ton of fun tearing shit up in this world when you're a shifter yourself."

His gaze slipped to Marisa. "Looks like pretty kitty found herself a new group, huh?" He looked back at Riley. "That's why I had to take out your old mate."

His casual shrug almost made Marisa leap at him to tear out his ugly throat.

"I just got lucky one day, happened to see her and your little kids go out in the woods. She couldn't move too fast since they were so little. But she was clever, that woman of yours, oo-eee." His ugly cackle scraped the air. "She realized I was following her. She hid them kids and made me follow her. I never wanted them. Those little brats couldn't have helped me. I wanted her for one reason."

A calculating look slipped into his face now. Now completely mad. "I wanted her to turn me into a shifter."

Marisa choked on her own cry, hearing Derek's snarls pitch upward to a volume that almost rose above the din of the continued fighting around them. Beside her, Riley didn't make a sound, didn't move an inch, his entire body so tense she thought he might explode.

Nefarious's expression turned into an outraged glare. "That fucking bitch. When I asked her to turn me into a bear like her, she flat out said no. Bitch said I'd make a shitty shifter." He shrugged again, casually. "So I shot her. She weren't of no use to me."

The sheer casualness of how he said that almost crushed Marisa's heart. No. She didn't want Riley to hear this. She was done with this bastard. She would end him now.

She lowered herself, tail quivering, ready to spring. Even if Nefarious shifted at the last second, she could still be on him before he was fully turned into his mountain lion.

Then everything changed.

Nefarious drew a gun from inside his jacket so quickly Marisa fell over her own paws making herself stop. Derek screeched in rage just as Riley blasted out, "You fucking coward."

Marisa knew enough about shifter culture to know that to them, guns were considered cowardly and purely pathetic. Silver bullets didn't kill shifters; regular guns could do that. But shifters never relied on them, instead only bringing their animal side to a fight, or their human side to the sanctioned fight rings such as the ones Slade fought in.

Then again, Nefarious wasn't an honorable shifter. He was the worst fucking monster she'd ever known. The blending of his hideous past with Riley and herself made her almost sick to her stomach.

She couldn't let this happen.

The oily, evil grin stretched over Nefarious's face again. "Hmm, pretty little kitty. I know how to really fuck you up now."

Turning his gun hand, he abruptly pointed it straight at Derek, his finger already pulling the trigger.

Marisa shrieked, instinctively launching herself to the side to throw herself in front of her brother, who was already shrieking and leaping toward Nefarious, heedless of the gun.

She heard the shattering, painful snarl as Riley finally shifted back into his bear, his rage flinging itself all over.

Riley launched at Nefarious just as Marisa launched herself in front of Derek.

The gun went off.

The gun went off, and everything exploded into a red haze.

Riley lunged, hurtling himself into Nefarious just as the gunshot went off. He knocked the bastard down, knocking the man's gun hand off-balance.

Immediately, he slashed into the murderous bastard's throat with his jaws, ripping it out in a gush of blood and gurgled cries. Nothing gleeful filled him as the man bled out in front of him. Just a small, cold satisfaction that it was finally over. The worthless piece of garbage was dead. Riley spat the man's blood out of his mouth, fury and disgust and new terror filling him as he whirled to find Marisa.

Horrified cries filled the air at the sound of the gunshot. There was sudden panic, but almost immediately all of the Silvertip shifters and their friends took the advantage. Most of the outcasts had been just as startled, but they did not have the advantage of the connection and training of all the other shifters. Swiftly, the battle was over.

Riley turned and bolted the few yards to where Marisa lay sprawled beside Derek. His heart squeezed so hard he thought he might hyperventilate, old trauma threatening to rise up and consume him.

Marisa struggled to her feet, a mixture of concerned whines and encouraging little purrs spilling out of her. Riley felt his heart start again as his warrior mate rose.

Derek blinked his golden eyes, mouth opening in a faint snarl of pain.

In a split second, Marisa had shifted back to human. Kneeling beside her brother, placing one hand on his fur-covered ribs and the other hand on his shoulder where blood flowed, she chanted, "Don't you dare give up on me, Derek. Don't you dare, don't you dare. Don't let him win. Stay with me. Stay with me!"

Coming to a stop, Riley approached cautiously, gently nuzzling around Derek's wound. He could smell the track the bullet had left, but he couldn't smell the copper and zinc of the bullet itself. It had gone straight through, only hitting Derek in the shoulder.

He would be fine.

Huffing in relief, Riley nuzzled Marisa, licking her shoulder in reassurance. She kept firmly saying to her brother, "You'll be fine, see? Don't you dare give up. Don't you dare. I came back to find you, Derek. Don't you dare give up!"

On the ground, Derek muttered out a snarl of pain, followed by a soft cry. Golden eyes blinked again as he struggled to stay there. To stay on this side of sanity.

Then, he rumbled low, his eyes clearing. He would be okay.

Marisa was okay, her brother was okay, and the fucking bastard who'd murdered Riley's first mate and almost killed his new, precious mate was finally gone forever. Vengeance had been his, and it had released him from the final pieces of rage that had dragged him and his bear down for so long.

Riley turned, threw his head back, and roared a deep cry to the world, letting his clan and friends know that they were safe. A thundering chorus of victorious howls and snarls answered him. They had won the battle. Everyone here was a warrior. Fiercely defending their home, their friends, their family. Never giving up.

Marisa leaned her bloody face into his fur and reached her hand up gently to stroke his snout while her other hand stayed on her brother's shoulder. Between her tears, she managed to say, "It's okay. Everything's okay now. I love you, Riley. I love you."

She leaned into him, the soft cadence of her voice washing over him like a balm. His mate, safe. His family and friends, safe. His entire world, safe.

Nothing else mattered now except their bright future.

EPILOGUE

As she snuggled into Riley's arms, Marisa felt her toes tapping to the irresistible beat of the music. The smile stretching her face no longer felt weird. It was beginning to feel really normal. *She* felt normal. Well, as normal as a human-turned-mountain-lion-shifter ever could. Which, she had to admit, now actually felt just right.

Riley squeezed her gently, settling his chin onto her shoulder as he surveyed the happy bustle inside the barn. "Happy Valentine's Day, babe. Will you be mine?" His hand rose up and uncurled to reveal a pink candy heart nestled into his palm with those words on it.

Marisa felt laughter bubbling out of her, mingling with the purrs from her cat, everything swirling around in time to the music and the cheerful laughter of the guests of the Silvertip Lodge as well as the clan members and many friends from town. She nodded against his chest. "Any day of the week. Every day of the week. I'll be yours forever."

His kiss on her earlobe made her shiver with delight before he lifted his hand toward her mouth. She leaned down and gently grabbed the candy off it with her lips, whispering a kiss over his warm skin as she did. An appreciative groan rumbled through his entire body as her lips touched him.

Eating the sweet little treat, she looked around as she snuggled securely into Riley's embrace. It felt like a lifetime ago that she had sat here in the barn while it was being decorated for this dance. She felt completely different too. She no longer had the need to keep every doorway under her watchful eye. Nor did she feel inexplicably angry and resentful at all the happiness clearly present in here. The sense of family and camaraderie. Now all she felt was happiness. An utterly amazing joy that she got to live here after all. That this was her family too. Her new friends.

Watching them all as they danced and goofed off among the guests, she smiled so hard she thought she might never stop. Abby and Quentin, laughing as they danced in fluid synchronicity. Haley and Cortez, smiling at one another as dopily as Marisa was sure she looked at Riley pretty much every second of the day. Pix and Beckett, returned from their trip back east to visit her family, arms wrapped around one another and slowly swaying together despite it being a fast song, seeming like they were about to start making out right there on the dance floor. Riley's boss and human friend Joe with his wife Natalie, who Marisa had instantly liked when she met her. Slade, darkly brooding as he leaned against a stall door, frowning hard at a small, pretty woman dancing with a guy so big he might be an elephant shifter, if there were such a thing. Ooh, trouble. Marisa figured there was a backstory there, but she didn't know it. Sending a mental hug to Slade, who had grown on her, she looked around the room for the cubs. Her smile got even bigger when she saw them. Laney was in hysterics as she and her best friend Laurel performed jerky moves that made Marisa think they were imitating robots, while Finn danced more solemnly with Willow, though he had an excited if somewhat shy grin.

Contentment purred out of her even more strongly. Yes. Her true family, all here.

Then she looked for the one other person who topped her list. There. Derek, healing fast from his wound and with a less haggard appearance every day, was tucked into a corner, watchful but with a faint smile lighting up his face. Beside him, that cute waitress from Whatchu Want sat on the bench, clearly doing her best to chat him up. Derek seemed slightly nervous, but Marisa knew her brother. He was interested. Definitely.

"What kind of shifter is she?" she idly asked Riley, gesturing toward Derek and the woman. She wondered if the waitress would be able to handle Derek and the mountain lion that he too was slowly getting to know better. Marisa's sheer love for him, combined with the loving bonds of a genuinely caring family for the first time in his life, was ensuring Derek wouldn't succumb to madness. He was like her. A fighter. A warrior. He wouldn't give up. He would, however, need a really strong woman to handle him.

"Casey? Oh, you're wondering if she can take on Derek." Riley's voice rumbled into her ear. "No worries there. She grew up in Alaska. That woman is a Kodiak brown bear. Trust me, she'll be able to handle your brother and his cat."

Marisa's cat purred harder. Good. Marisa needed to know that everyone she loved was safe.

Watching as the cubs danced with their friends, looking at the adoration on Jessie's and Shane's faces as they did a little family twirl out on the dance floor with Grant, Marisa sighed in utter contentment and nestled even deeper into Riley. Turning her head more, scooting up his chest so her lips were closer to his ear, she made herself be bold. "I have a question for you. I don't mean right now, it's too soon. But one day—" She paused. Her cat urged her on. Softly, she continued. "One day, would you like to have even more of a family? With me?"

Riley shifted to the side, turning his head so he could look at her. The excited, hopeful shine of his eyes

229

warmed her. "Do you mean, would I one day like to have a child with you?"

She nodded, holding her breath as she waited for the answer.

His smile almost touched his ears before he crushed her close again in a huge hug. "Yes. Definitely. One hundred percent, Marisa. I think the cubs would love it too."

She let the breath she'd been holding out of her in a little chuckle against his chest, nodding against him. "They've already asked. They say they want to teach a little brother or sister all that they know. Which might mean they're going to teach a sibling all sorts of ways to get up to mischief."

Riley laughed as well. "They probably will. We'll deal with that when the time comes. I can hardly wait," he added in a whisper. "But I'll definitely wait as long as you need. Always."

A happy glow of joy felt like it covered her entire body. This man. This stunning, incredible, patient man. He would die to protect her and his children, and he would also give her all the space in the world she needed. Always.

She was the luckiest woman in the history of the world.

"Okay, then." Riley's voice suddenly turned brisk. "I can feel your foot tapping in time to the song. Feel like taking a whirl on the dance floor with me, beautiful lion woman?"

Marisa's laugh rang out into the bubble of conversation and laughter throughout the room as she nodded. Jumping to her feet, she tugged him up. "Definitely. I got moves I can't wait for you to see."

Riley gave her an appreciative little smack on the behind, making her half gasp, half giggle as they whirled out onto the dance floor to join everyone else. Her friends. Her family.

Laughing with joy as her sexy mate spun her around alongside all the guests, alongside all her new friends and family, Marisa and her cat purred as one. This was the place she had always been searching for. The place she fit into purr-fectly and loved with all her heart.

She was finally home.

The End

Hunter's Moon (*Black Mesa Wolves crossover*) (Quentin & Abby)
Mountain Bear's Baby (Shane & Jessie)
Rescue Bear: Cortez (Cortez & Haley)
Ranger Bear: Riley (Riley & Marisa)
Hotshot Bear: Slade (Slade & Everly)
Superstar Bear: Bodhi (Bodhi & McKenna)

ABOUT J.K.

J.K. Harper writes about paranormal romance because it's really fun. She lives in the rugged, gorgeous canyon country of the Southwest, which is a great place to let her imagination run wild.

For more information about her books, please visit her website at
www.jkharper.com

Rogue Wolf

Dragon Mates

Dazzled

Thrilled

Burned

Wicked Wolf Shifters

Surrendered to the Pack: Volume 1, Episode 1

Claimed by the Pack: Volume 1, Episode 2

Taken by the Pack: Volume 1, Episode 3

Mated to the Pack: Volume 1, Episode 4

Wicked Wolf Shifters: Complete Volume 1

Ruled by the Pack: Volume 2, Episode 1

Hunted by the Pack: Volume 2, Episode 2

Destined for the Pack: Volume 2, Episode 3

Wicked Wolf Shifters: Complete Volume 2